"I can't wait any longer to dance with you," Ben murmured.

Carolyn drifted into his arms. Pressing her face against his shoulder, she said, "How many times have you called to check on Lucy?"

He laughed, and they moved to the music, a seamless union of man and woman. "Only once, thank you. She wants me to bring her a flower from the bride's bouquet."

"I'll go snatch one before Lily tosses it to the crowd."

Ben framed her face with his hands and looked into her eyes. "Don't go away, Carolyn. I have a confession to make."

She stared, lost in his suddenly serious expression. "I'm listening."

"The thought occurred to me that this could have been us if we'd gotten married." He leaned to brush his lips against hers. "I guess what I'm trying to say is, you'll always be part of my soul."

"Ben, don't," she said quickly, "because I—I'm—"

He put his chin against her forehead, holding her close. "Only putting up a brave front?"

Dear Reader,

I was immediately intrigued when I was asked to participate in the TRUEBLOOD, TEXAS series, because *A Father's Vow* deals with the issue of how much a father is willing to do for his child. And isn't that a central theme that plays through most of our lives? I love the guardian aspect of a father's role in his child's life. In this romance we get to see Ben Mulholland's strengths—and even get a peek at his desperation and fragility—as he takes the role of front-and-center player in his daughter's life.

As readers, we love to meet and read about big, strong men who fight so hard for their kids! Ben Mulholland is based on real-life fathers I have seen. There's the dad who shows up in his suit after work, holding a younger baby in his arms, while he coaches soccer. Or the one who works two jobs so that the bills are paid. The dad who mentors and takes the time to lay his hands across another child's shoulders to say, "I'm here for you."

Hopefully, I've captured the meaning that a father has in his child's life in this book. I hope you enjoy it. Please visit me at www.tinaleonard.com and let me know!

Love,

Tina Leonard

TRUEBLOOD, TEXAS

Tina Leonard

A Father's Vow

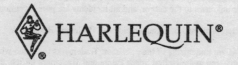

HARLEQUIN®

TORONTO • NEW YORK • LONDON
AMSTERDAM • PARIS • SYDNEY • HAMBURG
STOCKHOLM • ATHENS • TOKYO • MILAN • MADRID
PRAGUE • WARSAW • BUDAPEST • AUCKLAND

Tina Leonard is acknowledged as the author of this work.

Many thanks to Marsha Zinberg and Susan Sheppard, who helped me make this book the best I could make it.

Also, my sincere thanks to Peggy Hoffmann (aka Kate Hoffmann), without whom I'm pretty sure I would never have been able to write this story. Thanks, Peggy—it was fun!

And to my kids, Lisa and Dean, who are patient with their never-Betty-Crocker mom. I love you.

HARLEQUIN BOOKS
225 Duncan Mill Road, Don Mills,
Ontario, Canada M3B 3K9

ISBN 0-373-65080-9

A FATHER'S VOW

Copyright © 2001 by Harlequin Books S.A.

Visit us at www.eHarlequin.com

Printed In U.S.A.

TRUEBLOOD, TEXAS

THE TRUEBLOOD LEGACY

THE YEAR WAS 1918, and the Great War in Europe still raged, but Esau Porter was heading home to Texas.

The young sergeant arrived at his parents' ranch northwest of San Antonio on a Sunday night, only the celebration didn't go off as planned. Most of the townsfolk of Carmelita had come out to welcome Esau home, but when they saw the sorry condition of the boy, they gave their respects quickly and left.

The fever got so bad so fast that Mrs. Porter hardly knew what to do. By Monday night, before the doctor from San Antonio made it into town, Esau was dead.

The Porter family grieved. How could their son have survived the German peril, only to burn up and die in his own bed? It wasn't much of a surprise when Mrs. Porter took to her bed on Wednesday. But it was a hell of a shock when half the residents of Carmelita came down with the horrible illness. House after house was hit by death, and all the townspeople could do was pray for salvation.

None came. By the end of the year, over one hundred souls had perished. The influenza virus took those in the prime of life, leaving behind an unprecedented number of orphans. And the virus knew no boundaries. By the time the threat had passed, more than thirty-seven million people had succumbed worldwide.

But in one house, there was still hope.

Isabella Trueblood had come to Carmelita in the late 1800s with her father, blacksmith Saul Trueblood, and her mother, Teresa Collier Trueblood. The family had traveled from Indiana, leaving their Quaker roots behind.

Young Isabella grew up to be an intelligent woman who had a gift for healing and storytelling. Her dreams centered on the boy next door, Foster Carter, the son of Chester and Grace.

Just before the bad times came in 1918, Foster asked Isabella to be his wife, and the future of the Carter spread was secured. It was a happy union, and the future looked bright for the young couple.

Two years later, not one of their relatives was alive. How the young couple had survived was a miracle. And during the epidemic, Isabella and Foster had taken in more than twenty-two orphaned children from all over the county. They fed them, clothed them, taught them as if they were blood kin.

Then Isabella became pregnant, but there were complications. Love for her handsome son, Josiah, born in 1920, wasn't enough to stop her from growing weaker by the day. Knowing she couldn't leave her husband to tend to all the children if she died, she set out to find families for each one of her orphaned charges.

And so the Trueblood Foundation was born. Named in memory of Isabella's parents, it would become famous all over Texas. Some of the orphaned children went to strangers, but many were reunited with their families. After reading notices in newspapers and church bulletins, aunts, uncles, cousins and grandparents rushed to Carmelita to find the young ones they'd given up for dead.

Toward the end of Isabella's life, she'd brought together more than thirty families, and not just her orphans. Many others, old and young, made their way to her doorstep, and Isabella turned no one away.

At her death, the town's name was changed to Trueblood, in her honor. For years to come, her simple grave was adorned with flowers on the anniversary of her death, grateful tokens of appreciation from the families she had brought together.

Isabella's son, Josiah, grew into a fine rancher and married Rebecca Montgomery in 1938. They had a daughter, Elizabeth Trueblood Carter, in 1940. Elizabeth married her neighbor William Garrett in 1965, and gave birth to twins Lily and Dylan in 1971, and daughter Ashley a few years later. Home was the Double G ranch, about ten miles from Trueblood proper, and the Garrett children grew up listening to stories of their famous great-grandmother, Isabella. Because they were Truebloods, they knew that they, too, had a sacred duty to carry on the tradition passed down to them: finding lost souls and reuniting loved ones.

CHAPTER ONE

CAROLYN ST. CLAIR wasn't having the best day to begin with, but when the doors to Finders Keepers opened to reveal Ben Mulholland—her long-lost love—things went to heck in a handbasket.

Never mind that her pulse jumped erratically and a thrill set every one of her nerve endings on high alert.

Ben's intense hazel eyes settled on her with unyielding focus, and Carolyn managed the most difficult smile she'd ever forced to her face.

"Hello, Ben," she said.

"Carolyn." He shoved his hands into the pockets of his well-worn jeans and stared at her, clearly uncomfortable.

Time had made strangers of them. She reached for the platitude. "You're looking well."

His eyes flickered. "You are, too."

The response was too automatic to be a genuine compliment, so she decided to skip the small talk and say what she really wanted to say, no matter how awkward. "I was sorry to hear about your mom, Ben." She swallowed, hoping her stilted tone conveyed the sympathy she felt. But was it more sympathy than he'd welcome from an old girlfriend?

When he nodded in appreciation, Carolyn relaxed slightly.

"Thanks. Mom really liked you."

Eileen Mulholland had been certain Carolyn and Ben were perfect for each other. When Carolyn broke off the relationship, Eileen had personally called to tell her how sorry she was, and that she'd hoped Carolyn would one day become her daughter-in-law. Eileen never asked why Carolyn was breaking the engagement. She'd merely expressed her love.

Carolyn had felt so guilty.

Another woman had become Eileen's daughter-in-law, not too many months later. Sadly, she'd also become her ex-daughter-in-law, shortly before Eileen passed away.

"I saw the pot of daisies in Mom's hospital room," Ben said. "She told me you'd been by." He cleared his throat. "It was nice of you to visit her, Carolyn."

How could she not? She'd loved Eileen. She'd loved Ben. They were part of the family to which she had desperately wanted to belong; a family she'd always dreamed of.

She'd known for some time she would never have that family of her dreams.

"I hated to see her go, Ben. She had so much love of life."

"Thanks, Carolyn." His lips flattened for a moment, before he said, "Mom told me you were working here. I came by to ask a favor of you."

Carolyn's eyebrows rose. "A favor?"

"Actually, I'd like to hire Finders Keepers for a personal reason." He sighed. "I suppose nobody walks in the agency door unless it's a personal reason."

She tried to offer him a reassuring smile. He was obviously on edge, but she didn't feel it was because of her. On the other hand, she had tensed the moment their eyes met, despite the years since she'd last seen him. Now she needed to call on her professionalism to keep a wedge between the feelings she still had for Ben and the knowledge that those buried emotions would always be doomed to disappointment. "Please sit down." She gestured to a chair near the desk. "Can I get you something to drink? Coffee? A soda?"

He shook his head, drumming his fingers on the desk after he sat. One hand riffled absently through sandy hair that needed a trim. He looked tired Carolyn noted, or perhaps worried. Something other than happiness had etched itself into the sun lines around his eyes; the easy smile he'd once possessed hadn't surfaced since he'd walked in the door.

"How can Finders Keepers help you, Ben?"

"By taking my case."

"We'll certainly review whether our expertise is a match for your needs, but—"

"It's important to me that you be the one handling it," he stressed.

Startled, she shook her head. "I don't know if that would be in your best interest, Ben. Dylan and Lily Garrett really hired me to run the office. They're the experienced—"

"You haven't even heard the details," he reminded her. "Don't tell me no just yet, Carolyn. Please."

He hadn't missed her reluctance to agree to his request. She shifted in her chair, unable to meet his eyes for a moment. "I'm willing to listen, of course. And Finders Keepers will do the best they can to help you."

He frowned, furrowing the skin between his sandy brows. "You're uncomfortable."

She hesitated. "Perhaps a little."

Nodding, he said, "I understand that. I wouldn't be here if this wasn't a matter of urgency."

When he stared at her, those large hazel eyes pleading for her acquiescence, Carolyn wanted to close her own eyes and sigh. The memory of having to say no to him on another matter—marriage—crystallized painfully in her mind. She pushed the memory into a place she wouldn't let it escape from again today. "Do you mind if I tape you?" she asked. "I'll take notes, but it's better if I have a tape to go back over later, just in case I should miss anything."

He blinked at her sudden take-charge tone. "Does that mean you'll handle my case?"

She extinguished the pleasure she felt at the relief in his voice. "It means I need to get the particulars and discuss them with the Garretts, who run Finders Keepers. It's Dylan and Lily who do all the investigative work." She raised a hand to quell his instant protest. "I'll do my best to underscore your wishes that I handle this for you, Ben. I give you my word."

He nodded. "Your word was always good, Carolyn. I'll take it."

She set out a tape recorder on the desk, fitted it with a new cassette. The agency door opened, and a tall, beautiful blonde walked in, her stride graceful, but almost too long for the little girl beside her. Carolyn's heart stopped in her chest.

Marissa. Ben's ex-wife. The woman he'd married very quickly after Carolyn had turned down his marriage proposal. She made herself smile, girding her heart against the pain.

"This is Marissa," Ben said, not knowing that Carolyn had devoured the pictures of him and his new bride in the newspaper six years ago. Nor had she been able to keep from looking at the photos of Marissa in magazines over the years. Marissa in swimsuits, evening gowns, lingerie—it had hurt. For some reason, every photo of his glamorous wife had stung, maybe because Carolyn knew that beside Marissa's bright light, she was a nondescript shadow.

"Hello, Marissa," Carolyn said. "I'm Carolyn St. Clair."

"I know who you are," Marissa returned, her tone not warm, but not cool, either. Matter-of-fact. They assessed each other wordlessly, then the little girl Marissa held by the hand leaped into Ben's lap and they broke eye contact.

Carolyn was dead certain she'd be taking a hiatus from doughnuts with her hot tea from now on. And maybe she'd make an appointment for some highlights, start running on the track at the high school in the evenings...

"Carolyn," Ben said, his voice gentle, "this is my daughter, Lucy."

And his daughter's bright smile sent all the misgivings she'd been nursing right out of her head. "Hello, Lucy. You sure are pretty."

"I know." She grinned at Carolyn. "Everyone says I look like Mommy."

Carolyn smiled. "You do."

"But I'm going to look like my daddy when I grow up." She turned in her father's lap to brush the hair from his eyes. Then she kissed him on the nose and patted his cheek with a soft, pudgy hand. "I'm going to marry my daddy when I grow up."

Ben's laugh was quiet and proud. Marissa looked at her designer fingernails. *Well, that makes three of us in the same room who have considered marrying Ben Mulholland at one time,* Carolyn thought wryly. Lucy's childish wish was the most impractical, but it was obvious she had every centimeter of Ben's heart, and was guaranteed to keep it that way.

"I need a half hour or so," Ben said over Lucy's shoulder as he looked up at Marissa.

"Oh, Daddy!" Lucy protested, clearly unwilling to detach herself from her big, strong father.

Marissa nodded. Her gaze flicked to Carolyn as she reached to take Lucy's hand and guide her off her father's lap. "It was nice meeting you, Carolyn."

"You, too."

"Ben has a lot of faith in you," Marissa murmured. "I hope you can help us."

Help us. The plural caught Carolyn off guard. This was, then, a family situation that had brought Ben to her. Nothing she needed to fear. The past was not going to jump out at her with painful memories. "I'll do my best," she told Marissa sincerely. "Although I have yet to hear the situation, I certainly hope Finders Keepers can resolve it."

Marissa nodded, her eyes dark with something Carolyn couldn't define before she turned back to her husband. "Ben, my plane leaves in a few hours."

"I'll have you at the airport on time. Bye, honey." He kissed Lucy on the side of the cheek. She patted his face and then walked to the door with her elegant mother.

Carolyn glanced down as the door closed behind them. The pain she'd so determinedly avoided suddenly flayed her. "She's beautiful, Ben," she said automatically, meaning Lucy but knowing the word encompassed his wife, as well.

"Lucy is my soul's joy." He leaned forward and Carolyn's gaze involuntarily rose to his face. "She means the world to me. I can't even tell you how much I love my daughter." It seemed that the earnestness left his eyes for a moment as he focused inward. Then he said slowly, "She has leukemia, Carolyn."

Denial sprang into Carolyn's mind. "Oh, Ben!"

She didn't know what else to say. *I'm sorry* wouldn't cut it. *How terrifying!* was all wrong. Why Lucy? Why Ben? Why his mother *and* his child?

He put his head down, a slow surrender to pain, and sheltered his face with splayed fingers.

But she'd seen the tear. She heard his heart breaking. She'd seen the panic in his eyes, in Marissa's eyes.

Once again, Ben wanted a yes from her. This time, there was no way she could deny him. She took a deep, steadying breath and reached out her hand to cover the clenched fist he'd braced on his knee.

"I'm going to get you a soda from the kitchen," she said softly, knowing he needed a moment to pull himself back together. "And then you and I will get to work on whatever it is that brought you to Finders Keepers."

"I need to find a miracle," Ben said, his voice rasping with raw emotion.

She squeezed his hand briefly and rose from her seat, not at all certain she was the one he should have come to for a miracle.

"WHEN MOM WAS in the hospital, she was doing a lot of walking down memory lane." Ben had enjoyed hearing about his mother's childhood. He'd already known a lot about her past life, but it had brought them closer together to share the walk she needed to take. "In the final days, she focused on Lucy, and I probably don't have to tell you that Mom was intense. Lucy was...special to her." He smiled, somehow self-deprecatingly. "She's special to me, too, of course, but Lucy and Mom were really connected."

"Grandparents occupy a magical place in children's lives," Carolyn murmured.

He frowned, realizing he'd heard her say that a long time ago. It had been six years since they'd broken up, yet there was so much he could still remember about Carolyn. She'd been important to him in a way no one else had ever been. Maybe the innocence of youth had deepened the level of understanding between them. Tightened their connection.

It had been difficult to come here today, to face the woman he'd loved so deeply. No man willingly sought out a woman who'd rejected him. Avoiding pain was what a man did best. He would never have married Marissa if he hadn't been running from his shattered emotions. But his mother seemed to think

Carolyn could help Lucy. Heaven only knew, what he was going to ask of her was impossible. Unthinkable.

Carolyn was a woman, not a savior.

"In the hospital, Mom revealed to me that I'd had a twin. She gave birth to two children, both boys." He swallowed. It still felt strange to repeat his mother's incredible words. "The other child—" he couldn't say *my brother* "—was stillborn, according to the nurse who attended her."

Carolyn's hand flew to make a notation, then her gaze met his again. He saw calm in her eyes, none of the raging fear and panic he felt. Her acceptance of his pronouncement allowed him to continue.

"At the time Mom delivered, apparently a black market baby ring was in operation in Texas, ghastly as that sounds. Newborns have always fetched top dollar. Mom had two, and she believes that one of them may have been...stolen."

"But if one was stillborn, then why would the baby have been stolen?"

"Mom believes she heard the cry of another infant in the room. Two babies crying, but only for a few seconds. She was groggy from medication—even then women were often sedated to have children."

"I know. My mother said it was wonderful to wake up and be handed a baby."

He nodded. "Mom says she was already coming out of the anaesthesia when she heard the crying. But when she was told that one of her children had been stillborn, she didn't suspect that anyone would lie to her about it. She was young, seventeen, and my father was away at a farmer's market in Fort Worth, and…''

"She was overwhelmed and frightened. And too young to question what she'd heard.''

"Right.'' A sigh escaped him. "I won't tell you that I embraced this story of hers when she told me. I know Mom was desperate to find a bone marrow match for Lucy, and at a success rate of one in three million, we'd need an angel to guide us in finding one.''

Carolyn made no comment, didn't raise an eyebrow in disbelief. He'd gotten past the hard parts without rejection. She seemed to take in every word he said with complete empathy.

"Mom was rambling at the end somewhat, and this could easily be the wishful thinking of a dying woman. I know wishful thinking is more my companion every day, but even I know how implausible this sounds.''

"I'm sure you and Marissa have run through both sides of your family tree for possibilities?''

"Of course.''

Carolyn held his gaze for a second before looking at her notes. He had the feeling she was deep in thought. Her green eyes were alert, her posture erect. She'd always had a curvaceous, knock-out body, but the coral suit she wore gave her a professional demeanor. He liked the fact that the body he remembered so well was hidden beneath a jacket, knee-length skirt and gauzy blouse—a secret he would have preferred to keep his alone.

Pushing back auburn-tinted, rich brown hair, Carolyn met his gaze again. His heart stilled as he realized she was about to pronounce the time, dollars and energy this search would require.

"Ben, there are records which can be searched easily enough to get us started. It is true that long-lost relatives have been found as a result of searches by loved ones who suspect exactly what your mother did. But the outcome is a long shot, and I'm sure you know that."

He nodded.

"Still, it's not unthinkable."

"You'll do it, then?" The relief that swept through him was a crashing ocean wave flinging him onto a beach of hope.

"I'll present your case file to Lily and Dylan Garrett. They're better equipped to assist you. Lily has experience as a forensics expert for the FBI, and Dylan worked as an undercover detective. Actually, he was instrumental in breaking that baby-selling ring last spring. We've also started to refer cases to Budnicki-Morales Private Investigations in Midland-Odessa. Jennifer Rodriguez works there, and she is top-notch at locating missing persons."

"While I appreciate your advice to put my case in

experienced hands, you said yourself that records could be easily searched to start the ball rolling. That's something you can do yourself, isn't it?"

She nodded. "Yes, but—"

"Where are the Garretts right now?"

Her expressive emerald eyes widened. "Lily is getting married, so she's tied up with wedding details, and Dylan is out of town handling some of her caseload."

"So, they're otherwise occupied and not likely to give top priority to this case."

"The Garretts are thorough in their attention—"

"I know. My point is that my daughter is very ill with acute lymphocytic leukemia. I don't have the luxury of time. You said yourself the research process could easily be started. In fact, I'm here because of Carolyn St. Clair, not the Garretts. I trust you, and I know you well enough to know that you'll use all your energy to tear into the facts like a tenacious bull, Carolyn."

"Thanks, I think," she murmured.

He reached to touch her chin with his finger, so that she'd meet his eyes. "I need you for this, Carolyn. Mom sent me here with her last breath, to find you and ask you for your help. She knew you loved her…knew you'd fall in love with Lucy."

Knew you'd loved me. He didn't say it, but the words hung between them, implied and poignant. For whatever reason she'd left him—and that was a mystery he'd never unlock now—he knew in his heart that when Carolyn St. Clair loved someone, she loved with all her soul.

He was counting on that for Lucy.

CHAPTER TWO

WHEN BEN LOOKED at her like that, with his eyes full of hope that she'd say yes, Carolyn put her personal reservations aside for the moment. "Tell me everything your mother told you. Anything you can remember she said before she died."

"The doctor who delivered me was Douglas Benton. He worked with his wife, Vivian—she assisted him in a midwife capacity."

"Your mother didn't go to a hospital?"

"No. For one thing, she was from tough country stock. Her mother's children were born at home, and Mom didn't know there was another way to do it. Also, she and Dad simply didn't have the cash to go to a hospital. Remember, back then a person paid medical bills out of their own pocket. Ironically, Dad had gone to market to sell some crops, hoping to have enough money for whatever they needed when I was born." He withdrew a photo from his wallet of a smiling family: a tall man in an ill-fitting suit, a woman holding a blanket-wrapped baby in her arms.

Carolyn felt chills sweep her. "So if your mom

hadn't come out of the anesthetic early, she might never have thought there was another living child.''

He shook his head. ''If I really do have a brother, it's a miracle that we know to start looking for him. At the same time, I don't want to get my hopes up. Why did Mom never remember this before? That's what I keep coming back to.''

''I had surgery once for something minor,'' she said, not meeting his eyes and not about to tell him her deepest, darkest secret, ''and I was very groggy when I awakened. I was also more nauseated than I'd ever been in my life. To be honest, I was focused on the pain I'd begun to feel and not my surroundings.''

''Maybe that's what Mom experienced. Anyway, being in the hospital seemed to make Mom want to talk about her life. I never knew as much about my mother as I did during those days before she died. I wish I'd tape-recorded it for Lucy's sake, because I can't possibly remember everything she said.''

Carolyn smiled. ''You sound like it was a good experience for you.''

''It was. I could tell she'd made her peace with her situation, and that she wasn't afraid of—'' He took a deep breath. ''And that made me not afraid. But then all of a sudden, she became noticeably weaker. She began talking about my brother, and it was as if she couldn't…let herself die until she'd relived those moments of her delivery. I saw her turn into a frightened young girl who was upset that her baby was coming when her husband, her most trusted friend and provider, was out of town. Her parents weren't close enough to make it in time. She was young, alone, afraid.''

''Possibly a ripe target for a baby ring, if that is indeed what happened.''

''Maybe so. She was vulnerable, that's for sure. And there were no witnesses, except for the doctor's wife, and she's not going to want to tell us anything, if there is something to tell.''

''Did you happen to look through Eileen's records when she was in the hospital? Usually they're close at hand with the nurses.''

He shook his head. ''I never even thought to look at her chart. How would that have helped?''

''Probably it wouldn't have. But I would have been curious to know if your mother continued to see Dr. Benton after your birth.''

''I don't think she did. Otherwise I would have remembered him. Her oncologist is Dr. Tristan Collins. I can't say I liked him very well. He was overconfident and young. Perhaps if I'd met him under different circumstances... Actually, I believe I was put off by the fact that he was so young. The nurses were smitten with him, and so was Mom. She kind of glowed whenever he came into the room.'' He smiled wryly. ''I wanted a grizzled, mature doctor like the ones you see on television to miraculously heal my mother.''

Carolyn lowered her eyes for a second. "I'm so sorry, Ben."

"Oh, I was just mad at the world, I guess. Dr. Collins has an excellent medical record, and he made my mom happy because he didn't treat her as if she were sickly and fragile, which she was. He treated her as if she were still vibrant and beautiful, which was exactly what she needed at the time." He stared at his hands. "Dr. Collins is how we discovered Lucy was ill."

"What do you mean?"

"Mom was taking care of Lucy for me one day about six months ago. She went by Dr. Collins's office to get some paperwork, and he happened to walk through the waiting room. He stopped to chat to Lucy—she's quite a chatterbox—and he noticed a bruise on her arm. He asked Mom about it. Mom was astonished and assured Dr. Collins that the bruise hadn't been there when she'd helped Lucy dress. She couldn't remember Lucy bumping into anything, or getting knocked down by one of the dogs. Dr. Collins suggested Mom walk Lucy down the hall to one of his colleagues, a pediatrician. He called himself to have the doctor take a look at the bruise, which was ugly and big and greenish-blue."

He stopped, and Carolyn pinned her gaze on him, not wanting to hear the rest and yet knowing she had to. She gave Ben time to assemble his thoughts.

"And that," Ben said softly, "is how we came to

have Lucy tested for leukemia. I don't have to tell you that my whole world came undone.''

Carolyn sat very still.

''Perversely, I don't like Dr. Collins, when I know very well he is the only person who gave us a fighting chance with Lucy's life.''

She put a hand on his briefly. ''Ben, no one is going to blame you for wanting to shoot the messenger. You've lost your mom and your daughter is ill. You can have all the skewed emotions you want. I'm sure Dr. Collins would understand.''

''Lucy has tremendous regard for him. When she had her first round of chemotherapy, Dr. Collins came to visit her in the hospital.''

''I see.''

''With a giant teddy bear.''

She made a note on her pad. ''I should talk to Dr. Collins and see if he has anything he can share about your mother that isn't restricted to doctor-patient confidentiality.''

Ben remained silent.

''Ben?''

His gaze traveled over her, ever so slowly, and a strange sensation swept through her as he assessed her businesslike suit, her chin-length auburn hair, even her fingernails, which were short and coated with clear polish. Suddenly, she longed for sexy red polish and long, elegant nails.

"You haven't changed at all, Carolyn," Ben told her.

She didn't know if that was a compliment or just a general observation.

"Only you would understand that I was mad at that doctor for being the one to figure out Lucy was ill and for not being able to cure Mom. I wanted the impossible from him, and no matter how irrational that is, you just sit there and nod your head. Like you understand everything I'm feeling, even if I can't understand it very well myself." He paused for a moment before saying, "It feels great to talk to you again, Carolyn."

Searching around for something to say amid the morass of emotions that engulfed her, Carolyn found herself spared by the opening of the agency door. Marissa strode in, and Lucy sprang into her daddy's lap.

Marissa looked at Carolyn, a question mark in her eyes.

Carolyn stared at the beautiful woman who seemed on the surface to have everything, and then at the man holding the little girl who meant the world to him. "This is as good a place to start as any," she said to Ben. "Let me call a few people, and then we'll talk again."

They watched her, and Carolyn had the distinct feeling she was the point on a triangle the other two sides needed to retain their shape. She stood, arming herself with professional courtesy.

''I know you have to get to the airport, Marissa, so I won't keep you further. Lucy, I'll be seeing you soon.''

She smiled at the family as they walked in front of her to the door.

Ben turned back to stare at her, and she met his gaze as evenly as she could.

Then he left. She closed the door behind them, walked through the main reception area and into her own office.

She sat in the silence for a few moments, quietly thinking about Ben and everything he'd been through. Examining the feelings she'd once had for him.

Strangely enough, it had not been difficult to see him with Marissa. Not the way she'd always imagined it would be.

Breath stole back into her body. She was okay— her emotions surprisingly unscathed.

If Lily and Dylan wanted her to begin the initial casework, she could handle it. Eileen's faith in her gave her the backbone and desire to make certain everything in her power was done to find a miracle for Lucy.

The first thing she was going to do was put in a call to the hospital to find out how she herself could be tested as a donor match for Lucy. She knew the initial step was a simple blood test, but maybe, just maybe, she could justify Eileen's faith in her. Even if the missing brother turned out to be nothing but the wistful hallucination of a dying woman, Carolyn herself might be able to provide the miracle Lucy needed.

Ben would never have to know.

DR. COLLINS smiled at her when he met her in his office, and Carolyn recognized immediately that they shared a common interest.

"Thank you for seeing me, Doctor."

"My pleasure. I, too, fell under Lucy Mulholland's spell." He smiled at Carolyn. "She is a very sweet little girl. And she's going to be a heartbreaker when she grows up. Not of her own doing, of course. She's like her grandmother and father. A gentle species."

Carolyn blinked. "I couldn't agree more."

The doctor nodded, his blue eyes dark and serious now. "Eileen was a favorite patient of mine. We're not supposed to have favorites, I guess. All patients should be regarded equally. But Eileen had sparkle. She was a real trooper."

Carolyn cleared her throat, sensing the doctor's sadness. This was not the time to pry about Eileen, so she stuck with her basic question. "You were going to tell me about the blood testing process."

"The first stage is simple. You'll get a blood test, which we can do here at the hospital, and the results will be analyzed." He smiled, his eyes bright with humor. "I will admit to having been caught by Lucy's situation, and rendered up my own arm for a test."

Carolyn stared at him.

"Unfortunately, I'm not a match for her. Perhaps you'll have better luck."

"She's had the leukemia for a while, hasn't she?"

"I think she must have had it for a year before she was tested," the doctor said quietly. "Her leukemia is fairly advanced, which is creating greater havoc in finding a donor, as more selective matches must be found."

Carolyn felt Dr. Collins's intense gaze. Instinctively she knew that he missed nothing. If she had any outward symptoms of ill health, he would have seen them by now. She got up, told herself she was being irrational, but did her best to suck in her scarred abdomen anyway. "Thank you for your assistance, Dr. Collins. I appreciate your taking the time to see me."

"We'll keep our fingers crossed that you get better news than I did." He walked her to the office door. "Tell Mr. Mulholland hello if you see him."

"I will. Thank you." She forced a smile and hurried from the office. Once in her car, she dropped her purse into the front seat and let down the windows. September heat was stifling in Texas, but her breathlessness came from a different source. She turned on the car and hit the air conditioner button.

Hot air blasted her. She put her head back against the headrest and closed her eyes.

Control. Ben felt out of control—that's why he resented Dr. Collins. Ben wasn't confident these days of his own ability to protect his family.

Carolyn took a deep breath and glanced at the clock. In one hour, she would have the preliminary test that could prove her a match possibility for Lucy. She didn't feel in control, either.

She dialed a number on her cell phone. "Hi," she said when her best friend, Emily Chambers, answered.

"Hey, Caro."

"What would you say if I told you that Ben Mulholland came to see me yesterday?"

"That it was an interesting turn of events. How did he look?"

Carolyn smiled at the teasing tone in Emily's voice. "He hasn't changed much in the looks department."

"So your heart went pitty-pat?"

She rolled her eyes. "I met his daughter, and his wife. Ex-wife."

"And?"

"His daughter is sick with leukemia."

"Oh, no!"

"She's five, Em, and she's adorable. Precious. Demanding. Wants as much of her daddy as she can get."

"Ahem. And your heart…"

"Went right out the window. I'm waiting to have a blood test right now to see if I'm a preliminary match."

"Oh, God, Caro," Emily said on a sigh. "You were born a trouper."

"Don't tell anyone."

"Of course not. But I love you for being brave."

Carolyn thought about the lines of anxiety around Ben's eyes, the tightness around Marissa's million-dollar lips. "I'm not brave. I'm so afraid I'm looking for an easy way out."

"Meaning?"

"Ben came to me with a case request, and I'm not sure I'm the one to handle it."

"And you're calling me to get the green light."

"I'm calling you for a healthy dose of common sense."

Emily cleared her throat. "Let me see if I have the picture right. Ben wants you to help him with something, but already you feel the tugging of little heartstrings not just for him, but for his too cute daughter who is very ill. And you're not sure you can keep your heart from getting steamrolled flat again. So you're having the blood test done on the improbable chance that you're a match, so you could give him what his daughter needs and duck out on him."

"Without sparing me, you seem to have outlined my dilemma pretty well," Carolyn muttered.

"You're still in love with him."

"Would that shock you?"

"Would it shock me? No. Would it astound me

that you finally admitted it? Yes. Beyond words, actually.''

Carolyn closed her eyes. ''Oh, Emily. What a mess.''

''All right. I think you should have the test and pray for a miracle, for Lucy's sake. But if you're not a match, all you can do is talk to Dylan and Lily about the case. They're the ones who'll steer you right.''

She opened her eyes again. ''Emily? Do you remember when we first met each other, when we were working at the adoption center? And there were all those kids who needed families, and we always wanted to scoop them into our hearts and love them?''

''We tried to be pragmatic, though,'' Emily said. ''If you can't help Lucy and Ben, you can't, hon. There's only so much one person can do.''

''That's what I keep telling myself. Only this time, that knowledge doesn't make me feel any better.''

''The fact that you're personally involved is what Ben was counting on, Caro, or he wouldn't have specifically sought you out. He's hoping that because you cared about him and Eileen, you'll do your damnedest to help his daughter. But you can't save her, Caro. All you can really do is save him by being his friend.''

Friend. Could she be his friend? Sure. She could do that.

''Thanks, Em. I feel much better now.''

"Good. Go get your arm stuck, and let me know what you find out. It's too easy to work out this neatly, you know. The ex-girlfriend having the one thing the hero desperately needs. It's too romance novel, but I admire you terribly for trying."

Carolyn snorted. "You said I was looking for a cop-out to keep myself from having to fail if I couldn't solve the case in a satisfactory manner."

"I didn't say that," Emily told her, "you just did."

Carolyn was silent.

"Besides, what does motivation matter? The cold fact is Lucy needs a donor. So go get tested, and see if you can escape from the past that easily."

"Thanks, Em—I think." She wrinkled her nose and hung up the phone.

The thought of Ben alone in the world made her open the car door and get out, locking it behind her. On the surface, taking the test seemed like a brave thing to do, but what made her even more afraid was not being able to give Ben what he wanted most.

Again.

CHAPTER THREE

SUPPRESSING ANY lingering reservations, Carolyn called Dylan Garrett on his cell phone the following morning. ''There's a case which has been brought to Finders Keepers,'' she told him. ''Ben Mulholland wants us to see if there's any chance he had a twin who was taken from his mother at birth. His mother became suspicious because of the Austin baby ring which was broken. She was also convinced she heard two children crying when she gave birth.''

''She's waited all this time to mention that?''

''Ben believes medication may have jogged his mother's memory. She was dying of breast cancer and heavily medicated, which he believes helped unlock her memory of Ben's birth.''

''Or it could be the confused dream of a seriously ill woman.''

''Right. But I knew Eileen Mulholland, and she was firmly based in reality. I tend to believe the story's credible, mainly because of that.''

''And Mr. Mulholland wants this twin found to make his mother rest easier on her deathbed.''

''Actually, his mother has already passed away,''

she said with a lump in her throat. "It's his daughter he's concerned about now."

"Because?"

She sighed. "She has leukemia, and she needs a donor match."

"There's no guarantee the twin could provide one."

"Right."

"But a missing twin might provide what the bone marrow database hasn't been able to," he mused. "Hope."

"Ben gave his mother's story some credence once the shock wore off," Carolyn said. "If I didn't know the people involved, I wouldn't think it very likely. It's your agency, and your decision to accept or refuse the case—"

"This is what Finders Keepers does," Dylan interrupted. "Find the impossible. Start the preliminary search, and let me know what you find out. Lily's pretty swamped with wedding details, but this is more my area anyway. The first thing I'd do is get on the phone with Jennifer Rodriguez, and pick her brain as to what kinds of files are best and most available for this kind of search. Bounce it off her, and keep in touch."

"Thanks, Dylan," Carolyn said softly.

"No need to thank me. I know you can handle it, or I wouldn't have hired you to oversee the office."

That wasn't what she meant. She was grateful he

wanted Finders Keepers to take the case. But there was no need to correct his assumption. It meant a lot that he had that kind of faith in her abilities.

"Don't worry. You'll do fine. You're tenacious when you get into something, Carolyn."

"That's the same word someone else used to describe me."

"Well, it's a good trait in our business. Best of luck. Call me if you hit a pothole."

"I will." She hung up the phone, jumping when the door swung open. Ben walked inside, his little daughter at his side. Lucy headed straight for the candy dish, and Ben headed straight for Carolyn.

Her heart seemed to plummet downward like a fainting bird as his hazel eyes met hers.

"I'm glad you stopped by, Ben," Carolyn said, her voice friendly yet not more than that. "I just talked to Dylan Garrett about your case, and he believes Finders Keepers should try to obtain as much information for you as we can."

With those words, she steered them onto a business-like track. Immediately Ben realized Carolyn wasn't comfortable with what he'd asked of her. Taking this case went against her wishes to keep him at arm's length, which is what she'd tried to do from the moment he'd walked into the office. He'd insisted she be the one to help him, but he also respected the wall she'd erected to protect herself.

Okay. He didn't want to upset her. The fact was,

she was doing him a hell of a favor, and he wouldn't have come to Carolyn if his mother hadn't insisted. But Eileen had been correct. Carolyn of the soft heart would put her utmost into finding the truth of a twin, for Lucy's sake.

It had nothing to do with Ben.

"I appreciate that," he said briskly. "I feel better knowing that Lucy and I are in capable hands."

Carolyn looked at him evenly. "I'll need preliminary information, such as your place of birth. Also, I think we should be prepared for the consequences of what happens should we succeed with our search."

"Hopefully there's a match and…" His voice trailed off.

"There's always the possibility this twin won't want to have his or her life changed by the revelation of an unknown family."

Ben considered her. "I've thought of that. Selfish as it may seem, I'm not focusing on that right now."

"Donor matches are generally done anonymously," Carolyn said crisply. "In this case, we're counting on the family tie to secure the compliance of this person. But we have to be prepared that if you do have a missing twin, he may not be all that welcoming. It's a bridge we can cross when we come to it, but I feel we should take it into consideration at this point."

Ben bowed his head. "It must seem cold-blooded

of me, but I'd be willing to turn someone else's life upside down to save my daughter's.''

She shook her head. ''We just need to be prepared for the fact that this search is going to be very emotional. For everyone involved.''

He looked at her narrowly. ''I'd sell my soul to save my child. I swear I would.''

''You can discuss the retainer with us later,'' she said dryly. ''I doubt Finders Keepers wants your soul, exactly. However, we don't come cheaply, so let's get to work. Is Lucy going to be all right while we talk? There's a small TV in the reception area, and we could turn on 'Sesame Street,' or whatever it is kids watch these days.''

'' 'Sesame Street' would be perfect, but I warn you, she won't let me far out of her sight.''

''I had noticed that.'' They stood, and the three of them walked into the reception area outside Carolyn's office. It contained a sofa, two chairs, walls of books, a TV and a gum ball machine. ''This is sort of the lounge.'' She flipped on the TV, and Lucy bounced onto the sofa.

''Sit by me, Daddy,'' she commanded.

''I can't right now. I have to talk to Miss Carolyn.'' He glanced at Carolyn with his brows knit. ''*Miss* Carolyn?''

The blush that stole over her features was endearing. At twenty-seven, not many woman blushed. But Carolyn was not like any other woman he knew.

She would not get on a plane to go to a fashion shoot if her daughter was ill. Of course, he couldn't totally blame Marissa for running away. Sometimes he wanted to run as fast and as far as he could to get away from Lucy's illness.

The trouble was, his little girl had to be the one to outrun it. He couldn't do it for her.

"It is 'Miss,'" Carolyn said, her tone almost frosty to remind him to stay on his side of the wall.

"Miss St. Clair and I will be over here in her office," he said in the same crisp tone so she'd know he'd got the message. "Call me if you need anything, Lucy."

"Miss Carolyn is fine," she told Ben as they walked behind the stone half wall that separated Carolyn's office from the reception area. "Actually Carolyn is fine with me, if you don't mind Lucy calling me that." She motioned Ben to take a seat across from her.

"We prefer Miss or Mrs. or Mr.," Ben said firmly. "Lucy is a handful, and we're trying to teach her proper manners from the start. It's easier than undoing bad ones, and believe me, she appears angelic, but she'll try the patience of the saints. Once we found out she was ill, it was more difficult to be strict, but—" He stopped, realizing he sounded as if he were lecturing. As if he'd gone into teacher mode, stressing the explanation to a rebellious student.

Carolyn didn't seem to notice. She sat down at her

desk and pulled out a folder marked with his name and inserted a new tape into her ever present recorder. "Let's start with your birth certificate, of course. You were born on the outskirts of Austin, correct? A record of birth would have had to be filed at the county courthouse, and one with the state. We'll need to compare them."

He stared at her, realizing she was asking for more than the rote repetition of what was on his insurance.

"Whatever you can't remember, we need to make notes so that we can look up this information."

"Jeez, I wish Mom was alive," he said slowly. "I'm not sure I can remember all of it, and she could rattle off family details like a professor."

"Well, we'll have to do this without her," Carolyn said, her voice gentle. "Ben, we have to determine the best way to begin searching for the existence of this person. We've got a good start but these are the things we have to know. Whatever you can remember will be crucial in saving us time."

He let her straightforward manner wash over him. She was right, of course. He had to rely upon himself now.

And Carolyn. He wasn't totally alone and defenseless in the world as long as he had her on his side.

"IT SEEMS TO ME that the first person we should speak to is this Dr. Benton." Carolyn looked at Ben to see if he agreed. "Everything we've discussed leads back to the fact that the doctor is more than likely the only person who knows what really happened when your mother gave birth.''

He nodded. ''How do we proceed on a matter like this? Do you think this falls under physician-patient privilege, even though Mom is gone?''

Caroline tightened her lips thoughtfully. ''A patient's records would still be confidential after death. However, talking to the doctor is a logical first step. I, for one, would be quite interested to hear what he has to say. First of all, he's going to be quite surprised to have us show up out of the blue asking questions about the delivery.''

''What compelling excuse can we use to get him to pull Mom's records from the file? After all these years, there's a good possibility the records no longer even exist. How long are doctors obligated to keep a patient's records?''

''Even after a patient is deceased, most doctors keep the files in what is known as a dead file or something along that line. Patients change doctors, and those histories have to be moved from an active file into another system. They're somewhere. The question is, would he still have Eileen's files in his office or would he have moved them into a storage facility?''

''I'll go to Mom's lockbox at the bank,'' Ben suggested. ''I know that's where she kept my original birth certificate. It's probably a good idea to look at that before we see Dr. Benton.''

Carolyn nodded, opening an appointment book. ''I'll call and schedule an appointment with Dr. Benton.''

Ben put his hand over hers, surprising her. The contact sent warmth shimmering through her, and she found it difficult to meet his eyes.

''Maybe an unannounced visit would be best.''

Carolyn held her breath until Ben removed his hand from hers. She exhaled, forcing herself to think about the words and not the man. ''The element of surprise can't hurt, but we shouldn't assume Dr. Benton would be unhelpful,'' she reminded him.

''Sorry.'' He dipped his head somewhat sheepishly. ''I don't mean to sound combative. But Mom's story has begun to be very real to me. That makes Dr. Benton a bad guy.''

Carolyn nodded slowly. ''I can't blame you for the way you feel.'' Whether Douglas Benton was a bad guy or not remained to be seen, but she understood Ben's need to hope that there was an enemy out there that could be defeated. It had to be hellish to be fighting the enemy he was pitted against—his daughter's disease—with no weapons to rely on.

The love for his daughter was strong in this father. She admired that he so desperately wanted to be able to ride up on a charger and save her. But it also broke her heart. What if he failed? ''Leave Lucy with me, if you like, and see if you can locate your birth certificate. We can proceed from there.''

"You don't mind Lucy staying?"

She shook her head. "Not at all."

His eyes settled on her with some unidentifiable emotion. "Thanks, Carolyn. She could use a friend right now."

Then he got up and walked out the door without saying another word, his shoulders stiff, his back straight. Carolyn bowed her head.

It wasn't sympathy that made her see Ben in such a rose-colored light. She simply had never stopped loving him, and in the moment when he was suffering the most, she found herself tearing her own heart in two as she struggled not to let herself fall for him all over again.

Falling for Ben Mulholland had been the easiest thing she had ever done—getting over him had been impossible.

BEN'S BIRTH certificate appeared to be like any other she had seen. Carolyn wasn't sure what she'd been expecting, but maybe she'd been hoping against hope that some clue would pop out from the stamped page and point her in the right direction.

But the slightly yellowed Texas state document lay on the desk before her, innocuous and ordinary. She blew out a breath.

"Nothing special there," Ben said.

She smiled to herself at the tandem tracking of their minds and picked up her purse. "I'll head to Dr. Benton's now and see what I can find out."

"I'm going with you."

"You don't need to do that, Ben. Investigating this case is what you're paying Finders Keepers to do."

"Trust me. I need to do this."

Under the circumstances, she could understand how he felt—and she had to admit that she looked forward to his and Lucy's company as well. "Will a long drive be too hard on Lucy?"

"I don't think so. She can sleep in the car, and anyway, she enjoys small outings away from the house. She gets cabin fever."

Carolyn smiled as Ben rose and went into the lounge, where Lucy was engrossed in a conversation with stuffed animals and a plastic tea set Carolyn had unearthed from the main house. She heard Lucy mildly protest at having to leave the new toys behind, before acquiescing to her father's coaxing. Carolyn's lungs seemed to squeeze tight inside her. Ben was the parent she'd known he would be. She'd made the right decision all those years ago, and if she'd paid for that choice with unimaginable emotional pain, then it had been the right thing to do. Ben and Lucy adored each other—Carolyn couldn't imagine one without the other.

She started to call to Ben that Lucy was welcome to take the stuffed animals in the car with her, but then he appeared with Lucy riding on his back. "*Someone* had taken off their shoes and socks," he said with a grin.

Carolyn smiled at Lucy. "That sounds like a good thing to do."

"Mm-hm," Lucy agreed. She squeezed her thin little arms around her daddy's shoulders in a sweet hug.

It was like looking at a face full of sunshine. Those corners of Carolyn's heart that had never known that sunshine absorbed the light wistfully. "Come on," she said softly. "Let's go see what we can find out."

They drove approximately eighty miles north to the Austin address listed as Dr. Benton's in the phone book. Parking the car, Carolyn didn't allow herself to become apprehensive about the questions they would pose to Douglas Benton. Because of Lucy's situation, she wouldn't allow herself to feel anything but hope. She tapped on the front door of the house and gave Ben a smile that felt weak, though she meant it to be comforting.

The wooden inside door opened, and a woman peered through the screen door at them.

"Can I help you?"

"We're looking for Douglas Benton," Carolyn said.

"Why?" the woman asked, her tone suspicious.

Somewhat taken aback, Carolyn looked over the middle-aged woman more carefully. Her hair was unkempt, her figure rounded with lack of exercise. She wore orange polyester pants and a short-sleeved brown shirt. Somehow she didn't look like the wife of a prominent local doctor. "I'm Carolyn St. Clair," she said, forgoing introducing Ben for the moment, in case his name alerted the woman to the reason for their presence. "Would you be Mrs. Benton?"

The woman raised her eyebrows and studied the threesome, her gaze hovering on Lucy for a second before returning to Carolyn. "Luckily for me, no."

Uncertain how to take that, Carolyn pressed forward. "This is the Benton home?"

"It is. But only Mrs. Benton lives here. Dr. Benton died the first week of August, so you've just missed him, you might say," the woman said with a snort.

CHAPTER FOUR

BEN'S HEART contracted at the unwelcome news. He clutched Lucy's hand tighter in his to calm himself. The unhelpful woman was clearly annoyed with their presence. He decided to allow Carolyn to continue on her course—after all, she was doing her job. He stood still on the porch, torn between giving in to despair and chewing the woman out for her dismissive attitude.

Of course, she had no way of knowing that their mission was one of life-and-death. He had too much invested in the situation, and his desperation was setting his emotions at flashpoint.

Carolyn's calm voice pushed back the rush of disappointment swelling his heart. "I am sorry to hear of his passing. We were unaware that he was ill."

The woman shrugged. "What is it you wanted with him, anyway?"

"Actually, it's a private matter. Could you possibly direct us to Mrs. Benton?"

"I can, but it'll do you as little good as Dr. Benton."

To Ben's surprise, the contrary woman opened the

screen door. They stepped into the dark hallway, the musty smell of the house oppressive. A very unpleasant place to live, he thought suddenly. And this was the residence of the man who had helped his mother deliver him. He frowned. If this doctor had been guilty of baby smuggling, wouldn't he have chosen somewhere better to live?

"Thank you for allowing us to see Mrs. Benton," Carolyn said. "I realize this is something of an imposition, and I hope she won't mind us coming without an appointment."

The woman looked at them for a moment, her expression amused but not in a kind way. "Down the hall," was all she said.

Ben followed Carolyn, deciding to scoop Lucy into his arms. Something about this house rattled him, though he couldn't put his finger on it.

He moved into a large room, almost empty, it seemed, of personal effects. Only an overstuffed sofa and a television filled the space—and an old woman in a chair who sat watching "Hollywood Squares," her back to them.

Carolyn went over to her. "Mrs. Benton?"

The elderly woman ignored her.

"Mrs. Benton?" she repeated. When there was no response, Carolyn glanced at Ben, concerned. "I don't think she can hear me."

"Sometimes she can, sometimes she can't—depends on whether her mind's fixed or not," the woman informed them. "She's got a rare form of brain cancer. Lately she's more out than in, if you know what I mean. The doctor's wife ain't in, ain't in her right mind."

"Are you her caregiver?" Ben asked, his disgust growing with every word she uttered.

"As much as I can be. Heaven only knows I'm more of a guard most of the time."

"A guard?" Carolyn asked.

"She'll get it into her head that she's going to drive her car, and if I so much as turn away for a second, she's out there behind the wheel, angry at the car because she can't get it to go. I hid the keys, but still she tries."

Carolyn looked at Mrs. Benton for a few more seconds, her gaze searching the woman's profile. After a moment, she said, "We're looking for some records. Is there anyone in charge of the doctor's records?"

"Just her," the woman said. "She was his nurse, and his office manager, I suppose. They pretty much worked as a team. You're not from around here, are ya, or you'd know that."

"I'm not," Carolyn said. "This is Ben Mulholland, and his daughter, Lucy. We think that Dr. Benton assisted Ben's mother in her delivery. We're looking for Eileen Mulholland's records."

"I can't give you none of that," the caregiver said, "even if I knew where they were."

Mrs. Benton turned her head. "Eileen?" she asked in a quavering voice. "Eileen?"

"Eileen Mulholland," Carolyn repeated softly. Ben's heart seemed to pause.

Mrs. Benton frowned, obviously trying to sort through something in her mind. "Eileen."

"Mulholland," Carolyn said again.

The woman scratched at her hand. "Is she here?"

"No." Carolyn's voice was soft. "She died."

"Oh, no," Mrs. Benton said. "She didn't die. She's a healthy farm girl. I took her vital signs."

Carolyn's gaze met Ben's in triumph, but all he felt was a keyed-up sense of fear. He wanted answers, but how were they going to get them out of this addled woman?

Mrs. Benton turned toward the television again, apparently finished.

"Won't get much out of her," the caregiver informed them. "You're lucky you got that much. Say, if this Eileen Mulholland is dead, what are you wanting to see her records for?"

"Eileen Mulholland is not dead," Mrs. Benton disagreed without taking her attention from "Hollywood Squares." "I took her vital signs myself."

"Her health history could help us determine whether little Lucy here is predisposed to any medical problems."

Ben admired Carolyn's quick and logical answer. If nothing else, she was managing to squeeze some water from a very difficult stone. He'd have walked away with an empty cup if he'd been in charge of the questioning.

Carolyn took Lucy from Ben's arms and brought her near to Mrs. Benton, as if to engender a bond between them. To his surprise, Mrs. Benton glanced at the child—then drew back as if she were afraid.

"Is there something wrong with her?" the caregiver asked bluntly, her voice hard as she stared at Lucy. "She looks sick to me."

Ben took Lucy back from Carolyn and held her more tightly to his chest, willing his anger to burn itself out. *Let Carolyn handle this,* he reminded himself. *If you give this old witch a righteous asschewing, you're going to blow any chance of learning what you need to know.*

"I think I'll go for a drive," Mrs. Benton said. "I need to drive."

The caregiver sighed. "No, Mrs. Benton, no drive for you. But if you be quiet, I'll push your wheelchair in the garden." She brought a wheelchair over from a side room and helped her charge up, then glanced at the guests. "I think you've gotten all you're going to out of her. Could you see yourselves out? If I leave her while she's taken a notion to go driving, I'll come back here and find her gone. One time she walked down the street and tried to get into someone's house. She kept repeating over and over that she was an orphan and needed a home. Poor devil."

"We can see ourselves out," Carolyn assured her. "Thank you for your time."

"But—" Ben began, but Carolyn shook her head.

The wheelchair moved toward the back of the house, and they heard a door open and shut.

"I'll bet she tells everyone she sees that she's being kept prisoner. She's probably 'out' a lot more of the time than she's 'in' just to survive living with that battle-ax."

"No," Carolyn disagreed. "Mrs. Benton's suffering is real. The interesting thing was, she totally clicked in when anything was mentioned about patients or nursing. Did you notice how that really caught her attention? I have a feeling she was a very competent nurse. It's the part of her life she seemed very cognizant of. She remembered your mother had been a patient, and that she'd taken her vitals."

"Great, so Nurse Ratched was a nurse down to her cuticles. How does that help us?"

"It's something to go on."

He followed Carolyn as she moved to the front of the house.

"Daddy, can we go yet?" Lucy asked.

"We'll go, sweetie. I know you're getting tired." He was frustrated by the lack of information they'd found, but he injected his voice with kindness for Lucy's sake. Inside, he cursed, hating the brick wall they'd hit.

Carolyn walked into another room off the hallway,

her gaze on the steel filing cabinets lining one wall. "There's probably a gold mine of information hidden in those steel drawers."

"I think you need a search warrant or a request or something, Carolyn," he said worriedly. He'd hired her for her tenacity, but he didn't know if this much was a good thing. She had a determined gleam in her eye that hinted at her intentions. "Carolyn, if you go through those cabinets and the harpy catches you, she may call the police on us. I wouldn't put it past her."

"We don't have a lot of time for legal dancing," Carolyn said. She pointed to the garden, where they could see the wheelchair being pushed by the unenthusiastic caregiver. "Why don't you go settle Lucy in the car? I'll be right behind you."

"Getting fired from your job isn't something I want to have you do on my behalf," Ben said, watching as she walked into the office.

Carolyn ignored him as she opened the first set of steel drawers. "I'm not doing this on your behalf," she said, her voice preoccupied as she looked into some files. "These files are in a feminine hand, rather than masculine, which makes me think Mrs. Benton was far more than just a simple temperature taker. She was his partner."

"Miss Carolyn," Lucy said. "You're not 'posed to touch people's things without asking."

Ben patted his daughter's back. "In our home, we

teach that it's not good to just take things we want, Carolyn."

She glanced up at him, then at Lucy. "I always knew you'd be an excellent father, Ben."

He frowned. "What does that mean? You make it sound so strange."

She smiled at his harsh tone. "Sh. You two go outside—you're wrecking my concentration. I think I'm onto something here."

"You'd better be. The harpy's on her way back inside."

Carolyn flipped a page in a file. "There's no way that's possible," she said.

"Oh, yes, it is. She sees our car hasn't moved, and she knows exactly what we're doing. Come on, Carolyn."

"No, I mean, how could the good doctor have been on the outskirts of Austin to deliver you, then deliver a baby four hours away at the same time?"

"I don't know, damn it! Come on, Carolyn!"

"Daddy! Don't say *damn it*," Lucy protested, but Ben held his daughter tighter and grabbed Carolyn's arm with his free hand. She stuffed the file back into the cabinet and closed it just as they heard the wheelchair bumping the porch door.

"You are the most hardheaded, intractable, tenacious person I know," he said between gritted teeth as he hauled her toward the car. He opened the driver side door for her, then went around to the passenger side, so he could strap Lucy in the back seat. Glancing over his shoulder, he was relieved to see that the caregiver wasn't brandishing a broom or some other weapon at them.

"That's what you hired me for," Carolyn snapped. "It was the trait you were specifically looking for."

"Buckle up," he commanded. He slammed the door and hurried to the driver's side, getting in and cranking the engine. The car pulled away from the curb, and he allowed himself a breath. "I don't want you bending laws, Carolyn. I'm desperate, yeah, but not enough for you to put yourself at risk."

She ignored him, her forehead creased in thought. "Your mother was about twenty years younger than Dr. Benton's wife," she mused.

"So?"

"For someone whose husband had so many patients, it's odd that she remembered your mother. And her handwriting was clear in that file. She doesn't strike me as the kind of person who allowed herself to make errors. We saw how quickly her memory snapped back into place when the nurse in her was called up. Kind of like a policeman or military personnel, who make it a habit to remember times, places, dates and other pertinent facts."

"What are you getting at?" Ben demanded. "That precise Nurse Ratched made an incorrect entry? That she recorded the wrong time on one occasion?"

"I think she recorded exactly what she wanted to. The question is, why did she misrepresent the facts?"

"Can you know that she did?"

"I know a doctor doesn't deliver two children at the same time in locations that are four hours apart. According to her daily notations for your birth date, that's exactly what happened."

"It could have been a simple error—"

"I don't think so. She remembered your mother, she remembered that her status was healthy. I have the strangest feeling that she might have remembered more—she just didn't feel like revealing it. Or maybe she couldn't. The memory suppresses difficult things over time."

"What difficult thing might she have been suppressing?"

Carolyn looked at him with clear eyes. "That her husband stole babies and sold them for a profit. And that she was an accessory."

CAROLYN DROVE Ben back to Finders Keepers to pick up his car and, at his request, followed him out to the farmhouse where he lived on the outskirts of San Antonio so that he could feed Lucy and put her to bed. Then they needed to discuss what they'd learned and decide on the next course of action. At first she was nervous going to his house. She was afraid she'd see traces of Marissa everywhere. Then she was ashamed of herself for being so spiteful. For Lucy's sake, she should hope that there was much of Marissa's presence in evidence.

But to Carolyn's surprise, the small house was devoid of pictures or anything else that spoke of the beautiful model. Instantly, the word that came to Carolyn's mind was *comfortable*. Clean. Home. *Ben*.

She lowered her gaze, thinking that her heart had never been in the jeopardy it was in at this very moment. Ben was a protector, and she'd always sensed that with him, she would find warmth. Security.

To distract herself, she glanced around Ben's home. Log cabin style, the small house welcomed her. The main room was decorated with a blue-and-red Mexican blanket on one wall and another on the rough floor. A brown leather sofa, well-worn and all the more inviting for it, sat directly across from a long picture window. In front of the sofa rested a scarred pine table. Small pillows and two lamps of an indeterminable metal adorned the room. Carolyn wanted to kick off her shoes, sink into the sofa and wrap herself in Ben.

Carolyn St. Clair, you'd be a lot safer if you found a blanket to wrap yourself in.

Grimacing at her fancies, she perched on a chair in the kitchen instead. She spread some papers from her briefcase onto the dark wooden table and waited for Ben to return from changing Lucy into her pajamas.

Her gaze resumed its restless perusal of the room.

It was very difficult to imagine Marissa being happy in this house.

"Lucy was tired," Ben said, coming into the room. "She didn't want to eat. She just wanted her back rubbed, and then she went to sleep. The chemo she's undergone has taken a lot of her strength. She's getting spunkier, but then she'll suddenly fold like a wet piece of paper."

"Ben, I am so sorry the two of you are going through this. I wish there was something more I could do."

He sat down across from her, leaning back into the chair in an exhausted sprawl. His worn boots jutted across the floor, and his faded jeans gave him a long, lean line that made her unwillingly think about how sexy he was.

"You're doing the only thing that needs to be done, Carolyn. As far as I'm concerned, you're trying to single-handedly find me a miracle."

He gave her a tired smile, the small lines around his eyes reinforcing the warmth of his words.

"What if I can't?" she asked softly. "Ben, I'm so afraid."

Slowly, he shook his head, still wearing that soft smile as if he understood. "Don't be. I didn't say I expected you to single-handedly produce the miracle, Carolyn. That's for God to do. But I've got you on my team, and I'm not half so lonely and afraid when you're with me."

She had to look away from the kindness in his eyes. Her mind went back too fast to their time together. He had always been the strength she reached out to. Now he was saying she was his strength. It was an unspoken ebb-and-flow between them that had always existed. Maybe that was the way it should happen in a relationship: when one person was weak, the other offered strength.

Maybe it could have all been different if she'd gone to Ben when she'd been at her weakest point, and accepted his strength.

But confiding that her weakness was her woman's body would have been too…devastating. There was no point in thinking about the past now, anyway. What was done was done, and the trait of hers she was most proud of was her ability to keep her emotions in check.

I haven't been doing a very good job of that lately. Ben and Lucy were reviving emotions in her that she'd thought long laid to rest. Forgotten. The way she wanted them.

Ben's voice, low and warm, suddenly asked, "Speaking of lonely and afraid, Carolyn, I've been meaning to ask you if you ever hear from your sister, Christine."

CHAPTER FIVE

CAROLYN LOWERED her lashes, not wanting to think about her older sister. She had enough pain at hand to conquer.

She met Ben's gaze. "No," she said softly, "it's been quite some time since Christine and I have communicated."

And that was all she intended to say on the matter. Before he could speak, before the sorrow could cut any deeper, she changed the topic. "Ben, I'd like to suggest that we try to speak to Mrs. Benton once more."

He raised a brow. "What's the point?"

"I want to catch her on a different day. Maybe her lucidity goes by turns. I don't know." She exhaled wistfully. "It's a long shot, but somewhere in the tangled recess of her mind, she remembered your mother. I'd like to give her another chance to tell us more before we proceed further."

"I'm game." He shrugged. "And after that?"

"I'm going to ask Jennifer Rodriguez to help me with a computer search of children born on that day in that location. If we can narrow the living births for that day and time, then we can compare them with your own. Should one be a close match, we can search for a birth record. Somewhere, there'll be a birth certificate that would tell us more.'' She shoved the papers back into her briefcase after making some notes on them and looked up. ''Of course, this is all a what-if scenario. I'm just outlining the steps I'd suggest we follow if the pieces should fall into place.''

''If there is a birth certificate, it would have bogus information on it.''

''Yes. I would expect that. But Jennifer could dig deeper for us at that point.''

''If we had that many lucky breaks, Carolyn, I'm not certain I'd want to trust my daughter's only chance to a woman I don't know, this Jennifer Rodriguez.''

She understood that. ''Dylan has great faith in her. I'm relying on her expertise. But we could certainly set up a meeting with Jennifer for you, if you'd like.''

He leaned his head against the sofa for a moment and closed his eyes. ''Not now. I'm going to trust your instincts.''

A cat jumped into his lap, startling Carolyn since she hadn't realized it was in the room. Without opening his eyes, Ben covered the cat's back with his large hand, stroking lightly. Obviously, this was a routine man and pet both expected and enjoyed. Carolyn felt a swift stab of envy for the cherished warmth of the Mulholland home.

Counterproductive. She got to her feet and picked up her briefcase. "I'm going to let myself out, Ben, but I suggest we try one more visit with Mrs. Benton tomorrow. If that doesn't work into your schedule, I'm more than happy to go alone."

"I may get Lucy's favorite sitter to come over. I don't want to wear her out with a lot of running around. I'm taking time off from teaching, and hired someone to help with the ranch, so I'm flexible." He rose to his feet and walked toward her with the clear intention of showing her to the door. A polite gesture, nothing more—but Carolyn winced at the unexpected surge of attraction she felt as Ben approached. He stared down at her, his eyes shadowed with questions. "I can't let you go alone," he said softly. "The truth is, I want to be there if you find out anything from Benton's wife. If the wildest case scenario pans out and she and her husband did steal my brother, she's responsible for tearing our family apart and cheating my mother of her child. I just can't take the coward's way out on this one, Carolyn."

She stared at him. "Ben, the woman is old and sick—"

He held up a hand, his eyes clear with purpose. "I wouldn't look for compensation or revenge, Carolyn. I'm merely saying I need to face this, not let you handle it for me. But I thank you for wanting to do it.'' Pausing for just a moment, he reached up and stroked a strand of hair from her cheek to behind her ear. ''I don't think she has much more to say, frankly. But it would be a miracle and a heartbreak for me if it turned out that Doc Benton was up to more than the good country doctor routine.''

They stared at each other assessingly.

Then he leaned and brushed a kiss against her lips, so fast that Carolyn might have called it friends-only if he hadn't lingered at the last second. Her pulse quickened, the old heartache flared—and she stepped away as quickly as she could. ''Meet me at my office as early as you can.''

Without waiting for him to open the door, Carolyn did so, hurrying outside to her car. Through the windshield, she could see Ben's silhouette in the lighted doorway. Heart pounding, she pulled from the driveway, willing herself not to look back at the past.

BEN COULDN'T SAY why he'd kissed Carolyn. It had started out as a friendly thank-you, or so he thought. But once he got there, the feeling had been so good, he hadn't wanted to stop. So he'd lingered, realizing he was doing what he'd wanted to since… The realization struck him. He'd never stopped wanting to kiss her. To be with her.

She was the one who had ended their relationship. That was a long time ago, before Marissa, before Lucy, before acute lymphocytic leukemia. Except for wishing away Lucy's disease, he wouldn't change the past for anything, of course. Neither would Carolyn, from the way she'd stayed still beneath his lips and then fled as quickly as her feet could carry her.

He sighed, going out back to set out the pet bowls, which brought Lucy's menagerie running in anticipation. For all he knew, Carolyn had some type of romantic involvement going. All she'd said was that she was still single, not that she was currently available.

"Okay, so a friendly, sincere thank-you got out of hand," he said to the cats and dogs as he scooped dry food into bowls. "I should have known better than to stir up the past."

Looking at Lucy's assortment of furry friends, he sighed. "Maybe I was just in need of some human contact. You'd know how that is. Something more sustaining than divorce and hospital stays and being so scared out of my gut that…" No. He wouldn't say that, not even out loud. There was a miracle out there, and Carolyn was the one to find it. His mother had believed it, and he would, too.

"Hey, I can apologize tomorrow. Maybe."

Each furry head got a quick pat, and then he went back inside the house. He couldn't apologize for kissing Carolyn, even if he hadn't meant it as anything more than brotherly at first. The truth was, it had been a long time since any warmth had touched his soul— and kissing Carolyn had brought a fire blazing to life.

It had only lasted a moment, but it was enough to keep him going.

"AND THEN HE kissed me," Carolyn told Emily.

"Ben is clearly pleased with your services so far." Emily Chambers grinned. "Kidding, of course."

They sat at the kitchen table in the Garrett house, drinking tea and chatting about nothing and everything. It was difficult for Carolyn to think about anything except Ben and Lucy.

"I liked Ben kissing me," Carolyn said softly. "Liking it so much caught me by surprise, but what really panicked me was that it felt as if all our years apart seemed to wash away like yesterday's rain."

"So, maybe there's a rainbow to find," Emily suggested.

"It unnerved me, Em, that I could feel as if we'd never been apart. As if I'd only been waiting for Ben to walk back into my life."

Emily shook her head. "You were very close to Ben and his mother. Since they were pretty much the family you turned to when yours hit a rough patch, I'm not surprised you'd feel this remarkable reconnection. There's nothing wrong with that, Caro."

"I don't know." She sighed, tracing her finger along the white saucer edge. "I don't want to feel all that emotion again. The likelihood of a miraculous brother out there is slim to impossible. If this search doesn't work out, I'll feel like I let Ben down."

"Carolyn," Emily said, her voice sympathetic, "look. You're not responsible for Ben's happiness. His mother died, he dealt with it. There may not be a brother, he'll deal with it. His daughter may die, hon, and his heart will be broken, but he's not going to blame it on you. He's going to suffer, and he's going to grieve." She shrugged. "You've got to get past thinking that you owe him perfection, that you have to be some fantastic maximum madonna for him to truly love you. He had a child without you, and he could have another. But maybe, just maybe, he'd rather have you, hysterectomy and all."

Carolyn closed her eyes and felt Emily's hand cover hers lightly. "It's just so hard. Marissa—"

"Marissa is not some golden goddess of the ovaries. She is not Ben's perfect woman, or they wouldn't be divorced. Stop selling yourself short, and wait to see if the kiss leads to anything more than just a kiss."

Emily's hand moved away, and Carolyn opened her eyes, smiling slightly. "I am being silly."

"You are being normal. But let me put it into perspective for you. It's a deep dark secret, but people kiss their cats, their dogs, and sometimes their canaries." She smiled teasingly. "It may have meant something, and then again, it may have just been gratitude. And don't start doubting your value to Ben. He needs you to do the best job you can for him."

Carolyn stood. "Thanks, Emily. I feel so much better now."

"There is one last thing to think about, Carolyn. This isn't really the right time in Ben's life for a grand passion to crop up, is it? All his energy and focus have to be on his daughter. So whatever might have gotten started is no doubt not what he meant or intended. Not that I'm trying to discourage you. I just want to present the practical side of the matter, which is merely returning the favor to someone who is usually Miss Practical herself."

Carolyn laughed. "I'm back now."

"And ready to tackle the project of Mrs. Benton tomorrow?"

"That's the goal."

"How are Lily's wedding plans proceeding, by the way?" Emily asked.

Carolyn smiled. "To hear her tell it, everything is a disaster and everything is wonderful."

"That sounds like a typical bride-to-be," Emily observed. "Maybe you'll find out next."

Carolyn raised her brow. "And maybe I won't. Watching you go through it made me a bit wary."

Emily laughed. "The right man makes it all worthwhile."

AT NINE O'CLOCK sharp the next morning, Ben opened the door to Finders Keepers. He stood tall and slim in dark blue jeans and a polo shirt, and Carolyn made herself give him a brief smile. "Good morning, Ben."

He approached the desk. She gathered up her purse and allowed herself a swift swish at her skirt to make certain the wrinkles were swept out.

"I didn't sleep much last night," he said huskily.

"Did Lucy have a bad night?" Carolyn asked, instantly worried.

"No. And for the first time in months, I wasn't lying awake thinking about Lucy so much as I was thinking about something else."

Vague unease touched her. "Oh?"

"I have to admit that I was thinking about you."

She glanced away from his gaze. Emily's teasing words came back to her—*people kiss their canaries…it may have just been gratitude.* Maybe his kiss *had* been an impulsive gesture and nothing more.

"I can tell you're uncomfortable, Carolyn. And that's the last thing I want you to be."

"I'm not uncomfortable—"

"You won't look at me."

She made herself glance at him. "I just don't know what to think, Ben."

He sighed. "I realized I'd put you in an awkward position. Carolyn, I don't know what came over me. No, that's not exactly what I mean. You're a beautiful woman, and you bring me a lot of happy memories. I suppose I was reaching out for something. Anyway,

I hope we'll be able to continue to work together without too much..."

"Awkwardness?" she supplied, taking pity on him. "It's all right, Ben. A kiss between friends isn't going to turn me into Nervous Nellie."

He smiled, obviously relieved. "I hoped you'd feel that way."

She turned her lips up into an agreeable smile, though it was the last thing she felt like doing. It was best for all parties concerned if everything between her and Ben was strictly business—yet the last thing she'd ever feel toward him was coolly immune.

"Shall we go visit Mrs. Benton, then?"

"I'm ready." She went out the door as Ben held it open.

"Who's watching Lucy?"

"I know a great lady who's a nurse. We call her the 'baby-sitter' and she comes out whenever we need her. She's experienced with the type of illness Lucy has."

They walked toward Ben's truck, and he opened that door for her as well.

"Does she truly like the nurse?" Even though Ben would only be gone a few hours, Carolyn didn't want to think about Lucy being with a starchy person like Mrs. Benton's stern, disheveled caretaker.

"Lucy likes everybody. Haven't you figured that out by now?" He flashed her a grin as he got in the driver's side. They clipped on seat belts and Ben started the engine. "Anyway, to answer your question, this nurse is young and pretty and plays dolls and dollhouse with Lucy to her heart's content. It's my good fortune that she works the night shift."

"Oh," Carolyn murmured. "I see."

He glanced at her again. "She's married to a friend of mine."

"Oh," Carolyn repeated, wishing that piece of information didn't brighten her up so much. She had turned to look out the window so that Ben wouldn't see the dismay on her face at the mention of Lucy's young, pretty nurse, so she totally missed the happy realization lighting his expression.

They sat in silence for most of the eighty-mile drive, Carolyn reading through her notes while Ben listened to soft country-western music. Finally the small house appeared on the road ahead.

"We're here," he said.

CHAPTER SIX

THIS TIME, the caregiver was less anxious to allow them inside the house. She stared at Carolyn and Ben belligerently.

"Mrs. Benton doesn't see visitors. You got her overexcited yesterday, and it took me hours to calm her down."

Ben felt Carolyn's hand on his arm, signaling that she would handle the conversation. He heard Carolyn's calmness with a sense of relief as she began speaking.

"My name is Carolyn St. Clair," she began, "as I mentioned yesterday, and this is Ben Mulholland."

"I remember. That Mulholland business is what got her all stirred up. You ain't coming inside the house. And don't think I don't know you snooped in the office while I was outside. You need permission from Mrs. Benton for that."

"I'd like to get her permission," Carolyn said soothingly. "This is a matter of life and death. We desperately need to find someone."

"You ain't a policewoman, are ya? I don't need any trouble with the police."

Ben frowned. It was an odd statement for a caregiver to make.

"I am not a policewoman. I am merely looking for someone. But I could get a warrant to search the office, I suppose, if you think it would help. I do have friends who are investigators who could assist me—"

A shadow appeared behind the caregiver. Ben stared uneasily, until he realized it was only Mrs. Benton. She stepped forward and put one shaking hand on the screen as she supported herself with a black cane.

"You're back," she said to Carolyn, her eyes bright and lucid as she peered through the mesh.

"Yes, I am. And I'm still hoping to find answers."

Ben held his breath. Carolyn was being very direct—and Mrs. Benton didn't seem threatened by it.

"My husband is dead and he's not coming back," she told Carolyn.

"I know. I'm sorry."

"I don't know that I am. God only knows he's probably roasting in hell."

Ben put his hand at Carolyn's waist for support, but he couldn't have spoken if he'd wanted. Suddenly, it seemed all the breath was gone from his body.

"If you'll take me for a ride in your truck," Mrs. Benton said, "I'll give you thirty minutes to search for what you're looking for."

Carolyn's next words surprised him.

"Mrs. Benton, I know you remember Eileen Mulholland. I knew yesterday that you did. It would help us so much if we knew the truth."

Mrs. Benton held up a hand to silence Carolyn. "I can't help you. I don't want to think about the past. And I don't want to be arrested for it, either. So whatever information you need, you'll have to find it on your own, just as you tried to yesterday."

Emotions so strong hit Ben that the hair on his arms tingled. The woman was as near to admitting what his mother had suspected as she ever would be. He wanted to shout with relief. He wanted to scream with outrage.

He gritted his teeth and kept his hand tight to Carolyn's back. Whether he was supporting Carolyn or himself, he wasn't certain.

"Where do you want us to take you?" Carolyn asked.

"Not you. Him." Mrs. Benton's gaze settled on Ben. "You stay and poke around all you can in thirty minutes. I want my freedom, and I want to be alone with *him*."

He couldn't have been more startled if the skies had opened up and dumped rain solely on his head. The last thing he wanted was to be alone with a woman who might possibly have helped engineer the theft of his mother's child—his own sibling.

"I think we could arrange that, don't you, Ben?"

he heard Carolyn's soothing voice say over the freight train roaring through his head.

"I don't think—" he began.

"I don't think—" the caregiver interrupted.

"*I* think that it's the only way we're all going to get what we want," Mrs. Benton said. "And I probably won't be thinking clearly for long, so I suggest we all move along before I change my mind. Right now," she told Ben, "you have my permission to look through the records. In another five minutes, my condition could flare up and you won't ever have my permission."

He stared at her, pretty certain he was being threatened. It was the last thing he'd expected.

"All I'm asking for is thirty minutes away from this prison," Mrs. Benton said softly. "Your girlfriend gets what you want, I get what I want, and you," she said, turning to her caregiver, "can stick it."

The caregiver gasped. Carolyn grabbed the screen door, opening it wide. "Clock's ticking, Ben. Please take Mrs. Benton for a drive."

He stared at Carolyn. He didn't like leaving her alone in the house with a stranger, and he sure as hell didn't want to drive Mrs. Benton anywhere. Carolyn gently helped Mrs. Benton out the door, and he finally recovered enough to realize he didn't have a choice in the matter. Unflappable as always, Carolyn was ready to do what she had to do.

"One last thing," Mrs. Benton said as she leaned into Ben's supportive hand, "I don't want to know what you find or don't find. I was a damn fine nurse. I also have a pretty good idea why you've come. But if you bring the police here, I'll deny anything and everything. I'm not spending my last clear moments in jail. *She's* bad enough," she said with a jerk of her head toward the caregiver.

The other woman slammed the door and disappeared. Carolyn glanced at Ben, then at Mrs. Benton. "You've thought this through pretty well for someone with your condition. The police are not going to try to have a sick woman prosecuted."

"Trust me, I wish I didn't have this disease. But since I do, I prefer to use it to my best advantage. Consequently, I never think a thing about the past. And I wouldn't have if you hadn't come here yesterday. So," she said with a glance up at Ben, "let's get driving. I've done all the talking I'm gonna do. First thing I want is a cheeseburger."

Ben felt a wave of revulsion. "I'm not going to feed the woman who—"

"Yes, you are," Carolyn said, overruling him. "Ben, we can't change the past. But we *can* take our best shot at altering the future."

He heard the plea in her voice and knew that she was begging for Lucy's sake. Of course she was right.

"Would you like a soda with that cheeseburger?" was all he said as he helped Mrs. Benton up into the cab.

BEN DROVE down the street, wondering if he was crazy to leave Carolyn alone in the house with the harpy. The woman seemed mean-spirited, but not necessarily criminal. And he had to trust Carolyn's instincts.

He couldn't believe he was sitting in his truck with Vivian Benton.

"I want to talk to you," she said, making him start.

He couldn't even glance at her. "All I want to hear from you is the truth."

"I'm going to tell you a little more than what your girlfriend is going to find."

That was the second time she'd made the girlfriend reference, but he wasn't going to deny that Carolyn was anything more to him than a friend. It was none of Mrs. Benton's business.

"I remember your mother very well, you know."

A reply was impossible. He was too angry.

"You look like her. Of course she was very young—"

"Why did you do it? Why did you steal her child?"

Mrs. Benton didn't flinch. "Greed. The ultimate sin."

"That's disgusting."

"I don't expect you to be anything except angry. I

wanted to talk to you alone so that I could tell you that I wish my husband hadn't done some of the things he had. And I wish I hadn't helped him.''

''You don't expect me to care how you feel, do you? What about my mother's feelings? She was dying, and if the baby ring had been broken a few months later, she'd never have known. And then I would never have known that I have a sibling out there somewhere. You're a wretched woman, and nothing you can say can make me think anything good about you.''

''You are the crucible for any forgiveness I ever hope to achieve.''

''I don't think so,'' Ben said sharply.

''After I'm gone—or have totally lost my mind— all the records can be turned over to the state. Many people will find their lives affected in ways they never imagined. But you, I want you to have the information you need now. For Lucy's sake.''

''Don't try to bribe me with sympathy.''

She shrugged. ''Well, it's really all I have left to me. I'm hoping that if I do right by one person— you—that I can be forgiven in some small measure for all the others.''

''Does it work that way?''

''No, but I have to start somewhere. You know, I often wonder if the stress of what I did caused my health to deteriorate. Stress is a funny thing, you know, very damaging to the body.''

"Did you feel much stress when you were counting your money?" he asked harshly.

"Truth is, I never saw any of the money. My husband took care of the monetary arrangements. When he died, I found myself financially embarrassed, anyway. To be quite candid, Dr. Benton gambled. Frequently. So I'm not living on the proceeds of my sins, if you get my meaning. I'm mainly squeaking by on Medicare and the like."

He shook his head, unswayed.

"But that's neither here nor there. What I want to tell you is that I am sorry for what I did to your mother. Eileen was very young, and she was very afraid. I'll never forget the night you were born because it was storming, and she called at the last minute, terrified. We barely got out there in time. In fact, my husband hadn't planned on your mother's delivery, because she wasn't a patient of his. When she had twins, he said it was too good to be true. Your mother and father were so poor—"

"That's no excuse," he interrupted, his voice cutting. "We would have been raised just fine."

"No, but it was what popped the idea into my husband's mind. The house was so barren, your family's position so obvious, that Dr. Benton said it was a pity to burden them further. And he figured he'd probably never see a dime of his fee. When Eileen had twins, I honestly believe Doug thought he was doing your family a favor."

"Well, he wasn't."

"No, I know that," she said softly. "I'm very sorry, more sorry than you can ever know."

"But you unequivocally admit that there was another child—a boy?" he asked.

"Your twin brother was born healthy."

The words rang in Ben's ears.

"It could have been *me* you took," he said starkly. "You could have stolen *my* life."

"You cried the loudest," Mrs. Benton said. "My husband said your brother would make less noise as we left the house. He didn't cry much."

"Oh, my God," Ben said. "You sure nailed down all the details."

The energy seemed to leave her eyes, and she slumped in the seat a bit. "Yes," she said dully. "Yes, we did."

THE CAREGIVER didn't bother Carolyn as she tore through the records, copying notes and digging for anything else that could help them. The house was strangely quiet without the TV blaring, and the air felt excessively still and hot.

Perspiration broke out along her upper lip as she swiftly moved through more files. There was no air-conditioning in the small office. Impatiently, she got up and went to the window, lifting it to let in whatever breeze might be outside.

And that's when she saw it, as if it had been laid

out for her to find. A black leather journal, marked
with a sticky note that read only Mulholland. It lay
on the right-hand side of a filing cabinet. The handwriting was shaky, not the firm hand she'd noted
when she'd hastily read over the daily notations yesterday.

She opened the file and gasped.

Inside were at least twenty notations of sale, written
in a man's hand.

CHAPTER SEVEN

CAROLYN COULD hardly believe it. The last page of the journal was marked Baby Mulholland. She wanted to scream with relief and joy—and frustration for Ben's sake. And Eileen's.

She snatched her cell phone out of her purse and dialed Jennifer Rodriguez. "Jennifer, I've got a record here that tells the whole story, basically. There *was* another baby. It was sold to...a couple in a FoodSavers grocery store parking lot."

"Where are you?" Jennifer demanded.

"In the doctor's house, looking through his records."

"That's my job!"

"No, no, it's fine. I was allowed in by the wife. But I've got to hurry. Anyway, that's all the record says. I also learned that on the same night Ben was delivered, the doctor is supposed to have delivered another baby, same time, different place." She took a deep breath and organized her whirling thoughts. "I'll send a picture of Ben to you, in case his brother should look anything like him. Since we don't know whether the twin was fraternal or identical, it's a long shot, but it may come in handy.''

Examining the journal more closely, she saw the word *Madison* written in tiny letters. ''Someone has written Madison here, under the name of the grocery store. Madison, Texas, maybe. That could be where they sold the baby. It looks like the doctor's penmanship, only very small, almost as an afterthought, or a notation he didn't feel was very important.''

''Madison could be the name of the family he sold the baby to, as well,'' Jennifer suggested. ''That's worth a try. I'll start with an Internet search.''

''Okay.'' She heard the front door slam and knew that her time in the office was up. ''I have to go,'' she said abruptly. ''I'll call you if I find out more.''

Ben appeared in the room. ''Mrs. Benton is ready for us to leave.''

Searching his face, she noted the strain around his eyes. Clearly, he had not enjoyed the outing. ''I'm all set to go.'' She glanced at the journal, wondering if she dared sneak it out. There were other people who would never know the truth of their lives—

''No,'' Ben said firmly. ''Leave it.''

''All right,'' she murmured reluctantly. Walking to his side, she looked up at him. ''Do I thank her for allowing me to go through her husband's files to search for a crime that they committed? What's the etiquette for this?''

''It doesn't matter.'' Taking her by the hand, he

led her into the TV room where Mrs. Benton sat watching the television. The caregiver sat in the corner, knitting, as if they weren't in the room.

"We're leaving," Carolyn said, but neither woman looked up. Ben shrugged at her, and they left.

"It smells wonderful out here," Carolyn said once she was on the porch. "I didn't realize how suffocating it was inside the house."

"I know." He grabbed her hand and they ran to the truck. She opened the door and jumped inside before he could offer to help her. He got in the driver's side, and for a moment, they both stared at the house.

"It's sad," Carolyn said. "She should be legally punished, but actually, she's already suffering for her crimes."

He started the engine and pulled into the street without lingering further. "I couldn't stop worrying about you alone at the house with that weird woman."

"She didn't bother me a bit. And Mrs. Benton left a journal out for me to find that clearly referenced that your mother had another living baby boy. Baby Mulholland was the notation."

Even though he was hoping for it, hearing that written proof existed shocked Ben. "Baby Mulholland," he said in stunned amazement.

"And a reference to Madison was on the same line, in smaller letters."

"Madison. What the hell does that mean, I wonder?"

"It was either the town where the transaction was made, or it's the name of the family your sibling was sold to. Jennifer Rodriguez is checking out both angles."

"Mrs. Benton admitted a lot of this, but finding actual proof is stunning. I can hardly believe it. Mom was right," he said, his voice full of wonder. "Somewhere, someone may be able to help Lucy."

She smiled at him. "That's our hope."

"It's very thin hope, but still… Had Mrs. Benton died before you saw the journal, maybe no one going through her personal effects would have ever known an illegal activity was being referenced."

"The references were fairly obscure. They could have been notations for any of the babies Dr. Benton delivered. I doubt anyone would have suspected he sold babies if your mother hadn't begun remembering. Imagine that, Ben. And there were approximately nineteen other records in that journal. I wish I could have appropriated it."

"That's for the police to do," he said sternly. "You can't do anything illegal, Carolyn. We'll let the authorities know, and they'll handle it."

"I know you're right, but I sure would have liked to look at the other records. I didn't have time to, but I've got to wonder if there were any other names I might have recognized. Small-town syndrome, I guess.''

He stopped the truck once again, this time to stare at her. ''I know I said I admired your tenacity, but on this, I have to insist that you let it go. You've found exactly what I hired you to do, and if I have to fire you, Carolyn, I will. You are not going to jail because I've piqued your curiosity.''

She laughed at him, and his heart rose in spite of his vow to keep his feelings light. ''All right. But I *am* telling the authorities.''

''I'll dial the phone for you.''

And then he kissed the tip of her nose to express gratitude for what she'd done for him and Lucy. That's all it was, Carolyn told herself. Gratitude that she had found the proof he'd hired her to—and maybe, just maybe, a miracle for Lucy.

IT WAS ELEVEN-THIRTY by the time they drove into town, and Carolyn was starving. She was pretty certain Ben had not enjoyed his outing with Mrs. Benton, so she wouldn't suggest that they stop for a bite. Besides, he'd need to hurry home to Lucy.

So she was surprised when Ben asked her if she wanted lunch.

''Let's go to Perk at The Park,'' she agreed, ''if you think Lucy won't be upset that you're gone this long.''

''I'm going to call her on my phone when we get

there, but I'm sure she'd be disappointed if I came home this soon. She likes her baby-sitter.'' He winked at Carolyn. ''Besides, she might even be napping, and she wouldn't miss me at all in that case.''

Carolyn told herself not to be so pleased that they were going to spend a business lunch together, but when she walked beside Ben along the River Walk, it reminded her of other times they'd eaten at the outdoor coffee bar.

''Hasn't changed,'' he said.

''Not much.''

They sat at a table beneath a giant green-striped umbrella.

''I know I want a turkey sandwich,'' Carolyn said.

''I think I'll have vegetable soup, and a turkey sandwich as well. I'll go place our order.''

He smiled at her as he stood, and Carolyn's appetite suddenly turned to something besides food. *Why?* she thought wistfully. *Why can't I feel about him the same way I do about any other man?*

Ben looked at her thoughtfully when he returned a few moments later. ''Why would Mrs. Benton leave the journal out for you to find?'' he wondered.

''It was labeled and sitting where I couldn't miss it, so I figure she was motivated by guilt. Years of guilt.''

He shrugged his shoulders. ''She indicated those feelings to me.''

''Was it difficult being with her?''

"It was uncomfortable. Distasteful. Repugnant. But I sensed that in her screwy way, she was trying to atone for her sins." He took a drink from one of the iced coffees he'd brought them and sighed.

"She wants to know that you're going to find your brother. It's probably the most she's ever going to know about the matter, because it's not as if you'll call her up and tell her there's been a happy reunion."

"I guess you're right."

She covered his hand with hers for just a moment. "Think about Lucy. This could make a difference for her."

He nodded. "Okay."

Then she pulled her fingers back from his.

He watched her silently.

"You're in good hands," she told him. "I'll call Jennifer as soon as I get back to the office, and maybe she's found something I can start with."

"It's unnerving to think that I could very soon be meeting a brother I never knew I had."

"I hope it happens," she said quietly.

"I'm glad Mom sent me to find you." His voice was husky and warm. "I have to tell you, Carolyn, I never forgot you."

She shifted uneasily in her seat. "It wouldn't have worked, Ben."

"Not then."

But maybe now?

Of course that was not what he was thinking. She was crazy to have even entertained the brief thought.

"We made the right decision," she murmured.

"*You* made the decision."

"And you didn't seem to suffer too long," she said, forcing a smile to her face and a teasing tone to her voice. "Let's not dwell on the past. Let's think about the future, which is starting to look pretty bright."

"After I release you from one misconception, we will." He took a deep breath. "Carolyn, I married Marissa on the rebound. I didn't know it then. I wouldn't allow myself to feel the pain of losing you. It was easy to tell myself I'd fallen in love with a beautiful woman. Years after the fact, I know I was running from your memories."

She didn't know what to say, so she stared at him, her eyes wide.

"I'm not telling you this to make you feel guilty or uncomfortable. I just want you to know that if you think I didn't suffer, I did. I didn't get over you like you seem to believe. It took a long time."

"You don't have to tell me this, Ben."

"I want you to know. If you were hurt that I married Marissa so soon after we broke up, it wasn't that I forgot you or that what we had wasn't special. It was. Damn special."

She reached for the only thing she could think of to say. "You have Lucy."

He nodded once. "I do. Believe me, she is the only light in my life."

"You wouldn't have had her with me, Ben."

"I'm not saying I have regrets," he said, completely unaware of the confession she'd been trying to make. "I just want you to know that even though I got married, you still had a place in my heart."

Ben glanced at the main cart of the coffee bar and saw that their order was ready. When he stood to retrieve it, Carolyn shifted her gaze away from him gratefully. Hadn't she wanted to hear that he'd still loved her back then, that he hadn't simply forgotten about their love affair when he married Marissa?

Yet what purpose did it serve now, except to salve the pain she'd suffered at the time?

Ben returned with the sandwiches and soup.

Carolyn looked up at him. "Thank you," she said simply. "I can tell you were trying very chivalrously to...explain what happened. But you don't owe me any explanations, Ben."

She smiled at him, schooling her expression to be sincere, yet less intense. She needed distance between her heart and Ben. "Any woman would love to hear that her ex-boyfriend had carried a torch for her, but you don't need to make me feel better. We have a good working relationship, and that's what counts now, isn't it?"

"I suppose so."

An awkward silence ensued until Ben said, "Excuse me.'' He got out his cell phone and called Lucy, smiling as he spoke to her.

At first glad for the diversion, Carolyn felt her heart begin to tighten inside her as she shamelessly listened to the father and daughter exchange loving words. Tears stung her eyes but she stubbornly blinked them back. Nothing made Ben happier than his little girl. All she could hope for now was a miracle for Lucy and him.

He clicked off his phone and put it in his shirt pocket. ''Lucy says to tell you that she wants you to come see her,'' Ben said, startling Carolyn. ''Of course, I'm simply relaying the message and there's no obligation at all, although I wholeheartedly second the invitation.''

Carolyn's gaze lingered on Ben's and then broke away. Unbidden, a question teased at the edges of her mind.

Is it possible that we could still be in love with each other?

CHAPTER EIGHT

THE THOUGHT was too intimidating to face. She quickly dug her cell phone out of her purse. "You know what, I'd better let Dylan know I'll be back at the office after lunch—and that we've made some progress in the case."

Ben just watched her. Carolyn smiled, trying to appear calm and self-assured, as if she hadn't been staring at his lips, remembering what it had been like to kiss him.

Ben was a man a woman could kiss for hours, getting lost and never caring if she found her way back.

She didn't want to experience those wild emotions again.

"Dylan," she said, watching as Ben began eating his sandwich, her gaze safe now that he was paying attention to his lunch. "It's Carolyn."

"Hey, Carolyn."

"I'm at Perk at The Park now, having lunch with Ben Mulholland. We just found what we think is our first major road sign in the case."

"Excellent."

"I wanted to let you know I'll be back in the office in, say, thirty minutes."

Ben glanced up to catch her watching him. She looked away hastily. So much for trying to appear self-assured.

"Can you meet me at the library, Carolyn? I'm on my way over there now and there's something I'd like to discuss with you."

"That's fine. In thirty?"

"Great. Bye."

She clicked off her cell phone and put it into her purse. "Not to rush our lunch, but—"

"I understand you've got to get back to work, Carolyn. That's fine. I'll drop you off at your car." He smiled at her easily. "I need to be getting home to Lucy, anyway."

"Okay." He was trying to put her at ease, Carolyn knew. She was struggling to be so cool around him, unwilling to reveal her turbulent feelings—and Ben knew it.

I'm about as sophisticated as an escaping doe. She sighed and picked up her sandwich. She was her own worst enemy, of course. She longed to be able to have Ben—and knew very well how much it would hurt if he rejected her because of her inability to have children. Oh, they could have a wonderful affair, like they'd had before. They could have a mindlessly passionate and thoroughly satisfying relationship, but she would always know it would end. It was impossible to throw herself headlong into that kind of pain again.

And if Lucy didn't make it…Ben would be alone.

She wrenched her mind from Lucy's dire plight, mortified that she had even let the thought into her mind. *Lucy is going to be fine, Lucy is going to be fine.*

"I can't eat," she told Ben. "I think I'll just sit here and sip my drink."

"Is there something wrong? Investigative letdown or something?"

"What?"

"You know, when someone achieves their goal, they expect to feel a high, but then are surprised when they feel a low instead, because they don't know what comes next. Letdown."

She raised an eyebrow at him. "The teacher in you is coming out, I guess?"

"Nah, the bad psychoanalyst. Sorry. Just seeing if you had a smile in there."

"I'm just thinking," she hedged. "There's an important phone call I need to make and it's weighing on my mind."

She wanted to know if she was a match for Lucy.

"HEY, DYLAN," Carolyn said breathlessly as she caught up to him at the San Antonio Public Library. "What are you reading?"

"The *San Antonio Express-News*." He closed the

paper and looked at her, his hands folded on the paper as he sat in the chair. "Have a seat and join me."

"I will. I think I ran my hose when I was at the doctor's house this morning—yes, darn it, I did." She shook her head. *Sophisticated* was definitely not the word for her today. She'd have to buy a new pair at the drugstore when she left the library. "So what are you doing here?"

He grinned. "Escaping. Lily's going a bit crazy with the wedding so close, and it's real quiet here. I know that twins are emotionally very close, but wedding angst is one bonding experience I'd rather not share."

"I'm sure you can find plenty of peace at the house somewhere," she teased. "But you said you had something to tell me?"

"Uh, yeah. There were some messages for you this morning. One was from your doctor's nurse."

She stared at him. "And?"

"The message was that there was no need for you to come in for further testing, whatever that meant."

Her heart fell. "Oh."

"That's all it said. I was assuming that was good news, but I can see by your face, you were hoping for something else?"

"Well—" She glanced away for a second before returning his gaze. "Yes, I was."

"Anything I can help with?"

She didn't know if it was appropriate to discuss her

emotional involvement in Ben's case with her employer, but she decided to throw caution to the winds. "I had tests run to see if I was a match for Lucy, Ben Mulholland's daughter." She shrugged. "It was a long shot, but I'd gotten my hopes up when the initial tests seemed positive. Now it looks as if the doctors have ruled me out as a candidate for donation."

"Sorry about that."

"You could, of course, go roll up your sleeve," Carolyn said, her tone teasing.

"I could, but I could also forget to give you a raise when we discuss your job performance," he quickly returned, his eyes twinkling.

Carolyn went solemn again. "If I thought that was all it would cost me, it would be a very small price to pay," she said softly.

"Oh, brother," he sighed. "I was convinced you were such a pragmatic woman, a bulwark of stoicism. Are you going to become emotionally involved with all the cases I let you work on? I may have to rein in your duties."

She looked at him, not certain if he was still teasing until she saw the gleam in his eye. "Just this one."

"Past history throwing you a curve."

"Probably."

"Probably my foot." He grinned at her. "Considering everything that's been going on around the ranch, this is actually a small thing. I'll go roll up my sleeve."

She smiled at him. "Thanks, Dylan."

He shook his head. "Now, for the real reason I wanted you here. Let's talk about adjusting your duties while Lily's on her honeymoon."

Carolyn opened her briefcase and told herself returning the call to the nurse to find out why she wasn't needed for further testing could wait—so could letting the authorities know what she'd found at Dr. Benton's house.

DYLAN WATCHED AS Carolyn left the library two hours later. He was actually quite satisfied with his new employee, despite the ribbing he'd given her concerning her emotional involvement in the Mulholland case.

Now that she was gone, he opened the paper again, staring at the line of Dylan Thomas poetry he'd found in the classified-personals section. "Do not go gentle into that good night," he read to himself. Julie Matthews and he had shared an admiration of Thomas's poetry; he never read it without thinking of her. The words tugged at his heart and he wished for the thousandth time that Julie could be found. She had disappeared shortly after New Year's without a trace, and her husband, Sebastian Cooper, was just about as crazy as a man could be with grief over his missing wife.

Dylan had never felt so powerless. He had not stopped loving Julie since their years at college together, but that was his secret—something only Lily knew.

Suddenly, he realized he'd seen Dylan Thomas's poetry in yesterday's newspaper. He got up and retrieved it from the stack of old papers, quickly finding the personals section.

And there, ten lines down, another line jumped out at him: "Light breaks where no sun shines; Where no sea runs, the waters of the heart/Push in their tides."

His eyes wide, his heart thundering, he read the words again. And again.

No. There was no reason for him to think that the ad had been placed there by Julie. It would mean she had access to funds, maybe to a phone or a computer. It would mean she was alive.

It would also mean she had relative freedom.

The hair stood up on the back of his neck. These were some of their favorite passages from English Lit.

He snatched up another paper, his gaze roaming the personal ads furiously. "All the sun long it was running, it was lovely, the hay/Fields high as the house, the tunes from the chimneys, it was air/And playing, lovely and watery/And fire green as grass."

His breath froze in his chest. How many times had he and Julie laughingly wished that they could visit Fern Hill?

"Dylan Garrett?" a voice said, shocking him out of his thoughts.

He glanced up, startled. "Hello, Rachel," he said, somehow disappointed that the object of his thoughts hadn't materialized at his elbow. He could have sworn he'd heard Julie's voice speaking the poet's words out loud....

The librarian smiled at him. "You were deep in thought. I hope I haven't disturbed you."

"No. Not at all." He stood, recovering his manners, and kissed her cheek. "It's good to see you, actually. How have you been?"

"Wonderful." Her eyes glowed with happiness. "You know I've been dating Max Santana."

Max was the foreman at the Double G ranch. "Oh?" Dylan asked curiously.

She laughed.

"Speaking of romance," he said, "I'll soon be in a tux and watching my twin embrace marital bliss. You'll be at the wedding, of course?"

"Yes. Wouldn't miss it." Rachel checked her watch, smiling at him. "I've got to run, but I'll see you at the wedding."

"I look forward to it. Seeing you, that is, not necessarily the wedding."

She laughed. "You're a great brother to Lily, though you try hard to hide it. See you then."

He gave a brief wave as she walked away. Then he turned his thoughts to the poetry, and his growing sense that somehow these words had been meant for him to see.

AT THE HOUSE, Carolyn ran into Lily, who held a to-do list in one hand and a phone in the other. She smiled at Carolyn, who gave her a mock horrified look. "My job looks easier than yours," Carolyn teased.

Lily laughed. "Maybe. But things are starting to look up. Dad hired a new housekeeper-cook named Gracie Fipps to help out with everything."

Carolyn smiled at the mention of William Garrett. "Good for you. I'd offer to help but—"

"Sure you would." Lily waved her on. "But you've got to get back to the office, right?"

"Exactly." Carolyn waved goodbye and left Lily to her preparations. She had to talk to Jennifer and see how the database search was going.

But first she had a more personal call to make.

"SPECIFICALLY, the problem with you being a match is your health history," the nurse told her. "While many other factors would have given us a reason to test you further, the physicians overseeing Lucy Mulholland's case concluded that your endometriosis and subsequent hysterectomy could make for a less than optimum match."

"If it's the best match you could find, wouldn't it be worth a try?" Carolyn asked desperately.

"I know that you care, Ms. St. Clair," the nurse said gently. "I'm sorry this isn't the news you wanted to get. We want the best for Lucy, and the doctor feels we should see if there's a better match."

Carolyn took a deep breath. There was nothing more she could say. "Thank you for returning my call."

"Thank you for being so concerned, Ms. St. Clair. Believe me, we are on your side."

She hung up the phone, seething. "Rats!" So close! And yet, not close enough. Closing her eyes, she thought about the donor-matching database. How could so many possibilities exist and there be no match for Lucy?

Thinking about databases turned her thoughts to Jennifer. Carolyn tugged at her hair, seeing clearly in her mind's eye the journal lying by the filing cabinet in Mrs. Benton's office. Records that could change so many people's lives had been in that journal.

People who might not want their lives changed, perhaps, but others who would.

Inexplicably, she thought about her sister, Christine. Fit, athletic, beautiful. Older than Carolyn by five years, and prone to think the world owed her something. Maybe that wasn't fair. It was their mother who had dragged Christine to every children's modeling studio, every peewee beauty pageant, every agent's office she could find to tout her fair-haired daughter's exquisiteness. The fact that Christine had turned out to be self-centered and divalike should have surprised no one.

Maybe it's a seed of jealousy that keeps you from wishing your sister true happiness.

Christine had not achieved the perfection in her personal life that she had in her career. First a sought after model, now a TV talk show host, she lived her life with one eye on the mirror's reflection.

Carolyn had nothing in common with her sister's glamorous life, and over the years they had drifted apart, especially after their parents' retirement in Florida. It wasn't that they disliked each other; it was simply that as children, their worlds had been so separate that they'd never developed a close relationship that could withstand time and distance.

Christine had sent flowers when Carolyn had her hysterectomy. It had been the most emotional time of Carolyn's life, and Christine had marked it with expensive blooms. "Feel better soon," the card had read. "Christine."

No phone call, no visit, and no follow-up except the usual card and expensive purse at Christmas. Carolyn didn't carry purses; she carried a black briefcase.

Sighing, she told herself not to be so hard on her sister. She thought of Ben and the brother he'd never known he had. He'd been denied the experience of growing up with a sibling—his twin—and nothing could ever change that now.

It was time to call the police about Dr. and Mrs.

Benton. She dialed the number and was put through to a woman who sounded fairly uninterested.

Well, at least she'd done her part, Carolyn thought, hanging up.

The phone immediately rang, startling her. "Finders Keepers," she said, answering on the first ring.

"There are several men by the last name of Madison living in Texas," Jennifer Rodriguez said without segue into her subject. "Only one of them, according to motor vehicle records, is the right age. He lives right here in Midland, he appears to be single, he has no children, and when I called the number I was given by directory assistance, I got an answering machine message in a male voice that sounds healthy and robust."

Carolyn smiled at Jennifer's obvious implication. But she also thought about Ben, who was healthy and robust. As a father, he was precluded from being a donor match; the bout of malaria he'd had in Africa excluded him from even being an emergency match for Lucy.

A sibling of Ben's would still be only an emergency match for Lucy, but a healthy and robust match would be more than anything they had right now. "How do we find out if this man is actually Ben's brother?"

"I'm on my way to see him right now. A blood test will do the trick."

Excitement thrilled through Carolyn.

"I'll think of something. Right now, I want to see if he looks anything like this picture you had couriered over."

"Could we be this lucky?" Carolyn breathed. "Could a miracle happen this easily?"

"I don't know. We'll find out. In the meantime, you might let Ben know what's going on."

"Good luck," Carolyn said. "Let me give you my cell phone number, and don't hesitate to call me the minute you find out anything at all."

Once she'd hung up, Carolyn said a quick prayer and called Ben.

CHAPTER NINE

BEN DIDN'T answer the phone, and Carolyn didn't want to leave a message on the answering machine with any details Lucy might hear. So she simply left a message for him to call her.

The office was quiet, there were few incoming calls she needed to field. Waiting to hear from Jennifer was difficult. She turned on the answering machine, locked up the office, and drove home.

To her astonishment, Ben knocked on her door five minutes after she'd pulled off her ruined stockings and hung up her suit. She'd gathered her hair up into a scraggly ponytail, slid jeans and a baggy blouse on, and decided macaroni and cheese in front of the TV would have to suffice.

The bottle of wine in his hands told Carolyn she might have to at least warm up a lasagna. ''Hello, Ben,'' she said, stepping back from the door so he could enter. ''Where's Lucy?''

''At home with her favorite sitter. Lucy was asleep when I left, worn out from her day, but the sitter said she would call me when she woke up.'' He took a deep breath. "I had to stop by and see you, Carolyn. I didn't want to say this over the phone."

Like her, he wore jeans and a comfortable shirt. He'd showered, and his hair lay damp along his collar. "I was at the doctor's office with Lucy today."

She closed the door and waited as he stared at her with some emotion she couldn't identify.

"I pried what you'd done out of Lucy's nurse, Carolyn."

"Oh." She shook her head and went to the sofa, curling one leg underneath her as she waved at him to take a seat across from her. "I thought donor matching was confidential."

He remained standing. "It can be. And doctor-patient privilege is exactly that. I just happened to come into the office when the nurse was ending your call. I heard the nurse say your name a couple of times, and thank you for being concerned. When I asked her if she'd been talking to you, she didn't deny it. But she didn't tell me to mind my own business, either."

"Why were you at the doctor's office with Lucy?" Carolyn asked, uncomfortable with discussing her failed attempt as a donor.

"We had a scheduled appointment. Lucy's having chemotherapy tomorrow."

"You didn't mention that before," she murmured.

"No reason to. You're working on our case, and that should be your main concern."

She looked at him. "Then why are you here with wine?"

"To thank you for caring about Lucy." He swallowed. "The wine is a bribe for you to let me in the door...."

"A bribe isn't necessary."

He finally took the seat she'd indicated. "I know. But I couldn't come empty-handed, and I wanted to see you. I wanted to thank you in person...for caring, and for trying."

She masked her feelings by lowering her eyelashes. "I wish I could have helped."

"You have."

Shaking her head, she changed the subject. "It's just as well you came by. I left a message at your house for you to call me. Jennifer Rodriguez is on her way to talk to a man who fits most of the data we know about the child who was taken from your mother."

His eyes went wide. "Already on her way?"

"There isn't any time to lose," she reminded him gently. "Jennifer understands the urgency of your situation."

"Maybe I should have gone with her."

Carolyn got up and took the wine from him, setting it on the coffee table. "I may have a glass of this. Do you want some?"

"No, I have to be going in a minute. Is she meeting him somewhere? Is there time for me to get there?"

"Wait until she lets us know if this is actually your missing twin," Carolyn told him. "There's no reason to get your hopes up just yet. I told her to call me immediately once she knows anything."

"Oh, boy." He ran a hand through his hair, shifted the collar of his denim shirt, and sat back down on the sofa. "I had no idea things would move so fast. How will she know if it's him?"

"She'll have to convince him to take a test, of course. I sent a picture of you over to her, in case he looks anything like you, which may or may not prove to be helpful."

"Where'd you get a picture of me?"

He looked at her, his gaze piercing with curiosity, and Carolyn nearly had to glance away. She forced herself to answer his question as if it were any other question in the case. "I had one, an old one," she said as nonchalantly as she could.

It was the expression on his face, at once knowing and pleased, that told her she had failed the it's-nothing-unusual attitude she'd tried to project. He liked knowing that she'd kept his picture—and the fact that she had spoke volumes about her feelings for him.

"Carolyn St. Clair," he said slowly, his gaze measuring, "one day I'm going to know the reason you broke up with me."

She shook her head, about to deny what she knew he had to be thinking, but he got up, walked to her, and took her chin gently in his hand. "We have unfinished business."

All she could do was stare up at him.

He looked down at her before giving her a brief kiss on the lips. "Call me ASAP if you hear from Jennifer," he said, and then walked out the door.

Carolyn crossed her arms over her chest, shivering at the sensations his kiss aroused in her. Unfinished business indeed. He knew it, she knew it, and he also knew she didn't want to admit it. It was as if he were waiting, waiting patiently for her to realize she couldn't deny the feelings they had for each other.

Unfinished business.

SO MANY EMOTIONS were running through Ben that he knew he had to leave before he spilled more of his feelings and went beyond the "professional" relationship Carolyn was comfortable with.

But the woman had been willing to be a marrow donor for Lucy, and it touched his heart beyond words. It had been very easy to fall in love with Carolyn years ago. He'd never really gotten over her. When she left him, she'd shattered his world. That world was in danger of shattering again, if Lucy didn't receive the treatment she needed.... But as his mother had said, Carolyn would care about Lucy and try to help her.

His mother had been so right. But even though his heart had known it as well, he would never have dreamed that she would want to help to that extent. Now he knew without doubt that she loved his Lucy.

Carolyn wasn't about to let herself love him, Ben knew. This knowledge was difficult, but he was older and wiser now and knew better than to rush her. Maybe she'd never love him, but if all he could ever have of Carolyn was friendship, then he'd still gain a gift he hadn't thought he had a prayer of receiving.

His cell phone rang, startling him. It might be Lucy calling, worried that he was gone. He answered quickly. "Hello?"

"Ben?"

Carolyn's voice warmed him, calmed him. "There's something I probably should tell you."

He heard her hesitation and frowned. Surely she hadn't suspected the depth of his feelings for her and was going to tell him something he simply didn't want to hear. "I'm just outside in my car. I haven't gone anywhere. Do you want me to come up, or do you want to tell me over the phone?"

"Oh. It's probably better in person, I guess," she said, her tone miserable.

"I'm already out of the car." He jogged up the steps, inside the door and up the stairs, his phone to his ear. "Are you okay?"

"I'm fine." She opened the door, staring at him before reaching to take the phone he hadn't realized he still held at his ear. She turned it off, tucked it in his pocket, drew him inside, and closed the door behind him.

"What is it?"

"I've been needing to tell you the truth about something for a long time." Taking a deep breath, she said, "I don't know if now's the time or not, but...I'm afraid some of the old feelings are coming back."

"Oh." That was the last thing he wanted to hear. "You're afraid?"

"Yes."

He thought she looked darling, hesitant and slightly rumpled in her casual clothes, her ponytail askew. No lipstick glossed her lips, and she'd removed her makeup. The last thing he'd ever want was this delightful, delicate woman to be afraid of anything about him. "Don't be afraid," was all he could say. "I would never hurt you."

She smiled a little sadly. "I know you wouldn't. It's just that I know I hurt you before...and I don't want it to happen again."

Oh, she thought *she* had to protect *him*. The knowledge smarted. Ben winced, but tried to smile and be brave. "You meant that you're afraid *my* feelings are coming back for you, and you don't welcome them. You have to work with me because I hired you, and you care about my daughter, so you want to help her, but that's why you wanted to be an anonymous donor, so that I wouldn't see it as—"

"Stop!" she cried, her face anguished. "Ben, I'm not handling this very well. Come sit down and let me try to tell you what I have to without making you jump to conclusions."

They sat down on the sofa, a foot between them, but Ben wanted to hold Carolyn and wipe the distress from her face. He didn't dare, so he sat still and stiff beside her, watching her fiddle with the simple gold-and-silver ring on her right hand, before she spoke again.

"Perhaps I'm afraid my feelings never completely went away," she said softly.

That was more than he'd hoped to hear. Ben perked up as his barely beating heart kicked into cautiously happy pounding. "I wouldn't be afraid of that. I would probably look upon it as a favorable thing."

She gave him a wry look. "Ben, you are the sweetest man I've ever known—"

"Not that!" he cried in mock horror. "Not the 'You're the sweetest man, let's just be friends' speech. I've heard that speech is silk-wrapped doom when a woman gives it to a man."

He could tell she refused to be swayed from the seriousness of her subject because she didn't smile.

"I don't think we'll ever be just friends, Ben."

"Someday I wouldn't mind being more. Of course, I don't expect you to feel the same way, so don't worry that you're going to hurt my feelings, Carolyn.

And I'd never force something more on you than what you want from me."

"Ben, there's no easy way to tell you this, so I'm just going to have to make myself be honest or you're going to sit here all night thinking all the wrong things. I broke off our relationship because I can't have children."

He stared at her, dumbstruck. Not a word came to mind. The stark truth lay in her eyes. It was fact, and one she had never wanted to tell him.

"Oh, my God," he said huskily. "Oh, my God." He pulled her into his arms, burying his lips in her hair. She began to sob, and he felt silly and selfish all at once, for all the times she must have needed him and he'd been too wounded with his own vanity to see. She had no family to lean on, and she could have leaned on him, but he'd never thought she needed him. Cool, calm, capable Carolyn—leaping tall buildings for everyone else and never asking anything in return. He wanted to say, "Why didn't you tell me?" but that would have been pointless, because right now, what she needed was a place to rest her heart.

AFTER A FEW moments of soaking up the warmth Ben offered her, Carolyn raised her head and smiled self-consciously. "At the risk of appearing like an overly dramatic heroine who prefers to stay locked in a tower rather than face her demons, I have to be honest and tell you that wanting to be a bone marrow donor for Lucy was purely selfish on my part.''

He smiled at her, stroking her hair as she spoke.

"It's true," she insisted. "I want you to be happy. I always knew children would make you happy, and the only way I could have a part in giving you one would be to—"

"Hush," he told her. "I never thought you were an angel, Carolyn, if that's what you're trying to tell me. I know that because of your family, you work extra-hard at being calm and levelheaded, but inside you beats the heart of a carefree gypsy."

She looked up at him silently.

"And you tamp her down diligently so she'll stay put, and you won't make any mistakes which will cost you. I know." He pressed a kiss at her hairline as she reclined against him. "We're kindred spirits that way."

"Do you think so?"

He shrugged. "Sure. I loved my teaching stint in Africa and South America. I would like to have worked for a humanitarian organization in some capacity, but then I met Marissa. Once I had a little girl, it seemed safer to stay closer to home while she was young. Besides, deep in my heart, I knew Marissa would probably never be much of a mother. I mean, she loves Lucy, but she just can't do the role of housewife and Brownie leader. So I do it. There are days when I think I'd be safer off in some jungle than surrounded by a pack of little Brownies.''

She smiled, putting her head back against his chest.

''A gypsy heart comes in handy when it meets tough circumstances,'' he told her.

''Really?''

''Sure. When we learned Lucy was sick, I kept sane by thinking of all the places I want to take her when she gets well.''

''She'll like that.''

''Yeah. Your gypsy heart has stood you in good stead, too, I'm sure.''

''I don't know....'' She didn't think she'd handled anything about her situation very well.

''Carolyn, you've got the gypsy under wraps right now, but your heart was free enough to let me go without telling me you couldn't give me what I wanted. Other women might have needed the man to know, needed his support. You chose not to need me—not to make me feel guilty. That makes you quite a woman.''

She *had* known he'd want children. Hearing him say she'd done the right thing somehow hurt, though.

''So now that we've gone through these phases of our lives without each other,'' he continued, ''maybe we know more about what a relationship takes to succeed than we did before. I'm divorced, my mom is gone, my daughter, who is my shining star, is ill. Your family situation is awkward, Christine is still out there winning no awards for sisterhood, and you can't have children.'' He held her a little tighter as he spoke. ''It's a lot to go through alone.''

She closed her eyes as she touched the cable-knit sweater he wore. ''Are you saying that the older versions of us might be better than the ones six years ago?''

''Would you have volunteered to be a bone marrow donor back then?''

Her eyes opened wide. ''Absolutely not. I'm terrified of needles.''

He chuckled. ''I'm terrified of needles being put in my daughter.''

She stared up at him. ''How do you watch that?''

Slowly, he shook his head, his gaze on hers. ''It's not easy. I hold Lucy and wish I could feel the pain instead of her. I've learned that real bravery is holding a sick child in your arms while they're undergoing treatment. I have the highest regard for all the parents who have gone through it longer than me and suffered a loss I hope I never have to.''

She put her hand up to touch his cheek. ''You *are* a hero.''

''It's necessary for my daughter to think that. Only you can know that my tough exterior is surrounding a soft, marshmallow center.''

She smiled. ''Your secret's safe with me.''

''So…share.''

''Share what?''

"I shared my survival story."

"Oh." He wanted her to confide in him, and Carolyn didn't know if she could reciprocate. "It's really not very attractive."

"What's not? The story?"

"Well, that, and the final results."

"Somehow I have this image of us crossing a bridge," he said softly. "Back on the other side we were kids, but six years of living has made us adults, and now that we're on the other side of the bridge, we've found out we're stronger."

She closed her eyes for a moment and took a deep breath. "This is hard." She felt his arms tighten, his hands run along her back and shoulders. This was a part of her she'd kept hidden for years. Telling him wouldn't change the future for them; she still felt the same way she had about not being able to give him children.

But talking about it would be closure. And somehow, she knew that he was right. She'd crossed the bridge; there was no changing the past. It was time to be honest with him.

"I had been sick off and on for some time with stomach pain, strange periods. There were days when I couldn't work because the pain was so bad. At first, I thought it was stomachaches, maybe ulcers or something. I finally realized these episodes had a cycle to them. So I went to a doctor, and he performed a laparoscopy."

"You told me you'd had a cyst."

"Well, that was a possibility, too." She looked up at him, suddenly drawing away slightly as the disturbing memories washed over her. "Once he went in, he found damage from endometriosis and adnomyosis. Parts of my body had been stuck together with the adnomyosis." She sat up straight on the sofa, twisting her ring as she spoke. "If it had just been endometriosis, he might have tried cauterization and hormonal treatments afterward. But he had serious concern that there would be further spreading, and possibly a rupture in other areas from the adhesion he'd seen. We scheduled a hysterectomy, and a few weeks later I was—" she shrugged, as if to downplay the seriousness "—a postmenopausal twenty-year-old."

"I wish you had told me." He sat up next to her, not touching her, but staying close beside her.

"I didn't want anyone to know. There are so many misconceptions people have about endometriosis. It's in a woman's mind, it's caused by sexual promiscuity—whatever. And then there were the scars. Forget about bikinis. You know how some girls show off belly button rings—well, I have a lap scar, too. Not that it's significant, you know, but I'm not going to be piercing that area of my body."

"Why do I have trouble seeing you as the type of girl who'd want a belly button ring?"

She pushed at him with her shoulder. "It's not that I would. It's that I can't."

"You could always rebel in other ways."

"I wear a hormone patch," she said softly. "It's not big, just an oval piece of tape. I shouldn't complain, because I've never had any hormone problems, but there's a secret side of me that envies Christine and her beauty and her ability to have children, while I wouldn't even want to be naked with a man anymore." She stared directly in his eyes. "So, if you thought I was being some kind of good martyr for wanting to donate to Lucy, now you know the truth. I thought being able to give your daughter life might make up for the fact that I could never bear a child of my own. So I'm actually quite selfish, you see," she told him quietly. "Now you know I'm a woman who envies her sister and has ulterior motives where your daughter is concerned."

They stared at each other for a few moments.

"I'm glad you told me," he said. "I needed to know."

Slowly, she nodded. "Yes," she said, her voice sad. "Closure is very healing."

CHAPTER TEN

THE APARTMENT doorbell rang, delaying whatever Ben was about to say to her. Carolyn jumped to her feet, glad to spare him the sympathy she knew he would probably offer—and which she didn't want. She hurried to the door, and her heart stalled at the sight of her glamorous sister on the other side. "Christine! What are you doing here?"

"Breaking up a tender moment with your ex-boyfriend?" Christine asked, her brow arching as she looked at Ben. "Hello, Ben." Her glance took in Carolyn's casual shirt and jeans. "Hope I'm not interrupting anything."

"You're not." Ben nodded at her. "I was just leaving."

Carolyn gaped at him.

"It's good to see you again, Christine," he said. "I'd stay and chat, but I've got to get home." He passed by Carolyn, leaning down to give her a swift kiss on the cheek. "Remember the bridge," he told her. "You'll be better on the other side." And then he left her alone with a sister she had hardly communicated with for years.

"I didn't know you and Ben had gotten back together." Christine walked inside and sat on the sofa where Ben had been a moment before.

"We haven't."

"Where's Marissa?"

Christine eyed her sister, and Carolyn immediately felt dowdy. Marissa and Christine had a lot in common, she decided. "On a modeling assignment, I think."

"You really shouldn't have an affair with a married man."

"Thanks for the advice, Sis," Carolyn said sharply. "But I'm neither having an affair nor seeing Ben, who is divorced, by the way. Anyway, what are you doing here?"

"Well, taking my own advice, I suppose." A shadow passed over her pretty face. "I fell in love with a married man, so I decided it was best to come home to Tara for a while. Do you mind if I stay with you? I could use some of your levelheadedness."

"I don't have any to spare," Carolyn said between gritted teeth.

Christine sighed. "I would really appreciate it if you could put me up for a day or so."

"There are hotels in New York, California and Paris, all your favorite haunts. Why do you have to stay here?"

Christine was silent for a few minutes. "Carolyn, can I ask you something?"

"If you must. What is it?"

"Why don't you like me?" Christine asked. "I mean, why aren't we close?"

The distress Carolyn felt at seeing her sister was increasing. "I don't know," she said, more sharply than she'd intended. "You're older than me. Our interests are different. We want different things out of life. Are those enough reasons?"

"But all that could be true and we'd still at least be close on some level," Christine said. "With this new crisis in my life, I'm trying to figure out why I keep making mistakes."

Carolyn sat on the floor cross-legged. "You're not having a crisis. A crisis is when you're dying of leukemia and you may never see your tenth birthday. That's why we're not close, Christine. You come barging in here without calling and start talking about your love life and yourself, and it isn't something I admire in my older sib."

Christine sat back against the sofa cushions. "I never saw myself like that before. You have a point."

Carolyn sighed. "And I'm being inconsiderate, too. You happened to arrive when Ben and I were discussing something we've waited too long to talk about, and—"

"And I barged in."

Carolyn winced as Christine repeated the word she'd used to describe her unexpected arrival. "Sorry."

"No, it's perfectly all right. I always thought you and Ben—" At the warning look on Carolyn's face, she cut herself short. "Okay, maybe I didn't think anything at all," she muttered.

"Now you're getting somewhere." Carolyn sighed. "Let me get you a glass of iced tea or wine. I'm sure you're tired from your flight."

"Without sounding pitiful, I am. Tea, please." Christine got up and followed her sister into the small kitchenette, which was connected to the living room.

"Being on the lam from a married man sounds tiring," Carolyn observed dryly. "Don't date married men, Christine, if you're sincere about finding happiness in your life instead of crises."

"I'm not dating him yet," she said hastily. "I'm avoiding temptation. He's rather Rasputinish, if you know what I mean."

Carolyn thought about how un-Rasputinish Ben was and smiled to herself.

"No, I'm serious," Christine exclaimed, mistaking her sister's smile. "He's tall and dark and very magnetic, and I want him like I want the world's best chocolate delivered right to my door every morning—only more!"

Carolyn laughed at her, handed her a glass of tea, then walked back to the living room, this time to sit at the opposite end of the sofa from her sister. "So what's holding you back? I'm not sure I could resist that, either."

"Oh, you could," Christine said. "You're so practical."

Carolyn rolled her eyes. "I am not as practical as everyone believes me to be."

"Well, there is no way you'd be fooled by my latest. He's not like Ben. Ben is so solid, isn't he, and, well, kind of boring."

"I think you've just listed the fundamental reason you're not happy, Christine. You don't want anyone 'solid' and 'boring.'"

Christine gasped. "I did, didn't I?"

"And what man could risk comparison with the world's best chocolates being delivered to your door every morning? That's tough on the male psyche."

"Well, maybe it wouldn't have to be *every* morning..."

They shared a laugh, which felt good to Carolyn. She couldn't remember the last time she and Christine had had a normal conversation. "I find Ben's solidness very sexy, very comforting, yet he—" Carolyn blushed and decided not to continue. "There has to be a reason you fall for men you know are not available."

"I've never had it happen with a married man before. And, Carolyn, I haven't even kissed this one. I just needed space away from him so that I could break the spell." Christine stared at her nails, ovals of pearl that matched the shining pearl half moons on her eyelids. "And the real truth is that I always leave a man before he can stop liking me so that I won't have to endure the pain of him not being under my spell." She pressed a palm to one of her tiger-striped boots. "So, are you going to marry Ben?"

Carolyn was startled. "No. Absolutely not."

Puzzlement wrinkled Christine's perfectly plucked brows. "Why not? He sure seemed happy to be here with you."

"I'm helping him with a case," she replied carefully. "And we started talking about old times. That's all."

"Does he have any children?"

"An adorable little girl named Lucy."

"Oh, you'd get to be a stepmommy," Christine said in a gently teasing voice. "Even if you can't have any of your own, a little girl for you to love would be kind of nice."

Carolyn wrapped herself against the hurt she knew her sister didn't mean to cause. "I've thought about it, believe me, but it's just not that simple. I'm not interested in getting married, and Ben may want more children one day."

"Why do you think neither one of us wants to get married?"

She sighed, not wanting to go down that lane, either. "If our parents were happily married, it might have made a difference. But since we have no experience with happily-ever-after, it seems better to avoid it."

Christine was quiet for a few seconds, and Carolyn sipped her drink, thinking about Lucy and how much she'd love to have a sibling.

"Would you really want to avoid marriage if you hadn't had your hysterectomy?" Christine asked suddenly.

"Well, I certainly wouldn't avoid it the way you're avoiding Rasputin, I'm sure." *The truth was, I'd probably jump at the chance if it were Ben doing the asking.*

"Carolyn, was it very bad? I mean, I'm afraid of needles and doctors and people looking at my anatomy." Christine stared at her. "I should have come to be with you, but…I avoided it. Selfishly. I was afraid you'd know how frightened I was for you, and I finally worked myself up into such a state that I realized I wouldn't be a comfort to you at all."

Carolyn raised a brow. "It was me having the operation."

"I know. But it isn't easy to watch someone you care about suffer. And I'm not good with needles and hospitals and things. I figured I'd be more of a hindrance than a comfort, and I didn't want to drag you down with having to worry about me."

"I didn't know you were that concerned."

"Why ever not? I sent flowers."

"Christine, I didn't need flowers. At the very least a card would have been more personal and made me feel less…alone."

"I actually found a card especially for the occasion. It said, 'Congrats! No more tampons!' But then I wasn't sure you'd think that was funny. I've always known how much you wanted children, Carolyn. The truth is, I couldn't believe it was me who had perfectly healthy organs, someone who never wanted any of the little brats. I'm sorry I didn't come to be with you. I felt very, very guilty that it was me, the wild sib, who was still functioning."

Carolyn closed her eyes, not sure the old wounds would heal quickly. She didn't know what to say. "I missed you," she finally whispered. "I understand now, but I didn't at the time, and I was quite depressed about everything."

"I did call you once, in the hospital," Christine said. "Did they tell you? You were sleeping at the time."

"No. I didn't get the message." And it was possible it wouldn't have mattered. It seemed to only matter now—now that she was beginning to understand how short life could be, thanks to Lucy. "You know what? I shouldn't have held that in my heart for so long. I should have known you were holding your feelings in, Christine. You've been doing that for years."

"Yes, I'm quite the woman of unresolved emotions," she snapped.

Obviously a nerve had been touched. Carolyn put her hand over her sister's and smiled. "I'm glad

GET 2

HOW TO GET YOUR
2 FREE BOOKS AND FREE GIFT!

1. Peel off the MIRA sticker on the front cover. Place it in the space provided at right. This automatically entitles you to receive two free books and an exciting mystery gift.

2. Send back this card and you'll get 2 "The Best of the Best™" novels. These books have a combined cover price of $11.00 or more in the U.S. and $13.00 or more in Canada, but they are yours to keep absolutely FREE!

3. There's <u>no</u> catch. You're under <u>no</u> obligation to buy anything. We charge nothing – ZERO – for your first shipment. And you don't have to make any minimum number of purchases – not even one!

4. We call this line "The Best of the Best" because each month you'll receive the best books by some of today's hottest authors. These authors show up time and time again on all the major bestseller lists and their books sell out as soon as they hit the stores. You'll like the convenience of getting them delivered to your home at our special discount prices . . . and you'll love your *Heart to Heart* subscriber newsletter featuring author news, horoscopes, recipes, book reviews and much more!

SPECIAL FREE GIFT!

We'll send you a fabulous surprise gift, absolutely FREE, simply for accepting our no-risk offer!

5. We hope that after receiving your free books you'll want to remain a subscriber. But the choice is yours – to continue or cancel, anytime at all! So why not take us up on our invitation, with no risk of any kind. You'll be glad you did!

6. And remember...we'll send you a mystery gift ABSOLUTELY FREE just for giving "The Best of the Best" a try.

Visit us online at
www.mirabooks.com

® and TM are trademarks of Harlequin Enterprises Limited.

ONE

■■■■■■■■■

LYDIA SCHOLTZ ARRIVED at the Hawley Funeral Home at six o'clock on the morning of Saturday, August 15th, right in the middle of the worst heat wave in Cleveland's history. It had been between ninety and one hundred degrees during the day for two solid weeks, and there didn't seem to be any end in sight. The grass was straw for lack of rain, and by the end of the month the police would be attributing twelve murders to short tempers brought on by the heat. She didn't call ahead, but just showed up, ringing the bell until I descended the stairs from the funeral home's second floor apartment that my wife and I share, unshaven, blinking, wearing a bathrobe and slippers. When I opened the door I found her, hands trembling, eyes red from crying, her whole body infused with nervous, directionless energy. In my office I made her some instant coffee while offering all the comforting words I could. And when she seemed reasonably composed, I asked her to excuse me while I ran upstairs to dress.

I returned fifteen minutes later, shaved and in a dark suit, to find her sitting exactly where I had left her: in a chair pulled up close to the front of my desk. As I walked in,

she turned to me and said, "I'm sorry for bothering you so early. I thought there was always someone here . . . ." Her voice trailed off, and she glanced back down at her lap.

"No problem," I said, spilling her cold, untouched coffee into the sink of a wet bar in a cabinet near the desk. "That's my job."

"I've been up all night," she said. "I came straight from the hospital."

Pulling a new file folder from a drawer, I seated myself and watched her grow preoccupied with her thoughts. She was a tall, statuesque woman who had retained her looks in flat defiance of age. As I would learn when we were setting up his newspaper death notice, her deceased husband, Chester, had been seventy years old. But she was only sixty, which still surprised me. I'd have pegged her at fifty, tops. Her face was flawlessly—perhaps even artificially—smooth, and her hair, though traced with grey, was of such a warm auburn color 'hat it looked almost as if it had been specifically chosen to accent her hazel eyes. She was on the slender side, dressed in a dark brown suit that set off all the gold she wore, and unlike many tall women who stoop because they feel self-conscious, she sat up straight in her seat, crossing a pair of very shapely legs.

The details of her problem went like this:

Her husband had been found late the night before, dead on the floor of a cheap motel on Brookings Road in an area of town known as the "Combat Zone." According to the police, the girl who had reported his death was a twenty-year-old "exotic dancer" employed at a place called the Lipstick Lounge. She said that she had been hired by Mr. Scholtz for a private exhibition after he came into the lounge looking for some action. Apparently his heart hadn't been up to the challenge, and the motel manager dialed 911. In her statement, the girl described herself as a completely legitimate entertainer who danced for her clients, and that was all—there was no touchie-feelie, and definitely nothing kinky. The motel manager corroborated her story, adding that this wasn't the first time he'd seen "Mr. Peters," as

Chester Scholtz had signed the register, meeting a girl from one of the show bars on the street.

"It was bad enough that he was dead," Mrs. Scholtz nearly whispered, her eyes fixed on her hands. "But when they told me how he died . . ."

She trailed off again as the tears came, and I said, "This must be very . . . embarrassing for you."

"It's not embarrassing," she replied, looking up sharply. "It's a lie! My husband didn't do it. None of it. And I want you to prove it for me."

Her approach took me off guard. As a funeral director, I'm accustomed to listening to people talk about the events surrounding the death of their loved ones. When someone dies, the people left behind invariably end up vocalizing certain questions to me, in confidence, because they seem to believe that, since my job brings me into daily contact with death, I must have some special understanding of its mysteries. "Were Mom's eyes open or closed?" "Do you really take the blood out?" and, "Have you ever had a body sit up?" are the most common inquiries I face. But there are also those that resonate from a deeper place, such as, "Do you think Dad suffered at the end?" and, "What made him bleed so much?" and they echo a desire for knowledge that resides very close to a person's heart.

One of the most important parts of my job is to recognize the volatility of bereavement and to ease its pain with sympathetic, discreet information. To have someone close yanked from your life is hard. By answering what questions he can in an up-front, candid manner, I feel that an undertaker can help his clients realize that, instead of the enigma so many people believe death to be, it is, at its root, just another part of life. True, it's an uncomfortable part, and one that's hard to bear. But human beings are incredibly resilient, and, though they might doubt it at the moment, even the most devastated widow or widower has the strength they need to get through somewhere inside. There's salvation in the ordinary . . . in the details. And it's

my job to help them find the strength to satisfy their own individual needs of the moment.

But Mrs. Scholtz apparently wanted something more, and when I tried to explain that I was by no means a private investigator, which, if I had understood her correctly, was what it sounded to me that she needed, she cut me off with a dismissive wave of her hand and a suddenly curt tone of voice.

"This whole thing's a farce," she said as she rose and began pacing the room like a caged panther. "Chester was blind; and blind men don't hire strippers! He told me he was doing something risky . . . but I never imagined he'd leave me like this . . . that he'd die . . . like this."

I rose and took her hand, saying, "Mrs. Scholtz. Please. I'm not following."

To which she replied, "The police have already made up their minds about what happened to my husband, Mr. Hawley. At the hospital they told me that since there was no sign of violence, and no unusual circumstances surrounding his death, there's not even going to be an investigation. They said that, as hard as it was going to be for me to accept, there just isn't anything they can do since there was no evidence of a crime."

"And you think otherwise?"

"Mr. Hawley," she said, taking back her hand and squaring her shoulders, "when Chester walked into that motel, he was carrying fifty thousand dollars."

"I think you better start from the beginning," I said, lowering myself into my seat.

And she did.

Chester Scholtz was a retired accountant who had started his career in the private sector and moved over to a position with the county auditor's office when he was about thirty. He and his wife were married for almost forty years, had two children, and loved each other a lot. Chester retired when he was sixty-four, and spent the last six years of his life trying to take it easy . . . which was hard because the kids became a problem.

"They needed money," Mrs. Scholtz explained, the effort of speaking apparently serving to focus her mind and balance her emotions. "It's not that they're bad kids, it's just that they had some trouble. Especially our oldest, who lives in Detroit. He was always the level-headed one, like his father—a businessman. Not like our daughter; she's a free spirit . . . one of those people who just drift from one situation to another. She had a bad marriage. No direction. She's like a child. But Terry—he's our son—he went into management with G.M. and did well. A house in Grosse Pointe, three lovely daughters, a wife with a degree who started her own catering business on the side. Chester was always so proud.

"And then two years ago Terry lost his job. The company blamed the recession, and middle management was the first thing to go. He lasted longer than most, but they still lost the house and ended up in an apartment, living off the catering business while he looked for work. Not long after that, Sharon, our daughter, moved back in with us. And that's when Chester slid into a funk."

"That's understandable," I offered, making her shake her head as she said:

"Not for Chester it isn't. He was a go-getter, a problem solver, and he never gave up on anything. But for weeks he did nothing but complain about how frustrated he was that he couldn't help the kids more. Not that we're poor, but he wanted them never to have to worry again . . . that's how he put it. 'Lee,' he said, 'when I die I want you and the kids to have it made.' I told him that nobody expected him to shoulder the burden forever, and that I didn't like hearing him talk about dying, but he wouldn't listen. When he got something under his skin like that, there was just no reasoning with him. He'd get obsessive. Like nothing else mattered.

"And then, one day about six months ago, he announced that he had come up with a terrific idea. It was going to be a little rough for a while, he said, but he made me promise not to worry, and to trust him."

"Trust him?" I said. "Trust him how?"

"Just trust him," she returned with a shrug. "That was his way. He didn't always tell me things. He just said that he had a line on a deal that would solve all our problems. When I asked him what kind of deal he was talking about, all he'd say was, 'Don't worry, everything'll be all right.' But everything wasn't all right, because the next morning he slipped getting out of the shower and broke his hip."

The rest sounded pretty typical.

Chester Scholtz was taken to Southwest General Hospital, where his physician, Dr. Leo Teeg, said that, though he wouldn't require surgery, he would need a great deal of bed rest. He was admitted to the Manor Care Assisted Living Facility to convalesce, but there he only got worse, saying how he'd reached the end of his life, and that he was useless and feeble. He grew withdrawn and sullen. And finally his mental state deteriorated so badly that he went blind.

"Psychosomatic hysterical blindness," his wife said, repeating what the doctor must have told her. "It came on gradually at first, starting about three months ago as dimming vision, and finally ending with him just staring blankly into space. His hip was getting better, but that didn't matter anymore because now he couldn't see."

I had been listening to her patiently. But I wasn't just being a professional; there was something about the way she spoke that touched me inside. It was a kind of human contact that I often feel on my job, but to which I can only respond by performing my duties. But this woman was leading me in a very different direction, and it frightened me a little when I realized that there was a part of me that wanted very much to follow.

"Early yesterday morning," she continued, visibly bracing herself as if her words were the product of great effort, "Chester left the nursing home, went to the bank, and took fifty thousand dollars in cash from our savings account. Then he disappeared. I spent the whole day in a panic . . .

and when the call came that he was dead, I knew I had to come to you."

"But you just said that he was blind, and recovering from a fractured hip. How could he have gotten from the nursing home to the bank?" I asked.

Mrs. Scholtz looked at me significantly.

"Mr. Hawley," she said, "nobody said a word about there being any money in that motel room. Not the police, nor the emergency squad who took Chester to the hospital. My husband's dead, and nearly a third of our life's savings is gone. You've got to help me. Please. You've just got to find out what Chester was doing when he died. I've read about you in the paper, and I need someone I can depend on to be discreet. Discretion's a part of your business, isn't it? Who better than you could I ask?"

Suddenly, it all made sense: it was that damned article! I had known that it would be trouble the moment I saw it, and here that trouble was, not two weeks after my name had appeared in the *Cleveland Plain Dealer*'s Sunday Magazine.

I like puzzles; mystery movies, plays, books, and stories are my hobby. I also like the murder mystery weekends that a local bed-and-breakfast place puts on downtown. My wife, Nat, and I, have been attending these things once a month for years. They're put on by a local writer who does mystery novels, and Nat and I have won so many times that we've gotten to know the author pretty well. Unfortunately, there's a woman named Agatha O'Toole who does human interest stories for the paper who likes our local mystery writer, and she's the nosiest, most meddlesome woman I've ever met. She did an article on our novelist friend a couple of months ago, and while they were having their interview he mentioned me: a funeral director with a flair for solving whodunits. Ms. O'Toole thought that sounded like a great hook, attended the next weekend, made sure that we were introduced, and ended up doing an article called, "Cleveland's Sleuthing Undertaker," for which I've taken a lot of ribbing. I've also gotten a couple of calls

similar to what was happening in my office right now: people wanting me to look into things for them. Always I was polite when I declined their offers. But I had secretly been fearing that someone was going to walk in one day with a request that I couldn't refuse.

"Mrs. Scholtz," I said, being polite, but feeling an underlying sensation of anticipation placing an edge on my voice, "just because some human interest story says that I'm good at solving fictional mysteries, it doesn't mean that I would be any good at it in real life. And besides, what you're asking is completely unethical. If the Ohio Organization of Funeral Professionals heard about it, I could lose my license."

"But they won't hear about it. This will remain strictly between you and me. All I'm asking is that you please see what you can find out. I've known Chester for forty years, and I'm telling you that, whatever he was doing when he died, it was designed to make a profit."

"Have you told the police about the money?"

"No."

"Why not?"

"I can't."

"But why?"

Her lower lip was trembling, and her eyes were tearing up again. Finally she whispered, "Because I'm afraid."

"Of what?"

"I'm not sure!" she cried, slapping her hands down on her knees in frustration. "Oh God, Mr. Hawley, I feel so alone! There've been calls . . . and a van watching my house. I know it sounds crazy, but I've been scared for weeks. I sensed that something was wrong from the beginning, but I never dreamed that it would end like this. Chester was always so clever, and he knew so many people . . ."

"Who's watching your house?" I cut in.

And her voice calmed as she said, "I wasn't sure that anyone was, at first. But one morning I noticed a yellow van parked across the street, and that night it was still there.

Then I'd see it in the parking lot at the grocery store, or the mall, and all the way home it would be in my rearview mirror."

"How long has this been going on?"

"A week. Maybe two."

"And the phone calls?"

"They come at all hours, and when I answer there's no one there. It's like someone's checking to see if I'm home."

I paused, studying her eyes. Finally I said, "I get the feeling that you're holding something back, Mrs. Scholtz, like maybe you're not telling me everything."

And she said, "Chester knew people."

"What kind of people?"

"In his business. He worked for the county in the tax fraud division, and over the years he helped the government trip people up. Famous people . . . names you'd know."

"Are you saying that someone might be looking for revenge?"

And with a quick, determined glance at the ceiling as if to draw strength, she said, "Chester worked for the county, but he reported to an office in Washington. He was around dishonest people all the time, and it disgusted him knowing what kind of money they got away with. He made a lot of enemies, and took a lot of risks."

"And you think that he was doing something risky for the government that would make him a lot of money if he pulled it off?"

She shook her head, pressing her lips into a tight, thin line.

"Then he was doing something dishonest," I said softly.

And she nodded, a single tear rolling down her cheek as she practically whispered, "From the beginning I suspected he had a reason for going into that nursing home. But I didn't dare say anything because he told me not to worry. Whenever he told me not to worry in the past, things always worked out. He's never let me down before. Not like this . . . not ever. Now he's not only gone, but

someone's watching me . . . and I'm afraid that it's the same people who were there when he died!"

I got up and handed her a box of Kleenex, a little shaken by her scenario, and trying to work out some pattern in my mind that made sense. It all seemed so improbable, so contrived, and yet I was intrigued. "How did you find out he took the money?" I asked.

From her purse she withdrew a photocopied page, which she handed to me, saying, "It's called a C.T.R., a Currency Transaction Report. Anytime someone withdraws ten thousand dollars or more in cash, the bank's required to file one. After he left, the teller called me at home."

I examined the page, saying, "And you're sure this is his signature?"

"Yes."

"You said that the police won't investigate because they didn't find any sign of violence. Are you telling me that you think they missed something?"

"Not at all. I don't doubt that Chester really did die of a heart attack. But he wasn't a well man. I believe that the shock of being robbed could easily have stopped his heart."

"So you think the girl robbed him?"

"I don't know!" she said, her voice rising with emotion. "But someone took that money, and now it looks like those same people are watching to see what I'll do about it. If I go to a private detective, or even to the police, there's no telling what might happen . . ."

"This is all conjecture, Mrs. Scholtz," I cut in, trying to bring things back down to earth. But it didn't work. Instead, she seemed all the more determined to make her point.

"All right," she conceded with a quick nod. "Let's say I'm wrong. So what's the harm in humoring me? I'll pay you as much as you ask . . . and if you don't find anything, I'll admit my mistake. But don't you see, if I'm not wrong and there is someone out there, then you're my only hope. What's more natural than a widow coming to a funeral director after her husband dies? They'll never suspect that

we're actually talking about something else . . ."

"Mrs. Scholtz," I began, determined to stop this before it went any further, "I really regret—"

"No! Look!" she insisted, jumping up from her chair and pointing at the window. "If you don't believe me, then look for yourself."

I was about to protest, but something in her stubborn expression made me sigh and draw back the sheer so that I could glance at the street. It was just after seven in the morning, and the sun was already bright with the promise of another scorching day. Traffic on State Road was light since it was the weekend, and an American flag hung limply on its pole in the school yard across the street. I was about to speak, but then I caught sight of something that stopped the words cold in my mouth. On the side street across from our lot, dark with a mottling of leafy shadow thrown by the tree overhead, was parked a yellow Dodge van. I couldn't tell if there was anyone inside, but just seeing it made my heart stutter.

I let the sheer fall back and turned back to Mrs. Scholtz, who, having stepped up close, said, "Now will you help me?"

I didn't respond, but there must have been something in my eyes that gave my thoughts away because, with a look of relief spreading over her face, she said, "Thank you," and kissed me on the cheek.

TWO
■■■■■■■■

MY WIFE'S NAME is Natalie, and she's my foundation. If it weren't for her, I honestly don't think that I would be alive today because my drinking would have killed me. She helped me realize that I'm a born addict, and that it's a part of my personality that I'll just have to live with. I get hooked on everything: booze, cigarettes, caffeine. But she changed all that by giving me something to live for, and making me want to change.

After I watched Mrs. Scholtz leave, with the yellow van pulling out after her, my first impulse was to call Nat at work and get her input on the situation; she's a reference librarian at the local college where we met, and Saturdays she works eight to noon. But, to tell you the truth, I was in the middle of the deepest emotional low of my life at that time. I was thirty-three years old, going nowhere, and working for my dad. I had been a funeral director for nearly eleven years, having jumped into the family business right out of college. And though there were certain aspects of my job that I really enjoyed, what I mostly felt was trapped. Part of it was my own fault, and part of it was my situation, but the gist of it is that I was so ready for a change that,

as ridiculous as it sounds, when a little devil whispered in my ear, "Go on, take a chance. You don't need your wife's permission to ask a few questions!" I made a quick call to a friend of my dad's on the Cleveland Police Department, threw the one-man cot in the van, and headed for the hospital.

I did it, I think, because I needed to feel . . . what? Autonomous? That's not really the proper word here, but it's got the right feel. The bottom line is that my father had given me my job . . . and while I appreciated the fact that I had a place in the family business, deep down, on the level where every man's fragile self-image stands vulnerable in the light of his accomplishments, I felt as if I had never really left the nest . . . as if, every time my father handed me my paycheck, I was actually receiving my allowance. It drove me nuts, and I needed a change.

So as I drove to the hospital, Mrs. Scholtz's scenario buzzed inside my head, tugging at my attention with an almost irresistible seductiveness. "He was an accountant," she'd said, capturing the essence of the thing in a single image. "He thought in terms of profit and loss, and I'm sure that he saw the money he took from our account as venture capital." I have to admit, the idea intrigued me. And as I saw it, my most logical first step was to see if I could come up with anything that would either strengthen or disprove her theory. I mean, so far all I had was her word, and, as my dad, the retired fireman who had spent ten years on the arson squad, says, "The first rule in any investigation is to verify everything you can, and then to take a hard look at those things you can't." I figured that the easiest way to be sure that things had really happened as she described them was to ask the people who were there . . . the cops and the rescue squad, the motel manager, and maybe even that dancer.

The security kid at the hospital didn't know a thing about the body I was picking up, and the guys who were on in the E.R. when Scholtz came in had gone home at seven. But the head nurse was in the lounge, eating raspberry Zingers

and finishing her reports. So I sat down across the table and waited for her to look up, which she finally did, irritably, smiling only after she saw who I was and saying, "Wild Bill Hawley! The return of the Prodigal."

Her name badge read "Louise McCarthy, Nursing Supervisor," though when I worked as an orderly in the X-ray department we called her Lou Lou because she always acted like one of the gang.

"How the hell have you been?" she asked. "Got any cigarettes?"

I told her that I'd quit, and she frowned as she said, "Me, too."

I'd always liked Lou Lou because, even though she was a nurse, she had every bad habit known to man—and, I suspect, a couple known only to women. I had a real crush on her before I met Nat, but she was married at the time, and I was way too young and innocent for her tastes. Years later, during her father's viewings at our funeral home, she admitted that she had considered giving me a tumble for the sheer perverted thrill of playing the cradle-robbing older woman. And when I asked her why she hadn't, for God's sake, she replied that I had never acted interested. Talk about your disappointments: to realize that you missed an opportunity like that because you were too stupid to even realize it was there? I kind of wish she'd never told me.

We went back and forth for a few minutes—How's so-and-so? Oh really? Married? Etc.—until I finally asked her about Chester Scholtz, which made her put the end of her pen in her mouth for a second to think before she said, "Oh yeah: D.O.A. Came in cold. So that's why you're here." In response to my questions she ran down the particulars, giving me the names of the cops who'd done the reports, and saying that C crew was on the ambulance.

"Let's see," she added, licking her thumb and running through the pages. "Here."

She handed me his emergency room report, which described his condition when he came into the hospital in unambiguous medical terms, which was fine, but not

what I was looking for. What I wanted to know was how Scholtz's arrival had made her feel.

"What do ya mean, *feel*?" she asked, cocking her head and putting down her pen. She was a pretty woman, about fifty, with freckles and a dimple in her chin.

"You know how it is," I said. "You do this long enough and you get a sense about these things. Was Scholtz a straight D.O.A., or was something up?"

"Why you asking?" she responded suspiciously.

And I said, "Haven't you read about me in the papers?"

"Oh shit, Bill," she groaned, slapping her forehead. "No! Please! Say it ain't so. Not a fucking Kojak . . . not you! Please!"

"Lou . . ."

"You know how sleazy those guys are! Christ, you don't wanna do this."

"I'm not sleazy."

"You will be. It can't be avoided."

"Lou . . ."

"You didn't quit your job, did you?"

"No."

"Good. Then just pick up the body, and go. Forget the rest of it; you don't need it."

"Lou, sincerely. Just tell me yes or no. Was it a straight D.O.A. or not?"

"Yeah," she said with a resigned shrug . . . as if she'd just warned an alcoholic friend not to take his first drink, and had then watched him go ahead and do it anyway. "Why wouldn't it be?"

Quickly I ran down some of the highlights of Mrs. Scholtz's visit. As I spoke, Lou Lou watched me, chewing her Zingers and sipping coffee from a Styrofoam cup smeared with lipstick and coconut shreds. I finished by assuring her that instead of planning anything extravagant, all I wanted to do was check Mrs. Scholtz's facts and see if I couldn't find something that would put her mind at ease.

"Grieving people get paranoid sometimes," I said, hoping to stoke the compassion for others that I knew to be Lou

Lou's strongest suit. "Maybe if I can show her that there aren't any plots simmering beneath the surface she'll bury her husband and get on with her life. Right now I think she's refusing to let him go by manufacturing all these suspicions about how he died. As long as there are unresolved questions, it's almost like a part of him is still alive."

Lou frowned and asked, "Is that really what you're doing?"

And I said, "Of course. What do you think?"

"I think you better watch your ass. Remember Fleckner?"

"That was different."

"Was it?"

Harvey Fleckner was a big drunk guy they'd brought in after a bar fight at two a.m. one Memorial Day weekend when I was working the graveyard shift in E.R. I was nineteen years old and had been a member of the hospital's staff since my freshman year of college, so I should have known better. When Mr. Fleckner got up off the table, insisting that he was going home and daring the petite X-ray tech named Tammi to stop him, I knocked him down and sat on top of him until security came. The trouble was, hospital rules strictly forbade any lower level staff member—orderlies, housekeeping crew, etc.—from physically restraining a patient without the supervision of a superior, unless there was absolutely no other alternative. What I should have done was lock Mr. Fleckner in the room and wait. If the guy would have been a little more sober we might have had a lawsuit on our hands. But he was so blitzed that when Lou Lou claimed that she had been in the room all along, he couldn't confidently say it wasn't true. Her lie saved my job. And after that she took to calling me Wild Bill because she said that sometimes I acted like a cowboy.

"You're cursed with a successful father," I remember her saying later, Marlboro smoke curling around her lips— she was a chain-smoker with a rattlesnake cough. "Your dad's an overachiever, and deep down you wanna be just like him."

"That's not true," was my reply. "What I want to be, is better."

Sliding a pair of half-rim reading glasses onto the end of her nose, she took the E.R. report back from me and glanced at it, asking, "So what do you want to know?"

"If he really broke his hip," I said.

Lou Lou looked at me over the top of her glasses.

"Scholtz was brought in six months ago after he fell in his shower," I pressed. "Dr. Teeg must have had him X-rayed, so the films should be on file."

"So?"

"So, Mrs. Scholtz said that she thinks her husband went into the Manor Care Nursing Home for a *reason*. I just want to see how sick he really was."

She looked at me skeptically.

"I know what you're thinking," I said. "But I just want to check the facts."

"You know I'm not supposed to do this," she said.

And I returned, "I'm forever in your debt."

"No shit." She laughed, rising and leading me down to the Barn, a huge, fireproof vault in the hospital's basement where the X-ray records are housed. As I watched, she chose an aisle out of the dozen or so rows of steel shelves, dragged a rolling ladder along until she found her spot, and climbed up to the top shelf, saying, "And don't look up my skirt." When she climbed back down she was holding an X-ray file containing all the films shot on Chester Scholtz at Southwest General over the years. According to the record he had only been in twice. Once, about five years ago for a fractured thumb. And then six months ago for his hip. Sorting through the floppy black plastic sheets with the file pressed under her arm, she held up one after another, aiming each at the fluorescent light overhead and squinting significantly. Finally she said, "Here we go. Hip shot." Studying the film for a moment, she frowned and added, "Let's go back upstairs."

In the radiologist's office she stuck Chester Scholtz's X-rays up on a glowing wall of white plastic so that they

were illuminated from behind. With a magnifying glass she leaned close, her face shimmering with sterile light and her eyebrows furrowed. Finally she handed me the glass and said, "Look," pointing to a spot on one film with her finger. I focused the glass, ran it over the spot, glanced at her, and repeated the exercise.

Finally, laying the glass down, I said, "Shit."

She nodded, saying, "Let's go over that E.R. report again."

Half an hour later I was sitting behind the wheel of my van with Chester Scholtz's body on the cot behind me, thinking about his X-rays and wondering what they'd meant. There hadn't been so much as a hint of a fracture anywhere I could see, and after Lou Lou looked up the case in the computer, we discovered that Dr. Teeg had superseded normal hospital procedure by not putting the films through to be read by the staff radiologist after his initial examination. Without a specialist report, there was only Dr. Teeg's word that Scholtz's hip was fractured, and not a single follow-up exam had been ordered after he was admitted to the nursing home, which was right across the street. Lou Lou's review of Chester's E.R. report served only to lay out the chronology of last evening's events. And succinctly, they went like this:

At 10:35 p.m., Friday, August 14th, C Crew, Station 5, Cleveland Rescue Squad responded to a man down call at the Cozy Inn, Brookings Road, by the airport, where they found their patient prone on the floor with no vitals signs, and no motor responses. But since he was still warm, and, according to a dancer named Cynthia Moore, had been unconscious less than fifteen minutes, they administered C.P.R. and removed him to the nearest emergency room, where he was finally pronounced dead at 12:02 a.m. His wife was notified, and provided Dr. Teeg's name as her husband's attending physician. Dr. Teeg stated that his patient had a long history of heart trouble, and that he would sign a death certificate to that effect, thus negating the need of involving the coroner.

Shortly after two in the morning, Mrs. Scholtz and Dr. Teeg exchanged heated words in the physicians' lounge, and Mrs. Scholtz stormed out of the hospital amid a flurry of vague accusations. Dr. Teeg attributed her response to stress, and went home. After being wrapped in plastic, Chester Scholtz was removed to the hospital's morgue, and a nurse at the E.R. desk began calling his wife at home because she had neglected to sign a body release before she left. There was no answer until almost four a.m.—making me think, Where the hell was she all night?, seeing that X-ray in my head and hearing Mrs. Scholtz's words as she repeated, "I was up all night," in a ghostly, remembered voice.

"Up where?" I said aloud, glancing up and seeing the Manor Care Assisted Living Facility just two hundred yards away. Starting the engine, I added, "Hey Chester, if it's all the same to you, instead of headin' straight home, how about we make a quick stop on the way?" He didn't object, so I headed over, parking the van way back in the lot and locking it up tight. Even though I didn't like leaving a body unattended, I figured if Chester got bored he could always play the radio.

The Manor Care was a fairly new building, all glass and landscaping, with a cheery little pond out front that was home to a family of plaster ducks, and a receptionist in the lobby who looked old enough to be a resident. With the silent eyes of a dozen or so wheelchair bound men and women following my every step, I worked my way down to the west wing, asking anyone I saw in a white uniform for help. Finally, after I had identified myself as "Bill Hawley, from the Hawley Funeral Home," for probably the tenth time, a young black nurse pointed at a door marked ACTIVITIES ROOM saying, "Pete's in there. He was Mr. Scholtz's best friend on the staff."

I thanked her, noticing how naturally she slipped into the past tense when referring to a deceased patient. I don't think I could ever get used to watching people die. In my business, the real, physical suffering is over long before

I'm ever called. But nursing homes are full of persistent, immediate pain. I don't even like visiting them on body calls because most of the time you have to wheel the cot right through the front lobby, and inevitably there are a couple of patients watching from the periphery, silently indifferent, motionless in their wheelchairs, moving only their eyes as you pass. No one ever speaks, but neither do they look away.

I opened the Activities Room door and stuck my head inside, finding an orderly pushing an old woman's wheelchair in a lazy figure eight pattern to the strains of some classical music concerto emanating from a jam box on the floor. The woman's eyes were so glazed over that she looked as if she were in a trance, but if the orderly—a good-looking young man with sandy blond hair and a quiet, almost refined demeanor—stopped pushing for so much as an instant, she immediately started shouting and kicking her feet.

"She was a dancing instructor," he explained in a perfectly natural voice, making no attempt to prevent his charge from hearing what he said. "I think she's performing when we do this . . . in her head, I mean. She won't let me stop until the music's over."

The Activities Room was large, and empty, with a parquet wood floor and folding chairs stacked in one corner near what looked like an elementary school's stage. The rubber of the wheelchair's wheels squeaked as I took a seat off to one side and waited until the invisible ballet was over. When the music stopped so did the orderly, letting go of the chair so that it rolled to a halt of its own volition as he stood behind it and clapped. I joined in, and the room rang with our applause until a nurse appeared to "Freshen Irene up for lunch." Irene didn't seem to hear, but sat silently, staring straight ahead, her feet still, and her eyes blank.

"It's a sin what happens to them," the young man said, standing close by and watching the nurse roll the woman away. "But she's more aware than you'd think. I'm Pete

Germaine; and you must be the grandson Irene's been expecting."

He extended his hand, and I shook it, introducing myself and explaining why I'd come through his look of amused surprise. When I asked him if he could spare a few minutes, he invited me back to the staff lounge, checking in with the floor nurse for a ten minute break and leading me to a tiny vestibule with four aluminum chairs, three standing ashtrays, and a coffee urn. I declined his offer of coffee, and was surprised when he asked the first question.

"So, just exactly what are you, Mr. Hawley?" he said, leaning back and lacing his fingers behind his head. He was one of those people who seem comfortable with whomever they're around, and he had a disarming, almost boyish charm that I found quite appealing. His eyes were bright blue, and his uniform completely white. There was a fine, gold down on the part of his arms that his short sleeves didn't cover. And his smile was easy, unforced. He looked to be about twenty-three years old, and briefly I wondered if I had looked like this in my orderly's uniform when I was his age.

"I mean," he continued, leaning forward and folding his hands on the table, "I've read about you. Are you a funeral director who plays detective, or an aspiring detective who owns a funeral home?"

"Neither," I said, explaining that the article in the *Plain Dealer* was embellished quite a bit, and that my father owned the funeral home where I worked.

"Really?" he asked, eyes twinkling. "How interesting. Most men with strong fathers end up suppressing a lot of resentment. Are you prone to ulcers? I'll bet that you are. And on a Myers-Briggs Personality Test I'd peg you as an I.N.T.J."

"Which is?"

"Introverted, Intuitive, Thinking, and Judgmental. I'm an I.N.F.P. myself: Introverted, Intuitive, Feeling, and Perceiving. It means that I'm a wimp, basically. A member of life's audience. I'd love to be an E."

"Extrovert?"

"You got it."

"So it's safe to assume that you're a psychology student?"

"I'm in my second year of a master's program over at Case Western. It's taking me a little longer because I have to work full-time to pay for it. But in the end I think it'll be worth the effort."

"And I assume you'll be working with old people once you've finished your degree."

"Oh, God no. Old people are depressing. Reminders of our mortality, and all that. In a place like this all a psychologist would have to do is sit around thinking of ways to keep the residents placid until they died. Not to be cruel about it . . . but old people are frustrated all the time. I want to work for a major corporation; with people in the prime of their lives. I study how individuals interact with groups. And I love money. It's a disease."

I was taken with Germaine's frankness, and would have loved to ease into the subject of Chester Scholtz more gracefully. But since he only had ten minutes, I told him flat out how the old man had died. To my disappointment, he didn't act the least bit surprised, saying that the details were all over the facility because Mrs. Scholtz had appeared early that morning to ransack her husband's room.

"The story goes that she acted like a wild woman," he confided. "Practically tore the place apart."

"Why?" I asked.

And he shrugged, saying, "How should I know?"

"Tell me about Scholtz."

He wrapped his fingers around his paper coffee cup, asking, "Is this an investigation?" When I shrugged, he grinned and added, "How exciting. In that case, let me see; I suppose I should start by saying that he was definitely my favorite patient. Of all the people here, he was the most alive. Actually, dynamic would be a better word. He gave stock tips to everybody, listened to the financial news, talked politics, and was the center of attention wherever he

went. You'd see him hobbling up and down the hall on his cane all day long, checking in on his friends and trying to stay involved. If it weren't for his accident, I'm sure he'd have chewed glass before allowing himself to be admitted to a place like this."

"That hardly sounds like a description of someone who'd slide into psychosomatic blindness," I cut in, making the young man's eyes light up.

"On the contrary," he said, suddenly enthusiastic. "His blindness was almost a textbook example of reflexive suppression. By denying his resentments he subconsciously turned his anger into something so powerful that it manifested itself as a physical symptom. People don't choose to have psychosomatic disorders, you know. And when they do happen, they're often more debilitating than real diseases because the people experiencing them realize that, even though they're self-inflicted, there's nothing they can do to stop them."

"So if he'd have been depressed all the time, he probably wouldn't have gone blind?"

"Right. If he was the depressive type, then his depression would have been his symptom. As it was, his psychological makeup wouldn't allow him to acknowledge his rage, so he suppressed it. He was like a pressure cooker, and he didn't even know it."

"When was the last time you saw him?"

"Well, let's see. What's today, Saturday? I work an eleven to seven shift during the week, and I was off Friday since I'm taking days this weekend for the overtime. So that would mean that I last saw him on Thursday."

"You worked from eleven at night to seven in the morning, and you saw Chester Scholtz during those hours?"

"He was always up by four, so we'd have coffee together."

"And you were off yesterday?"

"Yes."

"How'd you spend your day?"

"Sleeping."

"All day?"

"Mr. Hawley, I work nights and I go to school days. When I get a day off, I rest."

"What about school?"

"It's summer. Remember?"

"What did you and Scholtz do at four in the morning?"

"Well," he said. "I probably shouldn't be telling you this . . . but . . ." He got up and took a quick look into the hall outside the lounge, adding, "Can we keep this between the two of us?"

I nodded.

"Well, I sort of let him look at the files, sometimes."

"The files?"

"The ones we keep on our residents."

"What did he want to see those for?"

Germaine looked a little incredulous, as if I'd just asked an extremely stupid question, and then, in a tone of exaggerated patience, he said, "He wanted to know how much the people around him were worth."

"Did you read them to him or what?"

"Yeah. Sometimes the nursing supervisor goes home early, and since I've got passkeys, and Chester got up early anyway, sometimes we'd go sit in her office and I'd read him files. He had this incredible mind, just amazing. He could do things with figures in his head that I couldn't do with a calculator. Part of the home's regulation states that all residents have to disclose their financial status when they're admitted, and then update it every six months. I guess the owners are afraid of getting stuck with an unpaid bill if somebody runs out of cash, so the numbers in the files are always current."

"Were there any files in particular he wanted to see?"

"Any one that showed that somebody had a lot of money. He was always interested in those."

"Why? Didn't he have enough money of his own?"

Germaine shrugged as he said, "Maybe that's something you should ask his wife."

Just then a young nurse stepped into the lounge, glanced at us both, and seated herself at the table with a magazine.

"Can I see his room?" I asked.

"Why not?" Germaine replied.

He talked all the way there, describing the people in the rooms we passed.

"Julia Fredrickson, age ninety-one," he said, indicating a door bedecked with pink paper hearts that read "To Great Grandma" in scribbled, crayon letters. "Major stockholder of the 'Shop Stop' chain of convenience stores, four hundred outlets nationwide, mostly in the Midwest. She's lived here for almost ten years, and you can figure out for yourself how much cash that comes to, keeping in mind that Manor Care doesn't accept Medicare patients. The folks here pay out of their own pockets: three grand a month, plus doctor bills.

"Then there's Mr. Hulan San Marko," he continued, his voice loud, as if we were alone in the building, "age eighty-four, invented the low pressure bleeder nozzle used in General Motors' single line paint sprayers since the flood. All it says under personal worth on his form is, 'Shit-load.' It's an accounting term."

When I asked him why he was telling me this, he replied that, before his death, Chester Scholtz had been giving investment advice to six of the wealthiest old people in the state.

"What did their families have to say about that?"

"Who knows? And anyway, there's no law that says an old person can't take advice. With the kind of money these people have got, I figure that if their kids can't look out for themselves, then screw 'em."

As I stepped into Chester Scholtz's apartment, Germaine stood in the doorway and explained that Dr. Teeg, Scholtz's physician, was not only one of Manor Care's staff doctors, he was also one of the facility's owners. I silenced his chattering with a finger to my lips, surveying the damage he said Mrs. Scholtz had done late the night before. Judging by the thoroughness with which she'd searched the place, I

figured that she had been looking for something specific, and that since she had come to me with her proposition, she hadn't found it.

From the doorway Germaine said, "I've never actually seen someone investigate anything. What are you doing?"

And I said, "Trying to feel who Scholtz was."

"Like empathy?"

"Yeah."

"How?"

"You want me to explain it?"

"Yeah."

I stopped, sighed, and settled myself, saying, "Okay, I'm Chester Scholtz, the blind, retired accountant. Now, before my wife ripped my room apart, I lived here, unable to see, so I would have kept things organized so that I could always find them. If I put something down where it normally doesn't go, it's lost. I'll have to search for it with my hands since I can't see it. So I know where everything is. Never move a thing. Never rearrange the furniture . . ."

"He'd have a fit if we so much as closed the bathroom door," Germaine put in helpfully.

"Where was this?" I asked, indicating an overturned chair. And Germaine told me that it was normally positioned directly in the center of the room where Scholtz would sit in the sun for hours, staring at the wall.

I put the chair right and sat down in it, musing to myself, "They leave the doors open in these places. People are always walking back and forth. There's no privacy. Nurses and staff pop in with breezy smiles to see if we've gone to the bathroom today. It's always time for a pill. From out there you can see . . ."

I moved my finger as if aiming a pistol, sweeping it across my field of vision.

" . . . every part of the room, except . . ."

Then I jumped up and entered the bathroom, turning on the light and feeling Germaine hovering behind me. There was a sink, toilet, and tub, all done in white linoleum

and crisscrossed with silver aluminum grab bars bolted to the walls.

"In here, with the door closed, someone's not going to walk by like out there," I said, cocking a thumb over my shoulder. "So in here I can let down my guard. But they clean in here, so I'd have to put it . . . where?"

Germaine made a noise as if he were about to speak, but he apparently thought better of it, silently watching as I got down on my knees near the toilet and ran my hands over various surfaces.

"Toilet tank's too clumsy," I said. "Loose tile maybe? Back of the mirror?"

Then I said, "Hello," and pointed at the mounting for a grab bar on the left-hand side of the toilet.

"Missing screw," I said, running my finger down the bar to its other end. "And loose screws here."

I undid two screws at the end of the bar, and once they were removed, the bar, which ran at an angle next to the toilet, could be pivoted to reveal a hole in the wall where its opposite end had been mounted. Crouching down, I carefully withdrew a pencil from the hole, around which was wrapped a single scrap of paper, held tight with a rubber band. Undoing the rubber band, I examined the paper, with Germaine looking over my shoulder, and, after we had both read it, we looked at one another until he finally asked, "So, what the hell is it?"

To which I replied, "It's a start!"

After Germaine promised to call me the next time the nursing supervisor went home early so I could look at the files like Chester Scholtz had done, I went back to the funeral home, my "evidence" stored securely in my right pants pocket, and a sense of real involvement brooding somewhere near the back of my mind. Germaine would have liked nothing more than for me to stick around so he could psychoanalyze me some more, but once he asked the desk nurse when Chester Scholtz had signed himself out of the building—eleven a.m. the previous day—and how

he had departed—taxicab—I gave him a business card and told him I'd be in touch.

As I rolled the cot into the embalming room, I was a little surprised to find that my uncle Joe was nearly finished with the body he'd been working on when I left. I've never seen anyone who works as fast as my uncle. He spent a two-year tour of duty in Vietnam as an Army embalmer, which left him with skills other guys can only envy.

Personally, I've never understood embalming. It's like, "Oh gee, Grandma died? Well good; let's have her stuffed." But it's a part of my livelihood, so I never talk about it.

Uncle Joe was wearing his bunny suit—the surgical gear embalmers have taken to wearing the last couple of years because of their concern over AIDS: full-length gown, McDonald's burger-flipping hat, bootie shoe covers, mask, goggles, and two pairs of surgical gloves since the word is that the virus can pass through a single thickness of rubber . . . which simply fills me with no end of confidence. When I carried bodies for a private ambulance company in high school it used to be macho not to even use gloves, and blood on your clothes was a sign of a tough guy. Now it's a sign that you're either stupid or suicidal. And sometimes I can't help but wonder what's next. Super AIDS? Nuclear tuberculosis? I hate to even think about it.

"Some cop called," Uncle Joe mumbled over his shoulder without looking up from where he was putting the finishing stitches in the leg of the man he was embalming. The guy had donated his long bones to the Cleveland Lifebank, which meant that the harvesting team had cut him from hip to ankle on both legs. Uncle Joe had to close those wounds which required about a hundred stitches each, and, more to the point as far as I was concerned, meant that his legs between his hips and ankles would be like rubber, making him tough to dress.

Since our one embalming table was occupied, I parked Chester Scholtz in a corner and went to my office to return Officer Evans's call. Sheri Evans is a dispatcher whose father knows my dad. We're roughly the same age, but

she's tougher than me; a shorthaired, heavy-hipped, hard-ass-woman-cop with something to prove. I took her out once for not giving me a ticket when I rolled through a stop sign, and it was like dating my high school shop teacher.

"I ran the plates on that van you asked about," she said without preamble as soon as she came on the line. "Belongs to a guy named Fizner. He's got an investigator's license and a downtown address."

"A P.I.?" I asked, a little stunned.

"Yep."

"Do you know anything about him?"

"Only that he's been hauled in a few times."

"For what?"

"Assault once, unregistered firearm once, and breaking and entering about half a dozen times. You still married?"

"Yes. Any convictions?"

"No. According to a guy in records, he deals mainly with an unsavory element who are slow pressing charges."

I thanked her and hung up, thinking, Why would a private investigator be shadowing Mrs. Scholtz? While I was mulling it over, I withdrew the paper I'd found in Scholtz's nursing home bathroom, flattened it out, and laid it on my desk.

8 5 ROGER 4 7 SHOE NEIGHBOR
9 3 CUP BIRDBATH HOLLOW 2

It didn't mean a single thing to me, but Scholtz had obviously thought it was important. I rubbed my eyes and sighed, leaning on my elbows and trying to think, jumping a little when the phone rang. I answered it, but no one responded. So I repeated, "Hawley Funeral Home," listened, and put down the receiver. There had been no one there. I frowned, and checked the window, half expecting to see Larry Fizner's yellow Dodge van still parked across the street. As I was looking, Nat pulled into the lot, and as soon as I saw her, I knew what I had to do.

THREE
■■■■■■■■■■

WHEN I'M FIRST introduced, people tend to pigeonhole me in their minds strictly on the merits of my appearance. I'm five nine, weigh roughly two hundred and ten pounds, have sandy brown hair, blue eyes, and a round, boyish face that is made to look even younger by the silver, wire-rimmed glasses I've been wearing, in one incarnation or another, since I was nine years old. I carry most of my weight in my chest, though I also have a bit of a gut. And my legs are very thin. My wife describes me as a beer barrel on a ladder, and she's right. But it's not my build that gets me pegged before I even open my mouth; it's my clothes. I have to restrain myself from putting on a necktie when I get up to go to the john in the middle of the night. Being formally dressed is how I feel comfortable, which is strange since I owned two black T-shirts and a single pair of jeans all through college. But being a funeral director's a funny thing sometimes. Most people believe that all we do is stand around in a suit, looking important. And for some guys that might even be the case. But at the Hawley Funeral Home, with just my dad, my uncle, and me taking care of the place, I clean a lot of toilets and vacuum a lot

of floors in my suit. And after eleven years, a tie is just the way I dress.

I was tying my tie in front of my bedroom mirror at eight o'clock that evening as Nat said, "Don't you need a license or something to call yourself an investigator?" from where she sat on the bed, looking at my notes about the "case" I was putting together for Mrs. Scholtz, and occasionally poking Quincy, our new cream-colored Persian kitten, as he raced across the bed on the attack. I'd just taken a shower, and was preparing to go out after spending the afternoon taking care of the particulars of Chester Scholtz's funeral. I had also just finished dressing the man my uncle was embalming when I got back from the Manor Care Nursing Home . . . which is why I'd taken a shower. Bone donors are gross, their limbs are like tentacles that bend every which way as you're trying to stuff them into their clothes, and since they leak through their incisions we have to wrap them in plastic, making them feel like bags full of cold noodles.

"You need a license to carry a gun," I said in answer to her remark, still facing the mirror as I combed my hair. "A private investigator's license is almost like an honorary thing. You send thirty bucks to Columbus, and they fill your name in a blank. It's no big deal."

Nat didn't look convinced. She was sitting cross-legged on the bed behind me, with her waist-length black hair hanging down over her shoulders as she looked up skeptically and placed the notebook aside. There was something about the pose that emphasized her American Indian blood. She's part German and part Sioux, which means that she's inherited a very interesting mix of European and Native American features. She's tall, strong, and beautiful. She's also smart . . . and when she speaks, I listen. Which is why I'd put the notebook together in the first place: I wanted her opinion.

"Okay," she said, leaning back on the headboard with her hands behind her head and her long legs stretched straight out. She was wearing a white, frilly gown from Victoria's

Secret, and caught in the mirror as she was, looked like a page of their catalogue come to life. "Run through it for me again, and go slow on the stuff Bob said."

I turned and sat down on the edge of the bed, stroking her bare foot as I laid out what I knew. The gist of my argument went like this:

Mrs. Scholtz believed that her husband got himself admitted to the nursing home as part of some plan he had devised that would make him a lot of money. Two of the things I had learned during the day seemed to lend credence to that conclusion: one was the record of his "broken" hip, which was clearly shown to be very *not* broken on his X-rays, and the other was Pete Germaine's contention that Scholtz spent a lot of time studying the financial records of the people residing at the Manor Care with him. When I spoke to the funeral home's accountant, Bob Bryant, he told me that there could be any number of reasons why a man with Scholtz's experience might be interested in information about a retired person's estate.

"That's the part I want you to explain again," Nat said.

And I nodded, saying, "Bob said that a smart money man could make a killing by having himself named as a wealthy retired person's financial manager. All he'd have to do is invest the money he's been given, report that he made a ten percent profit when he actually made twenty percent, and pocket the difference. Or worse."

"But if he was bilking old people," Nat cut in, "why'd he need to withdraw money from his own savings account when he went to the motel?"

I told her I didn't know, adding that, at least so far, there wasn't any evidence that Scholtz had actually succeeded in getting himself named as anyone's fiduciary representative. It looked as if he'd been trying, but that was all we knew for sure.

"And what about this private eye in the yellow van?" she added. "Why's he hanging around?"

Again, I didn't know. But his presence led me to believe that whatever was going on, it still wasn't quite over.

"So you're going to the motel?"

"To see what the night manager has to say, yes," I said, rising and lifting my keys off the dresser. "According to the E.R. report, when the rescue squad arrived at the Cozy Inn, they found Scholtz lying next to the bed with his arms over his head and his pants bunched up around his ankles. When Uncle Joe and I unloaded him this afternoon, he was still like that, except that the paramedics had ripped his shirt open and cut his sleeves. They didn't undress him at the hospital. So when we got him on the table we had to strip him. That's when I noticed the stains. He'd voided his bowels when he hit the floor, so his underwear was all crapped up. *But so were his trousers.* That doesn't make sense. If he had his pants down when he had his heart attack, then only his underwear would get stained when he hit the floor. But if he had his pants on when he voided his bowels, why would they be down when the paramedics found him?"

"So someone pulled his pants down after he died?" Nat asked.

I nodded, saying, "It's almost as if someone were making sure that the way Scholtz was found was so embarrassing that anything his wife said about it would look like an excuse."

"But it's such a risk," Nat cut in. "The implication is that Scholtz met someone with this money, then he lost it, and whoever took it set up this thing with the dancer to cover the crime. Is that about it?"

"Yeah," I said.

And she shook her head, saying, "It doesn't make sense," as Quincy appeared on the bed, flipping his tail, ready to play.

"Why?"

"Because it would have been a lot simpler just to take the money and run. Why make a production out of it? What's the big deal? They'd have found Scholtz in a couple of days, and that would have been it: an old man with a heart attack. Why complicate it with a cover-up?"

"I don't know," I admitted.

"I haven't seen you this pumped up in months," Nat said. "This little investigation of yours obviously means a lot; so what can I do to help?"

I bristled at her reference to my "little" investigation. About the only point of contention between us was her contempt for what she called my "male ego," which she said I had inherited from my father, who got his from his father before him. Grandpa Hawlinski ran away from the Ukraine before the Second World War, choosing to walk across Europe instead of being conscripted into the Russian Army. In England he caught a boat bound for the U.S., where he worked on the railroad until he saved enough to buy a tavern on Fulton Avenue. He spent the rest of his life talking about the Ukraine, and swearing that he'd never go back. He never did. And though he passed his fiercely independent nature on to both my dad and my uncle, it was in my younger brother, Jaroslav—Americanized to Jerry—where it was manifested in its purest form. Nat's reference to my little investigation was obviously meant as a catchphrase pointing indirectly to my brother, who was a sore spot to me personally, making him a delicate topic for Nat and me as a couple.

Nat's eyes were big and dark, and seeing the genuine concern she had for me reflected in them, I leaned down to put my arms around her. When I did, Quincy made a kind of gargling noise and raced off the bed, making me pull back and smile as I said, "I swear, I haven't been beating him when you're not home."

But Nat wouldn't let me change the subject so easily. Holding on so that I couldn't pull away, she kept her face close to mine as she said, "I mean it. You know you haven't been right since it happened."

I tried to draw back, but she held on to my shoulders, insisting, "You can't just curl up every time you think about him. It wasn't your fault."

"I know." I sighed. "But it's like a reflex."

"Bill, my God. The last couple of years have been rough. Between the funeral home, your folks' divorce, and that

whole thing with Jerry . . . you should go easy on yourself. You're doing great. That's why I'm saying, if it eases your mind to do this, then I'm behind you."

"Really?"

"Really."

"You don't think it's macho bullshit?"

"What difference does it make? Just don't get yourself in any trouble."

"What kind of trouble can I get into on Brookings Road?" I asked, heading for the door.

She let that one slide, adding only that she'd wait up for me to come home.

The one big indulgence that Nat and I have made as a couple is her car. It's a 1990 Mazda Miata, which is that two-seater sports car they made such a big stink about in all the car magazines when it first came out. It's compact, nicely designed, and a convertible. Nat went goofy for it the moment she saw one on the lot, saying that she absolutely had to have it because it was so cute. My only gripe was that it was under-powered. So we compromised. She got the Miata, and I had a friend pull the engine and drop in a Ford 3.0 V-8. Our Miata's fire-engine-red, way cool, and will blow the doors off anything else on the street—not exactly your ideal, inconspicuous stakeout car, but great for riding through the park on warm summer nights, eating ice-cream cones, and watching your wife's long dark hair dance in the breeze.

I don't have a car. I usually drive the funeral home's navy-blue Dodge Grand Caravan . . . but not that night. That night was a Miata night, and I even put the top down. It's not that I wasn't taking things seriously—even that early on it was obvious to me that Chester Scholtz was up to something in that motel—it's just that I didn't see how my involvement could go much beyond asking a few questions.

According to Scholtz's E.R. report, the rescue squad was taking him down the stairs on the stretcher as the police pulled in, so there was no accurate statement about the

condition of the room on record. The firemen treated the case as a straight rescue, and in Ohio they call the shots. In some states you can't touch a body until the medical examiner pronounces it dead. But around here, if the paramedics think their patient might still have a chance, they move him, and since they own the scene, the cops can't do a thing to stop it. I was going to talk to the guys on the squad the next day they were on—which was Monday, since their shifts work twenty-four hours and have forty-eight off. But in the meantime I figured that the motel manager could walk me through. My only concern was whether or not he'd talk to me, since the night manager of a Brookings Road motel had to be a representative of a unique and interesting species.

As I've already said, the west end of Brookings Road is known as the Combat Zone. It got that name because it's more or less our red-light district. I say more or less because it's not downtown, and downtown has its own areas where the hookers hang out. But the downtown cops sweep certain streets periodically, so the action moves around. Brookings Road, on the other hand, is in kind of a nebulous zone between the city and a suburb for which neither side wants to assume responsibility. Therefore it never changes. On one side of the street is a row of the sleaziest skin joints around, and on the other are motels with bugs in the beds and rates by the hour. Right in the middle of this wholesome environment is the city's largest Catholic cemetery, and that's where I decided to leave the Miata, parked up close to a wrought iron gate, in the black, unlit shadows beneath a row of dark, flowering trees.

It was after ten at night, but it was still hot, a good eighty degrees that seemed hotter because the pavement virtually pulsated with waves of heat absorbed from the daytime's relentless sunshine. Stepping from the gloom into a haze of cheap neon, I briskly walked the three hundred yards or so to the Cozy Inn, being greeted along the way by three women in hot pants, and one guy on a bicycle who wanted to know if I needed anything to help get me through the night. As I stepped into the lobby, I found a desk before

me that looked like someone had picked it up at a garage sale in 1932, and behind it was a Peg-Board covered with hooks from which dangled room keys marked with numbers painted in nail polish. There was a bell on the desk and I pinged it once, got no response, and pinged it again. From an open door I heard the "Beverly Hillbillies," and just as Granny was shrieking Jethro's name, a man appeared, looking bored and holding a can of Fago Root Beer.

"Yeah?" He was short, thin, wearing a Harley-Davidson T-shirt and a pair of jeans, probably forty years old, maybe older, clean shaven, jet-black hair combed straight back, tattoo of something dark and angular on his upper arm . . . could have been a bird, or a flower.

I pulled out my wallet, and he accepted the business card I handed him, read it, and handed it back saying, "Wonderful. You want a room or what?"

The business card read "T. J. Baldwin; American Mutual Life Insurance." Before I left the funeral home I'd pulled it from the stack I've got rubber banded together in my desk drawer. Every time somebody gives me a business card, I add it to my stack because I feel bad throwing them away.

Folding my wallet back into my pocket, I explained that instead of selling insurance, I worked for the company in an investigative capacity. As soon as he heard the word "investigative," a light went on in his eyes and he said, "Who ya wanna know about, and how much ya payin'?" disappointing me a little because I thought I'd need to at least do a little convincing before he'd help me. As it was, he agreed to fifty bucks, got the key to the room where Chester Scholtz had died, and told me I could look around all I wanted. He sent me on ahead while he locked up the office, and as I stepped into the parking lot, I heard the TV go suddenly silent.

The Cozy Inn was one of those four-story motels where the rooms all have doors facing the front, lined up side by side along common balconies. The stairs were located on either side of the building, and the place needed a lot

of work. The paint was peeling, the brick was sooty, and the balconies were decorated with empty beer and wine bottles that caught the parking lot light and reflected it in brown and green twinkles that looked like cat's-eyes in the shadows. The freeway whooshed and rumbled with traffic about a hundred yards away. I only saw about three units that had lights on inside. The rest of the place was dark.

Scholtz had died in room 410, top floor, dead center of the line. At the door I turned and surveyed the surrounding area, finding a towering Holiday Inn looming across the street, and a trucking company beyond the parking lot that was lit and moving with dark men working on the docks. Turning to the door, I inserted the key, wondering what was taking the manager so long. Then I stepped inside.

In Scholtz's room at the nursing home I had gone in with a particular idea in mind; that is, with the evidence of the X-ray films I had seen proving that the man hadn't really fractured his hip before admitting himself to the facility, I accepted Mrs. Scholtz's implied conviction that her husband faked his symptoms. Using that theory as my starting point, I had surveyed the apartment from the perspective of a man playing a role, and found the hiding place in the bathroom wall only because there were so few areas of the room out of sight of someone in the hallway. So in the nursing home, Scholtz played the role of a blind man. But what role did he play in the motel?

"Don't know what you expect to find," the manager commented from the door, startling me and making me turn. He looked a little sallow in the face, and his eyes darted around nervously. "I didn't even hardly have to clean up after they took him away. The two of 'em were only in here a coupla minutes. Bed wasn't even unmade."

At my request, he showed me where Scholtz had been lying, explaining that he was watching TV at about eleven o'clock when this girl in a bathrobe came rushing in wearing sparkling red shoes and a lot of makeup on her face. She was yelling something about someone being dead, and

he jumped up and followed her upstairs, getting immediately pissed when he saw the body, since it wasn't good for business having the cops come around, no matter what the circumstances. It was his idea that the girl stay and talk to the cops since her yelling had attracted the attention of a couple of people who were poking their heads out to see what was going on. So instead of having the cops come to her house, he told her to sit down and get it over with so she could go home clean.

While he spoke, I looked around, but there wasn't much to see: double bed, bureau with four drawers, night table with a lamp bolted to it, bathroom off to the side. There was a sliding glass window over the bed and I looked at it, finding that it was closed, but not locked. I moved it with my finger and it slid easily on its track.

Fifty thousand dollars cash, in one-hundred-dollar denominations—which I assumed would be what the bank would offer—adds up to exactly five hundred bills. I figured that Scholtz probably carried it in two stacks of two hundred and fifty bills each, which meant that the stacks would be about an inch and three-quarters thick. He could fit one in each trouser pocket, so there wouldn't necessarily have to be any kind of satchel or briefcase involved—no classic cartoon money bag with a big dollar sign on the outside to attract attention; no leather attaché case handcuffed to his wrist; just two little piles of paper hidden in an old man's pockets. I asked about a bag, just to be thorough, but the manager shook his head.

"You said that this wasn't the first time he came here to meet a girl," I observed, looking at the window again. There was something about it that interested me, but I couldn't put my finger on just what it was.

"Yeah," the manager said. "He came a coupla times. Always signed 'B. Peters' in the book. Paid cash up front, and never had no luggage."

"And the room was just like this when you found it?"

"Yeah."

"No signs of a struggle?"

"Hell no."

"Nothing broken?"

"No."

"How about the window: open or closed?"

"Closed."

"Was this the only time he carried a cane, or did he have it those other times too?"

The man kind of stuttered when he said, "He might have had it the other times. I never noticed."

I kept my eyes on his face.

"So what happened to it?"

"What?"

"It wasn't at the hospital, and it isn't here. Where did it go?"

The cane was a shot in the dark. Pete Germaine had said that Chester Scholtz hobbled up and down the halls on a cane, visiting his neighbors to give them investment advice. Since I was functioning under the assumption that Scholtz was playing a role, what better thing for him to have than a prop? A white cane . . . I could just see it. It would add an air of authenticity to his performance. He could tap with it, and lean on it—because of the stiffness in his broken hip—and it's the kind of thing his audience would automatically associate with blind people. White canes and . . . "Did he wear dark glasses?" I asked.

The manager blinked as he replied, "No."

"Are you sure?"

"Yeah. It was nighttime."

"What color was his cane?"

"I don't know."

"Could it have been white?"

"I suppose it coulda been."

"But you're not sure if an old man who wound up dead in your motel was carrying a white cane or not. You know what a white cane means, right?"

"Listen, I said I'd let you look around. I didn't say nothing about you putting the heat on me. Not for fifty bucks . . . which I ain't even seen yet. Remember?"

"Yeah," I agreed, softening my voice and backing off so as not to scare him away.

I opened the window and stuck my head out. The freeway was at the end of a vacant lot bordered by a cyclone fence. Looking down I found a ledge running between the second and third floors.

"Can I look around outside?" I asked.

And the manager said, "Sure," apparently relieved to be getting rid of me. On the way past him I handed over the fifty dollars I'd promised, saying that I might have to call or stop by again. He nodded, somewhat grudgingly, but didn't complain, and before he returned to his office, I got the absurd urge to pat him on the cheek a little too hard like they used to do in those old Humphrey Bogart movies.

Behind the motel the freeway was noisy and the air smelled of diesel exhaust. Diffused light from the street made the area look monochromatic, like a scene from a black-and-white TV show, and since the lot was perfectly flat, there was nothing but the building casting a shadow. One of the windows on the first floor was lit, and I gave it a wide berth as I passed to avoid riling some sensitive resident who might mistake me for a Peeping Tom. Broken glass crunched beneath my feet, and something moved in the darkness surrounding a dumpster at the motel's far end. That area too I avoided, reasoning that I wasn't interested in encountering the dumpster's occupant, rodent or otherwise.

I stepped back and examined the motel. From this perspective it was a perfect rectangle, colorless, severe of line, with four rows of identical windows bisected by the ledge I'd noticed from above which ran the building's length between the second and third floors. The ledge probably served as a work area for washing windows, which I counted off until I hit room 410. I put my hands on my hips and looked at it, dark like the rest on the top floor, closed, but not locked. The cane was bothering me. It was bothering me a lot. Again . . . it hadn't been at the nursing home, nor at the crime scene, nor with the body at the

hospital. So where was it now? Why would someone take a white cane?

Mentally I judged the distance from the window to the ledge one floor below to be about ten feet. If someone exited the room through that window, they could hang drop onto the ledge below . . . but then the window would be left open. The night manager had specifically said that he had found it closed. And even though I was sure that he had lied to me about something, just on principle, I figured that if he had found the window open, and had then closed it, he would have locked it too.

And then it hit me. Standing there in the dark with the trucks rumbling and invisible rats scratching rusty metal, I saw it, perfectly formed in my mind, almost as if it were happening at that instant:

The light is on in the room, making the cheap curtains glow a translucent amber that transforms itself into pale white as a man's silhouette parts them and slides open the window to poke out his head. He draws his head back, the light goes out, and through the now dark opening emerges first a leg, and then the rest of his body, dangling by his hands with a white cane held at an angle across his back where he's looped it through his belt. He drops, catches himself on the ledge below, and stands upright, removing the cane like a sword from a scabbard. Then he reaches up and slides the window shut with the cane since it's too far overhead to reach with his hand.

I saw it just that way, as if I were watching it in reality. A car entered the motel's lot and its headlights swept across the fence bordering the trucking company's property, but I paid no attention. Instead I was watching the shadowy figure making its way along the ledge, ducking its head down so as not to be seen against the windows of the rooms it passed until it finally reached the ladder at the ledge's end and worked its way to the ground. There it hesitated as a voice in my head said, "Then what?" And I glanced this way and that as I'm sure my phantom culprit had done. To my left was the motel parking lot, and to my right . . .

I swallowed, staring into the night. From where I stood I could plainly see the Lipstick Lounge across the street—a gaudy neon go-go girl shaking her hips in a jerky, perpetual shimmy. But what would he do with the stick? I wondered. Take it with him? No. Throw it into the field? In my mind I watched him do just that, and the white stick arced out and bounced in the grass . . . which was short and thin, parched brown from heat and lack of rain. I could see every beer bottle and scrap of garbage before me, even in the weak light thrown by the street lamps, and I realized that a white cane would virtually glow in that dusty lot. The dumpster? No, that would be the first place someone would look. Then I approached the building.

There was a down spout running from a gutter at the roof's edge straight to the ground, ending at a cinder block stained by runoff. The ladder from the second floor ledge ended right next to it, and when I touched it, it moved quite easily, grinding a little on the ground where it had been wedged against the block. I pulled it toward myself a little, and from its bent end appeared a sliver of white. I pulled it out further, watching as that white sliver elongated until, with a final wrench I was able to angle the spout away from the cinder block and a white cane clattered onto the gravel at my feet. A feeling of elation tingled my scalp as I picked it up, feeling its solidity in my hands verify my deductions:

Someone had slipped from the motel room through the window, and come this way. Someone had been in that room with Chester Scholtz, and had taken his money after he died. And someone had then crossed the street to the Lipstick Lounge and sent one of the girls who worked there back to tell the police a story about the old man's death. I didn't know who . . . and I wasn't sure why . . . but I had something solid in my hands that proved, at least in my own mind, that it had in fact happened just that way. The sensation of accomplishment surging through me felt wonderful . . .

Which made the fear that suddenly overtook me seem all the more intense.

"How ya doin'?" someone said, and I turned to find two men standing close. One reached out and took the cane from my unresisting fingers, and the other took me by the arm, saying, "We're gonna take a walk." I tried ever so gently to resist, but with a single tug he made it very clear that such a thought was unwise. My knees felt wobbly, and my mouth went dry. I couldn't think of a single word to say, so silently we crossed Brookings Road, heading straight for the Lipstick Lounge.

Now, up until this moment, I thought that I had lived a fairly eventful life. I went to Catholic school when I was a kid, a Catholic high school following that, and a private college. I did all the things kids do . . . chased girls, played sports, and experimented with drugs; I even played in the world's worst garage band so that for one giddy year I thought of myself as being almost famous. I was arrested once for trespassing when I was cutting across some guy's backyard, and while I worked on the ambulance, and later at the emergency room at Southwest General Hospital, I saw all sorts of weird and interesting things. But my entire past fell to dust as I was hustled across the street between those two goons in their white shirts and creased slacks. One was big and burly, with close-cropped blond hair and wide-set eyes. The other was smaller, with wiry, long arms and a whistle when he breathed through his nose. Neither of them talked, and all I could hear was my own heart roaring in my ears.

We entered the Lipstick Lounge through a big steel door around back, walked down a hallway that was almost completely dark, and entered a corridor lined with about ten doors marked "Private." Over each door was a little red light bulb, two of which were lit. The big guy chose a door with an unlit bulb and the other hustled me inside. Then they closed the door and locked me in. My forehead was wet with sweat, and my right arm hurt over the elbow where the one guy had been squeezing it. I don't know how long they left me in that pitch dark, but it seemed like a month. Finally a light snapped on behind me and I

turned, discovering for the first time where I was, and who I was with.

The room was tiny, no larger than the interior of a telephone booth. Its walls were painted black, and there was a stool, a roll of toilet paper hanging from a bent loop of coat hanger wire, and a wall of smudged Plexiglas through which I could see another room, just as small as mine, painted white, with a scrap of yellow shag carpet on the floor and another stool sitting in its center. Over the stool was a single naked light bulb hanging from a wire, and holding onto the end of its chain was an extremely fat man who barely fit into his cramped surroundings. He was wearing a plaid shirt, open at the collar so that the many folds of his gelatinous neck were free to quiver, and he had so many cheap-looking gold chains nestled in the hair covering his chest that for a second I wondered if Woolworth's hadn't had a sale. His buttons strained, his black pants were too tight, and even his loafers seemed a tad small on his feet. But unlike the rest of him, which moved with a kind of slow deliberation, his eyes were quick and sure, snapping up and down my body before he said, "Push your wallet through the slot," in a deep, commanding voice.

The Plexiglas wall separating us had holes drilled in it so that we could hear one another speak, and there was a slot positioned at waist level that was about six inches across and an inch wide. I did as I was told, and the fat man opened my wallet as he sat himself down on the stool. His armpits were stained with half-moons of sweat, and his forehead glistened wetly as he withdrew a handkerchief from his shirt pocket and mopped his face. He started with my driver's license, moved on to my credit cards, and sorted through the business cards I keep in a central compartment. When he was through he placed both hands on his knees and looked me straight in the eye as he said, "So, what's the deal, funeral director?"

His name was Jimmy Cecorno. I knew that from the TV news. He was the brother-in-law of a local crime boss who had spent a great deal of time in court recently. Cecorno's

reputation was that of an idiot, more or less. And the story went that the only reason he was involved in the family's business was because he had married well. But he wasn't smart enough to do anything responsible, so he had been given a couple of skin joints on the strip to manage as a way of insuring him a living without risking his making a monkey of himself in public. He was apparently grateful for his position because, of all the girlie bars in town, the ones that he ran were known as the most legitimate. He had never been arrested, nor had any of his places been raided. He seemed determined never to embarrass his prominent and dangerous brother-in-law.

Looking at him now, I decided to ignore his media reputation for slowness and treat him gingerly. The motel manager had obviously called him to say that I was poking around and asking questions about the old guy who'd snuffed it in the motel, which led me to believe that Cecorno had some interest in the matter . . . and I immediately wondered if he knew about the fifty grand that had gone missing. With great effort, I lowered myself onto my stool and told him that he was right about me being who my driver's license and stack of business cards said I was: William Hawley, undertaker. When he asked me why I was nosing around, I told him that the dead man's widow had asked me to, mentioning as I did that my wife and father both knew exactly where I was, just so he'd know I wasn't on my own. Then he said, "So, where's my girl?" and I blinked through my surprise.

It was hard making the transition, and for a moment I probably looked like a ventriloquist's dummy sitting on that stool, mouth hanging open, eyes blank and lifeless. But in my head my mind was turning from its preoccupation with my physical safety to the details of why I had come to Brookings Road in the first place.

"You mean, Cynthia Moore?" I asked.

And Cecorno nodded, his thick lips drooping into a swollen, purplish frown.

"She hasn't come back?"

"No. And she hasn't gone home."

"That doesn't sound good . . . unless she already knew the guy."

"She knew him all right."

"How do you know?"

He studied me for what seemed like a full minute. And then, almost grudgingly, he explained that some guy had come into his club at about ten-thirty the night before. He was young, maybe twenty-one, twenty-two, something like that, with fair hair and a nice face, looking real nervous and in a hurry. Cynthia Moore went right over to dance at his table as soon as he sat down, and he wasn't in the place more than five minutes before he was gone again and Cindy was grabbing her stuff and saying that she had to leave early because she had something important to do. That was the last he saw of her. And the cops had come around at closing time asking questions, which was a violation of his first rule of operation.

"I don't like cops," he said. "Not even a little bit."

I asked if Cynthia Moore had been more specific about the nature of her emergency to any of the girls working with her, but Cecorno said no. It was just "something important," and that was all.

"That fucking city councilman's been whistling up my butt for months as it is," he complained, my wallet still in his hand and a cigarette suddenly appearing between his lips. "All I need's some old fart biting the big one with one of my girls and I got shit on my hands on the front page. Know what I'm sayin'?"

I told him that I knew, and he looked at me.

"Listen," he said, glancing at my driver's license and reading my name, "William Hawley. Can I talk to you?"

I told him that he could talk to me.

"I ain't like Steve and Blue." He indicated the closed door behind me. "Those are the guys who brought you here. They're goons. This is a goon's business. But I ain't a goon. I got a sociology degree. You got a degree?"

I told him I had a degree.

"What's your degree?"

"English."

"Really?"

"Yeah, with a psychology minor."

"Then you're a man who can appreciate the nuances, right? So here it is: if my girl and that kid who came in here last night know each other, then we've got a hustle on our hands that killed an old guy. The fart . . . what's his name?"

"Chester Scholtz."

"Chester Scholtz: he never came in here. I'll swear to it. He never set foot in my place, I don't care what Cindy told the cops. But it don't matter what I say because the cops are gonna hear what they wanna hear, which is that one of my girls was meeting customers in a motel. That's solicitation, which is the kinda shit somebody could use to close me down. And I can't let that happen. Understand?"

I nodded.

"I don't know if you do. Remember what I was sayin' about goons?"

"So what's the point?"

"The point is a question. And the question is: what the fuck are *you* doin' here? A funeral director? Are you serious?"

I tried to respond, but he cut me off.

"Just shut up," he said, looking less angry than he did amused. "I'm gonna give you some advice, okay? You can take it or leave it, that's your prerogative. But I'm gonna give it anyway, 'cause that's the kind of guy I am: concerned for my fellow man. That kinda shit. Okay?"

"Okay."

His advice was simple, and to the point: I was out of my element, and if I didn't cool it, I was going to get hurt.

"See this?" he said, lifting his left hand. For the first time I noticed that the pinky was missing. "My brother-in-law did that," he explained grimly, holding his hand close to the Plexiglas. "My brother-in-law, okay? My wife's his sister.

It was like a warning. He did it himself, with a pair of wire cutters."

My eyes stayed on that hand as it traveled to his mouth and removed the cigarette bouncing on his lip.

"Anybody else but me on this strip gets a call that somebody's askin' questions like you were doin', and they bust heads," he said, smoke swirling so thickly that I could smell it through the holes in the plastic wall. "No questions asked, understand? Anybody else, and you'd be layin' in that field, bleedin' right now."

I didn't say a word.

"The point," he continued, "is that I'm doin' you a service here. I'm tellin' ya: go home, be whatever it is you are during the day, and forget the rest. This street's like another planet. Believe me. And whether you know it or not, whether you believe it or not, you got a rare and beautiful thing here tonight . . . you got a second chance. Now don't fuck it up."

Then he shouted, "Steve!" making me flinch. The door behind me opened, and a hand was on my arm again. Jimmy Cecorno pushed my wallet back through the slot and said, "Take him out front and give him a drink on the house." And then, looking directly at me, he added, "Now remember what I said. Drop it. It's the healthy thing to do. But if you don't, there's five thousand bucks in it for ya. I ain't suggestin' it; I'm just mentionin' it. You find something, tell me first, and it's worth five grand."

Then he was gone, and Steve took me up front to the bar. He tried to order me a drink, but I pushed past him and headed for the parking lot. He didn't follow, and I didn't stop moving until I was sitting in the Miata, sweat running down my face and my hands atremble. I started the car and turned it around to face the street, lights out, hidden in the shadows. The neon didn't look quite so gaudy anymore. And suddenly I felt like puking.

Cecorno had slipped one of my funeral home business cards into his shirt pocket before he returned my wallet. He knew my name, address, and phone number. And in my

mind I saw the stump of his missing finger, and wondered if the story he'd told me about how he'd lost it was true. I also heard him describe his men as "goons" again, and the juxtaposition of my business card and that word made me shudder. I thought about the funeral home, and all the work my dad and uncle had done to build it; I thought about the relief in Mrs. Scholtz's eyes as she kissed my cheek; and I thought about Nat. Most of all, I thought about Nat, and how much I loved her. Then I thought about goons, and missing fingers, and my younger brother, Jerry.

Drop it, a voice said in my head. Quite clear. Unambiguous. Just drop it and go home. Just bury the son of a bitch.

Her address was in my pocket—I'd put it there before I left . . . almost as if I had known . . . almost as if I'd done it deliberately. I put the car in gear, popped up the headlights, and pulled onto Brookings Road, realizing that I was wearing my drinking hat. That's what I call it: my drinking hat. It's that frame of mind I went through for so long before sobriety finally stuck. I'd say to myself, "Today I'm not going to drink," over and over, even while I was taking my first shot of vodka right after Nat left for work at eight in the morning. It was almost like my brain and body were two separate entities. It drove me nuts trying to explain how it felt to step back and watch myself doing something I knew was wrong, but that I did anyway, and regretted the instant I did it.

My drinking hat's made of stainless steel, it's shaped like a bowl, and it's got wires and electrodes sticking out of it that beep and emit sparks. It's also invisible, and when the power kicks on, it picks up signals from somewhere and transmits them directly into my brain. That's what an addiction is: an impulse that seems to come from somewhere outside your body, but that's as much a part of you as your blood. For a long time I made the mistake of thinking that if I just stayed away from the booze, I could take my drinking hat off. But that's stupid. You can't ever take it off because its terminals are planted right in

your flesh. If you've got the guts you might be able to *turn* it off for a while, but sooner or later it's going to pick up a new signal, and then the lights will start glowing again, and you'll be hooked . . . maybe not on booze this time, or drugs, or whatever, but on something: food, exercise, religion. It could be anything, and what it is doesn't matter anyway. It's just the way an addict's put together; the rush comes from the act of surrendering to a compulsion. Over and over again. Addicts are born to get hooked, because, in the end, the hook's the kick.

My entire body was stiff with nerve and shot through with adrenaline as I dropped the ragtop and hit the freeway, the sound of rushing air roaring over me and my hair whipping around on my head. The thought was clean and true, and it had occurred to me the instant I stepped from the Lipstick Lounge and felt a surge of unfocused gratitude that I hadn't been hurt by the goons inside. Simply put it was this: if I were Chester Scholtz, carrying fifty thousand dollars in cash to a meeting in a motel on Brookings Road, I'd have to be nuts to do it alone. I'd want someone watching my back. I'd want a professional.

She had a Westlake address . . . nice part of town, up close to the lakeshore where the houses were built by people with money long enough ago for the ceilings to be high and the windows to be made of leaded glass. The yards are deep, and the houses set far back off the street. The trees are generally tall, thick, and aged. And the neighborhoods are safe. From Brookings Road I took I-480 west to Clague and headed north. It was after midnight so there wasn't much traffic. Clague's only one lane each way, and the speed limit's thirty-five, so the drive gave me the chance to calm down a little, and to think. By the time I found Mrs. Scholtz's street my mental state had evened out, and I was focused on my task.

She lived in an area called the Royal Oaks that had a decorative ironwork gate nestled on a hillock planted with azaleas and rhododendrons. I half expected a uniformed security guard to jump out of a sentry box, but none did.

I parked at the end of the street, left the top down, and walked the rest of the way. Her house was about an eighth of a mile up, and the yellow van was parked across the street, under a tree. There was a dark shape in the driver's seat, and a pile of cigarette butts on the concrete below the open side-door window. It was very dark, and I crossed over a lawn, approaching the van at an angle so as to avoid getting caught in a rearview mirror. God, I was cranked. I stepped right up to the window, put my hands on my hips, and said, "We gotta talk," expecting Larry Fizner, the P.I. to whom the van was registered, and instead surprising the hell out of the woman sitting behind the wheel.

She was a real beauty, no more than twenty-five, with short blond hair and high, classic cheekbones that looked scrubbed and fresh. Her lips were full, but pressed together in a hard line. And her eyes sparkled with intelligence as she fixed her attention on my face and held it there. She didn't say a word, communicating with her expression such a sense of intense wariness that the hair on my neck prickled. Then a man's voice started asking sleepy questions, and Fizner appeared, disheveled and blinking as he put on his glasses and thrust himself forward from where he had been sleeping in back. He emerged on the sidewalk, trying to hustle me into the van's side door where we could talk, but I resisted loudly and he shushed me with a finger to his lips. He acted as if we knew one another, and when I angrily demanded to know why he had been harassing Mrs. Scholtz, he laughed in my face, saying, "I'm not harassing her, you asshole; I'm protecting her! Christ!"

He must have been the most nervous man in the world: sixty years old, maybe older, all but bald on top with oily grey hair around the sides, grown long over his right ear and folded across his shiny dome like braids of butcher's string. He wore thick glasses with black plastic rims, a cream-colored dress shirt with an open collar and no tie, and his lips were so thin it looked as if he didn't have any. When he spoke they barely moved. What did move was the rest of him: his hands, his head—jerking

around on his neck—and his eyebrows, which climbed all over his forehead. He was also one of those guys who move their false teeth around when they talk, so that he clicked and clattered and nearly drove me nuts. And for the life of me, I couldn't imagine how he had earned the assault charge Officer Sheri Evans had found in his record.

Not being in the mood for games, I hit him with what I knew:

"Chester Scholtz hired you," I said, laying out the scenario I had pieced together from what I'd seen that day. "He took a taxicab from the Manor Care Nursing Home at eleven o'clock yesterday morning, went to a bank, and then had you drive him to the Cozy Inn Motel. While you waited in the parking lot, he got a key and went up to room 410, where he expected someone to meet him. But the only person who showed up was a girl who only stayed a minute before coming back out, screaming so loud that the manager called the cops."

Larry Fizner squirmed, pulling at his collar like Rodney Dangerfield and grunting as if he were laughing at the absurdity of my contentions.

"Your first impulse was to run up to the room and see what was going on," I continued as the woman in the driver's seat opened her door and stepped out. I could feel her presence nearby, and it was as if someone had released a guard dog that was now prowling around loose. "But you didn't run. Instead, you sat in the van and watched as first an ambulance, and then a police cruiser, pulled in. It was after the ambulance was gone, but before the cops could notice you sitting there, that you took off. And you've been pasted to Lydia Scholtz ever since. You watched her a little before, because her husband was concerned for her safety since he was making deals with dangerous people. But now you're stuck to her like glue because she's your only link to Chester Scholtz, who promised you a percentage of what he was doing as your fee. That about it? Or did I leave something out?"

He looked at me with an expression as if he were smelling something terrible. Finally he asked, "Who the hell are you?" And I told him. Then he asked me how I knew that no one had shown up to meet Chester Scholtz at the motel other than the dancer, and I told him that he had that part wrong.

"Scholtz did meet his party," I said. "He'd gotten there before you and was waiting in the room for Scholtz to come. Once Scholtz was dead, he left through the back window because he'd watched you two pull up in the van and knew that you were still out there in the lot, keeping an eye on the door. I doubt if Scholtz was supposed to wind up dead. But since he did, the girl from the bar across the street came in handy."

"Why?" Fizner asked, cocking his head and looking at me from the corner of his eye.

"Why don't you tell me?" I replied.

And he frowned, making me realize that he didn't know either. The central question, as Nat had pointed out, was why the girl had been used in the first place. Why make a production out of it? Why try to cover it up?

"You don't know what the meeting was about either, do you?" I said.

And he admitted, "No," frowning and starting to talk.

Yeah, he said, Scholtz had hired him. But the thing was that the old guy really played things close to the chest. Fizner didn't like doing business that way, but times were tight, and Scholtz talked big. They'd known each other from the old days when Scholtz worked for the county in the tax fraud division, and he knew how sharp Chester was. He also knew that he didn't throw numbers around without good reason. Particularly numbers like these.

"What kind of numbers?" I asked.

And Fizner squinted as he said, "Not here," waving his hand to indicate the street. "It sounds like you and me got some business to transact, but I ain't gonna do it here." So he and I took my car to a Denny's restaurant near the freeway back down Clague Road, leaving Judy, his

apprentice, to watch Mrs. Scholtz's house.

We ordered breakfast, and Fizner insisted that I pay . . .
since it was my doing that we were there in the first place.
Then he accused me of trying to muscle in on his account,
establishing an adversarial relationship between us that I
suspected mirrored how he dealt with the world in general.
He seemed determined to be confrontational, and I decided
early on that he was a very hard little man. But as far as he
was concerned, Chester Scholtz was a saint, a genius, and
a friend. I didn't think that friends were something Larry
Fizner had a lot of, and that seemed to make Scholtz all the
more precious in his memory.

"Chet was one of the good ones," he said, digging into
his breakfast: a ham and cheese omelet, hash browns, toast,
juice, and coffee. "We went way back."

There was more to Chester Scholtz than simply being an
accountant, he explained, inflecting the word "accountant"
as if it referred to something shameful. Scholtz was also
an investigator, having been trained in the Army for intelligence work. Hearing that Scholtz was in the Army made
me think about his age, and for the first time I pegged
him as being of World War II stock. I've got a great uncle
who was a sergeant in that war, and I've always thought
that there was something about going through that period
in history that galvanized people into a particular frame
of mind. Chester Scholtz would have been twenty-one in
1942, putting him right in the middle of things. How much
did Larry Fizner know about Scholtz's wartime experience?
Only what Scholtz had told him.

"And how much was that?" I asked.

He shrugged. "Chet was a funny kind of guy that way."
He swallowed a slurp of coffee and added, "This is good,"
indicating his plate with his fork. "Thanks."

I nodded.

"I was too young for the war myself," he continued.
"But I served a hitch just before Korea, so me and Chet
had enough in common to get along. When we first ran
into each other—"

"When was that?" I cut in.

And Fizner squinted, tapping his fork on his front teeth as he thought aloud. "Nineteen . . . uh, fifty-seven, I guess. Fifty-eight. Something like that. He'd just started working for the county and I was fresh from the Army. He was upstairs, on the second floor of the fraud division, and I was a legman, running down goons and trailing their broads. It was a different world back then, sonny boy. But Chet had the training, so he walked right into it."

"What kind of training?"

"Secret Service," he whispered.

"Ooh," I said, feigning amazement.

"Listen," Fizner frowned, his mobile eyebrows dropping low and squeezing close together, "back then the Secret Service was a big deal."

"So what was he, a spy?"

"He was an interrogator. His family came over from Germany after the First World War. They spoke German at home, so since Chet knew the language, the Army used him to interrogate German prisoners. They trained him how to read people . . . how to tell when they were lying, or whatever. When he got out he used his G.I. Bill to get his accounting degree, spent a couple of years working for a company downtown, and ended up on the county payroll when the mayor put together a task force to investigate what we used to call the rackets. His specialty was finding out where crooks hid their money. And my specialty was finding out where crooks hid themselves. We were a team, a natural. We were pals."

He stopped talking for a second and stared straight ahead, his eyes misting up and his expression softening. Then he blinked and looked at me, saying, "But this shit's all ancient history to a guy your age. You're a hotshot, the new kid who's gonna show us old guys the way things oughta be done. Right?"

I could feel my face flush.

"Yeah, I know," he added before I could respond. "I been there myself. Kids always think they're the first ones

to ever feel anything . . . like old folks are born that way. Just remember, sonny, when you look at somebody like Chet, or me even, you're looking at a whole lotta life. And just 'cause I used up a good chunk of my time, that don't mean I used it all."

"Is that how Mr. Scholtz felt?"

"You bet your ass."

"And he contacted you when he needed somebody to watch his back because he knew he could trust you."

"Right."

"So you're following his wife . . ."

"Because I owe it to Chet to finish what he started. That's how we did things in our day. When you said you'd do something, you did it. We called that friendship."

"But what was he after?"

"I'm not sure."

"He didn't tell you? What about this friendship you've been talking about? What about trust?"

Fizner was shaking his head and chuckling as he lit a cigarette. Through the smoke of his first puff he squinted one eye and looked at me, suddenly taking on the appearance of a detective in a Mickey Spillane novel . . . and abruptly I realized that the relationship between those old stories and reality was much more complex than I had thought. Those books existed because of men like Larry Fizner . . . and men like Larry Fizner existed because of those books. Suddenly I felt a little dislocated, partially because of the lateness of the hour—I was dog tired, and buzzing from too much coffee—but also because it seemed as if I had fallen into a dream.

"Kid," he said, "what you don't understand is that when you're dealing with certain people, information can be like a bullet. If you get either one in your head, you're dead."

"So where do we stand?" I asked, almost removing a cigarette from the pack Fizner had placed on the table, but restraining myself.

He asked what I meant, and I explained:

"Mrs. Scholtz hired me. She's my client. Your client's dead. I found out more in the past twelve hours than you did in two weeks of sitting outside her house in a van. Even if the fifty grand ends up recovered, it belongs to her. You've got no claim on it. So why bother hanging around?"

I waited until he looked as if he were about to speak before I cut him off by saying, "Oh yeah, I forgot: friendship. People of your generation do things differently. Like shadowing a dead man's widow out of a sense of obligation for no reason, and to no purpose. Or is there a purpose, Mr. Fizner? There is, isn't there? You just think I'm too dumb to figure out what it is."

I leaned on my elbows, looking him right in the eye and saying, "I'm tired, and sick of fucking around. So I'll lay it out plain and simple: either you tell me a story I believe about why an experienced investigator is sitting in a bright yellow van outside a dead man's house, and being so goddamn conspicuous about it that a grieving widow was able to spot him, or I go to the cops and tell them that I think Jimmy Cecorno, our local representative of the pinky ring crowd, had something to do with the disappearance of fifty thousand dollars in a motel room where a retired civil servant died."

"You can't do that!" Fizner objected.

And I lifted one hand to interrupt.

"Oh yes I can," I said. "And I will. And even if everything I tell the cops turns out to be utter bullshit, all I've got to do is mention missing money and Jimmy Cecorno in the same sentence, and they'll come charging in like the cavalry."

"What do you want?" Fizner finally said, after a long pause during which I could virtually hear the wheels turning in his head.

"I want to know exactly what the arrangement you and Scholtz made between yourselves was," I responded. "And I also want you to pay for breakfast."

Fizner settled back in the booth, smoking as he looked at me, frowning and squinting one eye. Finally, with a sigh,

he said, "Chet came to me about a month ago and asked
me how I was doing. I told him that I was doing fine:
retired, set for life, a virtual Ross Perot. 'Well that's too
bad,' he says, ' 'cause I got a line on something interesting.
Something so big that if you were even the least bit hungry,
it would definitely be worth your while.' I told him I wasn't
interested. Honest to God. I told him I don't do it no more.
'It ain't like it used to be anyway,' I says. 'Bad cops, funny
laws, no respect. Shit, I got busted myself a year ago, and
I don't wanna push my luck.'

"But he don't like hearin' that, so he put on the pressure:

" 'Listen,' he says, 'I'll do all the work. All I need is a
legman to do the runnin'.'

" 'What kinda runnin'?' I ask, 'cause I couldn't help but
be curious.

"And he says, 'Easy shit. I gotta go undercover for a
while. Like we used to. So I need somebody on the outside.
That's all I can say.'

" 'That ain't enough,' I tell him, and he gets kinda frustrated, shifty, real persuasive, like he could be when he put
his mind to it.

" 'Listen,' he says, 'you know how it works. Need to
know . . . it's safer that way.'

"I tell him the safest way for me personally is for him
to get somebody else, and that's when he opened up.

" 'Okay,' he says. 'If that's the way it's gotta be, then
here it is. I want some for myself, Larry. You know what
I mean? All those years we got all that money back for
the government, and not a penny for us. You know? Just
a pension, and a pat on the back. Bullshit! I want some for
me. And I know just how I'm gonna get it.'

"I remember it word for word 'cause something in his
voice hit me. He was sayin' something I could understand.
See, when you're young, you do what you do because it
seems right. You don't think too much about what it means,
you just do it. But when you get to be my age, suddenly you
got the time to kinda look back on it all, and sometimes you

can't help but wonder, what the fuck? Where's mine? What have I got to show for it? Like I said, just 'cause I used up a lot of my time, don't mean I used it all. I ain't ready to die yet. There's shit left to do. So I listened, and he gave me the proposition:

"There was an old-timer, he said, one of the big ones, hid real good. He could make a bundle just for a name. That was it: one name. I told him that I didn't know what he was talkin' about, and he laughed. 'Yeah you do,' he said. 'And you'll work it out . . . I know you. But I'm not gonna explain that part right now 'cause it's risky. Real risky. All I'll say is that I'll pay you twenty thousand bucks to keep an eye on my wife, and maybe watch my back when I go in to make the drop.' I told him I didn't want in on no drug deal or anything like that. And he told me not to worry. 'It's a name,' he said. 'Just a name. No dope. No worries.'

"So I thought about it. A name? An old-timer, hid real good? Something for us? Then it hit me . . ."

He snapped his fingers.

"Just 'cause you're old don't mean you can't do shit no more, I thought. And just 'cause you're old, don't mean you don't know shit no more. Nobody knew more about the big-time hoods than Chet Scholtz. And a lot of those guys are still out there someplace. Old, retired, livin' the good life. If he got a line on one of 'em . . . one of the big ones, like he said . . . then he could really cash in. The feds would pay good to get their hands on some of those guys, even after all these years. And if Chet was offerin' me twenty g's for just watchin' his back, then he had already made his arrangements and knew exactly to the penny what his information was worth. Like I said before, he was one of the good ones. He didn't go around blowin' smoke. When he started talkin' numbers, I knew he was serious.

" 'I been workin' on it for months,' he says. 'Settin' up the deal, makin' the right contacts, and makin' sure of my information. It's guaranteed. You'll be comin' in on the end of a sweet thing . . . a couple weeks' work, and you're done.'

"It sounded good, I said, but why did he pick me as the object of his generosity? And he said that he felt more comfortable with somebody his own age . . . somebody who knew the ropes.

"So to make it short, I told him okay, I'd do it. 'Just tell me where and when.' "

The rest, Fizner said, crushing out his cigarette and lighting another, he didn't feel he needed to explain, since I'd told him the story exactly as it had happened on the sidewalk near his van in front of Mrs. Scholtz's house. He had picked Scholtz up from the bank at eleven-thirty Friday morning, just like I'd said. And they'd spent the day bowling and talking about the old days as a way of killing time until their meeting that night. At ten they went to the motel, and Fizner watched the door while Scholtz went inside. He was just getting worried because Scholtz had been gone so long when the girl showed up, all hell broke loose, and he got the hell out of there. He'd been watching Mrs. Scholtz ever since because he was worried about her.

"Believe it or not," he insisted. "I've been worried sick. I thought Chet got burned in there, you know, double-crossed. I figured that they set him up, and then paid the cops to keep it quiet. That kinda shit happens in situations where wise guys are involved. After that, I figured that whoever killed Chet might go after his wife too, since it wouldn't take a genius to realize that he must have told her about what he was doing. So I been sittin' out in the open like that, hopin' that if somebody came around lookin' to intimidate her, or whatever, that they'd see my van and figure she was being protected."

"Protected?" I asked. "Protected by whom?"

"The F.B.I.," he said. "Who else? I mean, if Chet had nailed down the name of an old hood, and had figured out where he was hiding, then who else would he have been selling that name to but the F.B.I.?"

"In a motel?"

"What're ya talkin' about?"

"Isn't it a little weird that he'd be meeting the F.B.I. in a motel to sell them the name of a crook?"

"Oh, for Christ's sake," Fizner said, accepting the check when the waitress brought it and reaching for his wallet. "He wasn't sellin' the name in the motel, he was *buyin*' it! What do you think he was doin' with that money?"

"I don't understand," I said.

And Fizner shook his head, saying, "I don't either, really. The best I can figure is that somehow he found out that there was somebody in that nursing home who had the information he wanted. He went in, nosed around, and finally arranged to buy what he needed at the motel Friday night."

"Which brings us back to my original question," I said. "Where do we stand?"

As it turned out, Larry Fizner had a proposition of his own.

FOUR

■■■■■■■■■

"SO, LET ME see if I've got this straight," my younger brother Jerry said after I had described everything I knew about Chester Scholtz to him early the next morning. "You think that Scholtz had himself admitted to this nursing home because he knew that one of its residents is actually a retired gangster hiding under a phony name. But even after studying the files, he couldn't figure out who it was, so he hooked up with someone who was willing to tell him for fifty thousand bucks. Right?"

"Right," I agreed, finishing it for him. "He then agreed to meet whoever he was dealing with at the Cozy Inn Motel to transact the deal. But somehow, he wound up dead, and an exotic dancer told the cops a cover story that looks like this . . ."

I lifted a newspaper for Jerry to see from where he was lying on his special bed, indicating Chester Scholtz's picture beneath the words, "Retired Auditor Found Dead With Dancer."

"This is yesterday's paper," I explained, holding the page so that Jerry might read the story, which was short and to the point. It insinuated a lot of things about the dead man,

and ended with a thinly veiled jab at the city for allowing the smut factories on Brookings Road to continue churning out their sludge. The *Plain Dealer* had been leading the charge to clean up the area for a long time.

"I didn't see it until this morning when Nat pointed it out to me," I said. "What's interesting about it is that Scholtz wasn't pronounced dead at the hospital until after midnight, so there's no way a reporter could have made the next day's edition . . . unless somebody called the story in earlier . . . like at ten or ten-thirty, which is when Scholtz really died. That would be before the rescue squad even showed up at the motel, which means that only one person could have made the call."

"That's not true," my father said, taking the newspaper from my hand and sitting down in a chair across the room, next to a window.

Jerry was grinning where he lay, his eyes aimed at the ceiling, but his attention directed at me.

"The way I figure it," I said, pacing back and forth as an old man in a wheelchair glided past the room's open door, "is that whoever took Scholtz's money knew that he had some kind of a deal going on the side. He knew that someone was waiting for Scholtz to give them this all-important name. So to make sure that these people saw that Scholtz was dead right away, he sent the dancer over to talk to the cops, and then called the newspaper himself with a story they couldn't possibly ignore. I mean, Christ, an old guy dead in a motel with a twenty-year-old stripper he got from one of the very bars that the paper's been writing nasty editorials about for a year? It was a natural . . . way too good for them to pass up."

"And what about this old private eye's proposition?" Jerry asked. "What about that?"

"He offered to be my teacher!" I said. "Honest, that's what he said. He thinks that if I don't get some instruction I'll wind up in trouble, so he offered to teach me the ropes as an investigator in exchange for me working for him on this one because he says it's a matter of personal honor for

him to find out what happened to his friend."

"And you don't believe him?" my dad asked from where he was sitting, his legs crossed, the newspaper folded on his lap.

"No," I said. "I don't. I think he's up to something and he isn't telling me what it is."

"No," my dad clarified, "I mean, you don't believe he's right when he says that if you don't get some professional training, you're going to screw yourself up?"

"I don't know," I admitted. "But we're not gonna fight about it now, are we?"

Jerry laughed and my father frowned. I was careful to keep my tone of voice light because I knew that I was treading on uncertain ground. Just being in the same room with my dad and brother was enough to make me uncomfortable because they tend to see things eye to eye, with me as odd man out. When we're together we almost always end up in an argument, with them on one side and me on the other.

"So what's the plan?" Jerry asked, cutting in with his happy voice because I had said that my proposal included him.

"First," I said, "I want Pop to explain why he thinks there could have been more than one person who called the newspaper on Friday night."

Dad smiled and said, "Because there's at least three people who knew that something was happening:

"Suspect number one is the motel manager. If the man who stole the money was already waiting in the room when Mr. Scholtz arrived, then he must have gotten the key from the manager first. Suspect number two is the dancing girl. She could have called from the room before she started screaming. And suspect number three is this private eye."

"Larry Fizner?" I cut in. "Why him?"

"Because who's to say that what he told you he did was the truth? Maybe he went up to the room, found the body, and made the call before the girl ever arrived."

"Why would he do that?" Jerry asked.

And my dad shrugged, saying, "Who knows? I'm just pointing out that, despite Bill's neat little scenario, there are other possibilities."

Before I could respond, Jerry asked me to explain my plan again, and I said, "I hate to suggest this, but I've got an idea about how we can get some information out of that nursing home."

"How?"

"By having you admitted there for a while."

His eyes sparkled as a smile blossomed on his face, and I found myself thinking about how he had gotten stuck in that bed in the first place.

As I said earlier, Jerry is the one in our family who most resembles Grandpa Hawlinski. And that's a double-edged sword. Grandpa's determination and guts got him to the U.S. despite the war in Europe, but once his journey was over, those attributes lost their focus and degenerated from a hard blue flame of desire to a smoldering irritability that made him seem resentful and ill-tempered. He was a grouch, plain and simple, and Jerry ended up just like him: stubborn, cocky, opinionated, and angry. When we were kids we were close, but that all changed when he turned sixteen and his testosterone kicked in. He lifted weights and worshiped Arnold Schwarzenegger. I smoked pot and worshiped Alice Cooper. He said I lacked drive and would float through life without ever accomplishing anything of value. And I said that he was a judgmental, tight-assed son of a bitch who spent all his time looking for flaws in the people around him. In his eyes, I would never measure up, and in my eyes, he was missing the point. But we still loved each other . . . we just didn't like to admit it. . . .

Until the accident.

And I don't care what Nat says, in my heart, I know that it was my fault.

He was protecting me, that's the bitch of it . . . the thing that will, very honestly, wake me up out of a dead sleep in the middle of the night and make me sit up in bed, wide-eyed and overcome with a feeling like someone's

squeezing my chest so that I can't breathe. My younger brother was sticking up for me the night he broke his neck, which means that if I would have done a better job sticking up for myself, the accident would never have happened. That's the truth, and its memory sends me back to that parking lot where the spit-shined black leather of rescue squad shoes crunched gravel as red lights revolved over my baby brother as he was loaded into the brightly lit interior of a city ambulance. He was strapped to a back board, his body immobilized, and his eyes black with fright. His mouth was moving, but I couldn't hear what he said. And in my mind that image will forever remain silent . . . all sight, no sound. I once read about a phenomenon called "night terrors," in which perfectly normal people suddenly find themselves overcome with panic for no apparent reason—and believe me, I can sympathize. But my episodes have a very specific object, and it's guilt: because of me, Jerry is paralyzed from the neck down.

Enthusiastically, he agreed to request a transfer to the Manor Care Assisted Living Facility from the nursing home where he had resided for the past two years. The opportunity to be involved with something important—even if it was only important because he allowed himself to see it that way—was the best gift I could have given him, because of all the adjustments his condition had forced him to make, inactivity was the hardest. Grumbling, my dad left to bring the car around, saying, "Well, it's time to go to work," leaving Jerry and me alone for a few minutes like he always does at the end of our Sunday morning visits.

Jerry turned his head to look at me. He's recovered the use of his arms, to a degree, but the process has been slow, and his physical therapy sessions leave him exhausted. His prognosis is hopeful, and someday he may use a wheelchair, but he has years of work ahead of him. He was fresh from an hour of mobility exercises, and the strain showed in his eyes.

"Can I really help?" he asked.

And I told him, "Yeah. I've got it all worked out. I even think I can get that orderly, Pete Germaine, to help you. You'll be right in there, my eyes and ears."

"It's lucky that's all you need," he joked, adding through his smile, "but really, Bill, thanks."

I told him not to mention it.

"No," he insisted. "I mean it. But Dad's right. You know? I mean about that private eye maybe teaching you stuff. If you're really serious about doin' this, what can it hurt?"

I told him that I'd think about it, putting my hand on his shoulder to indicate that I was about to leave. But the look in his eyes wouldn't let me go.

"Tell Nat that it's okay," he said. "You know what I mean? About her not coming. Tell her I understand. I wouldn't want to see me like this either, if I were her."

"That's not what it is," I insisted, not wanting to talk about it now, not feeling as if I could handle it. But he pressed on anyway, and there was nothing I could do to stop him.

"Did you see Jill this week?" he asked. The inevitable question.

I nodded.

"How's she look?"

"Fine."

"Did you talk to her?"

"No."

Jill was his former girlfriend. She worked in a bank not far from the funeral home, and I went in every once in a while specifically so I could describe her to Jerry, who hadn't seen her in nearly eight months. She came and held his hand for a time, right after the accident, but her visits grew progressively more infrequent, until they stopped altogether. When I went to the bank I never stepped up to her window, and she never looked at me. I only went in because Jerry asked me to.

"When are you going to ask her?" he said as I withdrew my hand.

"Soon," I sighed. "I promise."

"When?"

"This week."

"Really?"

"Yeah. After the last time, I wanted to give her a chance to cool off."

Jerry had driven Jill away . . . which was the subject of this exchange. After the accident he'd gone into a terrible depression during which he lashed out at everything and everyone, particularly Jill. I heard a couple of the outbursts he directed at her and they were nearly as frightening in their venom as the ones he hurled at me. In his mind he was dead. He had nothing left to offer. He never wanted to see anyone again . . . especially Jill, because he said that their former love would ruin her life. He wanted her to forget him and find someone else. And he wanted to die. He even asked me to help him commit suicide, and when I refused, he asked my dad, and anyone else who came by. When the doctors announced that he could expect to recover the use of his arms, he threw himself into the therapy sessions with all his old determination, making tremendous progress and enduring terrible pain. But his newfound purpose didn't change his mind about Jill: he wanted her out of his life. And it wasn't until recently that he had changed his mind.

"She's pretty screwed up," I said. "It's gonna take some time."

"I know," he admitted. "But just stick with it, okay? I know if you stay on her, she'll come."

"Okay," I said, "but she's got her own problems. You'll just have to be patient."

"I'm gonna be a patient for the rest of my life," he sighed.

And I left, relieved to be out in the sun again, and feeling like I would do anything for a drink.

At the funeral home I called Pete Germaine, explaining my idea about having my brother moved to the Manor Care for a while and convincing him to cooperate. It didn't take much. He was enthusiastic from the word go, saying

that it would be good to have someone who wasn't a hundred years old around to talk to. Then I faxed the sheet of numbers and words I had found hidden in the wall of Chester Scholtz's bathroom to Bob Bryant, the funeral home's accountant, scribbling on the bottom, "Does this mean anything to you at all?" And then I called the newspaper and found out that their deadline for articles appearing in the next day's edition was eleven o'clock at night. Then my dad and I got Chester Scholtz ready for his viewings.

The visitation process is one about which I have very ambivalent feelings. On the one hand, I understand that seeing the body is an important part of accepting the fact of a loved one's death, while on the other I think that it's cruel to put the family's grief on display before the burial. When I first started at the funeral home, two-day viewings were common, which was down from the three-day extravaganzas my uncle said were the norm when he got into the business twenty-five years ago. During visitations I don't have much to do other than stand by the front door and greet people as they walk in, and from that vantage point I've seen the toll the viewings can take on a family. For every person who arrives, there's the story of how Mom or Dad died to repeat, the sympathy to accept, and the whole process of social definition as extended families reacquaint themselves. It wears people down, and for the life of me, I don't understand how anyone survived for three solid days.

Mrs. Scholtz had decided on a one-day viewing, two to four in the afternoon, and seven until nine at night. Since her husband wasn't exactly a religious man, she asked if I could find her a Catholic priest who would be willing to come to the funeral home and say a few words over his casket . . . no church service, but a priest would be nice. I get that request a lot—"Could you just get us a priest?"—as if there's a room somewhere that's filled with on-call clergymen just waiting to come and perform funeral services for people they've never even met. The casket she

chose was a Batesville "Agean," solid copper, very smart, very expensive. Flowers started rolling in Saturday night, and by the time we had Chester in his crisp black suit and shiny copper casket, the service area was stuffed with baskets. He went into the big parlor, which seats about eighty people, has a pale blue curtain hanging over its feature wall, and ivory-white wallpaper that lets the bright burgundies and blues of the patterned carpet look their best. We arranged flowers for an hour, getting things to look good just in time to do it all over again when three or four new baskets were delivered, until, at noon, we put the coffee on to cook, and Dad went home. I was working the afternoon calling hours, and he was coming in at night. My uncle Joe was off that weekend, so he wouldn't be around until the funeral.

When we'd first come back from the nursing home where my brother lived, I'd noticed that the Miata wasn't in the garage. Nat left me a note on the kitchen counter saying that she had some work to do and that she'd be back soon. So I read the paper until one-thirty, turned on the lights, and opened up.

The Hawley Funeral Home is a really cool place, in my opinion. Unlike most of the funeral homes in town, which are converted mansions altered for the purpose, ours was built to be what it is, so it's functional, and lacks that sense of intrusion some funeral homes have, that feeling that you're roaming around somebody's house while they're not home. The building's a hundred and twenty feet long by sixty feet wide, is made of tan-colored brick, and has virtually no windows. Atop it is a dormer kind of thing that contains the living quarters, which jut out over the front entrance on six brick supports to create a carport beneath which we park the hearse on funeral days. Both the roof of the building and the roof of the living quarters are perfectly flat, and when viewed from above, the building looks like a capital T.

The interior was recently redecorated, entirely on commission, by a lady who came in with a clipboard and a

camera, looking the place over with one squinty eye and waving her arms over her head. A week later we got what looked like a wedding album via U.P.S., in which we found sketches and photographs . . . kind of like before and after pictures, showing us what we had, what we'd get—and two months after that, we got it. It's Victorian now . . . a lot of flower prints and flowing drapes, scrolled furniture and frosted glass. It's pretty, but from certain angles you'll catch a glimpse of say, the foyer, with a delicate love seat and a gloppy grandfather clock, and the words that pop into your head will be "French cathouse." No shit.

Mrs. Scholtz pulled up at a quarter of two, alone, which surprised me. She's got two kids, and I expected at least the unmarried daughter who lived with her to accompany her in for support. But she didn't. And instead of standing by the car and waiting for the kids to drive up and park so that they could enter the building as a united front, Mrs. Scholtz simply got out of her car and headed my way.

She looked a lot more together than the first time I'd met her, more composed, and a lot less likely to cry. I held the door for her to enter, and she glanced up at the board near the credenza that read "CHESTER SCHOLTZ, Parlor C. Funeral Services: Monday, 10:00 a.m.," glanced over the foyer, and found Parlor C's door where there was another small sign bearing her husband's name. She looked at me briefly, sighed, and went ahead in without ever saying a word. Her daughter didn't show up until two-fifteen, and the son from Detroit never came. But practically everybody else did, and for the entire afternoon the place was packed, so I never did get a chance to ask her what she had been looking for in her husband's nursing home room at two on the morning after he died.

Larry Fizner showed up at the stroke of two, wearing a hideous lemon-yellow sport coat and shaking my hand as if we were long lost friends. When I asked him where his assistant, Judy Newhardt, was, he winked and said, "Applying for a job," out of the corner of his mouth.

"What kind of job do you apply for on a Sunday afternoon?" I asked.

"One like a dancing job at the Lipstick Lounge, for example."

"No shit?" I whispered. "She's gonna be a dancer?"

"Can you think of a better way to keep an eye on the broad who was there when Chet died than having somebody undercover in the same place she works?" he responded, moving into the crowd and looking for "that book thingie you're supposed to sign."

Mrs. Scholtz's youngest child, her daughter Sharon, stepped in like a princess, and at first I wasn't sure who she was. From the way her mother had described her, a free spirit who had a bad marriage, I expected more of an aging flower child than the pleated, walking yardstick who sashayed her way past me with her hair cut and sprayed into layers so precise they looked sharp, and a mask of grim determination painted with makeup on her face.

Jimmy Cecorno lumbered in at two-thirty, and I only recognized him because of his size. Unlike the first time I'd seen him, he didn't look like a grease-ball; this time he looked smooth in a tailored baby-blue suit, tan loafers, and no goofy gold chains. He didn't speak to me, but simply nodded once and aimed his finger my way as he made a quick clucking sound with his tongue. He didn't sign the book, but just kind of floated around for about ten minutes. And then he left, again without a word.

When Pete Germaine pulled up in a rusted silver Toyota, I thought, Christ, the gang's all here, and I was going to go outside and try to talk to him, but Nat was just backing into the garage, so I went to say hi, and ended up helping her lug a stack of books from the car to my desk. Putting them down, I kissed her and asked, "So, what's up?" as she ran her fingers through her windblown hair and looked at herself in the mirror over my desk.

(Quickly: we've got this mirror in the office that I loathe. It's made of rose-colored glass and covers the entire wall behind my desk. It's beveled on the edges, and has our logo

etched into its center: a green laurel wreath arrangement with the black letters H.F.H. cut into it. It reflects the room in such a way as to make it look huge, reminding me of something you might see in an old James Bond movie . . . where a victim would stand before the desk of the head of K.A.O.S. or something, pleading his case, until a secret button is pressed and a trapdoor in the floor opens up to dump him into the dungeon below.)

"Remember what you said about a private investigator sending thirty bucks to Columbus for an 'honorary' license?" she asked, making me nod. "Well that's not how it works. It's closer to three hundred bucks, and it isn't honorary. It's a B.F.D."—Nat's abbreviation for Big Fucking Deal. "You've got to get character references from five citizens not related to you by blood or marriage, apply for a license, be interviewed by a board, and take a test. You also have to have the sheriff's department in the city where you plan to work run a complete background check on you, including your police record; and you can't have been convicted of a felony in the past twenty years. That's the law . . . Ohio Revised Code 4712.8"

"No shit?"

"No shit."

"You mean all those hard-drinking private eyes in the movies had to interview with a board?" I asked, trying to make a joke, but playing right into Nat's hands instead.

"That's fiction," she said. "And you look lousy."

"I feel lousy," I admitted, because I did. I hadn't slept the night before almost at all. I had drunk a gallon of coffee, which I never do anymore since caffeine's as much a drug as anything else, and getting buzzed up just makes me want to smoke. My hands were jittery, and I had a headache.

"You're pale," she said, feeling my forehead. "And clammy. Just wait here."

She ran upstairs and returned with two huge tumblers of ice water, one of which she handed to me along with a pill, which I took, saying, "What was that?" when I was through. She told me it was a Benadryl, and when

I protested that I didn't need any antihistamines to make me sleepy, she said that it would cut through the adrenaline in my system from too much caffeine and help the water to wash my insides clean. Nat's into health . . . and she says she's going to make me healthy, or kill me trying. Paradoxically, with both her parents being pharmacists, she's also a great believer in the wonders of drugs, so she's always distributing pills.

"And you don't need a gun," she said, out of the blue.

When I asked her why she thought I wanted a gun, she said, "Oh, get off it, Bill. All that shit you yammered last night about this Larry Fizner looking like Sam Spade, and how you just knew he carried a forty-five like Mike Hammer on TV. I know what you're thinking. You're like a twelve-year-old sometimes."

"I never said I wanted a gun," I mumbled, trying not to pout.

"And don't pout," she said, making me blink. "I honestly don't care what you do, but I know how you are when you get the bit in your teeth: you just run with it . . . and to hell with looking right or left. So this morning I looked up the details. Private investigators are carefully controlled by the state. You can't just run around asking questions without any supervision. It doesn't work that way. Already, if someone wanted to, they could have you arrested."

"Get out."

"I'm serious. They could slap a restraining order on you, and the penalties go up to a year in jail."

"For what?"

"Investigating without a license. And you know what else? You've got to be insured. Right now, today, because of the stuff you've been doing, you could get sued."

"Baloney."

"No baloney. Look." She opened a big, black reference book that was never supposed to leave the college library, but that she, as the reference librarian, could take with her anywhere she wanted. "Right there, see? It's in the law. You've engaged in practices pertaining to the act

of private investigation while representing yourself as a holder of a separate state license, namely, your funeral director's card. If somebody decided to sue, they could go after you personally, and the funeral home too. They might not win, but it would cost a bundle to defend. Now, is all this worth it?"

I stared at the books, and then looked up at her.

"Don't answer me now," she said. "But think about it. And, by the way. Remember when you said that the orderly at the nursing home said that Chester Scholtz's blindness was a 'textbook' example of an hysterical reaction?"

I nodded.

"Well, you had that part right anyway. It is a textbook case. I found it in a textbook . . . right down the line, every symptom you said Scholtz had. It reads like he was following a recipe. Now, I'm going to lie in the sun."

So I had to accept Larry Fizner's offer. I spent a half an hour looking at the statutes Nat had dug up before I realized why the old private eye had made his offer in the first place: he knew I would need to do it . . . it said so in the book. If I wanted a license—which I wasn't sure I did yet, really—then I had to serve an apprenticeship with a license holder in preparation for my service test. When I told him I was game, he just smiled and punched me on the shoulder, saying, "Good boy," which was such an oddly familiar gesture that it made me feel funny . . . kind of good on the one hand, and sneaky on the other.

At closing time Pete Germaine hung around and we talked while I turned off lamps and locked doors. He wanted to go out for a beer between viewings, but I gracefully declined, not mentioning why, but saying that I'd take a rain check.

After he left, I pulled my tape recorder out of the bottom drawer of my desk. It was one of those kinds that run miniature cassettes, about the size of a bottle cap, and it's voice activated. I used it in college to record lectures when I was too hung over to remember them well, and I hadn't turned it on in years. But a pair of fresh batteries got it going, and as I was testing it the phone rang, so that when

I was done talking I had a tape that sounded like this:

"Hawley Funeral Home. Oh, hi Bob. No luck with the fax, huh? Well, I didn't really think you would, but I figured I'd get you to look at it just in case. . . . Really? You knew Scholtz? How? . . . He was that well-known, huh? . . . Yeah, I guessed that he had to be some kind of a big shot judging by the crowd we had here this afternoon. What do you know about this Jimmy Cecorno guy . . . you know, that brother-in-law to what's his name, the Godfather with the nose? . . . Yeah, that's him. . . . Really? Who says? . . . Christ. . . . Yeah, okay Bob, I'll talk to you tonight."

That's what my tape sounded like, crisp and clear. But what wasn't on the tape was what our accountant had said, which was that Jimmy Cecorno, despite his carefully calculated public persona, was actually a lot smarter than anyone thought. As a matter of fact, the scoop in the business community was that playing dumb was the smartest thing he ever did.

At five I went upstairs and took a bath. Nat had just come in from the sun, wearing a black two-piece and sunglasses, and Quincy was sleeping on the shelf next to my computer. I didn't feel like eating dinner, but I did, after which I settled down on the couch with the remote control, popping through the stations until six-thirty when Nat took the remote away from me and said, "Just go. Okay? Don't mope."

I replied that I didn't know what she was talking about, and she poked me in the arm with her finger, saying, "The only person you haven't talked to is that girl."

"So?"

"So . . . go find her!"

And this time, I took the van.

Jimmy Cecorno had told me that Cynthia Moore hadn't gone home after she'd left the Lipstick Lounge the night Chester Scholtz died. She'd just walked off into the night clutching the canvas gym bag in which she carried her

street clothes, wearing a white satin bathrobe over the next-to-nothing panties and bra she wore at work, hobbling on her red rhinestone stiletto heels like a painted Dorothy in a neon Oz. Her address had appeared on the police addendum to the emergency room report I'd seen the day before, and I headed over, watching the neighborhood deteriorate as I got closer.

She lived within ten minutes of the airport, in a big, two-family house with top and bottom porches on the front. It was only seven in the evening, so the sun was blazing away overhead, and as I parked the van, kids rolled by on skateboards as parents watched from their lawn chairs.

Cynthia Moore's door was opened by a small, frazzled-looking woman wearing a dark blue housecoat and a plastic bag over the curlers in her hair. Through the screen I could hear a television playing cartoons and see the shape of a child on the living room floor.

I excused myself and asked if Miss Moore was home, to which the old woman responded by saying that she hadn't been home in a while. She made no offer to take a message, didn't ask me who I was, or anything. She just aimed a look of open hostility my way, telling me that "Cyn ain't home, and I don't know when she's comin' home neither. I'm just watchin' her kid is all. I don't know nothing." I squinted, examining the "kid" over her shoulder and finding a little boy of about five playing with the largest toy fire truck I had ever seen: shiny red, new, with a ladder and a bell. Fifty bucks, I thought. Maybe more, knowing how much toys cost these days . . . which I did because every so often Nat and I stopped in the "Kids R Us" at the mall just for fun. I looked back at the old woman with something goosing the back of my brain.

The little boy hadn't so much as looked up from his new toy when I clumped up the porch steps and rang the bell.

"And you say she hasn't been home in a while?" I asked.

The old woman shook her head as she insisted, "No. And I don't know where she is. I watch her kid. She don't tell

me where she goes, and I don't ask."

"So it's been a couple of days since she's been here?"

"Coupla days at least."

"Funny," I said. "But her son doesn't seem very concerned about his mother being away. He didn't even look up to see if I was her when I first got here."

The woman frowned, and made as if to move back into the gloom beyond the screen.

"Jimmy C don't like what she did," I said, raising my voice in hopes of sending my words through the house. "He says I'm supposed to tell her that in person. I don't want to be a pest, but I got my orders."

The old woman picked up the child and disappeared through a doorway inside, leaving me on the porch. I turned to go, catching the view from the front of the house, and seeing a car parked in the drive across the narrow, brick street that was cockeyed and rusted, glaring at me with one good headlight and a grill that was broken and dull. There were no curtains in the windows of the house across the street. And the lawn was overgrown with weeds. I put my hands in my pockets and headed down the stairs, trying to look nonchalant as I stepped thoughtfully around the side of the house and looked up at the windows.

I was being watched from inside, of that much I was sure. If someone came looking for me at my house and I had refused to be found, I'd be peeking through the window as they strolled around too. A path of sandstone led through the weeds along the side of the house, and I headed that way, looking up at the peeling paint on the shingles and saying loudly, "Yep, I sure hate having to tell Jimmy C I couldn't find Cindy. He'll probably get mad and send either Steve or Blue over next. Those goons. It's a shame, 'specially since all I'm supposed to do is talk this time. It's almost like Cindy thinks Jimmy C's as dumb as he wants folks to believe he is. Almost like she don't know no better."

Behind the house there was a tiny backyard surrounded by a sagging cyclone fence rusted completely brown, a line

of ancient garbage cans stuffed with torn, black plastic bags, and trash strewn everywhere, as if the neighborhood cats had been having a party the night before. The garage sagged precariously to the right, its old-style sliding buggy door permanently wedged open and what looked to be about a 1973 Buick Electra parked inside. The big, old, rust bucket gas-guzzler barely fit into the tiny building, and for a second I wondered how the driver had gotten out. Then I turned and looked up at the back of the house, which was in far worse shape than the front, with shingles missing and tar paper frayed to the bone. There were six dark windows to choose from, so I aimed my remarks at what I assumed was the kitchen, saying, "Well, her car's here, anyway. Wherever she went, she must have taken the bus. Guess I'll just tell Jimmy C he's gonna have to have somebody watch the house till she comes back . . . which he ain't gonna like at all. But I guess that's what I'll have to do."

"Who are you?" a voice asked, coming from one of the windows.

"A friend," I replied.

"Sure."

I shrugged, saying, "Fine. Whatever you think. But I only came to help."

Long pause while the owner of the voice apparently thought things over. Finally . . .

"The door's open."

And I said, "Thanks."

She sat at the kitchen table drinking Southern Comfort from a teacup and smoking Winstons without a break. She was the oldest twenty-year-old I had ever seen, and looking at her I couldn't help but feel pity . . . which I didn't express because I suspected that if I did she would either punch me out, or offer to have me move in. The old woman was her mother, and once I was inside she closed the kitchen door and stayed in the living room with her grandson, refusing to so much as look at me.

"Don't gimme that shit about Jimmy sending you here," were the first words out of Cynthia Moore's mouth. "He

doesn't even know anybody like you."

"What tipped you off?" I asked, looking the kitchen over while trying to appear as if I wasn't.

"Jimmy only hires dumb guys," she said from her seat at the table. Judging from the glazed look in her eyes and the nearly empty whiskey bottle near her left hand, I suspected that she had been sitting in that same place for quite a long time. The room was thick with the aroma of cigarettes, and she was dressed in a T-shirt. Beneath the table her legs and feet were bare, and I couldn't tell if she had any pants on or not.

"If the whole world's stupid," she said, crushing out her cigarette and immediately reaching for another from the pack near the overflowing ashtray, "then nobody knows the boss is a retard. Don't look for no college textbooks, by the way. Unlike every other slut in the world, I don't wanna be a nurse when I grow up. I don't even want to go into advertising. Sit down, you're makin' me nervous. Christ; you hover like my mother."

I sat down, and she asked me who I was again. When I told her the same story I had told the motel manager, about being an insurance investigator, she sighed and said, "That poor old fuck. Just keeled right over."

"I know that you weren't there when he died," I cut in, and she blinked slowly, as if the information took her a while to grasp.

"I ain't givin' the money back," she said.

And I told her that I didn't expect her to.

"Fucker stiffed me on half anyway."

"Stiffed you?"

"Twenty-five hundred up front, and twenty-five later. That's what he said. Waved around the cash and told me to meet him up the street when the cops were gone. But when I got there, no guy. Stiffed me. Shoulda seen it comin'."

"Had you ever seen him before?"

"No. But I'd sure like to see him again. Cute little ass for a nine-to-five."

"Nine-to-five?"

"Like you: Mr. Normal. Wife and kids and a steady job. See 'em all the time."

"If I showed you some pictures, would you be able to pick him out?"

"Maybe you do work for Jimmy after all. Suddenly you sound stupid."

"If you knew I didn't work for your boss, and you had no intention of answering any of my questions, then why'd you ask me in?"

"Because I didn't want you standin' in my yard yellin'," she said, rising from her seat and stepping over to the counter, which was piled with dirty dishes. Her T-shirt was long, so that even standing I couldn't tell if she was wearing anything underneath; and her toenails were painted neon pink. She was short and thin, with damaged blond hair and skinny legs. "People next door listen to every fucking thing that goes on over here," she added, shouting at the end, "Don't you, you nosy fucks?" aiming her words at the open window over the sink. She rinsed out a jelly jar which she placed on the table in front of me, saying, "Belly up to the bar." She looked at me a little funny when I didn't go for the bottle, but to my relief she didn't make an issue of it, sitting back down instead and saying that if I wanted, there was Coke in the icebox. I declined that too.

In the movies it seems that prostitutes and strippers are always depicted as essentially virtuous, world-weary women who have been beaten down by misfortune, but who retain a spark of humanity at the core of their beings. They're usually sympathetic characters that combine an explicitly sexual exterior with an essentially mothering nature to create what I believe is the ultimate male fantasy: the nurturing bombshell who can fix all your problems by laying your head on her breast after screwing your eyes out, with a twenty dollar bill taking the place of an emotional commitment.

Cynthia Moore, on the other hand, wasn't like that at all. And I think my description would have made her laugh. She had a soul made of leather, and it didn't take long to get to the heart of things: she wanted the rest of the five

thousand bucks she'd been promised . . . and she didn't care who paid her. She hadn't been home when Jimmy Cecorno's guys had come looking for her early Saturday morning because she was out spending a good part of the twenty-five hundred she had made, and if I'd have come an hour later that Sunday, I probably would have missed her too since she was planning on heading out to spend the rest. After all, she had to go to work on Monday.

"You're going back to work?" I asked.

And she shrugged, tipping her teacup and saying, "I got a kid to take care of."

Her son's father was long gone, her mother was a pain in the ass, she drank too much, loved cocaine and expensive clothes, and she couldn't hang on to money.

"So I work," she grumbled. "Ain't life a picnic? Beats McDonald's though. At the Lipstick I drag down a grand a week in dollar bills. I dance good . . . I know what guys like. If you got fifty bucks, I could send Mom and the kid out for ice cream and show ya what I mean."

I told her I appreciated the offer, but that I'd pass at the moment, trying to route things back to the man who had hired her to lie to the police.

"Twenty, twenty-five, thirty years old," she said. "Something like that. Short hair 'bout the same color as yours . . . light brown, sandy, whatever. Average height, average weight, big wad of money in his pocket."

"Hundred-dollar bills?" I asked.

"Hundred-dollar bills," she agreed with a slow nod.

"Two stacks, one in each pocket?"

"Yeah."

"And what exactly did he say that made you do it?"

"Not much. He comes in, I'm bored, I see a good-lookin' young guy—which is rare for the Lipstick, since it's mostly older guys come in there—so I go over to his table. I'm not there two seconds when he asks me if I'd like to make some quick cash. I think, cop, right away, but he pulls out a fistful of bills and holds it next to his leg so that only I can see it. 'Who do I have to kill?' I say. You know, like

a joke. And he says, 'Nobody. I already did that.' And then he laughs. So I laugh too, and he says to meet him in the parking lot.''

Which she did, asking the man with the money if he was serious about somebody being dead. When he said that he was, she got scared and tried to go back into the bar, but he grabbed her arm and explained that an old guy had dropped over of a heart attack, and that all she had to do was tell that to the police. When she heard that the police were going to be involved she nearly bolted, but the man was adamant, holding onto her upper arms and shaking her as he swore that he had never laid a finger on the guy, and that nobody would ever know the difference. He showed her the twenty-five hundred bucks again, and said that he'd give her twenty-five hundred more if she'd do what he asked before meeting him up the street when it was over . . . which she finally did. But he never showed up.

"The shit."

"Let's get to the details," I said.

But she said there weren't any details. I asked where she had been all day Saturday, and she told me that it was none of my business. I said that I thought she was with the money man, and that he had in fact given her her second twenty-five hundred bucks, and she said I was wrong. I said that I didn't believe her, and she told me to go fuck myself, putting us at an impasse. She obviously didn't give a shit whether I believed her or not. Actually, I didn't quite know what she gave a shit about, or what I was trying to accomplish, and I was about to give it up when she mumbled something intriguing.

"What?" I said.

And she looked up at me, saying, "I said that I should never have trusted a doctor. Too much education. They think they're smarter than anybody else."

How did she know he was a doctor?

Well, maybe he wasn't a doctor for sure, but he sure had the terminology down. Cardiovascular this, myocardial that. Sounded like fucking Marcus Welby. I blinked,

turning it over in my head and asking her to go through it all again, which irritated her—I could tell from the way her eyes narrowed—but which she did anyway, as if she grudgingly had to admit that she liked being the center of attention. As she spoke, I was thinking, Doctor? Doctor? Why does that sound right? And a thought had just occurred to me when a shadow crossed the kitchen floor as someone stepped up to the screen door, making Cynthia Moore lift her eyes to look as I turned in my seat.

"Oh shit," she said with a tone of resigned exasperation as the door opened, and I stood up, one hand on my chair, my other on the table.

"Who's the stiff?" he asked, filling the door frame with his body and speaking to the girl as if I were deaf.

"You better go," she said to me, her back hunched, her elbows still on the table and the teacup held between her hands.

"This the guy with the cash?" he asked, the screen door slapping shut behind him. "Is that who he is?"

He was grinning and looking at me now . . . still speaking to her . . . but looking at me.

I didn't speak, but she did, saying, "He's just some guy come wantin' me to dance."

"That right?" he asked, still looking at me with what was turning into a very stupid, very disturbing grin. "You lookin' for a good time, huh?"

"I'm tellin' ya," she insisted, still without moving from her chair, and for the first time I understood just how drunk she was. "He's just some guy . . ."

But before she could finish her sentence, the man in the doorway moved, throwing my chair aside with such force that it bounced off the cabinets and skipped over the linoleum like a stone on a pond. He was about my size as far as height and width, but he had one of those hard beer guts that stretched his T-shirt and a pair of hairy arms knotted with the kind of muscle you get after years of manual labor. His dark hair was long and pulled back in a ponytail, and he had a full, thick beard that made his teeth seem to

glow white from inside its depths. He wore a sleeveless leather vest over his T-shirt, and tattered black jeans that ended over scuffed motorcycle boots around which were wrapped two lengths of ornamental chain. His eyes were pink with what I took to be a chemically induced rage, and before I could react he brushed me aside and overturned the table, sending the whiskey bottle and ashtray smashing onto the floor.

"Taz, no!" Cynthia Moore shrieked, throwing herself back as he strode toward her.

"You must be fuckin' nuts!" he growled and struck her with his fist so that she slammed into the closed door leading into the living room where there was both an old lady and a little boy crying.

His fist was raised again as I shouted, "You're a faggot!"—because I thought it would make him mad—causing him to turn and look my way, a grin spreading over his face, and sweat running between his furrowed, bushy brows. Then I ran for the door.

I was down the three steps and into the backyard in a flash, not looking back, scared out of my mind. I was considering jumping the fence, hiding behind the garage, and climbing up on the roof of the house, all at the same time, as behind me I heard the screen door crash and the thunder of Taz's motorcycle boots on the hollow wood of the back porch. Almost instantly I heard another sound, and I turned to find Larry Fizner, his yellow sport coat draped carefully over the fence and the sleeves of his shirt rolled up, standing complacently by as Judy Newhardt, his apprentice, savagely beat the man in the leather vest with a black stick that looked like something a policeman might carry. The younger man looked startled as he lifted his hands in a vain attempt to block the young woman's blows, and within an instant there was blood on his face. He tried to fight back for a moment, absorbing a surprisingly rapid flurry of cracks from the stick, until he stumbled to the gate, the blood splashing freely now, and his entire body bent in an attitude of retreat.

Judy worked him over until he was practically to the street, where he limped to his motorcycle, and roared away, leaving me amazed. She hesitated for a moment, the stick hanging loosely at her side as if she expected the man to return, nodded, and walked back to where Larry Fizner's van was parked behind mine on the street.

For his part, Larry said, "PCP. Angel dust. That's why she had to hit him so many times. They don't feel any pain on that shit," as if we had been in the middle of a conversation before being interrupted.

"I'm callin' the cops!" someone shouted from inside the house next door.

But Larry just waved it off, saying, "Yeah yeah," at the voice, and, "Don't worry, even if she calls they won't come," to me.

As a group of people assembled curiously on the sidewalk, Judy casually sat smoking in the passenger's seat of Larry's van. I was trembling so badly that my voice broke when I asked Larry what the hell he was doing there, to which he replied, "What difference does it make?" shutting me up.

Cynthia Moore appeared on the back porch, her hand to her face, where already her left eye was swelling up black-and-blue, saying, "There goes work for a fucking week!"

And inexplicably the thought I had been chasing about doctors before Taz—whoever he was—started busting the place up, coalesced in my mind, making me exclaim, "The orderly!" with one finger pointed in the air, and my gut tied in a knot.

Cynthia Moore rode back to the funeral home with Judy in Larry Fizner's yellow van, and Larry rode with me in my blue one, explaining that he had followed me from the funeral home to see what I was up to. When I asked why he had abandoned his vigil on Mrs. Scholtz, he said that she had gone to dinner with her daughter, and that she would be safe enough at the funeral home during that evening's viewing. I was his concern, he said, because he didn't want

to see his new apprentice get himself in any trouble. He had parked out front of Cynthia Moore's house, and wasn't there ten minutes before Taz pulled up on his motorcycle, "blowing like a bull and red in the face. A neighbor must have called him when they saw you on the porch. In that kind of neighborhood, information gets around fast."

"But the nightstick?" I asked.

And he shrugged, saying, "I got all kinds of shit like that."

"But he was a big guy . . ."

"You mean that Judy's a girl, don't you?"

"Okay, Judy's a girl. He coulda taken that stick away from her and bashed her brains out with it."

"No way."

"Come on . . ."

"Listen, you seen too many movies. It ain't how big you are that makes you tough, it's how mean you are inside. Most people think they could hurt somebody if they had to, but when the time comes to actually do it, they pull back 'cause they ain't got it in 'em. Well, Judy does. She can be just awful sometimes. She's trained in all sorts of things, and she could tear your ears off if she wanted to. There was a time when I could too, truth be known. But I'm too old for that shit now, so I let her handle the physical stuff. Actually, it usually works out better in the end, since most guys think like you do, and by the time they get over their surprise, Judy's got their ass kicked all over the sidewalk."

I thought about the assault charge on Larry Fizner's record, and all those cases of burglary that had been dropped, and it made me wonder just what I was getting myself into with him and his bloodthirsty assistant. But I didn't dwell on it. Instead I thought about Taz—Cynthia Moore said that he was more or less her boyfriend, and that he must have heard that she scored some money and gotten pissed when she didn't offer to share it with him—then I thought about Pete Germaine . . . mostly, I thought about Pete Germaine.

His car was in the funeral home lot, and my dad was standing by the front door in a wine colored blazer and black slacks. We parked the vans near the back, approaching the building like an assault team, with me leading the way, then Cynthia Moore, followed by Judy and Larry, bringing up the rear. The dancer reeked of whiskey, and her idea of getting dressed was pulling on a pair of short jeans under her T-shirt and slipping on a pair of pumps. So I told Larry to take her around the side door to my office, and that I'd be there in a minute. Dad looked concerned when he saw us coming, but when I explained what I was up to, he disappeared inside, looking for our target.

We set it up quickly, with a minimum of fuss. Larry put Cynthia Moore behind my office door, which was open just enough for her to peek one eye through to the foyer. I stood straight in front of the door, across the foyer so that she could see me, and my dad went and got Pete Germaine from where he was sitting at the back of the parlor and walked him past me, offering to make him a cup of his "special" coffee downstairs in the smoking lounge. As they passed, I pointed clandestinely, indicating the orderly as Dad stopped for a moment, studying the grandfather clock as if he saw something amiss with it, giving Cynthia Moore a good long look. When they were gone I headed for the office, only to find that the girl hadn't recognized Pete Germaine at all.

"He looks sorta like the guy," she said, once I'd closed the door. "But he's taller. And the guy who gave me the money was better lookin'. This guy's all right. But that guy was different. He was a real . . ."

Her words trailed off, and she stared at the window behind me, stepping past and looking out for a moment before turning and heading to the foyer, where she stood in the hall, watching a man who had just come in from the parking lot. I stepped up behind her, following her line of sight and trying to see what it was that had caught her interest until I finally said, "What's going on?"

To which she replied, "That's the guy."

Making me grimace as I whispered, "Come on . . . you said the money man was between twenty and thirty years old. This guy's gotta be sixty."

"I know," she said vaguely, her face betraying a deep concern that seemed to cut through the booze she'd drunk, sobering her enough to be confused. Finally she added, "He was that guy"—pointing at an older gentleman with grey hair and a beautiful smoke-colored suit—"only he was younger."

"That guy only younger?" I repeated.

She nodded.

The man who had caught her interest was leaning over the register table signing the guest book. "But you said he was a doctor," I reminded her in a whisper. "That other guy's an orderly in a nursing home. He's a kind of male nurse. Something like a doctor, sorta. Are you positive it's not him?"

She nodded, still studying the grey-haired man as she said, "It's that guy, only it's not," her eyes narrow, and her lips slightly parted as if she were breathing through her mouth.

When the man had finished signing the book I casually made my way over to the table, straightened out the stack of memorial cards lying next to the contribution box, glanced at his name, and returned. Cynthia Moore asked me who he was as soon as I got back, while behind her, in my office doorway, Larry Fizner watched in silence.

"His name's Teeg," I said, simply. "Dr. Leo Teeg." Then, after a pause, I asked Judy, "Can you take Cindy home?" When she nodded I said, "Good, 'cause Larry and I have got some talking to do."

FIVE
■■■■■■■■

A FUNERAL DAY is like starting over. When people come in to make the initial arrangements, there's often a feeling of relief in the room by the time we're through. Everyone fears the unknown, and when a person dies, those left behind feel all sorts of pressures to do the "right" thing, whether or not they know what the right thing is. Not only is there the pain of loss to deal with, there's also a social expectation dictating that the deceased receive a proper memorial. But the definition of proper is subjective, so people turn to the funeral director to make sure some vital detail isn't overlooked.

But once the arrangements are made, the pressure's off, leaving people to concentrate on doing whatever it is they need to do to get themselves through the next few days. Men and women who've been keeping the death vigil at the bedsides of their spouses come into my office with their children and unload. They cry, ramble, get irritable and suspicious; and with every concern I erase—"What about flowers?" "How much should I give the priest?" "Can I come a little early and be alone with her for a while?"—they come back just that much from that place

grief has driven them, that dark corner where they feel so alone. They initiate more of the conversation, make eye contact more often, and mention family anecdotes with their relatives about the deceased until that golden moment when they smile for the first time, sometimes in a bittersweet way, but a smile all the same. That instant is like the parting of the clouds, and it's then that the healing begins.

The first time the body's viewed in the casket is another bad spot, usually ending as a moment of anticlimax. There just aren't any questions left, nor is there hope. The person's dead, it can't be denied, nor can it be changed. The tears come, but even they are pointless in the face of a creeping sense of acceptance that shifts the focus of the wake away from the body. People start talking, and laughing, and soon the deceased is all but forgotten. Amazingly, it's not unusual for the same people who originally said that they dreaded coming to the funeral home to linger at the end, not wanting to leave because of the pleasure they've discovered in the company of their family.

But on the funeral day the body's back to front and center, with an interment ceremony specifically designed to remind those in attendance that this is it, the final act, the last time we're going to see this person among us. We've laughed and cried and shared our memories, but now it's time to say good-bye. So it's like starting all over again, with fresh grief, fresh tears, and, quite often, fresh anger. That same man or woman who thanked you the night before for making the deceased look so good, and who said that they would never forget all your kindnesses, can arrive on the funeral morning pissed off and surly, blaming you for their pain. The first time it happens to a young funeral director it's an awkward moment that makes you feel lousy. But in the end you learn that it's just another part of your job.

We're the undertakers dressed in black. And it comforts people to believe that our association with death makes us

cold. Whether it's true that our job hardens us emotionally or not, it makes it easier for the public to believe that it does because that way they can say anything they want to us, since that's why we're there: to absorb their discomfort, and perform one of life's most unpleasant tasks. That's why we're called undertakers . . . in the old days we were the only people who would undertake the job . . . and, I think, given the derivation of the word, we're perceived as taking something precious away from people, which goes a long way toward explaining why Mrs. Scholtz arrived on the morning of her husband's funeral loaded for bear. She was in such a bad mood that I was glad that I wasn't staying for the funeral.

At the Hawley Funeral Home, we try to keep the same people on the same funeral all the way through, meaning that whoever makes the arrangements takes out the funeral. But because of the timing of Chester Scholtz's death—with his body coming in on a Saturday and his funeral being on a Monday so that all we had was the weekend to work with— there was some running around that had to be done pronto. And since the running around is my job, Uncle Joe decided that he'd take the funeral out while I chased down the death certificate.

The rules on death certificates and burial permits go like this:

Most people die under a doctor's care. Which only makes sense since most people who die are elderly. A solid eighty percent of any funeral home's business comes from nursing homes and hospitals. When a person passes away who is under a doctor's care, that doctor is notified and asked if he or she will sign the death certificate. If the doctor was treating the person for an illness that could conceivably have caused this person's death, the doctor will say, "Okay, I'll sign," and the body will be released to the funeral home. If for some reason the doctor refuses to sign, or if the person who died was not under a doctor's care, or if there was any kind of violence involved in the death—such as an accident or a broken bone—the case is automatically referred to the

coroner, who will fill out the death certificate in his or her own sweet time.

You can get a burial permit by either presenting a completed death certificate to the registrar at the city hall in the district where the death took place, or by applying for a provisional burial permit, which means that you sign a form that says that you gave a death certificate to the responsible physician, who hasn't finished it quite yet. When you get a provisional you've got five days to come up with a signed death certificate before city hall starts bugging you about it. The only exception to these rules is in the case of cremations. With cremations, you have to have a signed death certificate before you can get a cremation permit because, unlike in the case of a burial, where, if worse came to worst, you could always exhume the body, in a cremation the body is destroyed, so it has to be examined by a doctor before the cremation can take place.

Since Chester Scholtz had died over the weekend, the doctor hadn't been available to sign the death certificate, and even though I had seen him at the viewing, I learned a long time ago that you never approach a doctor at the funeral home. So while Uncle Joe took the funeral out, I ran to Dr. Teeg's office, and then to city hall, planning to drop the burial permit off at the cemetery by noon.

Not surprisingly, Dr. Teeg's office was located in the physicians' wing of Southwest General Hospital, right across the street from the nursing home of which he was part owner. On the way over I wondered about Cynthia Moore, hoping that she hadn't been bothered by her "boyfriend" any more last night, and wishing that she would have allowed Judy Newhardt to stay with her. But she had been adamant, saying that she didn't need anybody looking out for her, and that she could take care of herself. She said that Taz—short for Trevor . . . go figure—was always spouting off like that, and that she knew how to get her own back: usually what she did was wait until he was so drunk he could barely walk, then she beat the hell out of him. The last time, she said, Taz ended

up falling down the stairs and breaking his wrist. Ain't love grand?

The only thing about missing the funeral that I regretted was that I wasn't going to get to hear Mrs. Scholtz's reaction when Larry Fizner approached her with the news that he was officially taking over her case. Since I was now his apprentice, she would need to hire him if she wanted to keep me; and if she wanted to hire him, she was going to have to sign a contract. My opinion of Mrs. Scholtz wasn't quite fully formed yet, and the image of her ransacking her husband's nursing home room before she appeared at the funeral home still bothered me. I still hadn't asked her about that, but I couldn't imagine any answer she might produce that would put my mind completely at ease.

Normally when I get a death certificate signed I just show up in a doctor's waiting room during his office hours, hand the certificate to his receptionist, sit down, and read a *People* magazine or whatever's in the rack. I almost never see the doctor, and for all I know it's the receptionist who fills the thing out. But this time I was going to request an audience, and I wasn't taking no for an answer. Dr. Teeg's office was on the hospital's sixth floor, and the waiting room was empty. The receptionist opened the little frosted glass window when I knocked and accepted the certificate, asking me to take a seat, which I was just about to do when I noticed a young man standing by some filing cabinets in the office behind her. He was very good-looking, around twenty years old, dressed in white, and reading a clipboard.

"Who's that?" I asked pleasantly, indicating the man with a nod of my head.

"My son," she answered with a faint smile.

Just then the door leading from the waiting room to the inner office opened, and Dr. Teeg stuck his head through, asking me if I'd like to step inside. With a handshake he led me to his private office and closed the door, offering me coffee and waving the certificate nonchalantly in his left hand as he spoke. He was a tall man, probably six

feet, in his early to mid-fifties, with thick silver-grey hair and very Slavic features. He was wearing dark slacks and a knee-length white lab coat with his name stitched across the front pocket. His office wall was covered with framed diplomas.

"Sit down, sit down," he said pleasantly after I had my coffee. "I saw you at the funeral home last night, didn't I?"

I introduced myself, and we awkwardly shook hands a second time across his cluttered desk. He pulled out a pen and clicked its top before scribbling out a few words. Then he signed the certificate and handed it back. I took it, wondering what I was supposed to do now. He'd asked me into the office, and now that our business was apparently completed, we hadn't even said six words to each other. I was about to try a few opening lines when he said, "So, you're investigating Chet Scholtz's death?"

"Who told you that?" I responded.

"Lydia Scholtz," he said, forcing me to explain about how I really didn't normally do this kind of thing, et cetera, et cetera, until he stopped me with an upraised hand and leaned forward in his seat, looking all concerned and taking off his glasses with a tight little movement that made him seem slightly threatening.

"Chet Scholtz was a friend of mine," he said, making me think that Chet Scholtz seemed to be everybody's friend. "I've known him for years, and when Lydia told me that she'd approached you with this notion of having you investigate things, I must confess that it made me quite concerned. Investigations can get messy, especially when they're conducted by amateurs . . . no offense intended. Now, normally I wouldn't pry, but I don't want to see her have any more trouble than she's already gone through."

"Well then, if avoiding trouble is such a big concern," I began, hoping to get things rolling, "why did you deliberately misdiagnose Mr. Scholtz's hip injury when he first applied for residency at your nursing home? It would seem

to me that something like that's an invitation for trouble. Or didn't you think anyone would ever bother to look at the X-rays you took?"

The doctor sighed and leaned back, glancing at the ceiling as he apparently chose his words.

"Misdiagnose is an awfully strong term," he began, his tone of voice implying that he was about to launch into a lecture he thought his audience might not be quite sharp enough to follow. "But since you've obviously started poking around in places you don't belong, let me just explain that not all illnesses are necessarily physical in origin . . ."

"Dr. Teeg," I interrupted, "if you're going to tell me that Chester Scholtz had a psychosomatic disorder, you may as well save it. He might have convinced the Manor Care's staff that he was experiencing hysterical symptoms, but you know as well as I do that they only believed it because that's what they had been told to expect. His best friend at the home was an orderly in his second year of a psychology master's program who was just dying to see real-life examples of the disorders he read about in class. Mr. Scholtz was simply giving his audience what they wanted; and since you were his personal medical advisor, I can't imagine who would be more logical as his source of clinical information than you."

A hint of color rose in the doctor's cheeks, but before he could express his growing anger, I added, in a tone of voice that was much more confident than I actually felt, "Dr. Teeg, excuse me if I get right down to it, but I know that Chester Scholtz went into your nursing home with a specific task in mind. That fact's been borne out over and over again everywhere I've gone. And since it was you who faked the original hospital reports that admitted him, it seems obvious to me that you must have known what his task was and agreed to help him perform it."

"I didn't need to fake anything," he replied with an untroubled smile. "You don't have to have a broken bone to live at the Manor Care . . ."

"No," I cut in sharply, "but you do need to have the money, which you know damn well Mr. Scholtz lacked."

"He was hardly destitute."

"True. But he didn't have the kind of funds he'd need to pay his bills according to your institution's cash on the barrel head policy. His wife's told me about their financial situation, and at best he could have expected to stay a year. Maybe less. But that's if he was actually paying anything for the privilege. It might be interesting to find out what his bills really amounted to during the months he was there. And it might be even more interesting to find out who signed the checks . . . that is, if there were any checks to sign."

"Just who do you think you are?" Dr. Teeg asked.

And I got pissed.

"Let's cut the crap, okay, Dr. Teeg?" I said, standing and slamming both my hands down on his desk as I leaned forward and glared at his impassive face. "I know that somebody in your nursing home was worth a ton of money to Chester Scholtz, and I also have proof that in order to get him closer to that person, you faked his diagnosis and had him admitted as an invalid. I don't know what kind of deal you two worked out, but I do know that the lady working at the reception desk in your office is also your wife."

"That's an amazing deduction." The doctor smirked.

And I said, "Her being your wife makes the young man with the clipboard your son, doesn't it?"

When Dr. Teeg didn't answer, I added, "He was identified," the triumph naked in my voice. "He was there when Mr. Scholtz died, and I have a witness to prove it!"

"That's impossible," Dr. Teeg protested.

But I wouldn't be put off.

"I might have two witnesses," I mused, "now that I think of it. I forgot the motel manager. Three . . . including the bar owner."

"I think that you had better start explaining yourself . . ." Dr. Teeg began.

But I wouldn't let him finish.

"The deal you had with Chester Scholtz got him killed, Dr. Teeg," I said, sharp and fast. "The truth about it is bound to come out, sooner or later, and neither your medical degree, nor your intentions will change that fact. So far this has remained a private matter. But the more I find out, the more I think that maybe I should just go to the police and be done with it."

"Fine," the doctor responded, still without getting up from his seat. "Why don't you just do that?"

And I shrugged, rustling the death certificate as I said, "Thanks for this," and turned to the door.

It was then that I noticed that the door wasn't completely closed, but open about an inch. Before I could take another step it swung toward me, and there, on the other side, stood the doctor's son, frowning, and looking at me with sharp, haunted eyes. From behind me I could hear the sound of leather creaking as Dr. Teeg stood up, and I was careful not to break the tension with any move or word of my own. Silently, the young man stepped into the office and closed the door. Then he looked at his father, and his father looked at him, until finally, after some nonverbal communication had passed between them, the doctor said, "Oh hell, Steven," slapping his hands down on his legs in exasperation and turning away.

Then the young man looked at me and asked, "How'd you find out?"

To which I replied, "You just told me," making the doctor, with his back still turned to us both, grunt.

There's something about furniture, desks in particular, that's empowering. Even at that moment, when he had just been forced to realize that his son was in what could potentially be serious trouble, the doctor still insisted on maintaining a sense of decorum. He sat down behind his desk and had his son and me occupy a pair of chairs in front of him. It was like a professional consultation, which probably made him feel slightly more at ease. From where I sat, facing the doctor with his son to my left, I was able to draw back in my seat and compare the two of them

in my field of vision. The familial resemblance was truly striking. Cynthia Moore had said it exactly right: the man was his father, only younger. It was almost spooky when you looked at the two of them that way. It was like one of those movie special effects where they age an actor from twenty to seventy in a couple of seconds. My father and I don't really resemble one another that much. I've got his overall body shape, but facially I resemble my mother more than I do him. Briefly I wondered what it would be like to see yourself, only older, every single time you looked at your dad the way Steven Teeg would, and I concluded that if I were in his situation, I'd work somewhere else.

Dr. Teeg had appointments scheduled that morning, so he couldn't afford to, as he put it, "waste too much time on this thing." He actually said that. And the reason he did, I think, is because he wanted to create the impression that, even if it did turn out that he had done what I said he did, that it wasn't really any big deal, and that we could work out a solution like civilized human beings before he went on to more important things—like healing the sick—since he was, after all, a man of medicine.

"Your appointments can wait," I said, just to make sure that he knew that, at least in my opinion, what we were doing right at that moment was going to turn out to be the most important part of his day. His son said nothing, studying his hands, which were folded in his lap so hard that the knuckles were white. And looking at him I had a hard time reconciling the reality of this reserved, cringing young man with the image I had developed in my head of the cold, calculating perpetrator who had climbed from that motel room, closing the window behind him with a dead man's white cane before slinking across the street to a girlie bar where he promised a go-go girl five thousand dollars to lie to the police and save his "cute little ass."

"So, is accusing people with half-baked scenarios in hopes of making them believe that you know more than you actually do your standard operating style?" Dr. Teeg

asked, studying my face with what seemed to be a degree of newfound interest.

"It's worked so far," I admitted, realizing that I'd done it at least three times in the last couple of days, and deciding that I was going to cut it out before I got myself in hot water by accusing the wrong person of the wrong thing.

"But my scenario wasn't half-baked," I added in my own defense. "I really do have a witness. It's just that she picked you out, Doctor, and not your son." Then I explained about Cynthia Moore's less-than-successful ID at the funeral home the previous evening, concluding that, "I didn't have any of this worked out before I came here this morning. But it all fell into place when I saw how much your son resembled his father. Standing in your waiting room it struck me that he was the most obvious candidate for the man at the motel."

"Why?" Steve Teeg asked without looking at me.

And I explained that it was reasonably simple.

"Chester Scholtz didn't really break his hip," I said. "And yet that's how he was diagnosed by your father before he went into the nursing home. On the morning she made her husband's funeral arrangements, Scholtz's own wife told me that she suspected that he had faked his symptoms in order to get into that nursing home as part of some plan he had come up with to make a lot of money fast, a theory that was later verified by a friend of Scholtz's whom he had hired to watch his back while he took fifty thousand dollars to the motel, where he intended to exchange it for the name of a person living in the Manor Care under an assumed identity."

I was keeping an eye on Dr. Teeg while I spoke, and when I said the words, "fifty thousand dollars," his eyebrows shot up on his forehead.

"What made me connect you to the motel," I continued, "was the nagging suspicion that, since your father agreed to lie about Mr. Scholtz's broken hip, he was somehow involved in whatever he was doing in the nursing home. But if your father knew the identity of whoever it was that

Chester Scholtz was hoping to find, then why wouldn't he just tell him, instead of making him go through all the trouble of pretending to be a cripple?"

"Good question," Dr. Teeg observed. "How did you answer it?"

"By realizing that Chester Scholtz lied to you, Doctor," I said. "It only makes sense. If you wouldn't tell him the name of the man he was hunting, then you surely wouldn't help him lie his way into your own nursing home so he could ferret it out for himself. If you had known what he intended to do in the Manor Care, you wouldn't have helped him get in. That much is logical, and it begs the question: Why would you do it?"

"I'm listening, Mr. Hawley," the doctor put in.

And I said, "You did it because you thought you were doing something else. Chester Scholtz deceived you. He told you some story about why he wanted to live in your nursing home that had nothing to do with discovering the name of any incognito resident, but that instead played heavily on your years of friendship. Am I right?"

He nodded, saying, "He was a very sick man with a very bad heart."

"Which is why you agreed to admit him?"

"Yes."

"And the broken hip?"

"His wife would never have agreed to let him go to a nursing home unless his condition was serious enough to warrant constant attention. She would insist on taking care of him herself, no matter what the consequences to her own health. That, and he didn't want her to wake up one morning with a dead man in her bed, were the reasons he gave me."

"And you believed him?"

"More or less."

"But you had your suspicions?"

"Of course. It's not often someone proposes deception as a way of getting into a nursing home. People usually want to get out."

"Very well," I conceded. "Which all serves to make my point. Chester Scholtz convinced you that he had some other motive for entering the nursing home under false pretenses. He was apparently confident that, once there, he would either recognize whoever it was he was looking for, or find some way of discovering his name. But he obviously came up short. So, he got a psychology student with the keys to the nursing supervisor's office, who was working on his floor as an orderly, to read him resident files by faking psychosomatic blindness. But that didn't work either. Finally, he arranged to meet someone in the motel, someone who was in a position to have access to the very sensitive information he wanted, information that a man like you, Dr. Teeg, would never reveal to anyone except, perhaps, the members of your own family."

I looked at the young man sitting next to me.

"Like, for instance, a son who's involved in the administrative end of your practice."

"So what happened to the money?" Dr. Teeg asked.

"That's something you should ask your son," I replied.

And the doctor said, "I am."

"Do you know who we're talking about here?" the younger Teeg asked, directing his question at me.

"What?" I said.

"The man Scholtz was looking for," he said, "do you know who he was?"

"That doesn't matter," his father cut in.

And Steven Teeg came alive with a flash of fire that made his eyes suddenly meet mine as his teeth gleamed a quick lick of white and his lip curled. "It does matter. It was Constantine Stenetti. Recognize the name?"

"No."

"Steven!"

"Who gives a shit about a guy like that?" Steven Teeg suddenly shouted, standing bolt upright and projecting his words in an indignant fury. "So what if I told him? I'm supposed to worry that something might happen to a guy like Stenetti? He's been living like a king for all these years

and the taxpayers have been picking up the bill, and I'm supposed to pass up a chance like that? For what? Why, he's nothing but a—"

"Steven!" his father roared, also rising to his feet.

"I'm not giving the money back!" Steven Teeg announced, his voice changing from defiant to imploring in one disturbing cry. "I worked for that money! I risked a lot for it! I earned it and it's mine!"

"You're giving it back," I said softly, "or I'm going to the police."

Both men stopped and looked at me in silence. Then we all sat back down and worked out the details.

Later I felt like a man in a dream. Driving to city hall with the signed death certificate, and then over to the cemetery with the burial permit, and then back to the funeral home, was one of the most hazardous things I've ever done in my life because I couldn't keep my mind on the road. I was completely distracted, completely full of myself and my success. I laughed aloud a couple of times and pounded the steering wheel. I shook my head, and studied every pay phone I passed, thinking that I should call Nat, or Mrs. Scholtz, or Larry Fizner, or somebody. But I wasn't exactly sure what I'd say, so I didn't call anyone. Instead, I worked it all through in my head again and again. And by the time I got home, at about one in the afternoon, I was able to sit down and write the following conclusion to the notes I had already put together about the case.

"The solution," I wrote, "looking back now with the benefit of hindsight, and a confession from the principal suspect, is simple enough. What happened, according to Steven Teeg, the son of Dr. Leo Teeg, the man who faked Chester Scholtz's medical records when he first entered the Manor Care Assisted Living Facility, was that Scholtz knew who he was looking for *before* he ever set foot inside the nursing home, or outside the shower where he supposedly broke his hip. He knew the name, Constantine Stenetti—what he needed to find out was the assumed name

his target had taken as his own. The genesis of the thing apparently goes like this:

"As Larry Fizner has already said, Scholtz spent a great many years working in a special branch of the county auditor's office responsible for studying the disposition of illegally acquired funds by known criminals. In this position, he was exposed to a lot of highly sensitive knowledge. When his eldest son, Terry Scholtz, lost his job, Chester decided that it was time to turn at least one piece of the knowledge he had acquired earlier in his life to his advantage. Accordingly, he set out on a search for the man, Constantine Stenetti, a search that led him to the Manor Care Assisted Living Facility, and the Cozy Inn Motel, where he died."

Can you imagine how I felt writing this? I mean, Christ, this wasn't some bullshit murder mystery I had seen on *TV*. It was real life . . . *my* real life. I'm not kidding, my hands were shaking as I tapped the keys on my word processor. I've always wanted to be a novelist. When I was in college I was a Lit major, and off and on I've tried my hand at putting stuff together. But it never worked out. So to be sitting there describing what I was describing was something like a culmination of ambitions. And it made me desperate for a drink . . .

A cold beer!

One lousy, wonderful, ice-cold beer!

I could just taste it.

And a cigarette.

A Camel filter . . . like I used to smoke . . . or a Lucky Strike . . . no filter . . . so strong you'd cop a buzz off it.

Nonaddicts—or "easies" in the lingo of the compulsive personality group therapy world because they find it so easy to leave shit alone—tend to think of alcoholics as drinking when they're under stress . . . which we do. But we also drink when we're feeling good, or bored, or overworked, or any other strong emotion, even if it's not so strong. But the strong ones, at least for me, are the hardest. And feeling really good is actually my most dangerous time.

I literally had to restrain myself from running downstairs to the luncheon room in the basement of the funeral home where I knew there were at least twenty full bottles of whiskey in the kitchen cabinet and three cases of cold beer in the walk-in refrigerator. Nat wouldn't be home until five-thirty, and I had almost three and a half hours to get through sober. Once she got home I knew the craving would pass—it always does. But until then, I threw myself into my notes like a man dangling over a precipice, hanging onto a rope.

"Steven Teeg first heard about Chester Scholtz from the nursing supervisor on his floor," I wrote, my fingers virtually vibrating on the keys. "He works for his dad as a kind of administrative assistant, which is another way of saying that he doesn't have any ambition or talent of his own so he sponges off his father for a living . . . maybe like me . . ."

(Strike those last three words . . . I didn't mean to include them. Thank God for the delete button.)

"The nurse said that one of the new residents was asking strange questions about the people around him. Questions like, was there anybody living there who never got any visitors at all, or who might answer to a nickname . . . like maybe Stiv, or Stav, or Shiv, for example? After talking to the orderly Pete Germaine, who admitted to his early-morning forays into the nursing home's computer, Steven Teeg approached Mr. Scholtz, felt him out, and concluded that there was an accommodation that the two of them could reach. Apparently, Scholtz had known that Constantine Stenetti had turned government's evidence in a very well-publicized mob trial in New York City quite a few years ago.

"I had been under the impression, as was Larry Fizner, I believe, that whoever Scholtz was looking for was hiding with his own funds. The F.B.I. witness-protection program angle on this changed the entire complexion of Scholtz's motives, leading me to the inevitable understanding that, since the government already knew where this man was

hiding, and was in fact paying his bills, that the only place Scholtz could hope to trade his identity for money was with the underworld. Meaning that since Scholtz died before he could make his trade, innocent or not, Mr. Stenetti's life had been spared, since if the mob was willing to pay Scholtz enough to make all his efforts worthwhile, then they surely had serious plans for their pigeon once they knew where and who he was.

"But how had Scholtz known that Stenetti lived at the Manor Care?

"I don't know. Maybe Dr. Teeg slipped and said something like, 'We have somebody important here, but I'm not allowed to tell you who it is,' though he denies ever doing so. Or maybe it was through what he had seen of the company's books when he had done the doctor's taxes. I'll probably never know the details, and actually they don't really matter. What does matter is that Scholtz went into the Manor Care confident that the man he was looking for was on the premises, and that all he had to do was figure out who he was . . ."

I stopped.

Leaned back.

And sighed.

What about the paper with the numbers written on it that I'd found hidden in Scholtz's bathroom wall? I thought. What about that? Or the details of Scholtz's exchange? How was he going to contact whoever he was going to sell this name to after he had it . . . and when would the transaction take place? And who was Constantine Stenetti? I don't mean who was he as a person that someone should seek revenge on him after all these years, but which person in the nursing home was he? Steven Teeg hadn't told me that. He'd only told me Stenetti's real name, which Chester Scholtz had known all along. Actually, when you came down to it, even though Steven Teeg had admitted to meeting Scholtz and taking his money, I had no real proof that the kid even possessed the information he told Scholtz he did. It may have been a scam from the beginning, and

I hadn't even thought to ask him while I had the chance.

Suddenly, I was depressed. It just came over me, like a wave. It was like somebody let the air out of me, and right there, in my squeaky office chair, I settled back and stared at the blue computer screen as if the words written on it suddenly didn't make any difference at all. I saved my work on the hard disk and turned off the machine. Then I sat in my chair and looked out the window until the downstairs doorbell rang, and Mrs. Scholtz stepped in, looking to pick up some of the flowers left over after her husband's funeral. She had her kids with her, so I arranged the family in front of my desk, unconsciously imitating Dr. Teeg and his use of power furniture.

Mrs. Scholtz had calmed down considerably from her bad mood of the morning, so her smooth, pretty face seemed relaxed, the large hazel eyes somehow more peaceful than I had seen them in the short time I had known her. Sharon, the youngest child, had a face that was sharp and angular, with a thin mouth and very intense eyes that locked on me and stayed there, as if waiting for me to twitch in some secretly significant way. Terry Scholtz, the favored son from Detroit whom I had never formally met since he had only made it in for the funeral and had missed the viewings completely—no one ever explained why—was the image of his father: short, stocky, with closely cut dark hair and a bulldog look to the forward thrust of his head that made him seem to be always leaning in at you, as if he were hanging on your every word. He wanted to know about the funeral bill: when it would come, and how much it would be. Sharon didn't say a word. And Mrs. Scholtz wanted me to tell her kids everything I knew about the death of their father.

When I was done, the room was silent. I had laid it all out, holding nothing back, and, at the end, I produced from my desk drawer an envelope containing fifty thousand dollars in cash. (Steven Teeg's father had loaned him the twenty-five hundred he had given Cynthia Moore as payment for her lying to the police.) Mrs. Scholtz took it, examining a couple of the bills before she looked up at

me and said, "You actually did it," glancing back down at the money for a moment and then at her son.

"Yes, ma'am," I said. "But I think it's important for you to understand that, technically, Mr. Teeg committed no crime in that motel room."

"What do you mean, *no crime*?" Terry Scholtz piped up, thrusting his already prominent head toward me so hard I thought he'd topple out of his chair. "My father dropped dead because of this . . . this . . . informant!"

I'd been expecting this, although not from Terry, more from his sister Sharon, which was unfair on my part since I had only met her for a moment and was functioning on nothing more substantial than my first impression of her as being a tough customer. But I'd been expecting it, which was maybe why I'd gotten so depressed upstairs: I knew I'd have to say what I was about to say. And I was dreading it.

"The truth of the matter is," I began, addressing myself to Mrs. Scholtz, "that it was your husband who broke the law."

"What?" Terry Scholtz bellowed, rising to his feet.

"Terrence!" his mother snapped. "Sit down and shut up!" Which, like a little boy, he did.

"I'm afraid it's true," I continued. "Steven Teeg swears that he never touched your husband. And his father has signed a death certificate attributing the cause of death to a myocardial infarction stemming from a long history of arteriosclerotic heart disease, for which he has ample documentation from Mr. Scholtz's previous hospital stays. Mr. Scholtz's body was examined by the doctors in the emergency room at the hospital and found to be free of any marks of violence. So, though we may all feel that his heart attack was precipitated by something Mr. Teeg may have said or done, there's absolutely no way of proving it. All we can say for certain is that Mr. Scholtz died of natural causes while in the act of committing a crime, which is the identification of a ward of the federal government for the purpose of extortion. His plan was to sell the man he had

identified in the nursing home to people who were willing to pay a great deal for their revenge."

I went on to explain, since I had everyone's undivided attention, that Steven Teeg had described the scene at the motel to me in detail. His contention was that he had not gone there to accept the money, but to explain to Mr. Scholtz that he had changed his mind and was backing out of the deal. According to him, it was that information that set the old man off.

"He claims that he tried to explain that, after thinking it over, he had decided that he just couldn't have the death of another human being on his conscience," I said. "And no matter how much he wanted the money, the deal was off. It was at that point, he says, that Mr. Scholtz lost his temper and attacked him. To Mr. Teeg's horror, he says, it was just as Mr. Scholtz was coming at him that his face changed color and he lurched forward, landing dead on the floor. Teeg says that he admits to taking the money, but claims that it was an absolutely spontaneous reaction, and that he hadn't planned it at all. It was just that he knew there was fifty thousand dollars in cash in Mr. Scholtz's pockets, and he just couldn't leave it behind. So he took it, and, because he had been waiting in the motel room and had seen Mr. Scholtz arrive with another man in a yellow Dodge van, which was still waiting for him in the parking lot, he did all the things I've already described, hoping to cover his crime."

He chose the girlie bar on the spur of the moment, I explained as a kind of review, figuring that if he used a stripper, no one would ever connect him to what had happened in the motel because it would look like whoever had set things up hadn't known that Scholtz was pretending to be blind. Anyone associated with the nursing home where he lived would be familiar with his physical limitations, and sending a stripper would automatically imply that whoever had done it couldn't be associated with the Manor Care's staff. Also, since Scholtz had made a deal to sell the name he bought in the motel to some very dangerous people,

Teeg wanted those people to know that the deal was off as quickly as he could. Since he didn't know how to contact them himself, he called the *Plain Dealer* with the story of Scholtz's ignominious death as a kind of announcement intended to inform whoever might have been waiting that Scholtz wasn't coming.

"Our problem is that, though Mr. Teeg confessed all this to me, we don't have a shred of physical evidence to prove any of it," I concluded. "So that's why I felt it was best if we made a deal."

"What kind of deal?" Mrs. Scholtz asked.

Making me set my jaw as I said, "Steven Teeg agreed to return your money in exchange for my promise that you wouldn't start any legal proceedings against him."

"But you had no right to make a deal like that!" Terry Scholtz protested.

His mother raised her hand to silence him, asking me why she should honor such an arrangement.

"Because," I explained, "if you did take him to court, in the end things would boil down to his word against, well, no one's. He could simply say that Mr. Scholtz gave him the money, and that nothing else happened. . . ."

"But the dancer! What about her?" Terry Scholtz interrupted.

"He'll say she's lying," I said. "What jury's going to take her word over the word of a doctor's son? He'll just say Scholtz asked him to send over a girl and he agreed. Or, at worst, he'll say it was all part of their arrangement, and that when he left the room Scholtz was still alive. Who knows what he'll say, but you can bet that the lawyer his father hires for him will think of something. And, you'll probably lose the money again."

"What?" Mrs. Scholtz said, apparently shocked.

I nodded.

"Who knows how much it would cost to defend yourself against whatever countersuit Dr. Teeg and his son might decide to bring against you?"

"They might sue us?" Sharon asked.

"It's entirely possible," I responded, sadly. "This is a very subtle situation. The only hard facts we've got are that Mr. Scholtz definitely had a serious heart condition that ended up killing him, and you definitely got the money he lost back. Actually, since it was returned in cash, there's nothing to prove that you ever lost it. So the pool's muddy no matter how you look at it. I made the deal I did with the Teegs because I thought it was the simplest solution. They were concerned about keeping the doctor's reputation clean, and I was concerned with recovering your cash. I seriously recommend leaving it there, though I can't force you to do a thing. . . ."

"You're goddamn right you can't!" Terry Scholtz announced, slamming his fist into his palm and looking at me with murder in his eyes. "When I get my hands on the guy who left my father dead on that floor . . . !"

But Mrs. Scholtz's quiet words cut through her son's more voluminous ones and demanded all my attention.

"I've one question, Mr. Hawley," she said, looking straight at me from where she sat. "Why did the boy do it?"

And I was forced to admit that I didn't know. I had asked Steven Teeg that very question, and he had insisted that he had no deep motive beyond that obvious fact that he had seen an opportunity to make twice as much money in twenty minutes than he could make working full-time for a whole year. His intentions were never malicious; it was just too good a deal to pass up. But his conscience had gotten the better of him, he said, and things had gone sour. I didn't know if I believed him about that part or not . . . probably not . . . not completely. But I had to admit that I could at least understand how someone would be tempted.

"Easy money's a powerful motivator," I concluded.

And Mrs. Scholtz nodded, snapping the clasp on her purse as she rose to her feet. "Very well," she said. "It would seem best if we said nothing more about this matter."

"Mom!" Terry Scholtz shouted.

Mrs. Scholtz silenced him with a look. When she returned her eyes to me, they were cold, and curious.

"And what about you, Mr. Hawley?" she asked. "Since I haven't signed any contracts with Mr. Fizner as of yet, I feel this account should be settled between the two of us."

I rose and stepped around my desk, announcing that our conversation had come to an end and saying, without trying to sound sanctimonious, that I considered my fee paid. "I really didn't do anything but ask a few questions," I said, taking Mrs. Scholtz's hand. "I'm just glad everything worked out. I'd particularly like to thank you for agreeing to the terms of the deal I made with the doctor. That's going to be very helpful to me personally since my job brings me in contact with the medical community around here almost every day."

We spoke for a few more minutes, picked flowers in the service area, and said our farewells. Mrs. Scholtz kissed me, Sharon shook my hand, and Terry glared a lot. Then they went away, and . . .

I felt great again.

So great that I called Larry Fizner and told him all about it. Then I went upstairs and got out my guitar. Like I said before, in high school I played in the world's worst rock band, and to this day I still have my guitar, a white Gibson S.G., just like Tonni Iommi used to play when Black Sabbath was in its heavy metal heyday. I keep it in a walk-in closet we've got in the bedroom, all hooked up to a little amplifier and my series of effects pedals: phase shifter, wah-wah pedal, fuzz box, and some other wiring I did myself. For the next hour I cranked up the volume and played every riff I knew, bending strings, creating feedback, and generally blowing my brains out behind the closed closet door. When I had gotten it out of my system, I got in the hot tub on the patio off the living room, waiting for Nat, and chilling a bottle of sparkling grape juice in an ice bucket so that when she walked in the patio door was open, the tub was steaming, and James

Taylor was singing softly on the stereo. It was a long, sweet night . . .

It wasn't until morning that I got the call that Steven Teeg was dead.

SIX

■■■■■■■

I PULLED INTO the morgue's parking lot at almost exactly nine on the morning of Tuesday, August 18th. A thin rain was falling that did nothing to break the terrible heat that had been hanging over the city for so long, but that rose off the pavement instead as an oily steam. I didn't want to be there. I didn't want to go on. I had cried when the call came that Steven Teeg had been found dead, my tears as hot as the rain on my face, and my heart chilled with the certainty that he had died because of something I had done. Nat argued that I didn't have the least bit of evidence that there was any connection between the young man's death and what I had discovered about him. But the coincidence was too great, and the connection far too plain.

It was Larry Fizner who called to tell me about Teeg. He had called at seven in the morning, while Nat sat at the kitchen table reading the funnies and I was in the shower. He was hardly able to keep his voice steady as he described how and where Steven Teeg had been found, finishing by saying that he would meet me near the morgue, but that he wouldn't accompany me inside because of a little unpleasantness he had experienced with a couple of the

people behind the desk down there . . . well, specifically a couple of the county's investigators . . . and . . . well . . . technically he was barred from entering the building. I was standing in the bedroom, listening to him on a portable phone, and suddenly I burst out crying. It wasn't a sobbing kind of cry, no strangled exclamations of "Oh my God!" or anything like that. But I could see myself in the vanity's mirror and the tears were rolling down my face.

Nat tried to comfort me, but there was nothing she could say to change the way I felt. The guilt came like a wave, nearly knocking the wind out of me and making my hands shake. I sat down on the edge of the bed—Larry Fizner yammering away unattended in my ear—seeing the tall, strikingly handsome image of Steven Teeg in my mind as I groped for some indication of how things could have gone so tragically wrong. Finally, I said that no, I wouldn't meet anybody at the morgue, hanging up the phone and folding my arms around my wife so that when the phone started ringing again, I had to disentangle myself to answer it. It was Larry Fizner. And I repeated my answer, more stridently this time, and hung up.

When he called the third time he said, "For Christ's sake, just hear me out!" And I told him that I wasn't interested in hearing him out, in, or any other way. I wasn't interested at all. I should never have gotten involved with the whole mess in the first place, and I was sorry I had ever heard the name Chester Scholtz. I told him, in a bustle of words that began running into one another as my regret and shock evolved into anger and indignation, that originally I had thought that being an investigator would be fun.

There!

I had said it:

I thought it would be fun to play detective. But it wasn't fun . . . it was a serious business that could take really rotten turns for absolutely no apparent reason, and, because of my foolishness a man had died . . .

"But that's exactly my point!" Larry cut in. "Don't you see what this kid's turning up croaked means?"

"No," I responded, Nat's head on my shoulder so she could hear what Larry was saying as she sat on the bed next to me. "And I don't want to know. I'm out of it, retired, sorry I ever stuck my nose in . . . how can I say it so you'll understand? I don't want to play anymore! I don't ever want to see your lousy face again . . . I don't ever want anyone to ask me another question . . . and I don't ever want my name in the paper. I should have known better than to ever try doing anything on my own. And I've learned my lesson. I've had it! I—"

"Flushed them out!" Larry Fizner shouted, making me wince and pull the phone away. As I glanced at it, I noticed that Nat was studying my face rather carefully, but I could hear Larry's voice buzzing through the receiver excitedly and I turned my attention back to him.

The meat of it was that he thought that Steven Teeg's death proved that it wasn't over . . . the intrigue . . . the whatever you wanted to call it.

"There's still a shot at the money!" he practically shouted. And I asked him, very carefully, through tight, angry lips, to explain just what he meant. "I mean that somebody out there took a big risk and squeezed the Teeg kid until he spilled his guts," he said. "There's only one reason anyone would take a risk like that, and that's to keep the appointment Chet Scholtz made with the mob!"

I wanted to ask him then and there what Constantine Stenetti had done that would mark him with a sentence of death that would follow him for so many years. But I resisted because I realized that by so doing I would be falling right back into the frame of mind that had gotten me into the shit in the first place.

"The people who want Stenetti won't care who hands him over," Fizner continued, his words coming quickly as his excitement mounted with the cadence of his own voice. "Since Teeg knew who Stenetti was pretending to be, and he turned up dead, that obviously means that somebody still wants to keep the deal Chet made with his contacts. Somebody squeezed the kid for that name. . . ."

"How do you know somebody didn't kill him to keep him quiet?" I asked. "How do you know that somebody's not trying to stop this whole thing, and that whoever is stupid enough to fuck with it is going to wind up in the river?"

"Ain't you listening?" Fizner returned. "I just said that somebody squeezed him. I ain't makin' it up. I got it from a reliable source."

"They said that? Downtown?"

"They're postin' him this morning, but it was obvious from the marks they left that somebody worked him over pretty good. And whoever it was, they knew what they were doing."

"That son of a bitch!" I exclaimed.

"What?" Fizner shot back.

"Terry Scholtz . . . Chester's son! It's gotta be him. I knew he was a creep as soon as I saw his haircut."

"What are you talking about?"

"He said he wanted to get his hands on the man who left his dad dead on the floor. Well, obviously he did. I told him exactly who he needed to go after when I gave his mother back her money, and now he's going to cash in on my mistake. It was him, I know it was. Listen, I'm calling the police . . ."

"Hey!" Larry insisted, "Now just wait one minute."

He then proceeded to explain that I couldn't just call the police and tell them that so-and-so had committed first-degree murder because I didn't like his haircut. Plus, if I did call the cops, then they'd take it all away. Everything. And we'd lose whatever chance we might have had at the money.

"But I don't care about the money!" I cut in.

And Larry screamed, "Well I do! Don't you know how much we're talkin' about here? Don't you have any idea how much it would take to pull Chet across that fine white line from working for the good guys to making deals with the same bulldogs he spent his whole life putting in jail?"

"I don't care," I said, self-righteously.

"Do you care that somebody else is going to get it?" Fizner asked. "Huh? Do you care that, because of you, not only aren't we ever going to see any of it, but that somebody with a bad haircut is going to get it all . . . and that he killed the Teeg kid to do it? You and me both know Steve Teeg didn't kill Chet Scholtz. Chet died because he had a bad ticker. Steve Teeg died because somebody wanted what was in his head. And now that they've got it, Constantine Stenetti's next."

My mouth dropped as his points connected. He was right. Okay, yes, maybe something I had done had led to Steven Teeg's death. But if he had indeed betrayed his secret, then yet another man was going to die. I couldn't do anything now to prevent Teeg's death, but I could conceivably do something to prevent Stenetti's.

"But we don't know for sure he told them what they wanted to know!" I protested.

And Larry Fizner said, "Why wouldn't he? To keep from getting hurt, why would he hold out?"

So I was skunked. I hung up after agreeing to meet the old detective at the morgue, finding Nat still looking at me with that "cat that ate the canary" expression that made me say, "What else can I do?" as soon as I saw it. "I'm stuck any way I go."

"Are you?" she asked.

And I answered that, at least as far as I could tell, I was.

She got up and headed back to the kitchen with me following, still damp from the shower, a towel wrapped around my waist. She sat down at the table and resumed her reading of the funnies, ignoring my entreaties until she finally sighed, moved a strand of hair out of her eyes, and said, "Bill, stop trying to convince me. Okay? And don't kid yourself. You're not going anywhere because you have to; you're going because you want to. That's the only real reason anybody does anything, in the end: because they want to. Okay?"

I told her that she was wrong, and her face darkened, just a little, so that I realized that she was working very hard

at restraining herself. Just as when I had been a smoker, she was obviously watching me do something stupid while refusing to butt in because, as she had said a thousand times before, she loved me enough to let me live my own life without trying to change me.

"Come on," I said. "Tell me. I'm asking you."

"Okay," she said, placing her elbows on the table as she looked right at me. "No one's in any danger at all. All right? Not you, or Larry Fizner, or this Stenetti person, whoever he is that you should care what happens to him. Do you understand? Nobody's in any kind of danger at all."

"But you just heard . . ." I protested.

And she stopped me by saying, "I just heard that Larry Fizner thinks someone is going to betray Mr. Stenetti to the 'mob.' Okay. Let's say that it's true, and that someone is in fact going to do just that. You said yourself that Mr. Stenetti is a ward of the government, and that Dr. Teeg knows it."

"Yeah. So?"

"So, if there's any real danger, the government will move him somewhere else."

I stopped just as I was about to protest, and the import of her words cut into my understanding.

"Larry Fizner wants that money he thinks is out there so badly that he'll say and do anything to get it," she observed, almost casually. "That's his motivation: he wants the money and he's willing to do the same thing Chester Scholtz was going to do to get it. Your motivation is that you want to impress your dad. You said so on the phone just five minutes ago."

"No I didn't."

" 'I should have known better than to ever try doing any-thing on my own,' quote, unquote. You said it in so many words. You've been dealing with this image of yourself as being dependent on your dad for so long that you don't even realize when you come right out and say it. It's just a part of your world, Bill. So, okay: go do something on your

own. Go save Mr. Stenetti. That's what you've wanted to do all along. You want to be important on your own terms, independent and alone. You want someone to say, 'Oh, Mr. Hawley, you're so brave and strong.' Being the most important person in the world to me isn't enough for you. You need a testimonial . . . a medal . . . a big feature piece in the newspaper so people can point to you and say, 'There he is. That's the Bill Hawley I read about.'

"For a while booze served that purpose. When you drank you became the center of the universe . . . a legend in your own mind. Your inhibitions went away and all those repressed emotions came bubbling to the surface for a while. Then you stopped drinking and those feelings had no way to get out anymore. So now you've found a new drug. Okay, I'll accept it. But don't kid yourself about it, okay, Bill? And don't expect me to act dumb too. You need this . . . or you need something. It's the way you're drawn. Until you do something significant enough to convince yourself that you're a grown-up, mature, adult male human being, self-sufficient and capable of getting along without your father, you're going to keep bouncing from one addiction to another. You're going to go on searching for that special something that'll make you feel like a man. Regardless of anything I ever say, you'll always feel like something's missing. So if this is what makes you happy, then do it. Just don't lie about it; not to me, or to yourself. Okay?"

"But it doesn't make me happy," I observed. "I'm miserable, and I'm scared."

"Than maybe, deep down, being miserable and scared is what you think being a man is all about."

I didn't respond to that, and, as she looked back down at the cartoons spread out on the table before her, Nat's long dark hair fell forward, hiding her face as she said, "If you're going to save the world before noon, you'd better start getting dressed."

And I did.

● ● ●

The county morgue is located in a building on the campus of a medical college, and looks like an elementary school built in the fifties. It's made of that pale beige brick with the darker ones scattered here and there that they went in for back then. It's three stories high, has those wonderful windows where the bottom opens in at you, hinged along the sill with a single latch in the center the size of a piece of tall-ship rigging, and the upper one opens out so the rain can run off. There's a loading dock around back with a steel bay door and a city-painted sign that reads, POLICE, AMBULANCE, AND FUNERAL PERSONAL ONLY—and yes, it's supposed to be, PERSONNEL, but they got it wrong and nobody's ever fixed it. It's just like the sign on the laundry room door that reads, LAUNDY. Nobody's ever fixed that either.

Inside, the concrete floor's painted a deep maroon, there's a huge, stainless steel scale right in front of the bay door with a glass face that's calibrated up to fourteen hundred pounds, and every door has that frosted glass in it through which you can see the fuzzy shapes of ghosts moving through the mist. It stinks inside. Even on the upper floors where the business offices are, it stinks. And after nearly fifty years of corpses, I think that if you knocked the place down and hauled it away, every single brick would stink individually.

Let me tell you about the first time I ever saw the morgue:

My first job was carrying bodies for a private ambulance company called Northern Coast Medical Services, or just Northern Ambulance for short. I was sixteen, and my job was to help move bodies from wherever the person died—the hospital, nursing home, or wherever—to whatever funeral home was taking care of the arrangements. Not all funeral homes make their own removals, and most guys would rather pay the forty bucks than go out in the middle of the night anyway . . . which is when people die. It's a fact. Don't ask me why, but babies are born in the

morning, and people die in the middle of the night. It's a statistic. Look it up.

Anyway . . .

My first call came at one o'clock in the morning, and it took me to the morgue. The guy I was with was named Henry, and we went down to pick up the victim of a motorcycle accident and take him over to a funeral home on the east side. I was pretty nervous, and stayed more or less quiet during the ride downtown. Henry tried to distract me because he knew that I was scared, but nothing he could say made me relax, so he just gave up.

The morgue, back then anyway, still had those classic cooler drawers like you see in old detective movies. They were arranged floor to ceiling on two walls, and their doors swung on big black hinges with bolts set into them that were about the size of bottle caps. Inside, on stainless steel trays, the bodies lay covered with bloody sheets. When you opened a door, the smell had a metallic twang to it that combined the odor of raw meat and old blood in such a way as to make it all but unforgettable. We took care of our paperwork, got the number for our drawer—which turned out to be at about shin level—and dropped the cot so that it rested on the floor. Then we opened up the cooler door, and slid out the tray.

The man we had come to pick up had been riding his motorcycle on the freeway and had sideswiped a guardrail. Added to all the other traumas his body had been subjected to, his right leg had struck the rail right at a point where the steel had been bent back around by a previous accident to form a six-foot sharp edge. That leg had been cleanly severed at the hip . . . which I didn't know. The guys at the morgue had posted him (vernacular for postmortem, or autopsy), sewn him back up, more or less, and placed him in the drawer with his severed leg lying in its proper place. Then they had covered him with a sheet.

Because this was my first body, Henry wanted to go as easy on me as he could. So he told me not to worry about the sheet, or all the blood that had soaked through it, but

instead just to grab the corpse's ankles. He would take the shoulders, which was the heavy end, and then, on three, we would simply heave him over from the tray to the cot. I didn't know how much a corpse weighed, all I had ever heard about the subject was the term, "deadweight," so I decided that I had better put some back muscle into it. So I grabbed the ankles, which were ice-cold, I remember, and as hard as bone and, when Henry counted three, gave them one good, solid yank that had all one hundred and ninety of my teenaged pounds behind it.

I think I might have shouted. I don't really remember. What I do remember is that leg flying out of the drawer and landing with a wet slap on the concrete while I stumbled back and watched. Henry about laughed himself sick, as did one of the morgue guys who had come running in response to my shriek. And I, flustered, sweating, and with my heart racing like a hummingbird's, said, "Are they all gonna be like this?" which inspired another round of laughter and earned me a beer out of the icebox clandestinely stocked in the night janitor's office. For months I had to watch people bug their eyes at me and whine, "Are they all gonna be like this?" but I was such a good sport about it that eventually most everybody accepted me as one of the guys.

Larry Fizner was standing at a vendor's cart on the sidewalk out front, and he waved as I drove by. "Just get as much dope as you can," were my instructions. And, "They won't tell me nothing, but you . . . shit! You're practically one of the family down there," had been all the explanation for my mission he had felt it necessary to provide. When I asked how he knew I was "practically one of the family," he had responded that even he had heard of "Wild Bill Hawley." After all, the community of folks who worked the morgue was relatively small, and Larry had been around a long time.

I passed him where he stood examining a hot dog he had just purchased for breakfast beneath the aluminum pushcart's red and yellow striped umbrella, and parked the funeral home's Caravan around back. The morgue's

back door, near the loading dock, was open, as usual, and I went inside, finding about ten guys standing around the scale, looking at the body of a four-hundred-and-twenty-six pound Hispanic woman lying naked on the steel with blood running out of her nose. The men were all talking at once, so their voices formed what amounted to a babble as I walked by, and the only words I caught clearly were "hernia" and "boobs."

At the receiving desk I rang a bell, and Rusty Simmons appeared from around a corner. Rusty's about sixty years old, balding, black, and so good-natured that he's borne the brunt of some of the most tasteless jokes ever pulled at the coroner's office. His nickname's Rusty because his hair, before it turned grey and started falling out, had been red. He's been my best friend on the staff for years, and he smiled wide when he saw me. Then he looked a little confused, saying that he didn't remember seeing the Hawley Funeral Home's name written next to any of the people in his book. I told him that I wasn't there to pick up a body, asking him if he had a couple of minutes to spare. He nodded, getting serious right away, and indicating that I should follow him down to his "office," which was a utilities closet that he had claimed for himself by taking apart a steel office desk and reassembling it inside. There was just enough room in there for the desk and two chairs. But Rusty called it home.

He closed the door and offered me coffee from the pot he had sitting on a hot plate. After I declined, we sat down and I said, "Rusty, I came for a look at the book." To which he replied that the book was outside. I explained that the book I wanted to see was the one he kept in private.

"Why you wanna see that?" he asked.

And I said that I was investigating a murder, which pissed him off. But before we could reenact that tired routine about private investigators being such and such, I said, "Rusty, man, listen here. I need this. It's gone way beyond something I wanna do, and it's got to the point that I need it. No shit. It's important."

He looked at me, his big dark eyes narrowing to slits and his full lips pressed together in thought. Finally he sighed and said, "Nice boy like you," shaking his head disconsolately and pulling open the lower left-hand drawer of his desk.

Rusty's book is the stuff of legend, and though it isn't supposed to even exist, everybody at the coroner's office is proud of it, in a strange, possessive sort of way. Rusty's a collector, which is a phenomena strangely at home at the morgue. He's not the only one I've ever met . . . but he's surely the best. And he's been at it a long, long time.

There are three distinct types of dead bodies that go through the morgue on an average day. There's the natural causes death, which isn't very exciting. Then there's the accidental death, which can be spectacular, but that didn't interest Rusty. Then there's the homicide, which is where his fascination found its focus. He was a murder junkie, and he had amassed the most complete index of violent deeds anywhere in the city. What he did was Xerox the coroner's reports on anyone that was brought in as a homicide, including, when he could get them, copies of the on-site photographs taken by the investigators. "The Book," which is how his collection was known, was actually a whole series of scrapbooks he had amassed over the years. And the one in his lower desk drawer was just the most recent volume he had yet to fill. At first, Rusty's book was a source of irritation to the higher-ups, but eventually it became like a natural resource, and though it was never officially sanctioned, the investigators started using it like a reference guide whenever they needed to look something up. As it turned out, good old, uneducated Rusty, whose job it was to stand behind the receiving desk and sign out bodies, had a God-given talent for organizing and indexing. And the records he kept were the most complete, user-friendly accounts of Cleveland's murderous past ever assembled.

The book hit the desk with a whump. It was an enormous volume, all black vinyl stuffed with paper that spilled out the sides and was bound together with a series of steel

rings and tabs. Moistening his thumb, he opened it and lovingly turned the pages until he found the spot where Steven Teeg's report was listed, running his eyes briefly over what little there was recorded before he turned the book around to face me.

"He ain't been cut yet," he commented, as if explaining the thinness of Teeg's report. "So all I gots is the report about when they found him last night."

I nodded, losing myself in the material before me and turning the page to find a series of snapshots pasted in a row.

"And these?" I asked, wondering how Rusty had gotten ahold of pictures so quickly.

"One a the boys helps me out now and then," he replied. "Takes two setsa Polaroids so I get nice, clean shots for my book."

I nodded, concentrating on what I was seeing.

"So, you gonna tell me what's so important about you seein' this?" Rusty asked after a moment. "Or you gonna stay mysterious and make me die of curiosity?"

"Rusty," I said, looking up from the book and examining his friendly, familiar face, "you got a smoke on ya?"

He nodded, saying, "I thought you quit."

And I replied, "I did. Now, you gonna gimme a cigarette or what?"

As he produced his pack of Kools and expertly shook it so that just one cigarette popped out, he frowned, saying, "First the book, and then a smoke. Man, I feel like I'm presiding over the corruption of the innocent."

He finished this statement just as I was leaning my head forward to touch the end of my cigarette to his lighter's flame, and that drag, which was the first smoke I had tasted in almost a year, hit me so hard that it made me choke. He slapped me on the back, asking if I was all right. And, smiling as I removed my glasses to wipe my eyes, I said that I honestly wasn't sure.

Later, in a campus coffee shop down the street, I told Larry Fizner what I had found.

"Teeg was found in his apartment on the west side," I said, reading off a sheet of notes I'd taken. "Dead on his living room floor. And judging by the condition of the room, he did quite a bit of thrashing around before he died."

I lit a cigarette out of the pack of Camels I'd bought from the vending machine in the corner.

"How do you know?" Larry asked.

And I looked at him, squinting one eye through the smoke curling up the side of my face. That first Kool I had bummed from Rusty had been a B.F.D., tasting strong, making my head swim, burning my lungs. But already, only an hour later, I was right back in again, a smoker, like I had never quit.

"What do ya mean, how do I know?" I shot back. "You're the one who told me he'd been 'squeezed.' Dispatcher who owed you a favor let you know. Cost you twenty bucks. Or don't you remember saying that?"

"I remember. But I want to know what specific evidence the coroner's got in case the details might tell us something."

"Oh. Well, the examiner on the scene noted a couple of things. First, Teeg's hands were tied behind his back with a length of that plastic Sure-Grip shit cops use as handcuffs now, and he'd squeezed his fists together so hard his fingernails had cut his palms. Secondly, there was some pretty harsh soft tissue damage in his throat from where he swallowed his gag. And lastly, he had bruises on his face, chest, and arms, probably self-inflicted for the most part from when he was struggling on the floor, but some left by his assailant for sure. Body temperature, blood lividity, and the extent of the soft tissue bleeding all indicate Teeg died sometime after midnight but before three o'clock this morning. And according to some pathologist hocus pocus, the word going around the morgue is that he was probably alive for about an hour from the time he let his killer into the apartment—which I imagine would have been when he sustained his first injury—till the time he died."

"Cause of death?" Larry asked, spreading cream cheese on a bagel. Behind him I could see the street through a plate glass window, and because of the overcast sky the world seemed dark through the rivulets of streaming rain.

"They'll determine that later this morning, once the toxicology reports and other blood work are finished. But I'm pretty sure it's going to jive with the on-site investigator's determination."

"Which is?"

"I thought you knew already . . ."

"Just say it."

"He choked," I said, looking out the window again and feeling a kind of nausea twist in my gut. "He choked to death because somebody stuffed a dishrag in his mouth and wrapped duct tape around his head, covering his mouth, nose, and eyes."

"And this all happened right in the living room of his own apartment?" Larry said.

I nodded.

"No sign of forced entry?"

"None."

"Meaning?"

"Meaning that he probably knew whoever it was who did this to him, or, at the very least, he felt he had nothing to fear."

"Correct."

"What do ya mean, *correct*?" I asked, looking at him hard. "What, am I in class now?"

"You don't think you need it?"

I rested my chin on my hand, propping my elbow on the table as I devoted all my concentration to crushing my cigarette in an ashtray. I had almost forgotten what pleasure smoking gave me . . . all the little details that went along with it . . . wonderful . . . shameful . . . Nat was going to kill me when she got home. She could smell smoke on my breath over the fucking telephone.

"So, how's this going to work?" I asked.

Larry said that he wasn't following.

"This apprenticeship bullshit," I explained. "We gonna keep on going with me doin' all the work and you acting like a professor, or are we gonna compromise?"

He started to protest, but the appearance of a waitress to refill our coffee cups shut him up. The girl was young, and plain, but heavily made-up.

When she was gone, I said, "I'm on the list of people to question. Did your dispatcher friend happen to mention that? The cops are going to be coming to my door soon . . . probably even today yet. Steven Teeg's father dropped a dime on me. Told the whole goddamn thing to anybody who'd listen. I had half an argument with my wife this morning too. We never fight. And yet we almost did . . . and I'm not sure we're not going to later. And, as if I needed any other interesting surprises today, a state inspector called before I left this morning. It seems that there's a little matter of a conflict of interest between the funeral director's license I already hold, and the private investigator's license I never even applied for . . . but that's apparently in the works because somebody called down to the regulator's office on Monday morning and put my name on file as an apprentice, paperwork pending."

"Really?" Larry said, sounding genuinely surprised. "They made a stink about that?"

"Yeah," I returned. "They made a stink about that."

"I just didn't want you getting in any trouble, so I notified the board that you were working for me."

"That was very considerate."

"So what did the inspector say?"

"It was the Ohio Organization of Funeral Professionals, the O.O.F.P.," I explained. "It was their inspector who called. And he's not amused. I could conceivably have my license suspended."

"For what?"

"How the fuck do I know?" I exclaimed. Then, lowering my voice, I added, "How the fuck do I know what excuse he'll use? But the inspector never comes around for anything good. His sole function is to find violations of

the Ohio Revised Code. You remember that, don't you? It's
that pesky little book where they hide those . . . oh what the
hell do you call 'em? Oh yeah. Laws! Remember laws, Mr.
Big Shot Private Eye? As in, it's against the law to be such
a glorious asshole that your name can be associated with
somebody's being tortured to death, which, coincidentally,
happens to be against the law too!"

I bit down on the filter of a fresh cigarette and abandoned
myself to the act of scraping a match until it burned. Then
I used the smoking Camel as a pointer, aiming it at Larry
Fizner's grizzled face and saying, "You, Mr. Fizner, are a
pain in the ass, and that observation is not open to debate.
You're also a liar, just like everybody else I've met during the last couple of days. I've been thinking about this
whole thing very hard, and certain details just won't stop
bothering me."

"Such as?" he asked.

"Such as you telling me that Chester Scholtz approached
you with his plan. Or such as you sitting out in front of his
wife's house, even after he was dead. Or such as your claim
that he knew that this Stenetti guy was living at the Manor
Care *before* he ever got himself admitted there. That's the
such as that's been bugging me the most. But I finally figured it out . . . and I did it the minute you said that we *still*
had a shot at the money. As far as I can tell, we *never* had
a shot at any money, Mr. Fizner. Not *we* . . . not ever."

"So, what are you saying?" Fizner asked.

"What I'm saying is that the more I think about it, the
less the story you told me about this mess being Chester
Scholtz's idea makes sense."

"Why is that?"

"Because I just don't see where what you said you did
for Chester Scholtz would have been worth the twenty
thousand dollars you said he promised to pay you. He
had that money earmarked for his wife and kids, who were
supposed to use it to live on after he was gone. He wouldn't
have pissed away twenty grand of it just to be sure that a
retired private eye would be sitting in a broken-down van

while he took care of the hard part himself. I don't think he would have wanted you anywhere near that motel unless he absolutely couldn't help it. Which is why I think that it was you who approached him with the idea of ratting on Stenetti, and not the other way around. Since Scholtz was in such a tight financial position he went along with your plan, but when he died, instead of cutting your losses and getting out, you kept an eye on his wife in case she knew anything about what was going on. Then you saw your chance to sucker me into helping you . . . and you've been suckering me ever since."

"I didn't go to him," Fizner said. "You've got that part wrong."

"My ass!" I shot back.

"I'm serious," he said, taking a cigarette out of my pack and tapping it on the table. "You're right about the rest of it though. I'll admit to that. I didn't tell you about it in the first place because I didn't know who the hell you were. We're discussing some big bucks here, kid, and you just popped up out of the blue . . . and . . . I mean, hell. What would *you* have done?"

When I didn't respond, Fizner continued. "Originally, I approached Chet with Stenetti's name about a year ago. We never got along that good when we were younger, Chet and me. He was a highbrow big shot on the third floor, and I was just some punk kid outta the security department. So our reunion wasn't exactly what you'd call, emotional. First he heard me out, and then he threw me out. Didn't want anything to do with me or Stenetti, and said so flat out. Hurt my feelings, but hey, it was worth a shot, right?

"See, I needed him. Understand? I wasn't just looking for any partner . . . I needed him specifically because he knew the ropes. Stenetti's a commodity only if you know who to sell him to. The big shots in the syndicate today couldn't give a shit less about him. There's only a couple of old-timers who would be interested, and Chet knew who they were, and, what's more important, he knew how to make contact and set up a deal. But he said that he wasn't

interested, so I was fucked . . . until about three months ago . . . when he changed his mind and *came to me*. I swear."

"How'd you find out that Stenetti was at the Manor Care?" I asked.

Fizner shrugged, saying, "It was more or less an accident. I ran into an old friend from the department, and we got to talking about different guys we remembered. He mentioned how mosta the squealers who turned government's evidence got greased over the years, and that Stenetti was probably the only one still alive since he was hid so good in some nursing home on the east side. But the place had recently gone out of business, he said, and the patients were all transferred. He figured they probably ended up sending Stenetti out of state someplace, and we drank a toast to him, wherever he was.

"The next day I looked up any local nursing homes that had gone out of business, just as a long shot. And you know what I found? Nursing homes don't go out of business very often. There was only one in the last three years, and the patients had all been transferred to the Manor Care, which was a brand-new facility, freshly built. I didn't know what name he was living under, but I knew Stenetti was in that building somewhere. And if I could just get at him, I could make a ton."

Then, as the rain fell and the sky rumbled with thunder over the brooding Cleveland lakefront, I made the one statement that would determine the course of my entire future.

"The cops are going to catch whoever killed Steven Teeg," I said, feeling the tightness in my own voice, "and it's not going to take 'em long to do it. It's just going to be a matter of time. . . ." I trailed off, turning my attention inward to my own thoughts.

"Yeah?" Fizner said. "So?"

And I blinked as I replied, "So our killer is either supremely stupid, or he knows he's going to be far away before the cops have a chance to put together their case. So we've got

a timetable. Either we make some kind of move now, or we lose our options."

Larry Fizner looked at me for a moment, and then he said, "What are you gonna tell the cops when they ask you about Teeg?"

"The truth," I replied. "The absolute, unadulterated truth."

"And what about that funeral director inspector, or whatever he is? What about him?"

"He's another matter," I said. "What I tell him is gonna depend a lot on how I feel."

Larry sighed, saying, "I didn't have anything to do with what happened to Teeg, you know. You do believe me about that, right?"

"I don't know," I admitted.

And he nodded, as if I had answered just right. Then he leaned back in his chair and said, "You know, Bill, if you keep your head on straight, you could have a real future in this business . . . I mean, if you wanted it. You've got a good eye, and a lot of guts for a suburbanite."

I looked at him, saying nothing, but feeling my throat constrict. Accepting compliments is something I don't do very well because, during the course of my life, there wasn't exactly a lot of call for the skill. In my family the only time anything was ever said was when I did something wrong. My dad's point of view was that, "If you do it right, then you don't need me to point it out. But if you screw it up, I'll come down on you with both feet." My first impulse was to deny what Larry Fizner was saying with a modest, "Well gee, 'tweren't nothin'," like I had done the day before when Mrs. Scholtz asked me about my fee. But underneath, there was a tiny part of me that perked up and said, "Yes! You're right! I am good. I'm goddamn good . . . and finally somebody sees it!" But I didn't articulate either response; instead I sat silently and just let him talk.

"You've put together a lot of information, and your instincts have been right on the money almost every time," he said. "But you're still makin' the same mistake a lot of

new guys make the first time things go their way: you're startin' to think that you're special."

I tried to protest, but he cut me off.

"Don't shit me," he said, waving his hand dismissively. "I've seen it plenty of times before. Hell, I did it myself when I was your age. Success breeds contempt. Don't forget that. If you know you're right, it's a great temptation to think that everybody else must be wrong."

"I haven't the slightest idea what you're talking about," I said.

And Larry Fizner smiled as he asked, "Don't you? Then would you believe me if I said that I know who killed Steve Teeg?"

"I doubt it."

"See? I told you. You're smart, so I must be dumb."

"So who did it?"

"We've got a problem here, you know?"

"Who killed Teeg?"

"And our problem is that we don't know when or where the meeting Chet Scholtz set up is going to take place. That's really our central issue."

I closed my mouth and stared at him across the table, amazement spreading through me like alcohol.

"You think the meeting's still on?" I asked finally. "Is that what you're saying? That whoever killed Steven Teeg isn't worried about the cops because they set up another meeting with whoever Scholtz was planning to sell Stenetti to?"

"No," Larry Fizner responded with a wry smile. "Not another meeting, the *same* one."

"I don't get it."

"Then listen and learn, sonny boy. Listen and learn."

Twenty minutes later I was heading back to the funeral home with half a pack of Big Red chewing gum stuffed in my mouth in hopes of covering the smell of all those cigarettes, reeling under the assault of Larry Fizner's explanation, and half sick from the caffeine and nicotine in my

system. I'm really very sensitive to chemicals . . . and I don't know why I do these things to myself. I saw the funeral home's exit off the freeway and passed it, remembering that I had promised Jerry that I'd stop in and see him. While I drove through the rain toward the Manor Care, I reviewed Larry Fizner's theory, which went like this:

Not just anyone could approach the people who would be willing to buy Constantine Stenetti's name and hope to set up a meeting. Only someone with an extensive knowledge of some of the county's more shadowy historical crime figures could do that, which was why Fizner had needed Scholtz when he originally hatched the deal almost a year before. Now, with Scholtz known to be dead—as the newspaper article about him had so eloquently announced to the world—the deal would be off. Even if someone else were to come forward willing to take Scholtz's place, the chances that the purchasing parties would be willing to make fresh arrangements with someone new were extremely thin. These were careful men. One didn't live to a mature age in their profession without a healthy respect for security. But . . .

If whoever killed Steven Teeg also knew the details of the original meeting it would offer them an air of credibility too great to be ignored.

"Now just wait a second," I had said, stopping Larry Fizner on what was his verbal run. "How the hell would Steven Teeg's killer know the details of Scholtz's secret meeting? Even Teeg didn't know that, so he couldn't have told if he had wanted to."

"I don't know," he returned. "But those details are what we've got to figure out. They're the key to everything. If we knew where and when Stenetti's name is going to be turned over, we'd have a chance. Since we don't, we can either do something about finding out, or we can pack it up and call it a day. Those are absolutely our only remaining alternatives."

Then he told me who he thought had killed Teeg, and I didn't say a word in response because his reasoning was

just too damned sound. As much as I hated to admit it, he had to be right. And it just tore me up inside.

"So you in or not?" he had asked after he described what he thought we had to do.

And I said, "I'm in," going against every single one of my better instincts and proving once again that I have a positive talent for making the wrong decision when the chips are down.

The nursing home staff welcomed me like a partner, which confused me a little until one of the nurses mentioned Jerry's name. Then I understood: as had been the case during pretty much my whole life, I was again being the recipient of the goodwill my brother generated in the people around him. As much as I hate to say it, I really think it would have been better for everybody concerned if it had been me who was paralyzed. Then Jerry could have taken the job at the funeral home and made a million friends while bringing in a million funerals, and I could have lain in a bed and had people read me books. Despite the friction that existed between us when we were younger, he was always so gregarious and friendly that people ended up liking me too. And even though he had only been a full-time resident at the Manor Care for two days, having moved in Sunday afternoon, already he was obviously a favorite with the nurses.

Stepping into his room I couldn't believe the difference between the way he had been at the other place and the way he was now. His face actually seemed to shine, and there was a sparkle of life in his eyes like I hadn't seen in years. He and I look a lot alike now. It used to be that we didn't resemble one another at all because I've always been about twenty pounds overweight, and Jerry, Mr. Fitness, was always muscular and perfect. Where my face was round, his was long and angular. I was boyish, and he was ruggedly handsome. But now, with his having been confined to a bed for two years, and my wife having turned me into a vegetarian after the death of our first cat, Leonardo, I was thinner, and Jerry was heavier, so

we suddenly looked like brothers again.

When I walked in, he grinned wide from where he was propped up on his bed, welcoming me and saying, "Watch," as he looked down at his right arm and concentrated on moving it. I approached the side of the bed, and, without my help, Jerry reached over to the table next to me, and, very carefully, lifted one of the tiny tapes that fit the recorder I had given him, moved it over, and handed it to me. It was obviously a pretty delicate maneuver for him, and as his fingers brushed my hand after he had dropped the tape into my palm, I instinctively grabbed on . . . which got him semi-pissed because I had tears in my eyes.

"Oh, cut it out," he growled, just like—or almost just like—the Jerry I had known before the accident. His arm returned to its place across his lap, and he added, "I'm going to do it, Bill. The doctors say the chances for my legs ain't too good, but me and my arms are going to come to an understanding. It's coming slow, but it ain't like I don't have the time." Then he looked up and added, "Thanks, by the way. This is a better place than the other one. Expensive, but nice. And the physical therapist is a beast."

I said that I was sorry to hear that, and he told me that no, that's just what a physical therapist was supposed to be. Compassionate P.T.'s didn't do anybody any good, he said. Only the Nazi commandant types could get you pissed enough to get your ass in gear. I shrugged, saying that, in that case, I was glad he knew a Nazi. Then I pulled up a chair and, for the next hour, I reviewed what I had learned, including Steven Teeg's exposure as the man in the motel when Chester Scholtz died, and ending with his murder. Then I described what Larry Fizner and I had discussed that morning, detailing Fizner's plan, and emphasizing the importance of figuring out when and where Chester Scholtz had been planning to meet the people who wanted to kill Constantine Stenetti.

Jerry listened with an expression of utter delight, saying when I was finished, "That paper in the wall's got to be the key to the meeting."

"That's what I was thinking." I nodded. "Chester Scholtz could easily remember the name of the person he was looking for. Shit, with as much effort as he was expelling to find it out, he probably wouldn't be able to forget it if he tried. But a meeting with a big shot crook who was being careful to keep his ass safe would probably involve some security precautions—signs and countersigns, fallback procedures, and all that kind of secret agent shit . . ."

"Secret agent shit," Jerry cut in. "I love it."

"You know what I mean," I said. "Which is what I think those numbers were. I think that Scholtz wrote them down because he absolutely had to remember them, and he was terrified of forgetting. He hid them so he wouldn't lose them, and so that they wouldn't be discovered. But he wrote them cryptically so that, if they were discovered, no one would know what they meant."

"Which means that they aren't going to do us a lot of good unless we figure out the key to the code," Jerry observed. And I agreed, rising and saying, with one hand on his shoulder, that, since he was in the nursing home, he had the best chance of figuring out that part of the riddle. For a second he looked pained, as if he didn't like the idea of accepting that much responsibility. But then his expression hardened, and I could almost see the old Jerry coming up from inside, rising to the challenge and steeling his resolve.

"I'll do what I can," he said, and I told him that I knew he would. Then I left, promising to listen to the tape he had given me and telling him that I expected another one real soon. He laughed and said that he'd try. I stopped at the front desk to ask if Pete Germaine was on duty. I was told that he'd be in at seven. Then I left, cupping one hand over my mouth in the parking lot and smelling my breath. I could detect the cigarettes, even through the gum, and already it was nearly one in the afternoon. There was no way the smell would be gone before Nat came home. And I was sure my hair and clothes also smelled like smoke. I was going to have to pay the piper.

Back at the funeral home my dad was busy at the desk paying bills, my uncle was off somewhere lunching a priest, and I waxed the Cadillac in the big, five-car garage attached to the side of the building. Dad went home at three, leaving me to sit by the window and watch the rain. For something to do I popped the cassette my brother had given me into a machine and listened to it, wondering what the hell he had recorded, considering he had said that he hadn't found out anything interesting yet. Before his voice came on, I turned off the office lights so that the room became quite dim, and in the feeble grey of a stormy August afternoon, my younger brother spoke to me from the depths of a tiny, Japanese speaker.

"Jesus Christ," were the first words he said. "You gotta be a goddamn Hercules to push the record button on this little fucker."

I grinned, closing my eyes.

"Hi, Bill," he began. "It's now . . . what . . . cripes, it's after midnight so I guess that this is Tuesday morning, and I don't have shit to report. Actually, I feel a little stupid doing this. Here I am, lying in a dark room, whispering into a tape recorder. I feel like a half-assed secret agent . . ."

(Now I understood why he had laughed that afternoon when I referred to Chester Scholtz's secret agent shit.)

". . . and I'm not even sure what my mission is. Nobody around here knows a goddamn thing about Chester Scholtz, by the way . . . I mean other than what he told them, which was that he was blind. Everybody believes it too. And I mean everybody. That Pete Germaine's a good kid. A little too helpful for my taste, always trying to psychoanalyze you, but generally I think he's straight."

For twenty minutes Jerry described the tiniest incidentals involved in his move from one nursing home to the other, right down to his toilet requirements, which he had never mentioned to me before. For the first time I realized just how difficult, and insulting, his dependent condition must have been. He spoke about his daily routine, and his medications, about his physical therapy and the better looking

nurses who took care of him. And he spoke about how he felt. That's what intrigued me. He had never discussed his feelings like that before, and in my mind I could see him, lying in the dark, speaking to me, but not to me. Speaking to a machine and therefore more free somehow to say things he never would have said had there been an actual person in the room with him to hear. It was almost too much for me to stand, and twice I nearly stopped the tape. But I didn't; and when he got to the part about the accident, I was glad I'd let it go.

"You know," he began, his voice taking on a strangely faraway tone, "I never blamed you for what happened. No, that's a lie, Bill. I guess I did. Yeah, that's really more the truth . . . I blamed the piss out of you, and it took me a hell of a long time before I could even look at you without getting mad. I'm over it now. I really am. But God, for a while there you were lucky I couldn't move."

There was a long pause during which all I could hear was tape hiss before he added, "I didn't think I'd ever say that. They musta upped my medication or something. Christ. Maybe I oughta turn this thing off and go to sleep. There's no sense in draggin' it all out . . . or maybe, I don't know."

Pause.

And then . . .

"Why'd you do it, man?

"Seriously.

"Why?

"I mean . . . I know you were drunk . . . but . . . you were always drunk. Is it true what Dad says about you being sober ever since? Is that true?"

"Yeah," I whispered. "It's true."

"This is what I saw . . ." my brother said.

And I closed my eyes.

"I saw a bar downtown, where you really shouldn't have been since you were living in an apartment in the suburbs and had a long drive home, drunk as you were. I saw you in the parking lot, in the middle of a circle of people,

with another guy, no bigger than you, and just as drunk, scuffling around like two kids. I saw the guy swinging, and you covering your face with your arms, and ducking down so that the guy ended up pulling your shirt up out of your pants and over your head so that you stumbled around blind while he pounded you on the back with his fists. And I saw people laughing at you. And I saw myself coming in and breaking it up. And I saw you get pissed at me . . .

"At *me*!

"Why, Bill?

"Why the fuck, after I knocked the other guy down, did you have to get pissed at me?"

"Because you shouldn't have been there," I whispered, as I had said that night in the Prime Pump's parking lot, late, drunk, and bleeding. "You shouldn't have been following me around. What I do is none of your business . . ."

I paused.

That had been what I had said. It was what was in my mind then, the mind of an alcoholic denying that he needed help, denying that what he was doing was wrong in any way. I was full of resentment at anyone who tried to influence my behavior . . . but I was particularly prone to sparking off at my younger brother because he was so goddamn perfect. I couldn't stand the thought of him around me, particularly when I was drunk. It just set me off. I exploded. It was the same sensation a person would feel if ants were crawling all over his body, a prickling of the skin that could just drive me up the wall.

And he showed up, and it was two in the morning, and he wanted to rescue me! He just stepped into the haze of parking lot lights behind the Prime Pump, and it was like the Lone Ranger had ridden over the hill. He said that he had seen my car in the lot . . . he just happened to be passing and he noticed my car, so he had stopped in to buy me a drink. And wasn't it a lucky thing that he did? Wasn't it lucky he had noticed my car? Yeah, right! He had just noticed my car . . . at two in the morning, downtown . . . where he never went, but I always did, because he didn't.

He was looking for me . . . that's what he was doing. The little shit was out looking for me so he could take me home and put me to bed . . . like I couldn't take care of myself. Like I wasn't capable of doing anything on my own. Like I needed somebody to watch out for me . . .

Even though I did.

God.

Did I ever.

Those were all the feelings I felt that night when Jerry showed up and pulled off the guy who was beating me up. It wasn't the first time I was in a fight behind a bar. Even though I don't remember doing it most of the time, I guess when I drink enough I get obnoxious . . . and more than once I came home with a fat lip or black eye I couldn't explain. So Jerry, who had been out looking for me, stepped in and saved me from yet another ass whipping, and, instead of being grateful, or even quiet, I lashed out at him for being there, for being perfect, for being my pain-in-the-ass younger brother, the sight of whom, I said, was enough to make me puke.

"You remember what you said to me?" he was asking from the tape recorder, in the gloom, as the rain fell and I sat with my eyes squeezed tightly shut. I was nodding, though I really didn't remember the details. I could see the scene in my mind, but I couldn't hear the words . . . because, honestly, the scene I carry in my head is one that's more or less reconstructed because I was too drunk to remember it correctly. But I do remember it, even though I don't.

Both the tape recorder and I were quiet for a time, and then Jerry said, "So you got pissed at me, and yelled at me, and, while everybody stood around, drunk, laughing first at you, and then at me, you took a swing, and fell down, and I tried to pick you up but you pushed me away . . . and then you wanted to fight . . . and . . .

"I lost my temper and nailed you one in the mouth. God, did I ever unload. When you went down it was like somebody dropped a bag of cement out a third-floor

window. And I was so pissed . . . I'm still not sorry I hit you, but I suppose I shouldn't have done it. But I was just seeing red . . . and then I left you crawling around on all fours, got in my car, slammed the door, and stomped on the accelerator . . . and I was doing fifty by the time I hit the street, which is probably why I didn't make the turn . . .

"And the next thing I knew, I was in a hospital. And I didn't even remember getting there."

But I did.

From where I pulled myself to my feet, with my jaw aching and my lips swollen from where my brother had just punched me, I saw his red Camaro hurl around in a wicked circle on the parking lot gravel, straighten out, settle, and bite, throwing dust and aiming itself at the exit. I saw it— and this I remember, despite the booze . . . even though I don't remember most anything else, I do remember this— and I saw it . . .

Jesus, God.

I saw it miss the exit drive, just by a foot, and nail the telephone pole with its driver's side fender. It wasn't a tremendous crash like in the movies. There wasn't the sound of ripping steel and shattering glass. No dramatic music, no screaming sirens. Just a stupid, awful thump as the car smacked the pole and stopped, with the figure of my brother inside snapping forward in his seat and then falling back. Some asshole near me was giggling about it. Most everybody else was just quiet. But some asshole was giggling, and there was fluid running out from under the front of the car. I thought the car was bleeding. And I was standing there hoping, oh Christ, just let him get out. Jesus, he's gonna be pissed, I thought. Jerry's going to be so mad he'll kick my ass up and down the street. I pissed him off to the point that he couldn't drive, and now he fucked up his Camaro, his beloved Camaro, and it's my fault, and . . . please, Jesus, let him get out of that car and come over here and kick my ass, I was thinking. Please. Let him get out of the car.

But he didn't get out. And it was because he didn't that somebody—not me, but somebody—approached, tentatively, like there might be something inside the car that could jump out. I watched it all from the doorway of the bar, swaying, drifting in and out. I watched it, and I remembered it because I did, although I'm sure most of what I remember didn't happen that way at all. Most of it I remember because it was described for me later . . . partially by the guy I was fighting when Jerry pulled up . . . who felt nearly as awful as I did about what happened, and who stood like a zombie when the ambulance finally came. The ambulance finally came, and the men in it strapped my baby brother to a back board to immobilize his spine because it looked as if he'd broken his neck . . . or his back . . . they didn't know which . . . but there weren't any reflex responses in his legs . . . which wasn't a good sign . . . and . . .

I turned off the recorder, my heart beating so hard in my chest that it ached. I stared at the machine, and when I turned it back on Jerry said, "I love you, Bill. I guess, after it's all said and done, it all boils down to the fact that I love my brother. It wasn't your fault. And it wasn't mine. It was ours. We both did it together. Like it or not, we did. I always thought that one day, if I ever got up and walked again, I'd say, 'I forgive you, Bill,' and that would make everything all right. But now I realize that I'll never say it, Bill, because there isn't really anything to forgive. Okay? There's nothing to forgive."

And I said, "Bullshit," under my breath, holding that recorder in my hand and looking at it as if I could somehow make things different if I just looked hard enough.

"Scholtz had a couple of friends here at the home," Jerry said next, making me blink, so abrupt was his transition. I stopped the tape and rewound it a little, taking the time to drink a glass of water and throw away what was left of the pack of Camels I'd bought from the vending machine. Then I listened to the rest, which wasn't much, but went like this:

"Scholtz had a couple of friends here at the home," Jerry said. "There were about three guys he seemed particularly interested in, and he really earned a lot of brownie points with the staff for sitting with one guy who's just, like, totally zonked out because of Alzheimer's disease or something. The guy doesn't even know his own name, he's so screwed up. They call him the Parrot. Not the staff, but the old folks. No shit. They're just like young people, only older. That's what I've learned being in nursing homes these last couple of years. They kid around and have whatever fun they can manage. It's really sad sometimes, but it's enough to give you hope too. Anyway, they call this guy the Parrot because he just parrots words. You say something to him and he just says something back at you. It doesn't have anything to do with what you said, though. He just says words, so they call him the Parrot. I guess Scholtz spent a lot of time in his room, keeping him company, and the staff really loved him for it . . ."

There was more, but I didn't listen very carefully. In my mind I was still in that parking lot where my brother had stopped walking, and I had stopped drinking. When the tape finished, I rewound it and put it in a desk drawer, not thinking about it anymore until the phone rang at two o'clock the next morning.

"Hawley Funeral Home," I said, snapping on the small table lamp on the nightstand next to me and sitting up in bed, absolutely awake. You learn to do that when you live in a funeral home because you get your body calls in the middle of the night, and the people doing the calling are as awake as hell. They're usually in a hospital waiting room or a doctors' lounge, and sometimes they resent it if you answer the phone with sleep in your voice. As I've said before, when people are emotional, their behavior isn't always logical, but you have to respect it. I had a pen in my hand, ready to take down the name of the deceased, but instead I heard Pete Germaine's voice saying, "Mr. Hawley, we've got a really cool idea. It's kinda farfetched.

But it's still way cool. Hold on, your brother wants to say something to you."

There was the sound of a receiver being transferred, and then Jerry said, "Hey, big brother, I hope I woke you up. Man, you're gonna love this shit. No kidding. I thought of it just a little while ago. I was lying awake, staring at the ceiling, and it just hit me. Man! It was like an inspiration. . . ."

What was? I tried to ask, but the phone was being transferred back again, and Pete Germaine was on the line asking me if I had the paper that we had found in the bathroom wall of Chester Scholtz's room. When I said that I did, he asked me to read it to him, just like it was, one number or word at a time.

When I was done he said, "Okay. Now for the fun part. I'm going to put the phone down for a second, but the next voice you hear should be that of the Parrot."

The Parrot? I thought, looking at the clock again to verify that they really had called me at two in the morning for this. Nat was awake by now too, and after she asked me what was going on I snapped on the speakerphone and replaced the receiver so that we both could hear. She hadn't been pissed at me about the cigarettes, which was amazing. When she came home from work and smelled the smoke on me, she hadn't been pissed. Disappointed, but not angry . . . which was even worse, somehow.

"Okay, Bill," Jerry said, his voice cutting through the strange reverb of the speakerphone, "when you were here before you said that Chester Scholtz had set up a meeting with whoever was going to buy this Constantine Stenetti's name. Okay? And you said that, whenever and wherever this meeting was going to take place, that it probably involved some kind of security precautions which were a little too complicated for Scholtz to flat out remember, but too secret for him to just write down and save on a note card. So he wrote it in code and hid it in his bathroom wall. Right?"

When I nodded without speaking, Jerry asked, "Am I right?" louder this time.

"Yes," I said. "You are right."

"What bothered me about that," he continued, his voice sounding stronger and more alive than I had heard it since the accident, "is that the key to the code would probably be just as complicated as what he was trying to remember."

"Makes sense," I offered.

And Jerry said, "You're damn right it makes sense. And it made me nuts. I was lying here thinking, if he's got the coded message hidden in his room, the last place he'd hide the key to that code would be in the same room as the message. That would be stupid. So I figured the key was someplace else. Someplace he could get at it, so here in the building, but someplace where if somebody found his secret message, like you did, they couldn't just turn around and pick the key up off the coffee table. Dig?"

"Dug." I nodded, listening hard.

"At first I thought that maybe he gave it to one of his buddies here in the home," Jerry said. "But that would be really risky. Then I started going over what Pete told me about how Scholtz spent his time. And that's when it hit me: he sat with the Parrot a lot. The staff loved him for it—remember me telling you that on the tape? The Parrot's name is Matthew Taylor, by the way. And he's really kind of amazing. He just says words. You say a word, and he says a word. He's sitting right here next to me. Listen. Hey, Mr. Taylor, what do you think of when I say the word, blue?"

"Noodle," a voice responded.

"See what I mean?" Jerry asked. "They're the same fucking words every time too. Pete says it's some kind of language problem . . ."

"Disassociative Verbal Response Disorder," Pete Germaine offered in the background. "D.V.R."

"Yeah," my brother said. "That. Anyway, listen: book."

"Rummage," Matthew Taylor, the Parrot, returned.

"Shoe," my brother said.

"Liver," the Parrot replied.

"Plant."

"Airplane."

"Grandma."

"Bicycle."

"Blue."

"Noodle."

"Ya hear that, Bill?" Jerry asked. "Even when you mix shit up, he always says the same word for any word you say. Blue."

"Noodle," Mr. Taylor parroted.

"So?" I asked, feeling a little thick. "Where are you going with this?"

"He does it with numbers too," Jerry said.

And Nat touched my shoulder, moving closer to me as a chill washed over my skin.

"Bill?" Jerry asked. "You there?"

"I'm here," I replied. "Do it, Jer. Come on. Read him the paper."

"Oh, hey. That's a good idea," Jerry said. "I hadn't thought of that. Wait a minute, let me try it."

There was another moment's worth of rustling as, in my mind, I saw Jerry doing his Norton imitation. Art Carney as Norton on Jackie Gleason's "The Honeymooners" TV show used to flick his arm repeatedly before he was going to write something, driving Ralph Cramden, his best friend, into fits. Jerry liked to do the same thing, imitating Carney's movements until I complained. And in my mind's eye I could see him doing it now with the paper that had Chester Scholtz's numbers and words scribbled across it rustling in his hand.

"You doin' Norton?" I asked.

"Yeah," he replied. I could see him smiling. "I can't do it like I used to, but I'll learn. Okay. Here we go. Ready?"

"Will you just get on with it?"

"I thought you'd never ask. Okay. Mr. Taylor, what do you think of when I say the number, eight?"

"Tree."

"Five?"

"Silver."

"Roger?"

"Friday."

"Four?"

"Other."

Jerry went on like this for all thirteen of the numbers and words on the page. Then he said, "Shit," to which Mr. Taylor replied, "Coffee."

"Coffee?" Jerry repeated.

"Cowboy," Mr. Taylor returned.

"It's just gibberish," Jerry finally observed, sounding irritated. "I really thought it would work."

"Maybe we should try it backward," Pete Germaine offered from the background.

And Nat, who had taken the pencil from me to write out the words Mr. Taylor said in response to Jerry's prompting, read, "Tree; Silver; Friday; Other; Roses; Lamp; Jesus; Six; Foot; Hollow; Eleven; Nitwit; Sparrow," as if it were a sentence. She frowned, and I sat there watching her as she studied the page with the pencil's eraser resting on her lower lip. Finally she said, "Unless they're passwords, they don't add up to a thing."

And I said, "Jerry," prompted by something her statement had made me think of, "what did he say when you said 'shit' a minute ago?"

"Coffee," Jerry replied.

"Cowboy," Mr. Taylor piped up in the background.

"That's what I thought," I said. "Now try reading his answers back to him. But do it slowly, okay?"

And Jerry said, "I'm way ahead of ya, big brother. Okay, Mr. Taylor, for the big money, what do you think of when I say the word, tree?"

To which Mr. Taylor replied, "Railroad."

"Silver?" Jerry said.

"Locker," returned Mr. Taylor.

"Friday?"

"Twenty-one."

"Other?"

"Brooklyn."

"Roses?"

"Post office."

"Lamp?"

"Box."

"Jesus?"

"Seven."

"Six?"

"Airport."

"Foot?"

"Suitcase."

"Hollow?"

"Germany."

"Eleven?"

"Money."

"Nitwit?"

"White."

"Sparrow?"

"Hat."

When they were finished, Natalie, who'd been writing the whole time read, "Railroad; Locker; Twenty-one; Brooklyn; Post office; Box; Seven; Airport; Suitcase; Germany; Money; White; Hat."

I looked at her and she looked at me.

"Bill?" Jerry said, excitement hastening his pace. "What do ya think? Huh, Bill? What do ya think, for Christ's sake?"

"I'll be down there in about twenty minutes," I replied, and both Nat and I jumped out of bed at the same time.

At the nursing home we found Jerry sitting up in a wheelchair, which despite everything else that was on my mind made me stop for an instant and look. I hadn't seen him in an upright position—I hadn't seen him in anything but a bed—for so long, that it left me almost speechless. He smiled when he saw me, moved his arms, ever so slowly, a little ways apart, with the palms of his hands aimed up in imitation of a magician, and said, "Ta da!" as if he'd performed a trick. He was in the large Activities Room where I had first met Pete Germaine, with an old man

sitting on a chair next to him, and the orderly all but dancing around, he was so excited.

The nurses weren't exactly thrilled that two of their patients were up so late, but Germaine had apparently talked them into letting things go for a while, and after a little small talk as review we reenacted the exchange between Mr. Taylor and the words and numbers on Chester Scholtz's secret paper. In between words, Germaine explained some of the details involved with Mr. Taylor's disorder, describing it as a rare but by no means unheard-of condition in which a person loses the ability to construct cognitive expressions of thought with words. Words, he said, became somehow disassociated with their meaning, and apparently ended up producing a verbal response in the sufferer strictly for their sound. When Mr. Taylor heard a particular word, he produced another word that he apparently associated with the first. The meanings of any of the words were irrelevant, and the response word, when spoken independently, didn't necessarily produce the word that had originally prompted it in his mind. So when Nat said, "eight," Mr. Taylor said, "tree." But when she said, "tree," he didn't say, "eight," he said, "railroad." Which explained the amount of time Chester Scholtz had spent sitting with the man over the months he was a resident at the home.

"He was fishing for responses," Pete Germaine explained, which is what he apparently likes to do better than anything else: explain things. He'll make a good teacher someday, our Pete Germaine. "Scholtz had a list of words he wanted to remember," he said through a grin, "and he was first finding what key words would prompt them from Mr. Taylor here. And then he was trying to figure out what key words would prompt those responses in turn. It's really quite a clever code, and it must have taken a tremendous amount of patience on his part to devise."

Jerry agreed, but pointed out that Scholtz was killing time while waiting to discover who at the home was really Constantine Stenetti incognito, and, that like any good

businessman, he was simply making the best use of the raw materials around him.

Nat pretty much ignored our peripheral discussion, concentrating on verifying Matthew Taylor's responses, and, after about thirty minutes she had run her test four times. Each time, the results were identical.

"He's sticking to his story," she pronounced at last, presenting a page upon which she had written the thirteen words and numbers she was sure were correct. Mr. Taylor, who looked to be only about sixty years old, grinned and watched the proceedings around him with bright, eager eyes. He seemed very interested in everything, and his enthusiasm was touching . . . making me wonder what it was like to be inside his head. He wanted to be involved, and for all I knew he was, but he just couldn't tell us about it in any way we could understand. If his mind had been capable of grasping the meanings of words, Pete Germaine had pointed out, then it would have been theoretically possible to create a vocabulary that he could understand by discovering what word his brain was using in the place of whatever it was he was trying to say. But there had never been any indication that he grasped the meaning of any words at all. It was a tragedy really, since up until his particular disorder began manifesting itself, Mr. Taylor had apparently been a successful businessman in his own right.

I took the page from Nat, and after Pete Germaine took Mr. Taylor back to his room, the four of us assembled in Jerry's room and discussed our options. We finally decided that "Railroad; Locker; Twenty-one; Brooklyn; Post office; Box; Seven; Airport; Suitcase; Germany; Money; White; Hat" meant literally what it said. Or at least what we concluded it said, which was that whatever we were looking for could be found by going first to locker number twenty-one at the Amtrak station—since Amtrak, as far as we knew, was the only railroad station around that would have lockers—and then to post office box seven at the Brooklyn post office, and then to claim a German suitcase at the airport where we would either receive or need to produce some

money for a man in a white hat.

"Sounds a little crazy," Nat observed.

"Sounds great," Jerry offered in a tone of voice that implied that nothing would give him more pleasure than to go out and personally participate in what amounted to a scavenger hunt. Nat and I were planning on making the run immediately, and I asked Pete Germaine what he thought the chances were that we might in fact be able to take Jerry along with us in the car, seeing that he was able to sit up. But to our collective disappointment, he replied that he didn't think it would be a good idea.

"His muscles are still very weak," he said, making Jerry frown. "Those clowns at that other nursing home let him lie on his back so long that he's gone to butter. We've only been able to get him in the chair for very short intervals, and by the time we put him back to bed he's exhausted. Sitting up in a car for the two or three hours it would take to drive around town would be torture. By the time we were done, he'd be having muscle cramps all over his body. And since he can't feel most of what his nerves are reacting to, he'd probably end up with phantom pains for a week."

"It almost sounds worth it," Jerry offered.

But Pete Germaine added that we hadn't even considered how to deal with his catheter, and that, on a much more practical and serious level, if the muscles in his chest should cramp up too badly he might have a hard time breathing. So sadly we concluded that Jerry would have to sit this one out. . . .

"This time," I assured him. "But you're going on the next one. I promise."

"If there is a next one," Jerry said.

And Nat, speaking to Jerry while looking at me, said, "Oh, I wouldn't worry too much about that."

I glanced at her and caught in her eye a look that I can only describe as motherly. It was as if she were looking right into my heart and reading my deepest secrets. In the parking lot I asked her what her remark had meant. But instead of a reply she just said that she wanted to drive.

SEVEN
■■■■■■■■■■

I HAD NEVER been to the Amtrak station before, but its location, and the fact that we arrived at just after three-thirty in the morning, presented us with our first problem: namely, that we were downtown, in the middle of the night, with our Miata, which we were afraid would either be stolen or trashed the minute we tried to leave it in the parking lot unattended. I didn't want to send Nat in alone, nor did I want to leave her in the car while I went looking for the locker, so I suggested that she drive around the block a couple of times while I ran inside. She nixed that idea, saying that we'd just have to risk the car for five minutes. And I had to agree . . . but I didn't like it.

The station is located right on the lakefront, at the bottom of a steep ravine, under Cleveland Municipal Stadium. It's dark down there, and spooky . . . at least for a couple of white-bread young professionals like Nat and I who rarely spend any time in the city. As soon as we put the top up on the car and headed for the door it seemed like five or six figures that appeared to be loitering around without any obvious purpose turned to look at us. And we walked fast, holding hands. We were a little paranoid, no doubt about it.

But still we wanted to get in and out as quickly as we could. Our footsteps echoed on the concrete inside, and beneath the harsh white fluorescent lights I approached a counter like that in a bus station and asked the attendant where I might find the lockers. She pointed without even looking up from the magazine she was reading, and when she did, the gold post she had piercing one nostril gleamed.

We found locker number twenty-one, and I said, "So how are we supposed to open it?" stating the obvious since we didn't have a key. Nat shrugged, and I was about to go back and ask the attendant with the nose-ring—nostril bauble?—if we had to rent this particular locker or what, when Nat reached out and tried the handle, an experiment that hadn't even entered my mind. To my surprise, it opened, and looking inside Nat furrowed her brow.

"It's empty," she said.

"It can't be empty," I said, stepping forward and opening the door wide. Then I added, "You're right. It's empty."

"Thank God that's settled," Nat said. Then she looked around, spotted a young man in a uniform, and said, "Excuse me, but is there any way of finding out who had this locker last?"

To which the young man replied, "Are you nuts, or what?" as he walked past without even breaking his stride, leaving Nat irritated, and me with my head in the locker, completely perplexed.

"What's a 'Latin Knight'?" Nat asked, reading some graffiti off one of the station's walls.

I told her that it sounded like a Puerto Rican lounge singer's stage name, and then announced, "Aha!" as my searching fingers discovered something taped to the bottom of one of the locker's shelves. I disengaged the object and produced an envelope containing a key. I stuffed the key in my pocket and, glancing around quickly to see if we were being observed, grabbed Nat by the arm and hurried her back out to the car. On the way she asked questions, but I didn't speak again until we were moving, with me driving

this time, heading back to the freeway, and the Cleveland suburb named Brooklyn.

The key was large, brass, and had a number written on it. And just as Larry Fizner had warned me earlier, because I had found it I ended up feeling myself swell with a sensation of superiority that, I admit, made me talk down to Nat a little bit on the way to the Brooklyn post office. She didn't complain, but she got quiet, which I noticed but didn't acknowledge at first, feeling too heady about the ease with which we had performed the first part of our hunt, and sure that it was my brilliant reasoning that had seen us through. But at the post office my good mood fell flat, and I stood clutching the key like a kid holding the broken string of a kite that has just flown free. The post office boxes were located in a brightly lit antechamber that was open twenty-four hours a day, and there wasn't one there bearing a number that matched the one etched into my key since the boxes were numbered starting with ten.

"Okay, Columbo," Nat said behind me, "now what?"

"Let me think," I returned.

And she said, "Okay. Think."

So I thought, but it didn't do me a lot of good.

"Did you think?" she asked.

"Yeah," I said.

"And?"

"What kind of ideas have you got?"

"I asked you first."

"I'm going to try this key in every lock and see what happens."

"That's a thought," Nat said, apparently unimpressed. "But I wouldn't be too obvious about it, considering it's dark outside, and light in here, and with those windows behind us the people in the police station across the street can see every move we make."

I only had to try one lock to see that the key I held was of a completely different type than the one I needed. The post office boxes all had those tiny little aluminum keyholes that indicated that the locks were new. The key I held looked

as if it were from another era . . . large, heavy, and wide. Trying to fit it into such a tiny keyhole was like trying to fit the wide end of a baseball bat in your mouth.

"This key's made for a jail cell door out of a Jimmy Cagney movie," I observed, heading back to the car.

"Lemme see," Nat said, and I handed it to her. We sat in the Miata with the top down, and while Nat turned the key over in her fingers I stared at the sky. It was after four in the morning, the darkest time of night, and the sky overhead was so oppressive that it looked as if it were a solid, heavy object.

"You're right," she said at last, handing the key back to me. "The box this thing fits is a hundred years old. Too bad this post office is so new."

I snapped my head around and looked at her profile, sharply cut with shadows thrown by the light from the interior of the building.

"What did you say?" I asked.

And she repeated that it was too bad there wasn't an older post office in Brooklyn, because then we would find older post office boxes, and our key might work.

I spun the Miata's tires leaving the lot, making the eight-cylinder Ford engine I loved so dearly sing. Nat was holding onto the dashboard with one hand and her black Miata baseball cap with the other as I said, "Brooklyn!" over and over like an idiot. "Why the fuck didn't I think of that before?"

"What?" she asked.

And I didn't tell her until we were back on the freeway, heading back the way we had come . . . downtown, to where the Brooklyn Avenue post office was located, near the Justice Center, within spitting distance of the Amtrak station. There we found the right box, and our key fit. Inside the box there was a yellow baggage claim ticket with the words "Lufthansa Airlines" written across it next to a number. Nat grinned, tapping the ticket with her finger and saying, "Germany! Scholtz couldn't get Mr. Taylor to say Lufthansa, so he had him say Germany. That's kinda neat."

I agreed that it was neat and offered to race her to the car, where we could discuss it at length and drive at the same time.

The baggage claim area of Cleveland Hopkins International Airport is on the ground floor, which is actually below street level at some spots, while having streets running by at others. It's a little confusing, but then again most airports are. Nat and I parked in a lot, rode the people movers down a long glass causeway that was, again, well-lit—the electric bills for keeping relatively empty buildings bright at night must be enormous—and took an escalator down what must have been two stories only to ride back up on the other side of an alcove and down again to the baggage carousel, which never seems to stop moving. A few yawning business travelers were standing inside the roped-off area around the carousel, waiting for their bags to come tumbling by while red flight numbers flashed on TV screens overhead. Uniformed attendants laughed with one another between examinations of claim tickets as people asked about taxicabs and hotels. Not a single attendant was wearing a white hat, I noticed, which made me wonder if maybe we were supposed to come looking for our German suitcase on a particular day, or during a particular shift.

Finally I chose an attendant standing alone and asked him how long unclaimed suitcases were kept on the premises. He told me he didn't know, but that if I'd like to wait around, the office that took care of that kind of stuff would be open in about an hour. Nat shrugged, and we went back upstairs on the escalator and had an outrageously overpriced breakfast at some cafeteria-type restaurant with a cleverly aeronautical name and at least three rumpled men in uniform who looked as if they were trying to sober up after a long night of flying. The men were pilots, judging by their shoulder boards, and I told Nat to remind me never to fly on the airline they apparently worked for.

At exactly six we were back at the baggage office as the door was unlocked by a man with a ring of keys and a pleasant smile. Pretty much without preamble, I

produced my claim ticket and asked for my suitcase. When the man asked me to describe the bag, I said that I couldn't because I was picking it up for an elderly uncle who had neglected to tell me what kind of suitcase he had lost. The man, who was about fifty years old and had a stooping way of standing behind his desk, studied the ticket for a moment, then looked into my eyes and said, "I'm not certain I remember this flight number. Are you sure there isn't something you've forgotten?"

I told him that no, there wasn't anything I could think of . . . and he handed back the ticket and said that he couldn't help me. Nat tugged on my arm and whispered, "Money," in my ear, making me say, "Oh yeah," like a kid. But when I produced my wallet, it didn't faze the man, who just shook his head and insisted that he didn't recognize the flight.

Standing in the baggage claim area again, which was considerably more crowded than when we had first arrived, Nat and I looked at one another for a while, and then she produced the paper she had in her pocket and read our list of clues again. When she said the words, "White; Hat," our eyes snapped up to meet and she said, "*You're* supposed to be wearing one!"

"Come on!" I said.

We ran up the escalator, climbing over suitcases, and the people who had brought them, dashed down the concourse to the section where they had the gift shops, and bought a twelve-dollar white fishing hat that had the words, INSTANT ASSHOLE—ADD ALCOHOL, written across the front. Nat laughed when I put it on, stepping back for a better look and putting her hand to her mouth as she said, "You should wear hats more often. They do something for you."

I grouched something in return and dragged her by the hand down the escalator, only to find that the baggage claim office was stuffed full of angry travelers, one of whom fumed, "Nice hat," as he squeezed past me through the door.

We waited an hour before the office cleared out and we could reenact our little charade with the clerk. This time we

got our suitcase. He saw my hat, said, "Oh, *that* Lufthansa Airlines," and pulled a black leather overnight bag out from behind the counter. It cost me a hundred dollars to make him hand it over, and I gave him my hat as a bonus, mumbling to Nat that it was lucky he didn't want more because I wouldn't have been able to buy our way out of the parking lot. She elbowed me and said that there were bank machines all over the airport.

We could hardly keep ourselves from ripping the overnight bag open right there in the office. We waited until we got to the car, and, beneath the early morning sun of a fresh summer day, we sat in our convertible and peered into the suitcase it had taken us all night to find. Inside there were all the typical things you'd expect to find in a traveler's overnight bag: shaving cream, tooth comb, hairbrush, soap. But there was also one thing you don't normally run across in an average business day. Wrapped into a cylinder and hidden inside a box containing a tube of Crest Tartar Control toothpaste was a single sheet of paper bearing a map of the city, on the back of which was typed a set of instructions. There was also a bullet in that box, which Nat and I both took as a reminder, intended to emphasize to Chester Scholtz that the game he was playing was anything but a game.

We arranged to meet Larry Fizner and his associate, Judy Newhardt, later that day to plan our strategy. Of course I called my brother the moment I got back to the funeral home and spent an hour on the phone with him describing every detail of our search. And then I took a shower. Nat went to work, dragging like a zombie for lack of sleep, and I drank a pot of coffee . . . which I was seriously getting sick of by that point, perking up a little but still feeling pretty lousy. I hadn't been sleeping well at all the past few nights, and the wear was beginning to show.

At nine, three uniformed police officers arrived, eliciting some pretty strong glances from my father, who had been looking at me cockeyed anyway because of the dark circles under my eyes. He was wondering if I had been drinking

the night before, I knew it. But he was too nice to ask. The cops were almost apologetic—on account of my dad, I'm sure—saying that they knew I didn't have anything personally to do with the murder of Steven Teeg, but that the young man's father had been adamant, and quite specific in his statements about what I had said and done the other day in his office. They had to follow it up, they explained, hoping I'd understand.

I understood all right, and told them everything I knew . . . well . . . okay . . . maybe not everything. But a lot. Part of it, anyway. I left out the code and the key and the suitcase and the bullet, figuring that since Steven Teeg didn't know anything about those things, then the police didn't need to know either. The officers dutifully wrote everything I said down and left after about an hour. But on the way out one of them stopped at the door and gave me some advice, which boiled down to its bone went something like, "Watch your ass, kid. Don't fuck up." Deep words from a significant source. I thanked him and promised to be in touch.

At seven that evening, our intrepid little band assembled at an Italian restaurant near the funeral home, sitting in a booth with a red gingham tablecloth and a candle stuck into the top of an empty wine bottle, dribbled with wax for atmosphere. Nat and I sat together, with Larry Fizner and Judy Newhardt across the table from us. Larry was in an opulent mood, instructing us all to order anything we wanted, and saying, with an expansive series of hand gestures, that the meal was his treat, which made me instantly suspicious. We each had a copy of the map page Nat and I had found in the Lufthansa overnight bag, and we studied it until our salads came. No one spoke much, which created a strangely tight atmosphere around the table that I finally found tedious, and broke by saying, "So okay, it was definitely Terry Scholtz who killed the Teeg kid. What do we do now?"

Larry Fizner's eyes widened as he thrust his finger to his lips and said, "Shhh! Not so loud."

I looked around skeptically, saying, "Oh, I forgot. Maybe we should check the spaghetti for microphones." Nat rolled her eyes.

Judy Newhardt sat silently, studying us all as she chewed her salad. She was a hard-looking woman, made no more attractive to me by the things I had seen her do, nor the things her employer had said she was capable of doing. Her hair was peroxide blond, cut short and spiky. And her eyes were an icy blue. She spoke very little . . . and, now that I thought about it, I realized that I had never heard her voice. Inspired by that thought I looked at her and asked, "So, have you put in your two weeks' notice at the girlie bar yet, or are you thinking of maybe making a career change?" eliciting no reply save for a noncommittal shrug and a chilly glance from those hard little eyes. "Just do me a favor," I added, "if they should start playing music during the meal, dance on somebody else's table. Okay?"

The instructions on the back of the map we had found read:

> Meeting scheduled 8:00 p.m., Saturday, August 22.
> Arrive Cleveland Hopkins Airport—see map—7:30,
> go to Skyview Club bar, and put a drink on private
> flight number 1111's tab. Someone will approach
> you and take you where you need to go. Don't
> bring a weapon. And don't be late.

Larry Fizner read the instructions aloud for us, and then explained that during the day he had looked up flight 1111's owner, finding the plane registered to a publishing house operating out of Louisiana. Between bites of salad, Nat said that Louisiana made sense to her, since the most likely candidate for the man interested in buying Constantine Stenetti's identity was reported to be living in Mexico. "But he supposedly visits Texas quite a bit. Even has a couple of houses in Dallas, and one in a little town called Nacogdoches. He was a horse nut when he was younger, and he still runs a

few thoroughbreds. But he doesn't ride anymore."

"And who might that be?" Larry Fizner asked, just a little smugly.

To which Nat replied, "Anthony 'Pork Pie' Elestrano, old-timer out of Philadelphia. Made his bones in '26 in the Reglari killing. He was eighteen years old then, so that would make him eighty-four now. He ended up in the Gulf of Mexico area during the Second World War, hijacking consumer goods off the docks. But he didn't really hit it all that big until the early sixties, when he was one of the first old-timers to see that drugs were a permanent thing and not just a passing fad. He was fifty years old, and sharp enough to spot the hippies as a market, making him one of the first big-time importers of hashish and Colombian marijuana ever."

"How do you know all that?" Larry asked, obviously impressed.

And Nat replied, "I'm a research librarian. Today in the library, I researched."

"What else did you find out?"

"You really want to know?"

Larry nodded, and so did I. I had already heard Nat's report on the way to the restaurant, but I wanted to hear it again because it gave me a lot of pleasure just watching her speak.

Her sources, she said, were the *New York Times* and a couple of "true crime" books, including one called the *Who's Who of American Thuggery*, which was a particularly grisly affair that repulsed her with its graphic descriptions and photographs, and that she had ended up reading all afternoon. It was strange, she observed at one point, how something awful that happened to real people on a street corner in some city or another became almost mythical after someone wrote about it in a book. The nicknames of what was essentially a bunch of brutish, self-centered men, and the black-and-white photographs of the classic old cars and all the rest—the tommy guns and the bullet holes riddling restaurant windows—all added up to a picturesque, almost

Hollywood atmosphere that seemed to capture a powerful moment in time between a pair of dusty old covers while removing it from the real world . . . as if it had all happened to black-and-white people in a black-and-white reality. Larry Fizner, who had known more than his share of brutish men with nicknames like "Louie the Fish" and Eddie "Sharp Shoe" Lester, assured her that the crimes about which she had read had been anything but black-and-white when they occurred, and that the predominant color he associated with such incidents in his memory was the red of the victim's blood . . . which, coming from him, was a statement of such expressive vividness that I couldn't help but mark it in my mind.

The significant event, she said, occurred nearly twenty years before, in 1973. The city was New York, and the circumstances were fuzzy. Even after the trial, and its subsequent convictions, the events were still fuzzy, and the chances were that the only two people on earth who knew what really happened in all its grotesque detail were Constantine Stenetti, and his own personal avenging angel, Anthony "Pork Pie" Elestrano. By the way, they called Elestrano Pork Pie because, when he had been a street kid in Philadelphia in the very early twenties, the success of some crime or another he had pulled was invariably announced by his purchase of fresh pork—which at that time was very expensive—for his mother to make for dinner. At one point in his early career, he had even been tripped up because of this affectation, when a neighborhood beat cop noticed him emerging from a butcher shop carrying a paper bundle on the day after a clothing store robbery. Stopping him on suspicion—which I guess cops could do back then—the officer ended up arresting the young hood, who, it turned out, was wearing a pair of pants he'd lifted from the men's store while robbing it. Later, in his closet at home, the police discovered seventeen brand-new suits, all with the store's label inside, for which, it was later revealed, the young Elestrano had made two trips from the store and back.

While Anthony Elestrano had a colorful, and some might even say, romantic history, Constantine Stenetti's past was anything but elegant. He, like Elestrano, came from a poor, inner-city background. But where Elestrano used his cunning and imagination to build a thriving trade in what amounted to a commodities market, Stenetti earned his living, and what reputation he had, through acts of utter brutality. He was a thug, plain and simple: slow of thought, mean, uneducated, and violently vain. He lived from day to day, making a decent living as an enforcer for the local big shots, but pissing away the money on his own personal affectation: pornography. They even called him "Peep Show" for a while, but it was a nickname he despised, and he was reputed to have killed a number of men for using it. He was a heavy drinker, and a gambler. In short, he was everything the government could ever hope for in a witness . . . meaning, that once he was arrested and given the choice to cooperate or rot in jail, he was destined to betray his associates and concentrate on saving his own skin.

"How am I doing so far?" Nat asked, as a waitress set down plates of steaming pasta before us. Larry Fizner grunted as he nodded his approval, and I couldn't help but notice that the restaurant in which we were eating looked disturbingly like one where a classic mob hit might take place.

If it wasn't for what had happened in 1973, Constantine Stenetti would, in all likelihood, have spent his life as an unknown crook, and was probably fated to die while in the act of carrying out his brutal profession. As it was, he ended up infamous for a time, and his complicity irreparably altered the life of Anthony Elestrano, who swore vengeance on Stenetti with some of the most fearful oaths ever printed in any newspaper.

"It was all quite a big deal," Nat said with a kind of shrug I recognized as meaning that she personally found it all a little silly, despite the suffering of the participants, who, I knew, she saw as bringing their troubles on themselves by their poor behavior. "It was in the news for weeks. And

the trial . . . Jesus. The tabloids ran transcripts in special supplements on Sunday! It was ghoulish, but I guess it sold a lot of papers."

"It certainly did," Larry Fizner agreed, his eyes misting over a little as if they were looking back and seeing that time of his life again. "Stenetti changed the face of at least one part of the drug world. Fucked it up absolutely. And not only did he betray the trust of everyone he had ever known in the rackets, he sold out his friends to the cops."

The story went like this:

By 1970, the incredible amount of money generated by America's burgeoning illegal drug trade was putting a strain on the power structure of what could be called the traditional underworld in this country. Many of the most powerful families had divested their interest in the risky businesses, cleaning up their acts and raking it in through casinos in Vegas, silent partnerships in Hollywood movie studios, and soft contract jobs gotten through their political connections. The old-timers were getting tired, and maybe even a little gun-shy, and the young bloods moving up were undisciplined and prone to excessive behaviors that brought them more and more into the public eye. Instead of the quiet opulence of outwardly humble men enjoying their ill-gotten wealth in private, the new "gangsters" were flaunting their riches, hobnobbing with celebrities, and finding a peculiar kind of celebrity of their own that inevitably brought the authorities sniffing around. The clash between the old and the new was never more evident than in the case of Anthony "Pork Pie" Elestrano and a Young Turk in the drug trade named Santonio DeLuca Garcia, a Colombian-born American citizen living in Miami.

Garcia was blatantly cutting into Elestrano's market by employing private, free-lance pilots known as Lunch Boxes because they flew tin-pot planes into deserted areas in the dark, to deliver drugs from bases in Mexico to receiving points in Texas. Such private trade was reasonably rare at that time, and because of its insignificant volume, it was usually tolerated by the larger organizations. Maybe

there was a confrontation now and then between dealers on the street when different suppliers tried to work the same neighborhood, but normally business ran smoothly, and because of the richness of the market, there seemed to be enough for everybody.

But Garcia was greedy. Instead of accepting his place on the lower level of the hierarchy, he began what amounted to a guerrilla war against the established drug smugglers in the Gulf of Mexico. Three families ran the trade in that part of the country, and, though he had been the first to recognize the market, Anthony Elestrano's organization was the smallest of the three. So, Garcia chose Elestrano's turf as his starting point, viewing it as the most vulnerable to attack, which he orchestrated from his Miami headquarters as a series of harassment maneuvers intended to make conducting business so costly for Elestrano that he would be forced to either share his market with Garcia, or get out altogether. If Garcia's attack had come in the traditional manner of one family usurping the trade of another, Elestrano would have simply "gone to the mattresses," meaning that he would have had his soldiers hit back until the attacking family was destroyed. In a traditional confrontation, Elestrano would have held the advantage, and the war would have lasted a couple of months at most.

But Garcia didn't fight a traditional war. Instead he employed Latino youths in the ghettos of Texas cities to chop up not Elestrano's muscle men—the normal target in a mob dispute—but the families of Elestrano's daily business people. Wives were murdered, and children gunned down. Horrible acts of savagery aimed at what were traditionally considered to be off limits targets totally disrupted the Elestrano family, creating an environment of outrage that had people all over the country calling for an end to the violence. Elestrano hit back, and he hit back hard, aiming his attack not at the punks carrying out Garcia's orders, but at the people surrounding Garcia himself, and the war spread to Miami. Something had to give. This confrontation could not be allowed to continue. It was bad for business, and it

was causing the other larger and more powerful families concern. So Elestrano called for a meeting between himself and Garcia, to be held on neutral ground, in New York City, where together the old hood and the young general could sit down and work out some understanding. The meeting was set for the fifth of July, 1973, and elaborate precautions were taken to ensure the safety of both participants.

Here, Larry Fizner interrupted Nat's telling of the story, taking it up himself, since what she was saying had come from newspapers and books, and his knowledge of the affair had come from more personal experience.

"Naturally everybody was double-crossing everybody else," he said, pushing his dinner plate away. "And, through informants, the government knew that something big was going down somewhere. We just didn't know the details."

The plate was empty, and he had scraped it clean of sauce with slices of hot Italian bread. Leaning back, he put his hands on his stomach and, looking very satisfied, ran his gaze over each of us as he spoke, telling us all with his expression that he was trying his best to be perfectly frank.

"To make it short," he continued, "Elestrano hired Stenetti, who was about fifty-some-odd years old, and known as a reliable professional, to make the hit on Garcia in New York.

"And by the way," he interrupted himself, as if the thought had just occurred to him, "I wasn't personally involved in any of this. I just heard about it through the people I worked with. I was gumshoeing some other job, living in a fleabag hotel in Pittsburgh, and bored senseless most of the time because the guy I was shadowing wasn't doing shit . . . living like a fucking monk . . . pardon my French. Naturally I knew about the dispute between Elestrano and Garcia that was going on . . . everybody in the business knew about that. Nowadays a gang war with innocent bystanders getting cut down in the street's no big deal. Happens all the time. But back then it was something

unheard of . . . a new kind of thing. So naturally we were all interested.

"Anyway, when I wasn't actually working, I was hanging out with other guys in the business. You know . . . talking shop, that kinda shit. I didn't do nothing personally, but I heard a lot. When the shit finally hit the fan, you couldn't help but hear. Know what I mean?"

Judy, Nat, and I all nodded in unison, like a group of kids listening to their grandfather tell them a bedtime story.

"Now, according to Elestrano, he wanted Stenetti to hit Garcia before he could get himself too comfortable in the city. His thinking was that once he hunkered down in his hotel or whatever, he'd be out of reach. There was no way any of Elestrano's men could ever infiltrate Garcia's inner circle because Garcia surrounded himself with nothing but spics, and he didn't trust nobody else. So Elestrano wanted Stenetti to hit him from a distance. Kind of a Kennedy assassination type of thing. Or at least that was his plan.

"But here's where things get fuzzy, like Mrs. Hawley said earlier. Elestrano insisted later that he had hired Stenetti with a very specific task in mind: kill DeLuca Garcia. Stenetti's version is that he wasn't hired to kill Garcia, but rather to 'get him off Elestrano's back.' He said that the killing of Garcia had never been specifically planned, nor discussed. Leaving him free, in his own mind at least, to do whatever he could come up with that would so intimidate Garcia that he would be forced to withdraw from the field.

"So, while the mob's eyes were all focused on the events in New York City, and every federal agent who could get away was running around trying to pick up clues as to where and when the big meeting was going to take place, Stenetti traveled to the very village in Colombia where Garcia was born. And while he was there he did something that ended up being the bottom line as far as why Anthony Elestrano would be still interested in getting his hands on him, even after all these years.

"Two days before the meeting in New York was scheduled, Stenetti arrived in Miami from South America on one of Elestrano's private planes. He was carrying a plastic cooler packed with dry ice, which he immediately had delivered to Garcia's home, knowing that Garcia was out of town, but confident that he would get the message anyway. Garcia's wife was home at the time, and the house, which was a magnificent place, all done in an adobe style, was crawling with security people. Inside the cooler, wrapped in aluminum foil, was the head of Garcia's younger sister, seventeen years old and never having had anything to do with her brother's activities in America.

"When he got the news Garcia practically lost his mind, totally freaked out, went nuts. He punched the shit out of one of his own men in the hotel, screamed in Spanish for an hour, and had everybody convinced that he was going to throw himself out the window. The meeting in New York was cancelled; there would be no peace between Garcia and Elestrano no matter what the price. And a contract was put out that stated that whoever got to the man who had killed DeLuca Garcia's sister be given a permanent position of respect in Garcia's organization. Elestrano, for his part, was furious. Instead of removing his main rival from the game, Stenetti had enraged him, making him more dangerous than ever. And the meeting that Elestrano was counting on to be Garcia's death trap was transformed into a symbol of Elestrano's untrustworthiness and ineptitude. After he had so cleverly suckered his victim into a vulnerable position, he'd blown the hit, and now everything was gummed up but good. From Elestrano the word went out: 'Kill that son of a bitch Stenetti . . . that asshole nitwit fuck-head. I don't care who does it, but there's a fat commission for whoever makes the hit.'

"So in one day, Constantine Stenetti, who had thought that he was doing something smart, fucked himself up from both sides. Everybody wanted him. He had nowhere to turn but to the feds. Before either Garcia's men or Elestrano's could get to him, he literally walked into the F.B.I.'s office

in Miami and turned himself over. Bells went off from one end of the country to the other, and instantly Anthony Elestrano took off for the border.

"For nearly a year after that, Stenetti spilled his guts. In exchange for the government's protection he described mob killings all over the country, implicating people right and left, and pointing the finger at men who the cops had wanted to nail for decades, but who had been insulated from prosecution by a lack of witnesses. Maybe it was because he felt betrayed by Elestrano . . . after all, he had done what he thought he needed to do, and had received a death sentence for his trouble, or maybe he was just one of those men who needs to confess, but for whatever reason, he betrayed just about everyone he had ever known, and was the cause of the downfall of Anthony Elestrano's drug operation in the southwest. Garcia, enraged by his sister's killing, recklessly threw himself at Elestrano's organization, and Elestrano, preoccupied with the arrest of his associates on Stenetti's evidence, couldn't seem to fight back effectively. Eventually, years later, Elestrano got his own back against Garcia, but for almost fifteen years he was forced to rebuild his empire from his position of exile in Mexico. And during all that time, he blamed Constantine Stenetti for his trouble, and swore that, when he could, he would have his revenge, no matter how long it took for him to do it."

Larry Fizner stopped, and for a moment there was silence at the table. Then he said, "So now we all know the story. And we know when the meeting Chet Scholtz had set up with old man Elestrano is going to happen. But what we don't know is who in that nursing home is really Constantine Stenetti, and that, unfortunately, is really the key to our being able to do anything with our information."

I had been waiting for a moment such as this all evening, and I had known that it would have to come sooner or later. Clearing my throat, I said, "Supposing that we did know who Stenetti was at the Manor Care, what would we do about it?"

To which Larry Fizner replied that, as far as he was concerned, Constantine Stenetti was not a man worth too much compassion.

"I'd turn him over and get the money," he concluded.

"You would?" I asked seriously.

"Like a shot."

"But what about the fact that this Elestrano person would almost certainly have him killed?" Nat asked softly.

"Who cares?" Fizner returned.

We all seemed to think that over. Who did care? That was the essential question, and, unfortunately, no one seemed willing to offer an answer.

Finally, I said, "Since we've got to assume that Terry Scholtz made Steven Teeg tell him who Constantine Stenetti is before he left him to strangle on his living room floor, I'd think that it's also a safe bet that he was planning to keep his father's original appointment with Elestrano and collect the bounty money that was promised. Agreed?"

Larry Fizner nodded.

"But," Nat said, "how would he know the details of the appointment? Look how hard we had to work to figure it out."

"Maybe his father told him," I offered.

"Then why would Chester Scholtz go to all the trouble of encoding the instructions leading to the Lufthansa flight bag?" Nat asked.

"Maybe there was more than one copy of the instructions," Larry Fizner said. "Mrs. Scholtz ransacked her husband's room after she left the hospital the morning he died. Maybe she found that other copy and gave it to her son."

Nat was shaking her head. "No," she said, "I don't think so. She wasn't looking for coded messages that morning; she was looking for the money she knew her husband had taken out of the bank earlier in the day. It's as simple as that. I know if my husband took fifty thousand bucks from our account, I'd want to find it before somebody in the nursing home put it in their pocket. Wouldn't you?"

No one moved.

"And besides," Nat continued, "the suitcase was still at the airport counter for us to find. Nobody had been there before us. I don't think there's any way Terry Scholtz can know where he's supposed to be for the meeting. And it must be driving him crazy . . . he killed somebody for nothing. He's got a name worth a bundle, but he doesn't know what to do with it. And the four of us, who are the only people besides Elestrano himself who can possibly know when and where he and Chester Scholtz were going to meet, have no way of getting the name Elestrano wants."

"But what about the newspaper?" Judy Newhardt asked, making us all look at her. "It said in the paper that Scholtz was dead . . . and there was a death notice on Sunday, before his funeral. Why would Elestrano still keep the appointment if he knows that the person he was supposed to meet died last Friday night?"

Larry Fizner placed his hands flat down on the table and looked at each of us for a moment, as if measuring who we were. Finally, he said, "He'll come," as if announcing some unarguable truth. "The newspaper article won't change anything. He's got nothing to lose by keeping the meeting, and for all he knows, or cares, the article could be part of Scholtz's cover. Now, what we need to consider, is how much that piece of paper you found in that Lufthansa flight bag would be worth to Terry Scholtz?"

"You mean partner up with him?" Nat asked. "After he killed that boy, you want to make a deal with him?"

Leaning back in his chair, Larry Fizner sighed, saying, "I had a feeling you'd react that way," as if Nat had burst his bubble. "But it's our only option."

"We can tell the police," Nat countered. "That's another option. We can tell the police that Chester Scholtz told his son what he was doing, and that his son killed Steven Teeg to finish what his father started! That's the other thing we can do!"

"Not if we want the money," Fizner pointed out. "If we want the money, we make a deal with a killer . . . that's our only choice."

"Maybe not," I cut in, and everyone at the table looked at me expectantly. "There's a final option you haven't considered. We could keep the meeting at the airport ourselves, and cut Terry Scholtz out of it completely. We could leave him turning in the wind, and sooner or later the cops are bound to pick him up. His only hope of getting away with killing Teeg rested on his getting the money and getting out of town quickly, before the police could connect him with what his father was doing and start asking him questions. Without the money, he's a sitting duck."

"But how are we supposed to cut him out of it when he's the one with the name?" Judy Newhardt asked, obviously annoyed.

"But he's not the only one," I said. "Terry Scholtz may have gotten Constantine Stenetti's cover name out of Steven Teeg before he died, but he's not the only one who knows the secret anymore."

"Who else knows?" Larry Fizner asked.

To which I replied, "Me."

"You?" He almost laughed, his face breaking into a disbelieving grin. "Bullshit!"

Judy Newhardt was looking at me like a cat studying a blue jay.

"It's true," I said, taking Nat's hand for support. "While you were all out doing your individual things today, I was out doing mine. I was being a funeral director and talking to a few people I know. This afternoon, at the county registrar's office, I looked up birth certificates on their microfiche. It only took me a couple of hours to find the name of a man living at the Manor Care Nursing Home who doesn't have any birth certificate on file at all, which means that the name he's living under is assumed."

"But Stenetti wasn't born in Cleveland," Larry Fizner protested. "Just because a birth certificate's not on file at

Cleveland City Hall doesn't mean it doesn't exist someplace else!"

"I know," I said, placating him. "And for just that reason,
I also used the registrar's equipment to tap into the national
vital statistics computer mainframe. That program's like a
gigantic filing cabinet, and it hooks you up to records kept
all over the country. If a person's not recorded in there,
he's not recorded."

"But there are hundreds of patients at the Manor Care,"
Judy Newhardt protested. "You couldn't possibly have
looked them all up."

"I didn't need to. Mr. Fizner himself told me that the way
he had found out that Constantine Stenetti was at the Manor
Care in the first place was because another nursing home
had gone out of business and its patients were transferred
there. Well, I had Pete Germaine give me a list of the
people transferred from that other nursing home, narrowed
it down according to sex and age, since we know that
Stenetti's seventy-four years old, and then examined the
twelve men left on the list. Only one has no recorded
birth certificate, and, checking that man's Social Security
number through the Social Security office on York Road,
I found that that number came up as belonging to someone
else. There's absolutely no doubt in my mind that I know
exactly who Constantine Stenetti is at the Manor Care, and,
that if we wanted to, we could collect the money Chester
Scholtz died for last week."

"Meaning we could sell a human being's life for gold,"
Nat said.

And Larry Fizner narrowed his eyes.

"You know," he said, "if you're wrong about this, we're
all dead."

"I'm not wrong," I said.

"Then I think we should vote," he replied, somewhat
skeptically. "As to what we're going to do, I mean. It's the
only fair way. We should share whatever we get, and we
should share the decision too. We've all been through this
together. So what's it going to be? Do we take a chance and

make the meeting this Saturday in Chester Scholtz's place, or do we forget it and let it go?"

Three of us raised our hands. Only Nat voted no. So it was decided: armed with my information, we'd make the meeting.

EIGHT

■■■■■■■■■■

IT SEEMED TO take a hundred years for Saturday to come. And then, once the day had arrived, it took another two hundred years for the clock to move its hands around its face sufficiently to bring the evening home. The fact that it was August didn't help matters either; I couldn't even distract myself with my job because there was absolutely nothing to do around the funeral home. Believe it or not, death is seasonal. I'm not kidding. Funeral homes are busy in the winter and dead in the summer—no pun intended. When you tell someone that, they'll usually say something tasteless like, "Yeah, a lot of old people must kick off shoveling snow, huh?" But that's not really the case. I personally think that it's just a lot easier to give up the ghost in the middle of January, when the sky is grey and the air bitter cold, with nothing to look forward to but another ten weeks of the same oppressive weather, than it is to say good-bye to a world filled with singing birds and blooming flowers. Scientifically, I don't have a shred of evidence to support my conclusion, but the statistics will bear me out. More people die in the winter than in the summer . . . and that's just all there is to it.

So for three days I sat, waiting to go to the airport Saturday evening and meet a famous gangster. On Thursday, Larry Fizner made a big production out of going with me down to city hall and running through the process I had originally used to discover Constantine Stenetti's identity, and that evening, over yet another meal with the four of us sitting around a restaurant table, he announced that, according to his professional opinion, my conclusion was sound. I made a show of feeling relieved that his expertise had validated my efforts, but I could still practically taste the skepticism radiating off Judy Newhardt, who, though she had voted to go through with our plan because her boss had done so, didn't seem to be at all convinced, and who refused to say another word all week. Instead, she simply stared at me, and, by Friday, I was seeing those cold, unblinking eyes of hers in my sleep.

When Saturday finally came I paced around like a caged animal. Nat, on the other hand, seemed perfectly composed. Finally, around lunchtime, I broke down and asked her how the hell she could be so calm, and she said that she had examined our plan from every angle she could think of and had concluded that it was as good as she could expect it to be. We were committed to it, she said, and since worrying wasn't going to dissuade anyone from the course we had set for ourselves, what was the point in wasting the time or energy doing it?

"That's an awfully Zen kind of answer," I observed.

And she replied, "Look, Bill, there's obviously nothing I can say to make you not want that money, so all I can do is hope for the best."

"Yeah, but if you told me that you didn't want me to go through with the meeting, you know I'd do what you said."

"I know," she agreed. "But then things between us would be just like they are between you and your dad."

"Things are fine between me and my dad," I protested.

And Nat cut in, "Bill," taking both of my hands in hers and sitting me down so that we faced one another in a pair

of chairs in our living room. "When we got out of college we wanted to get married, but I didn't have a job, and neither did you. So instead of working for strangers, your dad said that you could come and work for him, which you did . . . not because you wanted to, but because you felt that you had an obligation to him as a son, and to me as a husband. You never wanted to be a funeral director . . . and you've resented working for your dad ever since."

"I feel like I never left home," I admitted, looking down at the carpet. "I feel like I can't make it on my own, and that I need my father to support me."

"I know," Nat said. "And I feel like your unhappiness is my fault because, when you asked me, I told you that I thought you should take the job. You and your dad get along fine, and you make a good living, but underneath there's that needling something that just won't let you have any peace. Until you make a change in your life, you're always going to be unhappy. Apparently, scoring this money is a part of the change you need. If I do anything to dissuade you now, I'll be responsible for yet another decision you made in favor of your obligations instead of your desires."

"But everybody has responsibilities," I said. "You've got to make concessions and compromises just to get along. It's a part of growing up."

"True," Nat agreed, growing quiet and studying my face. "And you've apparently made yours."

"I have to do this," I admitted, squeezing her hands and lowering my eyes.

"I know," she whispered.

"If I pull this off . . ." I said, pulling her to me and folding her up in my arms.

"What?"

"I don't know."

"Say it."

"Really, I just don't know. But it's a feeling like I've never had before."

"Is that honestly true?"

"Yeah. It is."

"Then I think you better just do it, and not question it anymore. You need to have your mind focused. You need to be sharp."

"You think I'm sharp?" I asked, pulling back and looking into my wife's dark eyes.

I thought she'd kiss me, or make some kind of joke to ease the tension a little. But instead she just looked at me for a long time before she finally said, "I'm the one person in the world who's never asked you to prove anything, Bill. I took you for what you are. You're the one who's doing the discovering."

"Do you think the plan will work?" I asked.

And she asked, "Do you?"

I hesitated for a moment, and then I said, "Yes."

And that was all.

I had badgered myself about this very question for hours and hours, and no matter how much I wanted to believe differently, deep down inside, I was simply convinced that we could pull it off. It was at that instant that I realized what Nat had meant when she said that she couldn't keep me from wanting the money. She could make me change the course of my behavior with a word, but there was, deep inside me, a spark of fire that cherished our plan. If I didn't get the chance to test my conviction, it would nag at me forever.

"Well then," she said, letting me go and standing up. "If you think it will, then it will."

"That's it?" I asked, a little disappointed.

"What else is there?" she asked.

And, you know, I couldn't think of a single thing to say in return.

"Okay, here we go," said Larry Fizner at seven o'clock that evening as Nat and I settled into the backseat of his big yellow van. The van was done up inside like a hippie crash pad; with shag carpet on the walls; big, puffy, overstuffed captain's chairs; and stereo equipment strung with dangling

speaker cable. It wasn't what I expected at all, and when I mentioned that to him, Larry Fizner replied, "What *did* you expect?"

"I don't know," I answered. "Surveillance equipment or something, I suppose."

"Like in the movies?" he said. "Revolving spy antennas and all that?"

"Well, maybe not exactly. But closer to that than this. This looks like Jethro Bodine's 'mobile bachelor pad' from 'The Beverly Hillbillies.' "

At that, both Larry Fizner and Judy Newhardt laughed in the front seat, and the sound of it went a long way toward making me feel a little more at ease. It also made me wonder, not for the first time, about the exact nature of their relationship. Judy Newhardt looked to be somewhere between twenty-five and thirty years old. Larry Fizner was sixty if he was a day, probably more. It made me wonder, especially the way they seemed to communicate nonverbally, as if they each knew what the other was thinking . . . which made me very nervous indeed.

I really didn't want Nat to come with us, but after just a minute or two's worth of discussion I had seen that trying to talk her out of it was useless. She sat next to me, holding my hand in silence. And the feeling of her skin on mine kept raising images in my mind about the evening's potential outcome. Larry Fizner and I had planned things very carefully. Even before our discussion in the Italian restaurant, we had gone over what we intended to do. And now all that was left for us to do it. But the idea of Nat's getting hurt made my stomach flip-flop; and maybe I was being a typical, ego-obsessed male, but I have to admit that I desperately wished that I could leave her at home and say something like, "You stay here, my dear. This is no job for a woman." I'd seen guys do shit like that in old movies, but I couldn't even imagine trying to pull anything like it with Nat. With Nat, it just wouldn't fly.

It had finally stopped raining, and now the weather was cool . . . I mean really cool. August in northeast Ohio can

get pretty beastly—hot and sticky dog days that seem to go on forever. So sixty degrees and overcast, which is what the weather was like that evening, made it feel like November. Larry Fizner drove, and I realized this was the first time I'd ever seen him do that. Usually he rode shotgun and left the driving to Judy Newhardt . . . but tonight he was in charge, and he talked almost incessantly, a cigarette stuck into the side of his mouth and his hands jumping around on the steering wheel as if he were playing an accordion. I didn't listen to most of what he said . . . it was all reminiscences from what I could tell, but what did catch my attention was the way Judy Newhardt's eyes fixed on the side of his face. He'd glance at her every once in a while, as if to see if she were listening, and she drank in what he said as if it were the most interesting thing in the world. They were a peculiar pair, and I couldn't help but wonder how in the world they had come together.

We took the freeway, Larry chattering away up front, Nat squeezing my hand as she looked out the window, and me just as tense as a spring. I even caught myself trying to decide if any of the cars around us were familiar, if I had seen them before, or if they could possibly be following us. As soon as I realized what I was doing I closed my eyes and leaned my head back, sighing so loudly that Nat ended up asking me if I was all right. I told her that I was, even though I felt like I was going to throw up on Larry Fizner's cheap stereo, which was bolted to a piece of plywood anchored to the wall next to me and included an ancient turntable with an arm that bounced back and forth with the motion of the car. When we got off the freeway I held on to my knees to keep myself from bounding up and shouting, "I changed my mind! Let's turn around and go home!" even though I knew Larry Fizner would never agree. And as we moved down the concourse on the people mover in the airport, I got a twitch in the muscle of my right thigh that felt like an unsteady heartbeat.

I don't know how he did it, but Larry Fizner took it all in stride, looking as if he were at the airport to meet a maiden

aunt coming back from a trip to Florida. He was dressed in another of his hideous outfits: checkered polyester slacks, white loafers complete with tassels, white matching belt, pink golf shirt, and his beloved lemon-yellow sport coat. Judy Newhardt was dressed in tight black slacks and what looked like the top half of a one-piece bathing suit, also in black. With her spiky hair and stiletto heels, walking next to Larry as she was, the pair looked like a sleazy used-car salesman and his young, all-night diner waitress friend on their way to Vegas for the weekend. Nat was wearing a black full-length dress covered with a pink rose pattern and the pearls I'd given her for our tenth anniversary. And I was wearing my usual black suit pants, white shirt, and dark tie. Together, the four of us couldn't have looked more unrelated. If it weren't for the fact that something about the tense nature of our mission made us all unconsciously walk in a group, we wouldn't even have looked as if we were together, which might have been for the best.

We took a seat in the Skyview Club bar—the first time I had been in a bar in a very long time, and I couldn't help but admire all the exotic liquor bottles arranged along the back wall beneath the glasses that hung from the ceiling over the cash register like crystal decorations. When the waitress appeared I tried to order a Diet Coke, but my voice caught in my throat and I shot a panicked look Larry Fizner's way so that he piped up and said, "I'll have a Scotch and water." I recovered, ordered my Coke, and listened as Judy and Nat did the same. While the waitress was gone, Larry asked me if maybe I'd like to wait in the van because I was acting like a complete asshole. When she returned, he casually told her to put the drinks on the tab of private flight 1111, which, by the way, wouldn't happen to be in yet, would it? She said that she didn't know, but she could find out. Then she went away, reappearing a moment later to say that flight 1111 had been in and gone again about an hour before.

I almost gave myself whiplash looking at my watch. Larry told me to relax. Nat sipped her Coke. Absolutely everybody

in the bar, which was very small and claustrophobically close to the busy concourse, seemed to turn at that instant into an undercover cop, and I was suddenly convinced that we had been followed. I was really flying the paranoid express, and after another couple of swallows of cold soda I was sure that we were in over our heads. But just as I was about to say that I thought we should get our asses out of there, a man stepped up to our table and said, "Mr. Scholtz's party?" To which Larry Fizner said, "Yes," and I nodded like an idiot.

The man, who was short and thin, darkly tanned, and very Latin looking in his white slacks and shirt, bowed as he respectfully asked us to accompany him to the private lounge on the other side of the airport. A courtesy car was waiting, which was one of those golf cart things you see whizzing up and down airports with old people and their poodles facing backward behind the driver, who's usually about sixteen years old and driving like he's mad at somebody. I was already standing, ready to go, when Larry said that the man in white would just have to wait because he wanted to finish his drink. I had to consciously keep my mouth from falling open I was so amazed at his audacity, but the man simply bowed politely again and stood quietly until we were ready to go.

The golf cart ride was really weird. People look at you. No shit. As you go gliding by, every person walking through the concourse turns and gives you a quick once-over, which I didn't really need right that minute. At the end of the concourse, the man in white—who said not another word after inviting us to join him on the "courtesy car"—led us to an elevator marked STAFF and indicated that we should get in. He did not join us. Instead he hit the button, and my last image of him was of his grim, expressionless face watching us as the doors closed before him.

"Now remember," Larry Fizner said, taking the opportunity of speaking in private as the elevator car rose through the building, "we present a united front. No dissension, about anything. Clear?"

We all nodded.

"And Bill," he continued, looking directly at me, "don't tell them what they want to know until I say it's okay. These guys are probably going to look pretty smooth on the surface, but remember how they made their money. They're killers, and crooks, and liars, and thieves. Don't give 'em an inch, 'cause if you do, they'll take the whole hand you offer it with. Capish?"

"Are you sure you can handle 'em?" I asked, watching the numbers on the wall go from dark to light to dark again. I was amazed that there were so many floors to the airport. What the hell, were we going to meet these guys in the control tower or what?

"If I wasn't sure," Larry replied, "you can bet your ass that I wouldn't be here."

When the doors opened we found ourselves in a large, circular lobby with sky-blue carpeting and windows running from floor to ceiling all the way around, except for the elevator door behind where we stood, and another door, directly in front of us, that was tall and made of a kind of carved wood that was so dark and heavy that it made me think it should be in a courthouse or some other kind of government building instead of an airport. There was no sign of life. Just the closed door. We all stepped into the lobby as a group as outside on the runway giant silver airplanes lined up to take off between rows of flickering yellow lights.

"Well?" I whispered.

"Just wait," Larry Fizner returned. "This is his show, so we have to play it at his pace."

I was going to take Nat's hand again, but then I thought better of it. I wanted to give an impression of toughness and imperturbability. And standing there hanging onto my wife didn't strike me as the kind of activity that might create such an impression. Finally, after what seemed an eternity, the great wooden door opened, eliciting only the slightest rustle of sound against the sky-blue carpet, and one of the most beautiful women I have ever seen in my life stepped forward to say, "Welcome," directing her comments to

Larry Fizner, and ignoring the rest of us as if we weren't even there.

I guess expecting a grizzled old man and getting a knock-out young lady is kind of hard on the senses, because it took me a second or two to recover. By the time I did, Larry Fizner had shaken the woman's hand and said, "You can't be Kelly, can you?"

Making her grin with pleasure and return, "All grown-up, eh, Mr. Scholtz?"

When Larry explained that he wasn't Chester Scholtz, the woman's eyes darkened, and for an awkward moment I thought that there was going to be trouble. I could see her disappointment rise as a kind of undercurrent that swept right through her limbs, practically shuddering her flesh as if it were a physical force. She was about five feet nine inches tall and built like a runner. Her skin was tanned to a baked brick color that indicated that she was a naturally dark-skinned person who had spent her life in a very sunny place. Her hair was curly, cut as short as a man's, and dark. And her eyes were large, and vividly cultured, like those of a lady who might appear in a fashion magazine—bright, yet aloof. She spoke with a Spanish accent, and when I saw the intensity of the anger that stiffened her muscles when Larry Fizner explained that Chester Scholtz had been unable to attend this meeting personally, I realized that she was a woman of passion, accustomed to having her own way. I don't know precisely what made me do it, but at that instant I pegged her in my mind as hot-blooded, and spoiled . . . a rich kid from a family with money.

Larry Fizner either missed her display of temper, or, much more likely, chose to ignore it, preferring instead to play the diplomat as he introduced the rest of us with a sweeping movement of his arm and a grin that stretched from one of his big ears to the other. After saying each of our names and explaining our relationship one to the other, he completed his pronouncement by saying, "And this lovely creature is Kelly Elestrano, granddaughter of our illustrious host, known as Pony to her friends. The

last time I saw her she was only six years old. That was when your grandfather took you to Mexico to live, wasn't it, Kelly?"

"That's about right, yes," the girl complied, looking at Larry Fizner more carefully for his apparent knowledge. "But I'm afraid I don't remember you."

"Oh, you wouldn't," Larry said with good-natured dismissiveness. "I was just one of the gang."

"One of what gang?" Kelly Elestrano asked.

And I held my breath.

"One of the gang of thousands watching events unfold in the press," Larry replied. "A disinterested party."

"And how exactly did you become interested, Mr. Fizner?" Kelly Elestrano asked, and in those bright eyes of hers I thought I detected just the slightest hint of that anger she had tried so valiantly to suppress just a few moments before.

Larry Fizner then explained how Chester Scholtz had taken him into his confidence regarding the deal he had struck with her grandfather, and that, since Mr. Scholtz had met with such an unfortunate and untimely end— as she and her grandfather might have noticed if they had been monitoring the Cleveland news during the past week or so—he had decided to carry through with the original plan in his place. Obviously, he said, lying as smoothly as I've ever seen anyone lie in my life, Chet Scholtz had trusted him with every detail of the meeting, or we wouldn't have been there now. And, he assured the solemn young lady, we were not only in possession of the item her grandfather wanted, but we were also ready and able to make the exchange in exactly the same way as Chester Scholtz would have done, had he lived to see his plans through.

It was a good performance, but when it was through Kelly Elestrano asked, if all that were the case, then why had Larry brought the rest of us along when the original agreement her grandfather had made with Chester Scholtz had been very clear about his coming to the meeting alone?

Unfortunately, he replied, there was no way to avoid it. Miss Newhardt was his assistant and accompanied him everywhere he went. "And Mr. Hawley here is the bearer of the information your grandfather wants."

"And you?" Kelly Elestrano asked, directing her question at Nat.

"My husband and I are a team," Nat replied.

"You've got some Indian blood in you," Kelly Elestrano observed. "Navaho, I think."

"Sioux," Nat said.

"I don't think so," Elestrano said, shaking her head thoughtfully. "I've known a lot of Indians, and you definitely look Navaho."

"If you say so," Nat acquiesced, which was apparently what Elestrano wanted because she immediately moved on to the next topic.

"Anyway, we monitored you all the way through the airport on the security cameras, so we knew there was more than one of you coming. My grandfather said that if I was satisfied with the way you answered my questions that I should let you in."

She looked at us appraisingly for a moment, and then announced, "I don't like it, but my grandfather's been waiting a long time. So I'm going to let you pass. But be forewarned, if there's any bullshit going on here, no one will ever find your bodies."

With that she turned and led us through the great wooden doors into what I can only describe as the most lavishly appointed series of offices I have ever seen. The windows all overlooked the runway, and the furnishings were amazingly masculine, heavy, and obviously expensive. As we walked she explained that this area was owned jointly by the airport's original developers and the executives of the airlines who leased space below. If it was operated by the people who ran the airport, Larry Fizner asked, did that mean her grandfather was one of their number, since we were using the offices for our meeting? Kelly Elestrano didn't answer that question, but smiled to herself, as if to

say that we should work it out for ourselves. We didn't
see any people along the way until we got to the end
of the corridor and approached a final door, twenty feet
high, I'd bet, and carved like the entrance to a church.
There we found two men in dark suits standing side by
side, to whom Kelly Elestrano nodded and said something in Spanish. They eyed us suspiciously, but moved
aside, and we were thus, unceremoniously, admitted to
the inner sanctum where Anthony "Pork Pie" Elestrano,
the street kid from the Philadelphia of the 1920's, awaited
our arrival near a mahogany desk the size of a king-size
bed.

The curtains were drawn and Tiffany lamps lit, making
the office seem meditative and still. The carpet, wallpaper,
and drapes were all done in earthy tones that lent the
place an air of intransigence, as if decisions were made in
this room that required perfect concentration and absolute
secrecy. Even the sound of jets taking off on the runway
below was muted by some dampening quality of the walls,
for as the doors closed behind us a faint rumble gently
swelled from outside, only to reverberate like the sigh of
some passing giant, invisible and unconcerned.

Anthony Elestrano was standing next to the desk, waiting. His granddaughter moved to stand behind him, and as
one of the guards who had just allowed us to pass leaned
through the doorway to close the door behind us, he made
a buzzer go off with his body, which I took as an indication
that there was a metal detector built into the frame of the
door. Everyone ignored the buzzing, and it soon stopped,
returning the focus of our attention to Anthony Elestrano
himself.

He was a tall man and as deeply tanned as his granddaughter. Though he was obviously old—eighty-four, by
Nat's estimation—he looked remarkably fit, with thick silver hair and the manner of a man who had spent a good
part of his life outdoors. I remembered Nat's saying that
Elestrano had always been a horseman, and looking at him
now I could imagine him riding with his granddaughter,

whose athletic grace and close-cut hair I suddenly understood as an outgrowth of her grandfather's influence. He was dressed in a brown suit that was flawlessly cut for his physique, and he wore delicate, wire-rimmed glasses that sparkled a subdued gold in the office's atmospheric light. Overall he reminded me of a retired archaeologist . . . which I suppose is an unusual description, but it's the only one I could think of to match each of the elements of his appearance. And I had to consciously remind myself that this refined, undeniably dignified man was the purchasing party in a transaction that would result in another man's death.

When Elestrano spoke, his facade of health and vigor crumbled. His voice was weak and rasping as he gingerly stepped forward, like a man whose feet hurt, extending his hand and saying, "So you guys are Chet's second string? That's good. I was kinda worried when I saw that he kicked off." Then he offered us drinks as he shook each of our hands in turn. His grip, I found when he took my hand in his, was strong, and dry . . . like how I imagined an alligator's claw might feel, his skin was that hard and coarse. He arranged us around a low coffee table near the center of the room, and the man in the white suit who had met us in the lounge downstairs appeared from a doorway off to one side of the room, moving to stand behind a small bar that was upholstered with dark brown leather and studded with shiny brass tacks. Kelly Elestrano didn't sit, but remained standing behind and to the right of her grandfather, as if to protect him should one of our company decide to lunge for his throat. We all politely declined the old man's offer of drinks, except for Larry, who accepted another Scotch and water. Watching him take the icy drink and swirl it in his hand, I ran my tongue over the roof of my mouth, absolutely aching for just one jolt of its cool amber fire.

There were a few amenities, a little small talk, and a lot of curious, searching glances from us all. After allowing time for Larry to take a couple of sips from his drink,

Anthony Elestrano got to the point, saying, "Show 'em the cash," over his shoulder to his granddaughter, who moved to the great desk and lifted a briefcase from the floor behind it. Laying it on the blotter, she snapped the clasps and opened it, turning it to face us so that we could all see that it was packed, top and bottom, with row after row of neatly wrapped bundles of one-hundred-dollar bills. Mentally I was doing the arithmetic: ten thousand dollars was one package, three inches or so thick, and ten of those packages was one hundred thousand dollars. Looking at the suitcase, I estimated that what was sitting on the desk before us was roughly . . .

"A half a million bucks," Anthony Elestrano said. "Five hundred thousand clams."

I felt the back of my neck tingle as I shot a quick glance at Nat, who, to my amazement, I found was looking not at the money, but at me. Our eyes met ever so briefly, and then Larry Fizner said, "I'd like to make sure." Elestrano nodded, and Larry set down his drink and went over to the desk. He picked up one of the bundles of money, riffled through it as casually as if it were a deck of playing cards, picked up another, did the same, and repeated the action three more times, digging here and there through the stacks and choosing at random which bundles he would examine. After a minute or two he shrugged and pronounced himself satisfied, returning to his seat and saying, "Okay. But how do we know that we get to keep it after you have what you want from us?"

Anthony Elestrano smiled, and returned, "I thought your buddy told you everything."

"Maybe you oughta just run through it all for me again, just to be sure," Larry offered, picking up his drink and leaning back in his deep leather seat.

Elestrano waved his hand, and his granddaughter snapped shut the briefcase, saying, "We've each got to be sure of the other. You want to know that you can get out of here with your money, and we want to know that the name you give us is really the one my grandfather wants. So, we're all

gonna go from here to wherever Stenetti's hiding, together. And when my grandfather looks into Constantine Stenetti's face and agrees that he is in fact who you say he is, then you get the cash and walk away. Until then, you don't touch the money. Now, where's Stenetti hiding, and how long will it take us to get there?"

I was trembling, unable to help but see in my mind the moment of truth when Anthony Elestrano heard me tell him where I knew Constantine Stenetti to be. But before I could speak, Larry Fizner said, "No good. I want half the money right now, in my hands. And I want Mrs. Hawley here to leave with it and take it to a place where we can meet her later. That way, if we're all not together again, with the entire amount we agreed on by a certain time, she can call the cops and have them pick up you and your goons . . . no offense intended, Kelly."

Elestrano was looking at Larry like a buzzard, and I was sure that he was going to put up a fight. But much to my surprise, he said, "Give 'em half," without moving his gaze so much as a flicker from Larry's face.

Kelly, like the good granddaughter she obviously was, did exactly as she was told, dumping half the money out of the briefcase into a big pile on the desk and handing what was left to Nat, who didn't rise, but accepted it where she was sitting, laying it on her lap as if it were nothing more significant than a newspaper. The room was hushed in the interval between the time Nat took possession of the suitcase and the time that Larry finally looked at Elestrano and said, "Now let her go."

Elestrano studied Larry Fizner for a moment, and then turned his attention to Nat, saying, "My dear, you're free to leave. But remember, you'll be followed. Don't go any-where near a police station. Understand?"

Nat didn't answer him, looking at me instead and asking, quite calmly, "Bill? Should I?"

I nodded, with my eyes on Elestrano. To my relief I saw Nat rise to her feet in my peripheral vision, step up to me, and kiss me on the cheek. I squeezed her hand,

and Larry Fizner said, "Wait for us where we planned." Without another word, Nat, suitcase in hand, stepped up to the office's great wooden door, waited, and then disappeared after the door was opened by one of the guards in the hall. Kelly Elestrano opened a cabinet on the wall near the desk, and on one of a dozen or so closed circuit TV monitor screens, we watched Nat ride the elevator down to the concourse, and then, on a different screen, step out into the street near the baggage claim area, where she hailed a cab.

Elestrano then said, "I got a guy tailin' her, so there'll be no bullshit . . . am I correct?"

I nodded.

And then Larry Fizner said, "Okay, Bill. Tell him about Stenetti."

I swallowed . . . this was my cue . . . my throat felt raw and my palms were sweating. I was desperate not to repeat my embarrassing performance in the bar when my voice squeaked, so it took me a long time to settle myself and say, "Mr. Elestrano, sir," reaching into my shirt pocket and withdrawing a folded sheet of paper. "It's my duty, sir, to inform you that, um . . ."

I unfolded the paper, feeling a little better because I had something to do with my hands.

"It's with my regrets that I tell you, Mr. Elestrano, that Constantine Stenetti passed away almost two years ago. He's dead, sir, unfortunately. Um, you have my condolences. Here . . ."

Elestrano didn't rise as he accepted the paper I handed him, which was a certified copy of a death certificate I had gotten from Cleveland City Hall the day I had spent looking through their files. He was smiling as he examined it, which made me very uncomfortable, and, lifting his eyes over his glasses to look at his granddaughter, who had approached him and was standing close by, he said, "He tells me the fucker's dead, Pony. It's the best they can come up with . . . that he kicked off. For that they want a half a million bucks."

He was still smiling, but Kelly Elestrano was not. In short order she had lovingly touched her grandfather's shoulder, glared at me, and shot an order in Spanish to the man in white behind the bar, who responded instantly by heading around the bar and positioning himself in front of the money on the desk. Instinctively I felt the need to convince him that what I was saying was true, and without prompting I said, "I'm serious, Mr. Elestrano! I spent a lot of time looking that up for you, and there's absolutely no doubt in my mind that I'm right. I can show you documented proof to back it up. It's no scam! It's a fact."

The man in white was so close to me that I could smell the sweetness of his after-shave. Glancing at Kelly Elestrano, he watched as the girl looked at her grandfather, who lifted his hand and smiled my way. Fingering the embossed seal stamped into the death certificate by the county registrar, the old man said, "Come over here," speaking to the certificate, but plainly summoning me. I took a step forward, and he glanced up, adding, "Come over here, close to me. I can tell when somebody's lying to me by looking into his eyes. So I want you right here . . . right up close. Come here."

I did as I was told, tentatively approaching the old gangster and stopping just a foot or so in front of where he sat. He motioned for me to lean down to him by curling his finger. And when I didn't move fast enough, I suddenly felt a strong hand on the back of my neck as the man in white grabbed me and bent me forward. As soon as he could reach it, Anthony Elestrano grabbed my necktie and pulled my face to within an inch of his own, so close that I could feel the heat of his skin and smell the coffee on his breath.

"Now say it!" he demanded, practically hissing the words. "Tell me how this thing can be Stenetti's death certificate when it doesn't even have his real name on it!"

What amazed me at that moment was not the fear I was feeling, which was substantial and deep. No, what amazed me was the anger that suddenly welled up from inside me and made me, before I consciously knew what I

was doing, slap Elestrano's withered hand from my tie and turn, pushing the man in white back so that I could stand without either of them touching me . . . which had been a feeling that I found I simply couldn't abide. I hadn't been manhandled since I was a child, and there was something about the sensation, the remarkable arrogance it took for someone to even presume to push me around, that shot through me like electricity and made me shout, "Get your fucking paws off me!" pointing my finger at the man in white and actually trembling with rage.

Like magic, a switchblade appeared in the dark man's hand, and its point hovered inches from my face. My knees felt watery, and a single sensation, like an ice cube sliding up and down my back, tingled my spine. But my voice was steady as I said, "I think you better make sure that's really what your boss wants you to do." Making the man in white's eyes flicker down to where Anthony Elestrano was sitting behind me.

Softly, Elestrano said, "Maybe later, Carlo. Put it away for now." And then to me, he added, "What did you say your name was, tough guy?"

I turned and replied, "Bill Hawley," breathing hard, clenching my fists.

Rising slowly to his feet, Elestrano added, "Well, Bill Hawley, your friend Larry over there told you not to fuck with me in the elevator on the way up here." When I glanced accusingly at Larry, Elestrano chuckled and waved the certificate casually, adding, "Don't worry . . . he ain't no squealer. They've got microphones and cameras all over this fuckin' place. You can't take a dump by yourself. I've heard every word you guys said since you got in the elevator, and that includes you askin' whether Larry was sure he could handle me."

He turned and met my stare with a cold, calculated one of his own, adding, "Well, he can't. And neither can you. I've been around hoods my whole life . . . and I mean real hoods; guys with brains . . . not like now. I've known some of the best, and I can promise you one thing: you clowns

can't shit me. I know you think you can 'cause I'm old. But you can't. Your dolly got away with half the money. Good for you. But you wanna know a secret? I don't care. I could kill you and have somebody take it back from her in a flash. Or, I could have Carlo slice you up and let you keep the dough for doctor bills. See . . . I don't care one way or the other. The money . . . shit . . ." He waved one hand carelessly at the desk as if the stack of cash on it were a pile of trash. "It don't mean nothin' to me. You hear that? Nothin'! Scholtz coulda talked me into givin' him a million if he'd have pushed a little harder. I'm at a point in my life where I got more money than I know what to do with. He thought it was a big deal so he settled for five hundred g's. I'd have given him twice, three times that much. And you know why? 'Cause you can't buy what's important to me anymore. Understand? We're talkin' about two different things here . . . you're talkin' about the money, and I'm talkin' about something that's real, and important, and solid. You're negotiating, and I'm tellin' you straight, I won't settle for anything less than Stenetti, on his knees. So don't bullshit me no more. Don't even try."

"Mr. Elestrano," I began, seeing that Larry Fizner was about to speak and deciding that it ought to be me instead, "I sincerely sympathize with your feelings. But the fact remains, Mr. Constantine Stenetti died of natural causes, on February 15th, 1990. He was under the care of the Federal Witness Protection Program, and they went so far as to mark his death certificate with his assumed name, probably to prevent anyone from ever knowing what became of him. If I could change things for you, believe me, I would. I almost . . . that is to say, *we* almost didn't come here today because we knew you'd be disappointed. And that's why we cooked up our plan to have my wife take half the money away before I told you the bad news. The rest of our plan was to settle for the half we got, since you're only getting half of what you originally agreed to buy."

"Half how?" Elestrano asked.

And I replied, "You said you wanted to buy Stenetti's name . . . but what you were really counting on was having your revenge for what he did to you and your family twenty years ago. I got you the name you wanted, it's on that death certificate, but I'm afraid nature, or God, beat you to your revenge."

I then explained how I had gotten the certificate, in detail, with Larry Fizner agreeing all the way and verifying what I said at the end by insisting, "It's all straight, Tony. I had the kid walk me through it myself at the vital statistics office. He's got it right. No shit. For a civilian, he's sharp."

Deep lines had etched themselves into Elestrano's forehead as he frowned and examined the death certificate afresh. He had listened carefully, had asked a couple of questions along the way, and he was buying my story . . . I really do believe that he was. If I'd have gotten just a couple more minutes with him, free of interruptions, I'm sure that we could have just walked out of that office, two hundred and fifty thousand dollars richer, and that would have been the end of it all. But things weren't meant to happen that easily for me. It just wasn't in the cards because, at the same moment that Kelly Elestrano moved close to her grandfather, who glanced up from the death certificate and asked, "So, what do ya think, Pony?" Judy Newhardt, who had been sitting silently, almost forgotten, watching everything that transpired before her, rose and said:

"Mr. Elestrano, it's all a load of crap."

Every head in the room snapped around and confronted Judy Newhardt openly, creating an ominous sensation of impending trouble. To her credit, she didn't back down one iota, but seemed to respond to the confusion her statement caused, adding, "It's a scam. They planned it all along. I wasn't gonna say nothing 'cause I thought they musta had the right name or they wouldn't have come. But I can't keep quiet after hearin' this garbage. I don't know how they thought they could pull this thing off . . . but it's all bullshit, plain and simple."

"Judy!" Larry Fizner shouted, the shock and outrage of her betrayal making his voice shrill. "What do ya think you're doin'?"

The look of contempt that spread over the young woman's face broke my heart because it illustrated just how little she truly felt for her boss.

"Get off it, Larry," she sneered, confronting him full faced and putting her hands on her hips. "You know damn well what I'm doin' . . . I'm makin' a half a million bucks." Then she turned to Anthony Elestrano with a sly grin and added, "Or should I hold out for a million, since money don't mean nothin' to you?"

It was at that moment that the door next to the little bar in the corner of the room opened, and Jimmy Cecorno, all three hundred pounds of him, entered the fray. As soon as I saw him, his clothes disheveled as usual, his collar open and his many chins quivering as he walked, I glanced over at Judy Newhardt and saw that her eyes were fixed on the fat man as if she had been waiting for him to arrive. It was that look of satisfaction on her face that made me shout, "You killed Steven Teeg?" pointing my finger Judy's way and trembling with rage.

She actually laughed when I did it. She threw back her head and laughed before she asked, "What the hell did you think, asshole? Did you honestly believe that some white-bread accountant from Detroit with a wife and kids had the balls to snuff that creep? You really are stupid. Your dumb must run to the bone."

Jimmy Cecorno lowered his head respectfully when he addressed Anthony Elestrano, saying, "Mr. Elestrano, I told you that they'd try to lie. Only my girl can give you what you want."

"*My girl*," Larry Fizner sneered, turning away from Judy Newhardt as if to deny her existence. "What a crock."

And I said, "I don't know what kinda bill of goods these two have been selling you, Mr. Elestrano," imagining Judy Newhardt and Jimmy Cecorno making their deals at the Lipstick Lounge after hours when Judy had finished

her shift dancing for tips, supposedly working undercover for us, but actually working undercover for herself, "but they're the ones who are lying. That certificate is absolutely authentic. I'd stake my life on it."

Looking at the certificate and then up at me, Anthony Elestrano frowned and said, "You are, tough guy. That's exactly what you're doing." And then he added, "So okay, let's go." His granddaughter pushed a button on the desk that summoned the guards in from their post in the hall, and I understood that this whole thing, from the very first moment we had stepped into the elevator, had been orchestrated to lead us to this point, and that the evening's activities were only just beginning.

NINE

■■■■■■■■■

WE RODE IN a limousine, long and dark, with Elestrano and his granddaughter sitting side by side, and Larry Fizner and I sharing a seat opposite them. In the third seat sat Jimmy Cecorno and Judy Newhardt. No one spoke, except for Kelly Elestrano, who mentioned at one point that she didn't know who was lying, but that whoever it was, was going to be very sorry. Her grandfather might have only been interested in one thing, which was finding Constantine Stenetti, but she looked at the big picture . . . and nobody made a fool of the Elestrano family and got away with it. It was then that I realized that this young woman, who could have been no more then twenty-five or twenty-six years old, wielded more power in her grandfather's organization than anyone else, and that her deference to him during the evening's proceedings was a measure of her respect for him, but not something she would allow to influence her better judgment. If I wasn't completely off base, she would let things go only so far before she pulled the plug. And I personally didn't want to be there when she did.

Before we left, Judy Newhardt explained that the man Elestrano was looking for was living at the Manor Care

Nursing Home, which was about fifteen minutes away. As she spoke, I imagined how she had gotten her information, seeing in my mind first the way she had beaten Cynthia Moore's boyfriend with the nightstick in the dancer's driveway, and feeling certain that the delicate, almost effeminate Steven Teeg had been no match for her calculated savagery. He had probably let her into his apartment, seeing just a lithe, pretty young woman with short blond hair, who, once inside, had transformed herself into a brutal, dangerous lioness. He was bruised, the coroner had said, on the chest, shoulders, and face, so what she had done was to knock him down . . . maybe even knocking him out. The police report I had seen said nothing about the neighbors in the apartment building hearing any kind of struggle, so the initial attack couldn't have lasted long. Teeg probably never even had a chance to fight back.

Then she demanded the name, which he gave her . . . she was probably sitting on top of him where he lay facedown on the carpet, twisting his arms, which she had bound with a plastic strap. I knew about the arm twisting because, as I had later learned from Rusty, the autopsy had shown that his left shoulder was dislocated. And then, with him struggling, or crying, on the floor, she opened a kitchen drawer, found the duct tape, and wrapped it around his head after stuffing a dishrag in his mouth, leaving him to die.

Imagining all this, I looked at her now—quiet and confident—and knew that her betrayal had been inevitable. All along, every time someone who knew me found out that I wanted to be a detective, they had protested that the people in this business were "sleazy." It was a word I heard over and over again, and suddenly, looking at Judy Newhardt, its true meaning drove itself home. This woman would have betrayed anyone for the money we had seen on Elestrano's desk—which was now riding in the front seat of the limousine in a brown paper bag next to the driver—and she'd sleep just fine when it was over.

It was almost nine-thirty when we pulled into the Manor Care's parking lot, so visiting hours were just ending and

people were drifting out to their cars. The limo got a lot of attention, especially from a couple of young boys who held their mother's hands and pointed as she dragged them by, and we waited for nearly fifteen minutes until the lot cleared out. Then we went inside. On the way Kelly Elestrano hesitated for a moment, looking the building over with a critical eye and instructing a couple of the men who had ridden in the car that had followed us from the airport to station guards at all the nursing home's exits and not to let anyone in or out until she said it was okay. The men, who were large, solemn, and silent, nodded, and went about their task, and Kelly Elestrano took her grandfather's arm and led him down the sidewalk as casually as if the pair had just returned from a drive in the park.

In the lobby, Judy Newhardt, who had never been to the Manor Care before, checked out one of those "You Are Here" diagrams, deciding where the nursing desk was and leading the way. The rest of us followed, marching quickly to match the young woman's pace and leaving Anthony Elestrano and his granddaughter far behind to catch up. Glancing over my shoulder, I noticed that there were two bodyguards accompanying the Elestranos, and that Jimmy Cecorno too had preferred to stick close to them, leaving his partner Judy to walk ahead alone. Out of the side of my mouth I said, "So, what do ya think?" quite softly to Larry Fizner.

"I think I'd like to slap her silly," he said, scowling.

"I mean about Elestrano."

"Kelly's the problem," Larry replied. "Tony's almost finished. He's frail. But Kelly's a rattlesnake. She won't let anybody off the hook."

On the walls bulletin boards covered with crayon drawings and happy little flowers cut from crepe paper jiggled into a brightly colored blur in my peripheral vision. And that horrible nursing home smell—disinfectant and urine mixed in warm air that never moves—started churning my already nervous stomach.

"You think Nat's okay?" I whispered as we turned the final corner and approached the main nursing desk.

"Right this second I'm a hell of a lot more worried about us," Larry returned.

Judy Newhardt rang the bell.

We all stood close together in front of the desk as Judy rang the bell a second time, summoning, after what seemed an interminable wait, a pretty young nurse from the office in the back. The girl, who was Oriental and dressed in a candy striper's uniform, told us that visiting hours had ended at nine, and that we'd have to come back tomorrow. Judy Newhardt explained that we were only going to stay a minute, and that this elderly gentleman had just come all the way from Mexico to see his brother . . . and couldn't we just bend the rules a little . . . this one time . . . be a sport?

The girl frowned and shrugged, saying that she supposed it was all right, if we were just going to stay a minute, and asked who we were there to see.

Everyone in our group stiffened.

Here it came.

The name we had all been waiting to hear.

"Frank Metcalf," Judy Newhardt said simply. "The man's name is Frank Metcalf."

The girl's eyes brightened visibly, and she smiled, saying, "Mr. Metcalf? Really? You're his brother? That's wonderful. Mr. Metcalf never gets any visitors. I'm really glad you came, it'll mean so much to him. He's in room 312. Take the elevator to the third floor, and then left down the hall. It'll be on your right. I'll buzz the nurse upstairs and let her know you're coming."

We walked like zombies, no one speaking, heading for the elevator like it was the gas chamber. All the way up I was running the name through my mind. Metcalf? Metcalf? I couldn't remember whether or not I'd seen it on any of the lists I'd examined over the last couple of days. But I knew one thing for sure, it definitely wasn't the name on the death certificate I'd given Mr. Elestrano back at the airport. And I'm sure he and his granddaughter were

thinking the same thing. Somebody was lying here . . . there was no doubt about it. And, as the elevator doors opened, admitting us to the third floor, where the desk nurse smiled and nodded as we passed, I knew we were on our way to finding out just who it was.

Approaching room 312's door, I had to wonder how accurate Anthony Elestrano's memory would be. True, Constantine Stenetti had been the root cause of a great deal of the man's misfortunes over the years, but Jesus Christ! It had been a solid twenty years since they had laid eyes on one another. Could we really depend on Elestrano's being able to recognize him after all that time? I was betting my life on it . . . we were all betting our lives on it, put that way. But what if he made a mistake? What if he couldn't make up his mind? What was I doing here in the first place? And was the money really worth it?

That's what I was thinking about as Judy Newhardt said, "Here we go," stepping aside and leaving the door for Kelly Elestrano and her grandfather to open.

It was a door just like all the others, with a name tag written in pencil that said FRANK METCALF and a plastic message pad with a pen hanging from an elastic string with instructions about medications scribbled over it in a great, squiggly mess. The only thing different about this door was that, unlike the other doors on the floor, it didn't have any decorations stuck to it with tape. No scribbled drawings with, "I love you, Grandpa," done in crayon, no paper hearts, no sign that anyone gave a damn about the man inside. I noticed it, as, I'm sure, did the rest of the group. It was just one of those little details you pick up when you know that the man inside is being hidden by the government. That he was being protected, living a lie, and completely alone. And that's when it really struck me how hellish this life of solitude and paranoia must have been. Twenty years like that? I thought. Stenetti had spent twenty years in a nursing home, unable to pronounce his own real name, and completely alone without a single visitor! How had he done it without going nuts?

I was amazed when Kelly Elestrano knocked on the door. We were here to pass judgment on the man inside, to pronounce whether he lived or died, and which of our party would share his fate. She and her grandfather had the power of life and death in their hands, and here she was, politely tapping on the door.

No one answered, so she tapped again.

When no one answered the third time, she opened the door, and we all stepped inside.

The room was dark, and warm. There were no lights on, and the curtains were drawn. But because of the halogen lamps in the parking lot outside, the drapes were described in grey along their edges, and the room, after a moment during which my eyes adjusted to the gloom, took on a flat, halftone atmosphere through which I made out a chair, straight ahead near the window, a table, off to the side, and a bed to the left in which the irregular, motionless shape of a man reclined.

"Don't let anybody in," Kelly Elestrano whispered behind me as the door closed and the light from the hall, which had stretched each of us into distorted shadows on the far wall, was cut off, leaving us in the dark. I could feel Larry Fizner's touch as he squeezed past me, and glancing back I discerned the shapes of Judy, Jimmy Cecorno, Kelly Elestrano, and her grandfather, huddled together in a group. No one moved. For thirty seconds, I doubt if anyone even breathed. There was a hush in the place that was almost reverent . . . as if we were all unconsciously savoring the anticipation, which I decided was exactly what Anthony Elestrano was doing. This was the culmination of twenty years' worth of hate. He'd been waiting for it all that time, and now, even though the suspense must have been killing him, he wasn't going to rush it through.

Finally, he said, quite softly, "Somebody turn on a light," and I made out Judy Newhardt's spiky outline moving toward the night table, where there was a reading lamp jutting up like a black flower, thin-necked with a tiny dark blossom on its tip. The light snapped on, sharp and

concentrated, not nearly enough to illuminate the room, but throwing a beam instead down onto the table. Judy stepped aside, and Anthony Elestrano disentangled himself from his granddaughter's grasp, adjusted his suit coat with a pair of forward thrusts of his arms—like Jimmy Cagney in an old gangster movie—and, in the virtual black-and-white of that feeble light, stepped forward and moved the gooseneck of the lamp to shine its beam on the face of the man in bed.

"Jesus Christ," Larry Fizner whispered, his voice husky and unsteady.

A single bead of sweat ran down my back.

And when I tried to swallow, I found nothing there.

From where I stood, the reading light silhouetted Anthony Elestrano as he leaned forward over the bed. The man reclining there, who was propped up on a couple of pillows and resting with his hands folded on his stomach, looked peaceful and reposed . . . as if he had been arranged this way for us to find and had been waiting until we arrived. His eyes were closed, and his features slack. Slowly, the eyelids flickered, and he turned his head, facing Elestrano's gaze and blinking, licking his lips, and blinking again. He needed a shave, and his wispy grey hair was thin and cut very short. Elestrano didn't move, didn't speak, didn't give any indication at all what he was thinking. Together, in the glow of that tiny book light, the two old men looked at one another, and finally, the man in the bed's lips quivered before stretching into a weak smile of apparent recognition.

With remarkable gentleness, Anthony Elestrano reached up and touched the man's face, running his fingertip ever so lightly down his cheek. The man blinked, still smiling. And Elestrano said, "Connie?"

The man didn't respond, or stir in any way.

Elestrano paused for a moment longer, and then straightened up, keeping his attention on the man before him, but addressing the rest of us in the group behind him when he said, "It ain't him. It's been a long time, but there's no way that this guy is Connie Stenetti. Somebody's pullin' some shit."

"What?" Judy Newhardt shrieked, and, as if her voice had activated some hidden device, the overhead fluorescent lights in the room snapped on, making me lift my hand to shield my eyes from the glare as I turned to find Jimmy Cecorno standing with his hand on the switch by the door.

"I told ya it was bullshit," Larry Fizner was saying, shaking his head regretfully and shrugging his shoulders.

Kelly Elestrano was looking at Judy Newhardt with an expression of undisguised malevolence.

"But it can't be!" Judy exclaimed, standing over the bed and pointing down at the man in it as she turned to confront Anthony Elestrano. "That's got to be him! It's just got to be! The kid told me so . . . I'm serious! He swore to God that the name was Metcalf! It's got to be him!"

"What's your name?" Anthony Elestrano asked the man in the bed, who was smiling happily and looking from face to face as if he were utterly delighted to be the focus of so much attention. When he didn't answer, Elestrano leaned over him, as if maybe the man were hard of hearing, and pronounced, "Name?" quite loudly.

To which the man responded, "Cucumber."

"Cucumber?" Elestrano said.

And the man said, "Butter," apparently with no more comprehension of the word's meaning than a parrot might have.

"Butter?" Elestrano said.

And the man replied, "Business card," smiling and enjoying the game.

"He's a retard," Kelly Elestrano said.

And I shook my head sadly, saying, "It's called Disassociative Verbal Response Disorder. D.V.R. It's a shame what can happen to a person when he gets old."

At that moment both Anthony and Kelly Elestrano seemed to have the same thought simultaneously, and they both lifted their eyes to Judy Newhardt, placing her at the center of their undivided attention. She glanced from one to the other of them, stammered half a word once or twice, and then smiled,

saying, "You don't think . . . I mean . . . I didn't know . . ." pointing down at the man on the bed, and then at herself. "I mean . . . I wouldn't . . ."

Then, her mind apparently forsaking any verbal argument as hopeless, she did what she always seemed to do when she found herself in a spot: she got physical. With a snarl she lashed out directly at Anthony Elestrano, who was standing the closest to her, and who, when she laid her hands on his shoulders, practically folded up while trying to protect his face. She bodily turned and thrust him forward, throwing him like a rag doll at his granddaughter, whose reflexive response was to cushion his fall with her body, and who took the brunt of his weight and collapsed in a heap with him atop her on the floor. Before any of the rest of us could move, Judy Newhardt was past us and through the door, running down the hall with the two men standing guard sticking their heads into the room and Kelly Elestrano screaming from where she was struggling to get out from under her grandfather, "Don't just stand there! Get her!"

The men blinked stupidly for a second, and then turned, galvanized to their task, to go barreling down the hall.

Jimmy Cecorno was standing like a cigar store Indian, arms at his sides, his expression one of simple mortification.

"Ain't you gonna run too, Jimmy?" Kelly Elestrano sneered.

Jimmy shook his big head sadly, saying, "I ain't exactly built for speed. And besides, where the hell can I go?"

"Good point," the girl said, bending and lifting her grandfather to his feet. Helping him over to a chair she added, "Did you really think you could get away with it? Was a coupla hundred g's so important that you decided to try something as stupid as all this?"

"I believed her," Cecorno answered, his voice hollow with defeat and compliance. "I honestly did, Miss Elestrano. She came to me one night early this week and explained how everything worked. She told me about the funeral director,

and her boss, the detective, teaming up. She told me about the doctor's son, that Teeg kid, how she'd gotten the name out of him, and how he swore it was the one she wanted. She said if I would set it up so that you and your grandfather would keep Scholtz's meeting, that she could guarantee the goods." He paused, shrugged, and finished simply by repeating, "I believed her. What can I say? I guess I must be as dumb as my brother-in-law says I am."

Anthony Elestrano had collapsed into the chair his granddaughter chose for him, his suit coat bunched up under his chin and his face flushed red as he puffed and caught his breath. In the hall outside, the sound of shouting which had greeted Judy Newhardt's escape was fading, and stepping to the window I looked down at the parking lot, seeing the men who had been guarding the doorway emerging into the night and signaling to the men standing around the limousine. After a moment of wild gesticulating, the group assembled and moved away from the building, drawing dark objects from under their jackets—guns, I assumed— and heading for the tree line bordering the parking lot to the south.

"What will they do to her?" I asked helplessly, already knowing the answer.

But no one paid any attention to me, they were busy with other matters.

"He's dead, Pony," Anthony Elestrano complained to the air around him, his eyes looking vacant, and his entire manner that of a man lost in the throes of utter disappointment. "After all this time, the son of a bitch cheated me again."

"It's okay, Grandpa." Kelly Elestrano was soothing, glancing around the room as if to catch anyone in it looking anything but respectful, and patting her grandfather's shoulder.

"It was gonna be great, Kelly. After twenty years, it was gonna be so sweet."

"I know, Grandpa. I know."

"Where's that paper with his name on it?"

"In your pocket."

"Mr. Elestrano?" Jimmy Cecorno said timidly.

But Elestrano didn't acknowledge him. He was too busy unfolding the wrinkled death certificate I had given him from where he had stuffed it into his pocket and mumbling about feeling cheated that he hadn't had the opportunity to commit murder that night. Looking at him, I saw an old man, and that was all. With all his money, and power, and reputation, with all the terrible things he had personally done in his life, and all the things he had ordered done from his haven in Mexico, seeing him sitting in that chair with his hair undone and his tie cocked to one side, grumbling and clucking to his granddaughter, I realized suddenly that he had lost any remnant of the dignity he had exuded before. And maybe it was seeing him for what he was, or maybe it was seeing him for what he wasn't, but suddenly I wasn't afraid of him anymore. Suddenly, this whole goddamn thing infuriated me, and I shouted, "What are they going to do to her?" meaning the men who were chasing Judy Newhardt, the men with the guns.

Neither Kelly Elestrano nor her grandfather answered. They were both engrossed in private thoughts, one with the other.

I repeated my question, more softly, feeling sick, suddenly drenched with sweat. She was a murderer, and she had betrayed us all. She had been willing to see us die so that she might collect the money we had all worked so hard for, the money we had made by selling another man's name to his most hated enemy. I stood there trembling, wondering, awestruck with the magnitude of what I had done, when Jimmy Cecorno, still standing at the door, looked up at me and said, "I told you, kid. It's a goon's business."

He was holding up his hand, the one with the missing finger, the missing finger that his own brother-in-law had taken from him. Seeing that stump, I growled, "My ass!" and broke for the door. Behind me I heard Larry Fizner calling my name, but I didn't stop. I hit the stairs and raced down them, hitting the main lobby and shouting for Pete Germaine. He was standing by the front door,

looking confused and scared, pointing toward the trees and saying, "That way!" as I shouted, "You got your car here?" He pitched me the keys, and I found his rusted silver Toyota parked near the back of the lot. It was a manual transmission, which to me means that it was a pain in the ass. I hate driving those things. Clutch, shift, clutch, shift. It feels like you're pedaling a goddamn bicycle . . . especially the way I drive, which on a manual is lousy. I jerked and stalled twice trying to get the car out of the lot, cursing and pounding the steering wheel, bouncing in my seat and fumbling for the keys to restart the engine each time. I got the hang of it by the time I hit the street, racing the engine and shifting directly from first to third, where I intended to stay, even if I had to run somebody over to do it.

The trees behind the Manor Care Nursing Home were a part of a strip of park that ran through this part of the city. The Rocky Creek Parkway was about fifty yards wide and divided this particular suburb almost directly in half. Down its center ran the Rocky Creek, and, though it looked from the nursing home like a substantial patch of nature, I knew it would only take Judy Newhardt a few minutes to work her way through. With this in mind, I raced to the corner, ran a red light as I made a tire-squealing left turn—drawing horns and raised middle fingers from startled drivers, but, unfortunately, no police sirens, which I was sincerely hoping for—and flew over a small cross-bridge that cut through the park and emerged on the main street that ran parallel to the one on which the Manor Care was located. Counting the addresses up that side of the street I pulled over and crawled along the parking lane, scanning the tree line behind the businesses on the opposite side of the street, looking for movement, which I found, quickly enough, in the form of a dark shape pulling itself at a run from between the trees. As I watched, that shape stopped, turned its head both ways, and disappeared behind a Frosty Freeze ice cream store.

From the way she was moving, I determined that Judy Newhardt had kicked off her stiletto heels and was running

barefoot. She was like a night animal, all speed and agility, alight with attentive nerve and fear. Behind her came Elestrano's men, two, four, five of them total, crashing through the trees and underbrush like gorillas and pulling up short in the shadows behind the Frosty Freeze to look both ways before the man in front, who seemed to be in charge, sent three of his guys one way, while he and the last went the other. They were bound to catch her, I saw, observing the chase from a distance. She was quicker than they were, and she was probably familiar with the streets. But there were five of them, and, as I watched, the dark blue Mercury Grand Marque that had followed the limousine from the airport trolled down the street with yet another man behind the wheel, scanning the sidewalks.

What was I going to do?

What did I want to do?

She was a killer, and a traitor to us all. She was capable of terrible violence, and she had proven that she possessed not an ounce of scruples or loyalty. And yet, I couldn't leave her to the mercies of these men. I kept seeing Jimmy Cecorno's stump of a finger in my mind, and I knew I simply couldn't abandon her to the retribution of Anthony Elestrano and his rattlesnake granddaughter. I had to find her, get her in the car with me, and get her away from here. But how? I had to think . . . and I didn't have a lot of time to do it . . .

While I was watching Judy Newhardt's life-and-death chase across the park from the nursing home, what was going on at the Manor Care was important too. And, as it was described to me later by Larry Fizner, it went like this:

In response to all the commotion of Judy Newhardt running down the hall with the guards at her heels, the Manor Care's two-person security team showed up to see what the hell was going on. One was a very heavy woman, about forty years old, who was so tightly stuffed into her uniform that, Larry said, she looked like a navy-blue sausage with

silver buttons. And the other was a young man with a flattop haircut and a tiepin shaped like a pair of handcuffs. They arrived to find Jimmy Cecorno on his knees, begging for mercy in front of Anthony Elestrano, who was looking down at the big man from where he sat, collapsed in his chair, while his granddaughter shouted from where she was standing at the window, "There's nobody in the limo! They left the fucking money in the car and just took off!"

When the security people demanded to know what was happening, Larry Fizner told them to stay out of it, if they knew what was good for them, which bruised their authoritative natures and made the young man draw his nightstick, which was a mistake. Jimmy Cecorno, desperate to make some points with Anthony Elestrano, who seemed to be debating whether or not he should have the fat man killed for his part in Judy Newhardt's attempted deception, rose from his feet and rushed the boy, shouting, "Don't worry, Mr. Elestrano! I'll handle him!" plowing into the kid and knocking his hat off. The fat woman barked something about calling the police into her walkie-talkie and disappeared into the hall. And Kelly Elestrano said, "I can't believe those morons didn't leave one guy with the cash!" as she too headed for the door.

Jimmy Cecorno disarmed the kid with the nightstick, who took the first opportunity he found to retreat before the fat man could use the stick on him, leaving Cecorno, Larry Fizner, and Anthony Elestrano in the room with Matthew Taylor, the Parrot, who was still grinning happily and all but bouncing up and down on his bed with delight at all the activity going on in his room. Fizner offered Elestrano his arm, and Larry helped the older man up while Cecorno stood by with his newly acquired nightstick, which Elestrano grouchily barked at him to throw away because, "It makes you look ridiculous. And don't worry, nothing's going to happen to you. I've known your brother-in-law for years. I'll let him straighten your ass out." That last statement, although essentially saying that Elestrano had decided not to have Cecorno killed, didn't seem to cheer

the big man up all that much, and morosely he fell in behind as Larry Fizner helped the old gangster down the hall. As they went, the two contemporaries spoke as if they were the closest of friends, and when they emerged into the parking lot, they found Kelly Elestrano standing next to the limousine, with the front passenger's door open and her face practically glowing with rage beneath the light of one of the parking lot lamps.

"It's gone!" she announced as soon as her grandfather stepped from the Manor Care, finally pulling himself free of Larry's helping grasp and standing on his own. "I'm gonna break every bone in that asshole's body myself. I swear I am!" Kelly added, trembling and clenching her fists. "He knew the money was in the car and he left it! Look!" She pointed as if everyone needed a reminder as to where the bag of cash had been resting.

There was a moment's silence in the parking lot as Anthony Elestrano looked into the car. He stood, perfectly still, gazing down at the empty front seat, and then, as Larry describes it, a light went on in his eyes, and, as if speaking to himself, he said, "Good," looking up and around him to the street. "Some punk got it. That's just how I got started, lifting whatever I could get. Good. What a haul, huh?" He turned, not to his granddaughter, but to Larry, as if he would appreciate what he had to say more than she, and added, "Can you imagine that kid's face when he opens that bag? Makes a snatch from a car like this, runs down the street wondering what he coulda got out of a limo in a paper bag, and then finds all that dough? Christ! He'll drop over on the spot. He'll faint dead away."

Larry Fizner smiled thinking about it, and then Anthony Elestrano made a face like somebody discovering something surprising, and then the two old men looked at each other, and laughed. That's just what they did, Larry said. They laughed and laughed, and Elestrano ended up putting his hand on Larry's shoulder, and they laughed together until the tears came, and still they laughed, with Kelly Elestrano practically jumping up and down she was so indignant while

her grandfather told her to lighten up because it was only money, and, "Think about that kid. . . ." Then he turned and to the empty street around him he shouted in a loud clear voice that was stronger than Larry Fizner would have thought him capable of producing, "Good for you, sonny boy! At least somebody made out tonight! You're welcome to it! You hear that? I said you're goddamn welcome to it!"

And then he and his granddaughter got in the backseat of the limo, closed the doors, and left Larry Fizner alone with Jimmy Cecorno in the lot. Together, grandfather and granddaughter sat behind the big Cadillac's darkened glass, waiting for their driver to come back and take them away.

Meanwhile, I was sweating bullets. I had spotted a phone booth down the street, and had even considered stopping at it and dialing the police. But I didn't have time. That fact was made painfully clear to me as Judy Newhardt's running shape materialized briefly, only to disappear again as she moved between two buildings about a block down from where I was sitting. Pressing the clutch and crossing my fingers that I wouldn't jerk the car forward and squeal its tires, I moved ahead, watching for any indication that Elestrano's men were close, and seeing immediately that they were, as two big shapes followed Judy's path between the same two buildings. I had to move fast, and I had only one option left.

Stomping on the accelerator I blasted the little Toyota into the thin traffic on the street. Judy was heading due west, passing behind building after building and generally keeping to the shadows, probably looking for someplace to hide. Ahead there was a video rental place, well lit and busy, next to an Amish furniture store, which was closed, with its windows dark and its doors locked. Beyond that was a strip mall with convenience stores, a haircutting place, and a drugstore, and after that was a bar. If I were Judy, I'd be heading for the bar. I didn't know why, but that was just my gut reaction. To get to it, she'd have to pass behind the strip center, and that's where I headed,

racing the Toyota's engine and picking up speed.

Behind me I saw the driver of the dark-colored Mercury turn and glance briefly my way before returning his attention to his study of the pedestrians milling around in front of the Frosty Freeze. When I got to the strip center's parking lot I cruised to the end, hung a left around the corner of the last building, and turned off my headlights, emerging on the other side which was little more than a narrow driveway, wide enough for a garbage truck to navigate while emptying the row of dumpsters that lined the rear of the building. It was dark back there, and I aimed the car down the center of the drive, rolling down my window and hoping that I hadn't missed Judy by moving too slow.

"Judy?" I called questioningly, hanging my head out the window as I rolled along, heading in the opposite direction from which I figured she would be running. I imagined her, pressed up against the building, moving quickly through the shadows, barefoot and careful in the dark, particularly around the dumpsters, where there would probably be broken glass. . . .

"Judy?" I called again. "It's me! Bill! Judy, answer me!"

The Toyota's tires crunched as I approached the middle of the strip center, passing a door that was open about a foot to ventilate the kitchen of a Mr. Hero out front. Inside I caught sight of a couple of kids in paper hats standing amid brightly lit, stainless steel equipment, and then I moved on, back into the dark.

"Judy! I'm here to help!" I called, catching a glimpse of something up ahead in the dark and hoping that it wasn't one of Elestrano's men, waiting with a pistol.

I stopped the car and turned off the engine, sitting in dead silence and holding my breath.

"Judy?" I finally said in little more than a hoarse whisper. "Quit fucking around and get in the car!"

The only sound I heard was a kind of clicking that was actually something in my throat responding to my heart, which was beating so hard in my chest that it hurt.

"I'm not gonna ask again!" I whispered. "Ten seconds and you're on your own."

The dark shape I had seen moved suddenly, flitting across the front of the car and around to the side where the door opened and Judy Newhardt slid into the seat beside me. She was puffing and scared, but alive with suspicion as she took her place and looked at me, her eyes bright in the darkness and her voice husky as she asked, "Why you helping me?"

"I'm not sure," I responded, cranking the Toyota's engine and snapping on the headlights. "Now keep your head down."

When the headlights came on, they illuminated the alley in front of the car abruptly, like a searchlight beam from some prison camp's tower. Instantly, the brick wall to my left became crystal clear in all its rough, mundane detail, as did the dumpster straight ahead of me, and the trees to my right. And standing directly in the path of the car were the two big men I had watched break off from the other three goons. They were standing shoulder to shoulder as if to block my escape, holding pistols, I saw, as their free hands jumped up to their faces, shadowing their eyes from my high beams. Both their mouths were open, forming dark o's under their protective hands. And in that moment during which they seemed immobilized in the light I shouted, "Hang on!" and sounded the horn as I popped the clutch and stomped on the gas.

The car jerked forward, and for a terrifying instant I was afraid that it would stall out and I'd be left there like a sitting duck trying to crank it back to life as the men in front of me ran up to the car and stuck their guns in through the open windows . . . or worse, just started shooting . . .

Shooting!

Now that's a word that never really had a lot of meaning for me before that moment. Naturally, like every other American I had seen more than my share of shootings on Westerns and cop shows on TV and in the movies, but I had never actually fired a gun, and my only personal exposure

to the results of what a gun could do came in the form of picking up the bodies of shooting victims over the years, particularly when I worked as an orderly at Southwest General Hospital. Gunshot wounds, for those who have never seen one, aren't neat little holes, they're gaping, bruised, torn flesh, leaking blood and guts. They're ugly, and they happen fast. And just the idea of those men raising their weapons my way and firing, blind, directly into the haze that the car must have been to them—nothing but a shimmering white blur—nearly made me piss my pants.

With a cry I squeezed the steering wheel as a very satisfying shudder ran through me and the car's wheels spun. The engine didn't stall, but wound up hard, propelling us toward the men with the guns, who, taking a split second to judge their positions, ended up diving out of our way. My seat belt and shoulder harness were fastened, and I was hunkered down for the worst. Judy Newhardt was perched in her seat, one hand on the dashboard, the other on the side door. And as we shot past the two men who went rolling on the pavement out of our way, I was actually screaming, feeling like a fighter pilot in a jet.

In the rearview mirror I caught a quick glance of the man on my side of the car, who, rolling once, jumped back up to his feet, dropped his arms to his sides, and then disappeared into the open Mr. Hero door I had just passed. The other man was gone as far as I could tell, and I hoped that he was rolling down an embankment into the park in the dark. The most important thing to me at that moment was that there were no pops behind me, no shattering glass, and no one shooting.

Judy Newhardt hadn't made a sound, and I closed my mouth as we approached the end of the building, feeling a little embarrassed at all the noise I had been making and pulling the steering wheel hard to the left. Heads snapped our way up and down the street as people looked to see what all the commotion was as we came bursting out from behind the building, tires smoking and the gear shift firmly planted back in third, my favorite gear. I aimed us at the

street, charging across the parking lot and scanning the area for any sign of Elestrano's men as, from the front of the Mr. Hero in the strip, the man who we had so nearly run over emerged, gun in hand as customers screamed and dove under tables. He ran into the parking lot as we turned left on the street and headed past the strip center, waving his arms over his head and finally letting a single shot off into the air, clearing the area around him and immediately drawing the attention of the dark Mercury, which was about a block away, still checking out the area around the video store.

"Shit!" Judy Newhardt growled, her body twisted in the seat as she watched through the back window. "We got trouble."

I nodded, not bothering to respond, pushing the Toyota as hard as it would go and winding up the speedometer to fifty. Behind us the Mercury, with its V-8, zillion horsepower engine, settled into pursuit. And ahead there loomed a four-way intersection, complete with traffic lights and four turning lanes.

"He's on us!" Judy shouted. "We've gotta move!"

"I'm moving!" I shouted, as ahead the light changed to red and traffic blocked my path.

What happened next happened fast. The car was racing straight toward the crossing traffic and my nerve gave out. I balked, slamming on the brakes and yanking the wheel hard right, burning rubber in a pair of long, snaking black marks on the street and sending us bouncing up on the sidewalk. Judy screamed and flew forward, hitting the dashboard with her body and the windshield with her head, as behind me the Mercury did a strange kind of wobble that indicated that its driver too was struggling for control of a car sliding on locked brakes. I was lucky, letting the brakes go and fishing the front end back around so that we crashed down onto the street off the curb again, having cut off one end of the turn to end up heading the proper way in traffic, now going due south. The driver of the Mercury wasn't so fortunate. The last thing I saw in my mirror was the big dark car turned sideways on the pavement, sliding

and weaving an instant before it rammed into a telephone pole, bouncing its driver so hard that he disappeared under the dash.

Judy was cursing, holding her head down, her body bunched into a ball in the passenger's seat beneath a dark splashing stain on the windshield that I knew was her blood. The Toyota was still moving fast, and I was blinking through the lines of sweat running down my face. Behind us there was no sign of pursuit, and not so much as a single police car. Bearing down and picking up speed, I said, "Where were you planning to go when you ran?"

It took Judy a couple of seconds to settle herself, as if my question had come unexpectedly and she had to think about her answer. From the corner of my eye I saw her reorder herself in her seat, still holding her hand on the back of her head and exhaling hard. Finally, she said, "You can pull over anywhere here and get out."

"You're hurt," I exclaimed. "And you killed Stephen Teeg."

She had a knife—it didn't take me long to see it in her hand—and actually, I think I sensed the danger of it before I actually registered it with my eyes. It was in her right hand, and she was turning to look at me, her eyes set with pain and her posture stiffening.

"I said that you can pull over anywhere here," she commanded. "I want this car—"

I interrupted her, turning my head to face her and shouting, "Did you really think I risked my neck to save you? You think I'm on your side?"

She was shaking her head, lifting the knife, but I couldn't stop myself from screaming, "You *killed* him! Doesn't that mean anything? You killed that boy!"

"Fuck you!" she sneered, removing her bloody hand from behind her head and bracing herself to lunge.

The Toyota was doing fifty, hard and steady. The street ahead was nearly empty, and the trees of the parkway were far behind, lost to my sight. Around me there were nothing but buildings and concrete.

"I won't let you get away with murder!" I shouted. At the same instant that Judy Newhardt came at me with the knife, I turned the wheel hard to my right and aimed the car directly at a glass bus shelter beneath a wooden telephone pole.

Judy screamed—and so did I, but I didn't let go of the wheel as we skimmed past the pole, shearing off the mirror on the passenger's side and ripping back a sheet of steel as the window shattered and the bus shelter smashed into the front of the car . . . .

The impact was intense, and I was unable to resist throwing my hands up to protect my face as the car bounced and crashed, glass flying around us like glittering ice in a blizzard while the thunder of twisting metal blasted in my ears. When my brother Jerry's Camaro had hit that pole in the parking lot of the Prime Pump bar, the sound it had made from where I was standing had been quick, dull, and vaguely disappointing. But this sound, from the perspective of the car's interior was anything but disappointing. It was sickening, especially since I was belted down, and Judy was not.

I saw her, briefly, yet with such crystal clarity that it looked as if she were moving in slow motion, as she was thrown violently forward, striking the dashboard again, her head snapping around in an unnaturally loose fashion and the knife in her hand flying free. I snapped forward too, the breath being knocked out of me as the restraining strap seized up and held me back, snapping my head forward so that my teeth came down hard, crunching between my ears as my arms flew straight ahead, bashing into something hard and sending hot stabs of pain all through me. Judy crumpled. My head bounced back against the headrest. The car lurched, tangled itself in the wood of the bench inside the bus kiosk, ripped through, scattered glass, and rammed into a fireplug about twenty yards up the street. When we hit that, it was like hitting a wall, and the car simply stopped, every ounce of its forward momentum arrested, throwing Judy and me around inside one last time before

everything went perfectly quiet except for the wonderful sound of sirens in the distance.

I sat there shaking as if I were cold, which was a sign of shock, I knew. Judy didn't move at all. She had been thrust into a wad of tangled arms and legs, wedged half under the dashboard, with her head lying facedown on the passenger seat. I couldn't tell if she was breathing or not, and it shames me to admit that, at that moment, I really didn't care. I was shaking, and something was running down my chin. I thought it was drool, but when I lifted my hand to my face—an action that seemed to take every bit of effort and concentration I could muster—I felt a warmth on my lips that stained my fingers red. I reached up and twisted the mirror down so that I might see my face, and when I did I found that my chin was bathed with blood. I smiled at myself, and my teeth were bloody. I stuck out my tongue, and it was bloody too. I didn't feel any pain though, so, as the sirens cried, approaching with each moment just that much closer, I closed my eyes and waited for the police.

TEN

■■■■■■■■

THE WORDS "THIRD degree" don't really mean that much to you until you've been through one yourself. I went through a third degree like nothing I'd ever seen before starting that night and stretching through the next couple of days after the accident. I never lost consciousness, which I regretted once or twice since I was just as sore as hell, especially across my hands where they had banged into the Toyota's dashboard. The blood on my face made me look as if I were injured a lot worse than I actually was, and after one look the ambulance attendants passed over me to concentrate their efforts on Judy Newhardt, who was banged up but good. It turned out the blood on my chin came from a gash I had cut into my lower lip when my teeth gnashed together. But by the time an attendant helped me out of the car that gash had closed and swelled up, looking and feeling lousy without endangering my life at all.

I staggered around for a while, and a couple of cops talked to me, starting slowly and working their way up to the big questions . . . like what the hell was I doing driving so fast on a street that ran down the center of their city's business district? After I'd sat for a while,

sucking my throbbing lip and clenching and unclenching my sore fingers, I explained a little of what had happened, mentioning Stephen Teeg's name and saying that the woman in the car with me was the young man's killer. One of the cops actually recognized Teeg's name, and he got very serious, asking me how many fingers he was holding up, if I understood what I was saying, and what kind of proof I had that I had the right person. I was too sore to explain it all on the spot, and I waved the man away, giving him a business card from the funeral home instead of having to go over the spelling of my name three times and backing it up with my driver's license.

To make it short, it seemed that the whole world was mad at me for the rest of the night and most of the following day. I ended up down at the police station, very goddamn close to being placed under arrest myself, and explaining my ass off through my swollen lip. Larry Fizner and Nat showed up at about midnight, backing up my story and eventually calling my dad, hoping that he might have a little pull. When he arrived I thought the roof was going to come down, but he rolled up his sleeves and waded in behind me until the detective who was giving me the most trouble finally backed off, ran his hand over his sweaty hair, and said, "Okay. So let's start this again. And we'll go slowly this time."

So, slowly, I told him the whole thing. All of it. Including the part about the money. When I was through, Larry Fizner chimed in that what I had said was true. But when the detective asked Nat what had happened to the two hundred and fifty thousand dollars she had left the airport with, she told him to ask Larry, who frowned deeply and expressed his most sincere regrets as he explained that he had given it back to Elestrano.

"You gave it back?" the detective shouted, slamming down his pen and looking at Larry in astonishment. "Why?"

"Because even a quarter of a million bucks isn't worth dying for," he explained. Then he added, "Even though

Anthony Elestrano said he believed us, I knew that deep down inside he had his doubts. He's old and sick, but his granddaughter's not. She would have gone back to Mexico and chewed on what had happened until she pissed herself off enough to believe that she and her grandfather had been screwed. Then she'd send somebody to get their money back, probably with instructions to teach either me or Bill a lesson in the bargain. Instead of risking a problem like that, I just gave them their money now so they wouldn't have any gripe with us in the future."

The detective looked at Nat and asked, "Is that true?"

To which she responded, "If Mr. Fizner says so, then it's true."

"Did you actually see him hand over the money?"

"No."

"Then all we have is his word."

"That's right," Larry cut in, smiling. "And that should be good enough for you."

It obviously wasn't, but in the end, the detective let it slide. But my dad didn't, and later he demanded an explanation, which I gave him back at the funeral home, in the office, with all of us sitting around as the sun came up outside.

"We had a plan," I said, speaking slowly and with care. "And it was a reasonably simple one once you understand that Larry and I knew that it was Judy Newhardt who wasted Steven Teeg all along."

My dad tried to protest that we couldn't have been sure of our facts, and I told him to hold on to his questions till the end, and that I thought I could lay all his doubts to rest.

What I said was that, once you examined it logically, it simply had to be Judy Newhardt who was the killer. Even if Terry Scholtz did have the guts to kill Teeg after I had revealed the kid's name to him when I returned his mother's money, there was no way he could have kept the meeting his father had arranged. If Chester Scholtz hadn't hidden the details of that meeting in the wall of

his bathroom at the nursing home, then we would have thought he must have told his son. But the coded message proved that Chester Scholtz hadn't told another living soul, which meant that his son would never have risked murder for a name he could not have used.

Judy Newhardt knew everything we did about Steven Teeg, and she knew something even more important . . . namely, that her boss, Jimmy Cecorno, could, if sufficiently motivated, use his brother-in-law's connections to get a message through to Anthony Elestrano's people that it would be worth his while to keep the appointment he had made. If we hadn't discovered the secret of Scholtz's coded message, Jimmy Cecorno and Judy Newhardt would simply have gone to the airport, turned over the name, Frank Metcalf, ridden back to the Manor Care Nursing Home, and collected their money once Anthony Elestrano was satisfied that Mr. Metcalf was in fact Constantine Stenetti incognito. But when I announced at the restaurant that we had cracked the code, it left Judy with the inconvenience of having to accompany us to the airport that Saturday night.

If things had gone as she had planned, the three of us, Nat, Larry, and I, would have disappeared that night after she exposed the deception we had planned with the phony death certificate I had brought. That death certificate, by the way, belonged to a man the same age as Stenetti whom we had buried two years before, so that if Elestrano ever decided to look it up himself it would be there. There was no birth certificate on file for the man because he had been born in Europe—all a part of the cover, or so Elestrano would think—and he had resided at the Manor Care for a number of years before his death, having no family in this country for Elestrano to bother. But since Larry and I knew Judy was going to sell us out, we had cooked up a plan.

Everything we had said in the restaurant, and in fact anything we said anytime Judy was around, was carefully calculated to lead her to believe that we were planning one thing, when in fact we were counting on another. We knew she'd betray us, and that the only way Elestrano could

possibly know who was telling the truth was by looking directly at the man in question. So, we had arranged for Pete Germaine to be waiting for us behind the nursing desk at the Manor Care, and when we arrived, no matter who we asked for, he was supposed to have the nurse there send us up to room 312, where Matthew Taylor, the Parrot lived. The Parrot couldn't give us away because he couldn't form coherent sentences, and there was no way he could actually turn out to be Constantine Stenetti because he was way too young. It would look like it was Judy Newhardt and Jimmy Cecorno who were pulling the scam, and Anthony Elestrano would have no choice but to believe that what we had told him about Stenetti's having died in 1990 was the truth.

I had never planned to go crashing Pete Germaine's car into a bus stop, I said, not wanting to appear as either a hero or an idiot in my father's eyes. But once she ran away, I realized that I couldn't just let her go, and I couldn't let the gangsters kill her. It was foolhardy, I admitted, and things would probably have been simpler had I not done it, but I hadn't been thinking clearly, I supposed. Or maybe I had actually been thinking too much.

When Nat produced the cash, laying it out in a stack on the desk, we divided it exactly in half, giving a hundred and twenty-five thousand to Larry Fizner and keeping the other hundred and twenty-five thousand for ourselves. We let him have the suitcase it came in to carry it in, and as soon as he had his money he decided that it was time for him to leave. At the door, he turned and asked me two questions. The first was whether or not I had anything to say about the rest of the money that had disappeared from the limousine. Like maybe that I had picked it up as I ran through the parking lot heading for Pete Germaine's Toyota. I swore that I hadn't touched it, citing the fact that it hadn't been found in the car after I wrecked it and drawing a skeptical, sideways glance from the grizzled old detective.

The second question was, did I want to cancel my apprenticeship? I blinked when he asked me that, having

to stop for a moment and reassemble my thoughts. It hadn't even occurred to me that I might continue pursuing my private investigator's license once this "case" was finished. Thinking about it at that moment, the notion seemed absurd. And yet . . .

"I'll let you know," I said, holding open the door and extending my hand for Larry to shake. "I promise. In a couple of days, I'll let you know."

"A hundred and twenty-five grand's a nice piece of change," he said, leaning his head toward me and looking me carefully in the eye. "But you can't live on it the rest of your life. And besides that, you got the bug, Bill. I can tell."

"I'll let you know," I repeated, and closed the door.

After I had stepped back into the office, my dad, Nat, and I watched Larry Fizner's yellow van pull out of the lot, and then Nat stepped over to the closet next to the wet bar and produced a brown paper bag, which she emptied onto the desk next to the stack of money already there. The packs of hundred-dollar bills thumped one after the other, rolling from the bag and creating a veritable mound on the blotter. When she was through, I looked at her, thunderstruck. It had never occurred to me that it might have been her who took the money out of the limo, and now, seeing the evidence of the risk she had taken, I asked simply, "How?"

"I had somebody following me all the way from the airport to the funeral home," she explained, crumpling the paper bag into a ball and dropping it into the trash can behind the desk. Then, moving a strand of her long hair from where it hung in front of her face, she continued, "So I had the taxi drop me off out front and came inside. The car that followed me stayed parked right across the street, so I went upstairs, stashed the cash in the safe in case he decided to try and come up and get it, and then I went out the window around back."

"What window around back?" I asked. "There aren't any windows around back except up on the second floor."

"That's the one I'm talking about," she answered.

"But how'd you get down?"

"I was careful."

"Careful," I repeated, letting it go. "But how'd you get to the nursing home without a car?"

"I walked down the street and borrowed your mom's. Then I drove over to where I knew you'd be, saw the guard leave the limo, figured I'd see if the rest of the money was inside or with you and Elestrano, saw the bag, and took it. I feel awful about it, but I did. And now I'm giving it to you."

"Because you want to start your own business," my father said.

And I looked at Nat searchingly.

"I told him," she said simply. "And he's got an idea."

"You wanna hear it?" he asked.

And as tired and sore as I was, I nodded, flopped myself down in a chair, and listened.

"We're gonna build another funeral home," he said, lifting a package of hundred-dollar bills and turning it over in his hand. "The mortgage is going to be in your name, and I'm going to cosign it using this funeral home as security. The money's going in our safe, and I'm paying the mortgage from the operating capital of our business, reimbursing myself in cash from the safe."

"You can do that?" I asked, feeling very tired.

He nodded, saying, "It'll take some finagling. But we can do it."

"It ain't exactly honest," I observed.

And he smiled, ignoring my remark.

"The new place is going to be yours," he continued, stepping up to the window and looking out at the parking lot. "It'll be yours because you earned it, not because I gave it to you. From now on, you'll be your own man, and you can do as you please. You won't be in my shadow anymore."

I glanced at Nat, knowing that she had told him what I had said about feeling as if I had never left home, and

realizing that it was something I should have done myself a long time ago.

"So what do you say?" he asked.

"What do we have, three hundred and seventy-five thousand? Will that be enough?" I returned.

"No," he replied. "The funeral business is one of the only ones in the world where you've got to look successful the minute you open your doors. Folks want the chandeliers and the Cadillacs from day one. You can't work your way up. I'll have to help you a little . . . if that's okay."

I glanced down at my bruised hands, realizing what was happening around me. Nat had gone along with the risk for the money even though she had disagreed with the morality of it from the first, because she knew it represented something so important to me that it was all but irresistible. And now my dad was offering to make a dream of mine come true. They were both doing so much for me that it was all I could do to keep from crying. I stood up and nodded, saying, "Yeah, it's okay."

Then I left the room.

EPILOGUE
■■■■■■■■■■■■■

ONCE THEY HAD her in custody, the police were able
to find all sorts of evidence linking Judy Newhardt to
Stephen Teeg's death. She was in the hospital for a couple
of weeks after the accident, but she's out now, and in jail,
awaiting trial.

Jill, Jerry's estranged girlfriend whom I promised I would
approach, said that she'd think about calling him. That was
as good as I could do. Jerry wasn't thrilled with the result,
but told me to keep at it and that she would come around.
He's now working his ass off in physical therapy, learning
to use his arms again so that he'll be able to take the
position of office manager I offered him at the new Hawley
funeral home, which is under construction in Berea, the
suburb south of Cleveland where Nat works. The physical
therapist predicts that it will take about a year for Jerry to
be able to dial a phone and operate a computer keyboard,
which, coincidentally, is about as long as it will probably
take for the new funeral home to be built. Ain't it funny
how things work out?

The inspector from the Ohio Organization of Funeral
Professionals didn't appreciate my decision to finish my

apprenticeship under Larry Fizner, saying that if I took and passed the state's private investigator's test I might be defrocked, or disbarred, or whatever it is they do to undertakers who get drummed out of the corps. I told him that I'd worry about that when it happened. He'll be keeping an eye on me, he said. So I had better watch my step.

Yeah.

Right.

A friend of mine finally told me the ultimate result of all of Anthony Elestrano's hate and trouble, though he didn't realize he was doing it. He works as a security guard at the Holy Word Cemetery, which is where the man whose death certificate I gave Elestrano is buried. My friend mentioned to me last week that, about a month ago, on Friday, August 28th, he was working the graveyard shift when a limousine rolled up to the cemetery gates. This was like eleven o'clock at night, he said, and he went out to see why the limo was sitting there honking its horn. When he got there, the driver gave him a hundred bucks to look up a particular grave, and to let the man in the car visit that grave for a minute. For a hundred bucks the guy was not only willing to bend the cemetery's rules, he would have been willing to wash the limo too, so he did it, leading the big black car out to the section and pointing out the grave the old man in the back wanted to see.

"And you know what the guy did when we got there?" my friend asked. When I shook my head to indicate that I didn't, he said, "The old guy in the back had this young chick help him out of the car, and then he wobbled up to the grave by himself, and pissed on it. Can you believe that?"

I said that yes, I could believe it.

"People are strange," was my friend's conclusion.

And I was forced to agree.

I too paid a final visit, just to wrap everything up in my mind. It wasn't to the Holy Word Cemetery, but to the Manor Care Nursing Home, about a week after everything had settled. Pete Germaine let me in, seeing that it was after

midnight, thanking me for the new Honda I'd bought him to replace the Toyota of his that I'd wrecked, and leading me to a room where he left me alone at the door, saying, "I've already done it myself. I hope the experience means more to you than it did to me."

I opened the door, allowing the light from the hall to fall on the bed, where there was an old man sleeping, mouth open so that it yawned toothlessly at the ceiling, wet tongue moving slowly inside as he dreamed whatever dreams an old man calls his own when he's alone in the night. And this old man had been alone for years and years. Twenty, that I knew of, and who knew how many more before that? I looked at him, realizing that I had saved his life, and that he was responsible for changing my life forever. He gurgled in his sleep. And smacked his lips. I closed the door, my sore hand wrapped in gauze, my swollen lip pressed into a tender frown.

Pete Germaine was waiting for me at the end of the hall.

"Well?" he asked.

"Well," I replied. "The earth didn't move."

"It didn't move for me either when I first looked in on him. I don't know what I expected after I found out who he was, but it wasn't what I got."

"What's he like?" I asked, heading for the lobby.

"He's a grouchy old man who hasn't had a single visitor since he came here," Pete Germaine replied.

"He had one," I corrected, smiling. "I wonder what he'd say if we ever told him what he missed."

"Do you think he'd care?" Pete Germaine asked.

And I replied, "No," stepping into the night and taking a deep breath of the clean, fresh air. "To tell you the truth, after all these years alone, I'm not really sure that he'd care at all."

SPECIAL PREVIEW!

If you enjoyed *Final Viewing*—and would like to see Bill Hawley undertake another murderous mystery—be sure to watch for...

DOUBLE PLOT

A BILL HAWLEY UNDERTAKING

The second chilling whodunit in the marvelously macabre mystery series—coming soon from Berkley Prime Crime.

Here's an exclusive excerpt from the next Bill Hawley Undertaking...

I WAS JUST starting to dial the casket company when the doorbell rang. Thinking Mrs. Kane had forgotten something, I opened the door to find, instead of her rock-steady gaze, a whisper-thin young man with longish blond hair, eyes that had been cried almost raw, and a high-pitched, tremulous voice that was filled with so much emotion that it cracked as he exclaimed, "I've been waiting across the street for over an hour. I thought she'd never leave!"

He was dressed in a white, V-neck sweater, tan slacks, and brown loafers with no socks. (Why don't kids wear socks anymore?) His entire body radiated irritation, and every time he spoke I received a blast of booze breath—probably gin, I deduced from long, personal experience. I knew he was Edward Kane because his facial resemblance to his mother was almost eerie. And the first question out of his mouth was, "Tell me, please, what did they put down as my father's cause of death?" In return I asked him if he'd spoken to his mother since she left, in reply to which he flapped his hand dismissively and glowered. "Don't worry about that. Just tell me what killed my dad."

"Unspecified internal injuries," I said, quoting what I'd been told over the phone by the Wittmere County Hospital, since Mr. Kane's body had yet to be released.

"Oh my God!" he moaned, flopping himself down on the same chair his mother had occupied for the previous hour and throwing his arm up so that the back of his hand covered his eyes like a lady having a swoon in a Gothic romance. I thought he was reacting to the tragedy of his father's death after bracing his nerve in a college bar somewhere, but when I tried to express my sympathies his face snapped up and he reached into his pocket, producing a black plastic audio cassette and saying, "I've read about how you help people in trouble, Mr. Hawley. There were those articles in the *Plain Dealer* . . . and I've seen you on the local T.V. news. Well, nobody has ever needed your help more than I do now. You can believe me when I say that. And I can pay you whatever you ask."

His words made the back of my neck tingle, and I glanced first at the tape, and then at his face, saying, "I'm not following," with as noncommittal a tone as I could manage, even though the prospect of a "case" had my palms feeling a little damp. I'm known as the "sleuthing undertaker," and even though I think the title's a little silly, it goes a long way toward capturing the essence of who and what I really am.

"It's a suicide note," he explained, rising and laying the tape on the blotter before me. "I found it on my father's desk this morning. I got home after my mother left. I was a little late. I was upset. I must have just missed her. I let myself in with my key, but she was already gone and the house was just so empty and quiet that this horrible sadness washed right over me. When I was a little boy my dad used to sit me on his knee when he was working at his desk, and, I don't know why, but I wandered into his office and threw myself down in his chair, crying like a baby. That's when I noticed the tape, sitting right in the middle of the blotter next to the recorder he must have used to make it with. I don't know what made me do it, but I put it in the

machine and turned it on . . . and that's when I heard my father saying that he was going to Logan's Town to *kill himself.*"

He paused as if collecting his thoughts, sighed, and continued with a shrug, "Well, I didn't know what to do. Mom had said that he died in a car wreck. But she obviously hadn't heard the tape. God, could you imagine? I knew she'd be here, so I waited across the street until she left so I could turn it over to you."

When I asked him what he wanted me to do with it, he got very excited and said, "I want you to find out what happened to my dad! This tape says that he was planning to kill himself, but those redneck cops in that jerk-water town say he died in an accident. Something's going on, Mr. Hawley! Don't you see? My father was a very influential man, and he had business dealings all over the world. Coincidences don't happen to men like him. They just don't!"

I picked up the cassette and turned it over, thinking that, even if there was something to this, the kid had handled the tape, so any fingerprints on it were already ruined. Looking up, I said, "Okay, so let's say, for argument's sake, that your father did in fact take his own life, and that for whatever reason, the Logan's Town police got it wrong. Why is that something you'd want to prove?"

He eyed me intently, tears welling and lips pale as he said, "What do you mean?"

"Well," I began, trying to be tactful, "suicide usually cancels life insurance payments, and it's hell on the family. If the coroner ruled your father's death accidental, why don't you just let it go?"

"If it was *your* father," Edward Kane said, his eyes going cold, "would you let it go?"

It was a good question. So good, in fact, that I didn't even try to answer it. Instead I asked, "What kind of insurance did he have?"

"Tons."

"So by asking me to disprove suicide . . ."

Edward Kane stood up, suddenly looking, and sounding, more like his mother. "I'm not asking you to prove, or disprove anything," he announced. "What I want is the truth. That's all. He was my father, and I owe it to him."

"What you want to know is whether or not someone killed him. Isn't that it?" I asked.

"Exactly," he returned.

I examined the tape again, more as a way of moving my eyes from his face than because I expected to find anything I'd missed before. I didn't like the authoritarian demeanor he'd suddenly assumed. All that people who try to push me around usually succeed in doing is pissing me off.

"This isn't a television drama," I said. "And by nature I'm an extremely skeptical person." I cocked a thumb toward the door, adding, "People come through that door ten times a day"—I was exaggerating a little, but he didn't know it—"and they almost never talk like you're talking now. It's not normal for someone to suspect things without a reason. Do you have a reason, Mr. Kane?"

"Yes," he said, simply.

"Well, what is it?"

"My father was rich."

"And?"

"And it's not his voice on that tape."

"What?"

"It just doesn't sound like him," he exclaimed, wringing his hands and losing that look of determination he'd assumed so briefly in favor of the "little boy lost" expression I suspected was more his natural state. "That's why I waited for my mother to leave. I sat at the desk at home and listened to that tape over and over again . . . and no matter how many times I did I couldn't get it out of my mind that it was all a load of bullshit! It's not my dad. Don't you see? I don't know who would do such a thing, but that's somebody else imitating him—and doing a pretty fair job of it too. But they can't fool me. He was my father, after all. I know his voice. And that one's bullshit, Mr. Hawley. Somebody left it for us to find!"

My thoughts were suddenly tangled, and all I could think to say was, "Are you sure?"

He looked at me with exactly the cross expression I deserved.

Finally I said, "Well . . . if you're right, that does, uhm . . ."

"Fuck things up?" he asked, with some of his mother's confidence returning to his face.

"Yeah," I agreed.

He had me interested, and I think he knew it. Crossing his arms over his chest he looked suddenly grim and said, "My proposition is this: I'll pay you to look into it. That's all I'm asking. I'm not suggesting that you go out and chase down any killers or anything like that. I just want you to poke around until you're satisfied that there's enough here for me to go to the police. As it stands, all I've got is my word that my father didn't make that tape. He's dead, so there's no way to prove he did or didn't make it. But if I'm right, and someone did do something to him . . . there," he closed his eyes and sighed, "I've said it. If someone did do something to him . . . then I want to be able to go to the police with something in my hand that will make them listen to me. Find that something for me, Mr. Hawley. Please. If you don't I'm sure I'll go crazy knowing what I know."

"And you're certain this isn't your father's voice?" I asked, unnecessarily. "I mean, you're *convinced*?"

"Absolutely." He nodded, resolutely. "There's just no way to prove it."

But that's where he was wrong.

It was eleven o'clock that night before I figured out how I was going to check the accuracy of Edward Kane's suspicions. Flipping on the prep room's fluorescent lights, I imagined video cameras and microphone stands arrayed around the embalming table, with klieg lights hitting the stainless steel, and me standing over the body, narrating the proceedings. Being an audio-visual junkie, I had everything

I'd need stuffed in my bedroom closet upstairs to re-create the scene. But a video tape of what I had decided to do could land me in court. So, appropriately outfitted in a pair of red boxer shorts and a black "Batman Returns" T-shirt, I approached the embalming table armed with a portable cassette recorder, and convinced that making a dead man "talk" was the only way I was going to settle the nag of worry that had been playing on my mind.

This book is dedicated to my uncle,
Dennis Lazuta.
Everything I know about the funeral business,
I learned from him.

CHRISTMAS STALKING

Margaret Daley

Love Inspired

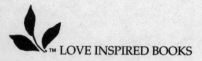

PLEASE RECYCLE · THIS PRODUCT IS RECYCLABLE ·

Recycling programs
for this product may
not exist in your area.

™ LOVE INSPIRED BOOKS

ISBN-13: 978-0-373-44512-7

CHRISTMAS STALKING

www.LoveInspiredBooks.com

Printed in U.S.A.

For if ye forgive men their trespasses,
your heavenly Father will also forgive you.
—*Matthew* 6:14

To Shaun and Kim, my son and daughter-in-law

ONE

In the dark, Ellie St. James scanned the mountainous terrain out her bedroom window at her new client's home in Colorado, checking the shadows for any sign of trouble before she went to sleep. The large two-story house of redwood and glass blended in well with the rugged landscape seven thousand feet above sea level. Any other time she would appreciate the beauty, but she was here to protect Mrs. Rachel Winfield.

A faint sound punched through her musing. She whirled away from the window and snatched her gun off the bedside table a few feet from her. Fitting the weapon into her right palm and finding its weight comforting, she crept toward her door and eased it open to listen. None of the guard dogs were barking. Maybe she'd imagined the noise.

A creak, like a floorboard being stepped on, drifted up the stairs. Someone was ascending to the second floor. She and her employer were the only ones in the main house. She glanced at Mrs. Winfield's door two down from hers and noticed it was closed. Her client kept it that way only when she was in her bedroom.

So who was on the stairs? Had someone gotten past

the dogs outside and the security system? And did that someone not care that he was being heard coming up the steps? Because he didn't intend to leave any witnesses?

The latest threat against Mrs. Winfield urged her into action. She slipped out of her room and into the shadows of the long hallway that led to the staircase. Having memorized all the floorboards that squeaked, Ellie avoided the left side of the corridor as she snuck forward—past Mrs. Winfield's door.

Another sound echoed through the hall. Whoever was on the steps was at the top. She increased her speed, probing every dark recess around her for any other persons. Near the wooden railing of the balcony that overlooked the front entrance, she found the light switch, planted her bare feet a foot apart, preparing herself to confront the intruder, and then flipped on the hall light.

Even though she expected the bright illumination, her eyes needed a few seconds to adjust to it. The large man before her lifted his hand to shield his eyes from the glare. Which gave Ellie the advantage.

"Don't move," she said in her toughest voice, a husky resonance she often used to her advantage.

The stranger dropped his hand to his side, his gray-blue eyes drilling into her then fixing on her Wilson combat aimed at his chest. Anger washed all surprise from his expression. "Who are you?" The question came out in a deep, booming voice, all the fury in his features reflected in it.

"You don't get to ask the questions. Who are—"

The click of the door opening to Mrs. Winfield's bedroom slightly behind and to the left of Ellie halted her words as she shifted her attention for an instant to make sure the man didn't have an accomplice already with her client.

"Winnie, get back," the intruder yelled.

By the time Ellie's gaze reconnected with the man, he was charging toward her. She had less than a second to decide what to do. The use of her client's nickname caused Ellie to hesitate. In that moment the stranger barreled into her, slamming her into the hardwood floor. The impact jolted her, knocking the Wilson Combat from her hand. The thud of her weapon hitting the floor behind her barely registered as she lay pinned beneath two hundred pounds of solid muscle. Pressed into her, the man robbed her of a decent breath.

Her training flooded her with extra adrenaline. Before he could capture her arms, she brought them up and struck him on the sides of his head. His light-colored gaze widened at the blow. She latched onto his face, going for his eyes with her thumbs.

"Miss St. James, stop!" Mrs. Winfield's high-pitched voice cut into the battle between Ellie and her attacker.

The man shifted and clasped her wrists in a bone-crushing grip.

Ellie swung her attention from the brute on top of her to her employer standing over them with Ellie's gun in her quivering hand. Pointed at her!

"He's my grandson," Mrs. Winfield said. "Colt, get up. She can hardly breathe."

The man rolled off her, shaking his head as though his ears rang. After her attack they probably did.

Sitting up, he stared at his grandmother who still held the weapon. "Please give me the gun, Winnie." His soft, calm words, interspersed with heavy pants, contradicted his earlier authoritative tone.

Ellie gulped in oxygen-rich breaths while he pushed to his feet and gently removed the weapon from Mrs. Winfield's hand. He dwarfed his petite grandmother by over a foot.

With her gun in his grasp, he stood next to her client and glared down at Ellie. "Now I would like an answer. Who are you?" Anger still coated each word.

She slowly rose from the floor. "Ellie St. James."

He put his arm around his grandmother, who stood there trembling, staring at Ellie as though she was trying to understand what had just happened. "What are you doing here, Miss St. James?" he asked.

With a shake of her head, Mrs. Winfield blinked then peered up at her grandson. "She's my new assistant."

"What in the world are you doing carrying a gun?"

His question thundered through the air, none of the gentle tone he'd used with his grandmother evident. He glared at her, his sharp gaze intent on Ellie's face. Although he'd lowered the gun, Ellie didn't think it would take much for him to aim it again. Fury was etched into his hard-planed face.

"My dear, why *do* you have a gun?"

Mrs. Winfield's light, musical voice finally pulled Ellie's attention from the man. Her employer had regained her regal bearing, her hands clasped together in front of her to control their trembling.

"I've lived alone for so long in a big city I've always had a gun for protection," Ellie finally answered.

Although Mrs. Winfield was her client—the person she'd been assigned to guard—the older woman didn't know it. Her lawyer and second-in-charge at Glamour Sensations, Harold Jefferson, had hired Guardians, Inc., to protect her. Ellie was undercover, posing as her new assistant. Her cover had her growing up in Chicago—the south side—and still living there. But in reality, at the first opportunity she'd had she'd hightailed it out of Chicago and enlisted in the army. When she'd left the military, she hadn't gone back home but instead she'd gone to Dallas to work for Guardians, Inc., and Kyra Morgan—now Kyra Hunt.

"You don't need a weapon now. This isn't a big city. I have security around the estate. You're safe. I prefer you do something with that gun. I don't like weapons." A gentle smile on her face, Mrs. Winfield moved toward her as though she were placating a gun-toting woman gone crazy.

Ellie didn't trust anyone's security enough to give up her gun, but she bit the inside of her cheeks to keep from voicing that thought. She would need to call Mr. Jefferson and see how he wanted to proceed. Ellie had wanted to tell Mrs. Winfield that her life was in danger, but he'd refused. Now something would have to give here.

"I'll take care of it, Winnie. I'll lock it in the safe until she can remove it from here." The grandson checked the Wilson Combat, slipped out the ammo clip and ejected the bullet in the chamber, then began to turn away.

"Wait. You can't—"

He peered over his shoulder, one brow arching. "I'm sure my grandmother will agree that this will have to be a condition of your continual employment. If I had any say in it, I'd send you packing tonight." He rubbed his ears. "They're still ringing. You have a mean punch. Where did you learn to take care of yourself?"

"A matter of survival in a tough neighborhood."

That was true, but she'd also had additional training in the army.

"As my grandmother said, that isn't an issue here. We're on a side of a mountain miles away from the nearest town. No one bothers us up here."

If you only knew. "I'm licensed to carry—"

But Mrs. Winfield's grandson ignored her protest and descended the staircase.

Ellie rushed to the railing overlooking the downstairs entrance. Clutching the wood, she leaned over and said, "That's my weapon. I'll take care of it."

"That's okay. I'm taking care of it." Then he disappeared into the hallway that led to the office where the safe was.

"I certainly understand why you got scared." Mrs. Winfield approached her at the railing and patted her back. "I did when I heard the noise from you two in the hallway. I didn't know what was happening. I appreciate you being willing to protect me, but thank goodness, it wasn't necessary."

This time. Ellie swung around to face the older woman. "Yeah, but you never know."

"The Lord watches out for His children. I'm in the best care."

"I agree, but that doesn't mean we shouldn't be proactive, Mrs. Winfield," Ellie said, hoping to convince Mr. Jefferson to tell her about the threats tomorrow.

"Please call me Winnie. Christy, my previous assistant, did. I don't like standing on formality since you'll be helping me." She smiled. "Colt gave me that name years ago, and everyone calls me that now."

"Was he supposed to visit?"

"The last I heard he wasn't going to come back this

year for Christmas. He probably heard my disappointment when we talked on the phone a few days ago. If I had known Colt was coming, I would have said something to you."

She'd read the dossier Kyra Hunt had given her on Colt Winfield, the only grandson Mrs. Winfield had. She should have recognized him, but with a beard and scruffy hair and disheveled clothes he'd looked like a bum who had wandered into the house intent on ill gains.

"He was supposed to be in the South Pacific on the research vessel through Christmas and the New Year." Mrs. Winfield gave Ellie a smile, her blue eyes sparkling. "Just like him to forget to tell me he was coming home after all for Christmas. Knowing him, it could be a surprise from the very beginning. He loves doing that kind of thing. Such a sweet grandson." She leaned close to Ellie to whisper the last because Colt Winfield was coming back up the steps.

"I wish that were the case, Winnie." Colt paused on the top stair. "But I need to get back to the *Kaleidoscope*. I managed to get a few days off before we start the next phase of our project, and I know how important it is to you that we have some time together at Christmas."

Great, he'll be leaving soon.

"Just a few days?" His grandmother's face fell, the shine in her eyes dimming. "I haven't seen you in months. Can't you take a couple of weeks out of your busy schedule to enjoy the holidays like we used to?"

Please don't, Ellie thought, rolling her shoulders to ease the ache from their tussle on the hardwood floor.

He came to the older woman and drew her into his

embrace. "I wish I could. Maybe at the end of January. The government on the island is allowing a limited amount of time to explore the leeward side and the underwater caves."

Mrs. Winfield stepped away. "You aren't the only one on the research team. Let someone else do it for a while. You're one of three marine biologists. And the other two are married to each other. They get to spend Christmas together."

"I need to be there. Something is happening to the sea life in that part of the ocean. It's mutating over time. It's affected the seal population. You know how I feel about the environment and the oceans."

"Fine." Mrs. Winfield fluttered her hand in the air as she swept around and headed for the door to her bedroom. "I can't argue with you over something I taught you. Good night. I'll see you tomorrow morning. I hope you'll at least go for a power walk with Ellie and me. Seven o'clock sharp."

"Yes, Winnie. I've brought my running shoes. I figured you'd want me to."

When her employer shut the door to her room, Ellie immediately said, "I need my gun back."

"You do? What part of your duties as my grandmother's assistant requires you to have a gun?" His gaze skimmed down her length.

Ellie finally peered down at the clothes she wore— old sweats and a baggy T-shirt. With a glance at the mirror at the end of the hall, she noticed the wild disarray of her hair. She looked as scruffy as Colt Winfield. She certainly wouldn't appear to this man as a capable and efficient bodyguard. Or a woman who knew how to use a gun when she needed to. "Ask yourself. What if you had been a burglar? Would you have wanted me to let you rob the place or do worse?"

For half a moment he just stared at her, then he started chuckling. "Since I'm not and I'll be here for a few days, you'll be safe. Didn't you wonder why the three German shepherds didn't bark?"

"I know that dogs can be good for security purposes, but they can be taken out. It shouldn't be the only method a person uses." Which Mr. Jefferson was changing—just not fast enough for her liking. A new alarm system for the house would be in place by the end of the week. But even that didn't guarantee a person was totally safe. Hence the reason why Mr. Jefferson hired her to guard Mrs. Winfield—Winnie.

"So you decided to bring a gun."

"I'm very capable. I was in the army."

"Army? Even knowing that, I'm afraid, Miss St. James, we're not going to see eye to eye on this." He swiveled around and went to pick up a duffel bag by the steps. He hadn't had that when he'd first come upstairs. He must have brought it up when he put the gun in the safe. "Good night."

Ellie watched him stride down the corridor in the opposite direction of her bedroom. When he paused before a door at the far end, he slanted a look back at her. For a few seconds the corners of his mouth hitched up. He nodded his head once and then ducked inside.

She brought her hand up to comb her fingers through her hair and encountered a couple of tangles. "Ouch!"

Moving toward her bedroom, she kept her eye on his, half expecting him to pop back out with that gleam of humor dancing in his eyes. When he didn't, something akin to disappointment flowed through her until she shoved it away. She would have to call Mr. Jefferson to tell him that Colt was here. From what she'd read about the man he was smart, with a doctorate in marine biology as well as a degree in chemistry. Currently he worked on a research vessel as the head marine biologist for a think tank formed to preserve the world's oceans.

His grandmother hadn't ever questioned why Ellie was always around, even in her lab, but she had a feeling Colt would. Then he would demand an answer.

After traveling for almost twenty-four hours the day before, Colt dragged himself out of bed at a quarter to seven in his old room where he'd grown up. Winnie hadn't changed anything in here, and he doubted she ever would. She would always think of him as her little boy. Although Winnie was his grandmother, she'd raised him when his own mother had died from a massive infection shortly after he was born. Thinking of his past brought both heartache and joy. Heartache because he'd lost so many people he cared about. But he'd rather not dwell on his past. Besides, he had Winnie. She had given him so much.

After dressing in his sweats to power walk in the crisp December air in the Colorado mountains, he made his way toward the kitchen and the scent of coffee. Just its aroma made his body crave caffeine. He'd need it if he was going to keep up with Winnie. At seventy-three, she was an amazing woman, owner of Glamour Sensations and creator of both women's and men's fragrances. Not to mention her latest development— a line of antiaging products rumored to revolutionize the cosmetic industry. This had been a dream of Winnie and his granddad for fifteen years. Although his

tiring. Not to mention he can hold his breath underwater for two minutes. I think that's from growing up here in the mountains. Great lung capacity."

His grandmother's remark to her assistant slid his attention to the tall woman who lunged to the left then right. "So you're into power walking, too?"

Ellie brought her feet together, raised one leg behind her and clasped her ankle. "When I can get the chance, I usually jog, but I've been enjoying our early morning jaunts."

"Who did you work for before this?"

Pausing, she stretched her other leg. "A small company," she said finally.

Winnie didn't seem to notice the slight hesitation in Ellie's reply, but he did. Was something going on? When he got back from his power walk, he would catch Harold before he talked with Winnie. He didn't want to upset his grandmother unless there was a good reason, but who exactly was Ellie St. James? A woman who carried a gun and, based on last night, wasn't afraid to use it.

"I'm glad I caught you before you talked with Winnie." Ellie shut the library door after the lawyer entered.

"Ah, I see you've made good progress with Winnie," Harold Jefferson said. "She doesn't usually have someone call her Winnie unless she likes you."

"I think that's because she appreciated my attempt to protect her last night."

His eyebrows shot up. "Someone got in the house? Why didn't you call me?"

"Because it turned out to be her grandson."

His forehead wrinkled. "Colt's here?"

"Yes, for a few days. I thought he was an intruder

and I pulled my gun on him in the upstairs hallway. Without her knowing why I'm here, she doesn't understand why I would have a gun. It's now sitting in her safe in her office. That ties my hands protecting her. She needs to be told."

"She will stress and shut down. She's under a tight deadline with this new product she's coming up with. That's why I'm here to talk to her about the publicity campaign now that her former assistant, Christy, has agreed to be the new face for the company."

"The Winnie I've seen this past week is tough when she needs to be."

"It's all a show. I've been through a lot with her. Years ago her company nearly fell apart because of her son's death. Then she had a heart attack ten years ago, and we went through another rough patch. That was followed by her husband passing away five Christmases ago. Finally she's close to going public with Glamour Sensations and offering stock as she brings out her new line, Endless Youth. She's been working toward this for years. She feels she needs to fulfill her late husband's vision for the business."

Ellie placed her hand on her waist, trying to control her frustration and impatience. "If she is dead, she won't be able to fulfill his vision."

"That's why you're here. To keep her alive. The fewer people who know someone has sent her threats the better. She *is* the company. The brains and creative force behind it. We need the infusion of money to make a successful campaign for the new products in the spring that will lead up to the unveiling of the signature cream next Christmas."

"If the company is going public, don't you have to disclose the threats?"

"Yes. When we reach that part of the process, we'll have to disclose the threats to the investment banker and lawyers. Fortunately, we have until right after Christmas to take care of the problem."

"I can't protect her without my weapon. It's that simple."

"What if we tell Colt and have him get the gun for you? She rarely goes into the safe. I imagine she's too busy in the lab downstairs."

Ellie looked out the floor-to-ceiling window across the back at the stand of pine trees. "Yes, but what if she does?"

She'd never liked the fact that Mrs. Winfield didn't know about the threats and the danger her life was in. The former assistant had given Mr. Jefferson each threatening letter. They had become more serious over the past month, and one also included a photo of Mrs. Winfield out power walking. That was when he had contacted Guardians, Inc. He was hoping nothing would come of the letters, but he knew he had to put some kind of protection in place. That was when Ellie had entered as the new assistant to replace Christy Boland, who was going to be the spokesperson for Glamour Sensations' Endless Youth line.

"On second thought, we probably shouldn't tell Colt. I don't want anyone else to know if possible. He might let something slip to his grandmother. It's probably better that he returns to the research ship." Mr. Jefferson snapped his fingers. "I've got it. I'll get you a gun to use. I can come back out here this afternoon with whatever you want. Maybe a smaller gun that you can keep concealed."

"Fine, unless I think there's a direct threat."

"I'm hoping I can catch the person behind the letters before then. The Bakersville police chief is working on the case personally, as well as a P.I. I hired. Winnie received another letter at headquarters yesterday."

"Another picture in it?"

"No, just threats of what the person is going to do to her."

Ellie thought of the sweet lady she'd spent the past week with—a woman who toiled long hours because she knew a lot of people who worked for her counted on her. "What in the world has she done to anger someone?"

"We're looking into disgruntled employees, but she was never directly responsible for firing anyone. If she had her way, everyone would still be working for her no matter if they didn't do their job. Thankfully I run that part of the business."

Ellie sighed. "I'll need you to bring me a Glock G27. It's smaller and easily concealed. It will have to do, even though I prefer my own weapon. At least you were able to get Winnie to stay and work from home this month. That will help the situation, but this home isn't secure."

"Is any place?"

"No, but there are some things we can do."

"Like what? I'm working on a better security system."

"That's good because the one she has is at least ten years old." Ellie paced the large room with bookcases full of books. "We could use bulletproof windows. Security guards to patrol the grounds and posted at the gate. Also cameras all over the house and the property being monitored 24/7."

"She won't go for anything else. She didn't even understand why I wanted to upgrade her security system. Told me the Lord was looking out for her and that's all she needs."

Ellie believed in the power of God, but Winnie was being naive. "What if someone gets to her? I've convinced her that I enjoy power walking, and she has graciously asked me to come with her, but she likes her independence. I'm running out of reasons to tag along with her when she leaves this house."

"It's only for a couple of more weeks at best. The P.I. on the case is tracking down some promising leads. If nothing changes after she has completed the last product for this new line, I'll tell her. She's fragile when she's in her creative mode. Easily distracted. Even Colt's visit will strain her schedule."

"And Christmas won't? I get the impression she enjoys the holiday." The wide-open space outside the window made her tense. Someone could be out there right now watching their every move.

"That's just a few days." Mr. Jefferson checked his watch. "I'd better find Winnie. She starts to worry when people are late."

"I've noticed that."

"Five years ago next week, Thomas was on the way home from work and lost control of his car. It went off the cliff. The sheriff thought he'd fallen asleep at the wheel from reports by witnesses. So anytime someone is late she begins to think the worst." He covered the distance to the door. "I'll meet with Winnie in the lab then come back later with your gun."

"So let me get this straight. You don't want to tell Colt?" Another secret she would have to keep.

Looking back at her, Mr. Jefferson opened the door. "No, not right now."

"Not right now what?" Colt stepped into the entrance of the library.

TWO

Mr. Jefferson waved his hand and passed Colt quickly in the hall. "I'll let Miss St. James tell you."

Ellie balled her hands at her sides. What was she supposed to tell Colt? Even worse, had he overheard anything they had been talking about? She started forward. "I'd better go and change for work."

He gripped her arm, halting her escape. "What aren't you telling me? Why were you and Harold talking in here?"

She schooled her expression into one of innocence. She would love to get her hands on Mr. Jefferson for putting her in this situation. "He wanted to know how my first week went with Winnie. Is there a reason we shouldn't talk? After all, he hired me."

"And how are you doing?" He stepped nearer until Ellie got a whiff of his coffee-laced breath. "Does he know about the gun?"

"Yes. I saw no reason not to tell him." Her heartbeat kicked up a notch. She moved back a few inches until her back encountered the wall behind her. "Your grandmother and I are getting along well. She's a special lady. Very talented. She's easy to talk to. To work for."

"Winnie?"

Hating the trapped feeling, she sidled away. "Who else are we talking about?"

"My grandmother is a private woman. She doesn't share much with anyone."

"I haven't found her that way. Maybe something has changed, since you've been gone for so long." There, she hoped that would keep Colt quiet and less curious about her relationship with Winnie. In some of her past jobs, she'd had to play a role, but it never was her favorite way to operate.

"Then maybe you can fill me in on what's going on with my grandmother."

"What we've talked about is private. If you want to know, go ask her." Before he could stop her again, she pivoted away and hurried down the hall to the foyer.

As she mounted the stairs to the second floor, she felt his eyes on her. It was so cold it reminded her of the icy mountain stream they'd passed on their walk today. Unable to shake loose of his frosty blue gaze, she felt the chill down to her bones.

After dinner that evening Ellie followed the small group to the den, a room with a roaring fire going in the fireplace and the dark rich wood of the mantel polished to a gleaming luster that reflected the lights. She sat on the plush, tan couch before a large glass-topped coffee table. In the middle an arrangement of sweet-smelling roses vied with the fireplace for attention. She'd quickly learned Bloomfield Flower Shop in the medium-size town at the foot of the mountain delivered a fresh bouquet twice weekly because Winnie loved looking at them in the evening. Their delicate aroma wafted up to

Ellie and surrounded her in their fragrance. Since working for Winnie, she'd become attuned to the smell of things. Like breakfast in the morning or a fresh winter day with pine heavy in the air when they were power walking. Winnie always pointed out scents wherever she went.

Colt took a forest-green wingback chair across from her. She caught his glance lingering on her for a few extra seconds while the others settled into their seats. She pulled her gaze away to finish assessing the placement of everyone, along with all the exits. Harold took the other end of the couch she sat on while Winnie eased down between them. Christy Boland, the face of the new line, and her fiancé, Peter Tyler, a Bakersville dentist, occupied the love seat.

"I can't imagine living on a research vessel for months on end," Christy said, taking up the conversation started at the dinner table.

"I have to admit it does take getting used to. It was an opportunity I couldn't pass up. I don't even have a place of my own right now."

"You don't need one. You're always welcome here when you're in the country," Winnie told her grandson. "After all, you've done so much to help me with my new line, especially this last product, which will be the coup d'état."

"How so, Winnie? I don't remember doing that."

"Your research on certain sea life sparked a breakthrough for me on this project."

Colt tilted his head to the side. "Which one?"

Winnie smiled. "I'm not telling. Right now I'm the only one who knows. It's all up here." She tapped the side of her temple. "But this will keep you busy for years, Christy. Harold isn't going to be able to count the money fast enough." Her grin grew. "At least that's what I predict. And all my predictions have been right in the past." She sat back and motioned the servers to bring in dessert.

Linda and Doug Miller, the middle-aged couple who lived on the property and took care of the house, carried in two trays, one with coffee and the other with finger sweets. Doug placed the coffee down in front of Winnie while his wife served the petite desserts to each person in the room.

"I will say I miss your cooking, Linda. No one on the vessel can cook like you." Colt selected four different sweets and put them on a small plate.

By the time the caretakers retreated to the kitchen ten minutes later, everyone had a cup of coffee and dessert.

Colt raised his cup in a toast. "To Christy. Congratulations again on becoming the face of Endless Youth. This is a big change for you from being Winnie's assistant to touring the country, your photo plastered everywhere."

"Yes. I haven't traveled like you have or Winnie. About as far as I've gone was Texas and California when Winnie did."

"That will definitely change, dear," Winnie said after taking a sip of her coffee. "I'm thrilled you agreed to do this. When you tested the product and it did such wonders for you, it became obvious you were perfect for this new job." She slid a glance toward Harold. "Thankfully, Harold found a new assistant for me who is working out great."

All eyes turned to Ellie. Never wanting to be the focus of attention, she pressed herself into the couch until she felt the Glock in its holster digging into her back. Harold had brought the gun when he'd returned for dinner. Having it holstered under her jacket was a constant reminder she was on a job. "I appreciate you helping me, Christy. Answering my hundreds of questions."

Christy laughed. "I wish I had someone to answer my hundreds of questions. I've never been a model and don't know one. Poor Peter has to listen to all my questions."

"And I don't have any answers for her. Actually, she's been gone so much lately that I haven't had to listen to them." Peter covered Christy's hand that lay between them on the love seat. "I'm looking forward to some togetherness at Christmas."

Harold bent forward to pour himself some more coffee. "I just finalized some plans for Christy to start the filming of the first commercial in L.A. next week."

Christy glanced at Peter then Harold. "But I'll be here for Christmas Day, won't I? It'll be our first Christmas together."

"Yes, but since we're launching part of the line in February for Valentine's Day, your time will be very limited."

Peter picked up her hand and moved it to his lap. "We'll work out something," he said to Christy, his adoring look roping her full attention.

As Ellie listened to the conversation shift to the launch of Endless Youth, she decided to call Kyra, her employer, and have her look into everyone around Winnie, including Harold Jefferson, who ran the day-to-day operation of Glamour Sensations as the CFO. She'd learned quickly not to take anything for granted, even the person who hired her.

The threats against Rachel Winfield had started when news of Endless Youth leaked to the press. What was it about that product line that would make someone angry with Winnie? From what Ellie had learned, the development and testing didn't upset any environmental groups. So did Endless Youth have anything to do with the threats or was its development and launch just a coincidence? Maybe it was a rival cosmetic company. Was the industry that cutthroat? Did this involve an industrial spy?

She kneaded her hand along her nape, trying to unravel the knots twisting tighter in her neck. Finding the person behind the threats wasn't her priority—keeping Winnie alive and unharmed was. She needed to leave the rest to the police and Harold's P.I.

Colt entered the kitchen that gleamed with clean counters, any evidence of a dinner party gone, but the scent of the roast that Linda had cooked still lingered in the room. The Millers did wonders behind the scenes for Winnie and had worked for the family for ten years. He wasn't sure what his grandmother would do if they decided to look for another job. He didn't worry about Winnie with Linda and Doug taking care of the property and house.

He raided the refrigerator to make himself a sandwich with the leftover roast beef. After piling it between slices of Linda's homemade bread, he turned away from the counter ready to take a bite. But he halted abruptly when he noticed Ellie hovering in the entrance, watching him.

She blinked and averted her gaze. "I heard a noise and came to check it out. Winnie just went to bed."

"She stayed up later than usual, but then when Christy and Harold come to dinner, she usually does. That's the extent of her entertaining here."

"I can see that. She spends most of her day in the lab."

"My grandmother is one of the few people in the world who has a 'nose,' as they say in the perfume industry. She can distinguish different scents and has a knack for putting them together to complement each other. That comes easy for her. But this new product line is something else, more Granddad's pet project. I'll be glad when she finishes and doesn't have to work so much."

Ellie came into the room. "She's being taken care of. Linda makes sure she eats healthy. Harold doesn't let her worry about the running of Glamour Sensations, and I do all the little things she has allowed to mount up."

"So she can focus on Endless Youth. I can remember when Granddad was alive. Those two talked about the line back then. He had already started the research. Winnie is just finishing up what they began in earnest eight years ago. I think he pushed her to help her recover from her heart attack. She loves a good challenge." He held up his plate. "I can fix you one."

Her chuckles floated through the air. "I think I'll pass on that. I ate more tonight than I usually do."

He put his sandwich on the kitchen table and gestured at a chair beside him. "Join me. I hate eating alone. When you live on a small ship with fifteen others, you're rarely alone except in your tiny cabin. You would think I would cherish this time."

"You don't?" Ellie slid into the seat next to him.

He noticed she didn't wear any fragrance and wondered if Winnie would change that. "I'm used to it so it's strange when I'm not here. When I've come back here, I've felt the isolation I never felt while I was growing up here."

"Well, it won't feel isolated too much longer. Winnie has several evening events the closer we get to the holidays."

"Let me guess. Most of them have to do with the business."

"Yes, and she is the mistress of ceremony at the lighting of the Christmas tree in Bakersville in a few days. This year the town is naming the park after your grandparents."

"They've been trying to get her to light the Christmas tree for years. I'm glad she finally accepted."

A tiny frown made grooves between Ellie's eyebrows.

"You aren't?" Colt asked.

Her expression evened out. "I'm only concerned she doesn't wear herself out. She has the big gala for Endless Youth and Christy's introduction to the press a few days after that."

"Yeah, she's been trying to get me to stay an extra week."

"I can understand the demands of work."

"Is this job demanding to you? Is the isolation getting to you?"

"I love the isolation. Remember, I grew up in Chicago where everywhere I turned there were people."

"How did you find out about this job?"

Ellie rose. "I think I'll fix a cup of tea. Do you want

any? Herbal, no caffeine." She walked to the cabinet where the tea was kept and withdrew a tin of lavender tea.

"No, thanks." He waited until she put the water on to boil then continued, "Harold said something about him finding you. How? Chicago is a far piece from here."

"Harold knew my former employer. She suggested me for the job."

"She let you go?"

"Not exactly. She knew how much I love the mountains and thought this would be perfect for me."

"What did you do at your former job?"

She laughed. "I feel I'm being interviewed again, but since I already have the job, that isn't it. So why the interest?"

"Because I love Winnie and have her best interest at heart."

Gripping the counter edge with both hands, Ellie lounged back, except that there was nothing casual about her stance. Something wasn't right. Colt lived in close quarters and had learned to read people accurately and quickly. It made his life much easier and calmer.

"What are you hiding, Ellie?"

THREE

"What makes you think I'm hiding something?" Ellie busied herself pouring the hot water into a mug and dunking the tea bag.

"I get the feeling there's something in your past you don't like to talk about. If it wasn't that Harold is thorough when it comes to my grandmother, I would be concerned at your evasiveness."

"But Harold is thorough." She drew herself up straight, cupping her hands around the mug. "I didn't know full disclosure about all the details of my life was necessary for me to get this job. Winnie seems satisfied. Is this something we should bring up to her?" Lifting her chin, she clamped her jaws together to keep from saying anything else that would get her fired.

He dipped his head in a curt nod. "Duly noted. Winnie is a great judge of character."

Meaning he had his doubts? Pain shot down her neck from the tense set of her teeth grinding together. She strode to the table and took the chair across from him. Though she would rather drink her tea in peace, she knew escaping to her bedroom would only confirm that she had something to hide.

One of the reasons she liked being a bodyguard was that she could blend into the background. Most of her clients didn't engage her in casual conversation. But Winnie had been different, and it seemed to run in the family. She kept a lock on her past—a past she didn't want to take out and reexamine. No point in going over it.

"If you must know, the short version of my life so far is—"

"That's okay—"

"I grew up in Chicago," she interrupted, "in a part of town where I had to learn to take care of myself and stick up for my brother, too. People weren't kind to him. He had a mental disability and talked 'funny.' Their word, not mine. When I could get out of the neighborhood, I did." She sipped her tea, gripping the mug tighter to keep her hands steady.

"Where's your brother?"

"Dead." The word hung in the air between them for a long moment while Ellie relived the moment when Toby had slipped away from congestive heart failure.

"I'm sorry. I didn't mean to bring up something painful."

"What did you mean to do, then?"

"To make sure Winnie was in good hands."

She stared into his light, gray-blue eyes. "She's in good hands. When I do a job, I do it one hundred percent."

Another long silence stretched between them as she felt the probe of his gaze, seeking, reading between the lines.

"Did I pass?" She raised her cup and drank, relishing the warm, soothing tea.

"This wasn't a test."

"You could have fooled me." After she scooted back her chair, the scraping sound filling the kitchen, she pushed to her feet. "While I would love to continue this interrogation—I mean conversation—I'm tired and plan to go to bed. Good night."

She left the kitchen. Out in the hallway she paused, a hand braced on the wall as images of her twin brother washed through her mind—running from the neighborhood bullies, falling and scraping his palms and shins, crying because he didn't understand why they didn't like him. But the worst picture was of Toby on the floor of their small, dirty apartment, taking his last breath. He looked straight at her. She held him while they waited for the ambulance. A light brightened his eyes, and a peace she'd never seen fell over his face. Then he went limp as the sirens came down the street. She'd been thirteen.

Tears crowded her eyes. She squeezed them closed. This was why she never dwelled in the past. She did not shed tears—hadn't since she was thirteen.

She slowly crossed to the front door and checked to make sure it was locked and the antiquated security system was on. After Colt went to bed, she would make a more thorough check of the house before she slept. Until then she would prowl her bedroom, hating the situation she'd been placed in. This secrecy handicapped her doing her job.

Standing in the dark, Colt stared out his bedroom window at the yard in front of the house; the outdoor lights illuminated the circular drive. Usually by this time of year there was a lot of snow on the ground, but not so far this winter. Most Christmases as a child, he remembered it being white. This year he'd be in the middle of the Pacific Ocean with blue water as far as he could see. One morning at the beginning of the week, a day after he'd talked to Winnie, a strong urge had overcome him. He needed to see his grandmother if only for a short time. He couldn't shake the feeling all that day. By nighttime he'd made a reservation to fly back to Colorado.

He glanced at his bed. He needed to sleep. Wanted to sleep. But he couldn't. Winnie's new assistant plagued his thoughts. Something didn't fit. First, although she and Winnie seemed to get along great, Ellie wasn't his grandmother's usual type of assistant. Christy had fit the mold well for three years. Accommodating. Almost meek. A follower, not a leader.

But Ellie certainly wasn't meek. He rubbed his ear, recalling her defensive tactic last night. And accommodating? Hardly. He had thought for a minute that she was going to tackle him for her gun. But mostly she wasn't a follower. Although she'd done everything his grandmother had requested of her today, her mannerisms and actions spoke of a woman in command. A woman who wouldn't admit to a vulnerability.

A couple of hours ago, though, he'd seen a crack in her defenses when she'd talked about her childhood, her brother. That was what he couldn't get out of his mind. The glimpse of pain in her eyes he suspected she didn't realize she'd shown. Or maybe she did and couldn't control it because the hurt went so deep.

Staring at the play of light and dark surrounding the front of the house, Colt plowed his fingers through his hair. His skin felt as if he was swimming through a swarm of jellyfish, their tentacles grazing across his arms and legs, their touch sending pain through him.

Something wasn't right. He couldn't shake that feeling, just as he couldn't deny the need to come see Winnie a few days ago.

One of the German shepherds that guarded the property pranced across the drive and disappeared into the dark. Squinting, Colt tried to follow the dog's trek. Something white flashed out of the corner of his eye, so briefly he wasn't sure he'd seen anything. He shoved away from the window and headed for the door. He wasn't sure why. It was probably nothing. One of the guard dogs had white fur.

Still. He wanted to check.

A sound in the foyer caught Ellie's attention. She'd just checked that part of the house. Was Winnie up? Colt? She crept down the hallway toward the front entrance, pulling her gun from the holster under her large sweatshirt. She found Colt crossing the foyer to the exit.

Relieved it was only him, she stuck the borrowed gun back into its holster and entered the entry hall. "Is something wrong?"

With his hand reaching for the doorknob, Colt jerked and pivoted toward her. "What are you doing down here? I thought you went to bed."

"And I thought you did, too."

"I did. Couldn't sleep."

"So you're going for a walk dressed like that? Won't you get cold?" She gestured at his sweatpants, T-shirt and bare feet.

He peered down. "I thought I saw something outside." Taking a few steps toward her, he took in her similar attire except for her bulky sweatshirt to cover her weapon and her tennis shoes, in case she had to give chase. "I'm sure it was nothing now that I think about it. Probably one of the dogs. If anyone had been outside, they would be barking."

Unless they were taken out, she thought, recalling her words to Colt earlier. "Dogs aren't invulnerable."

He paused. "True. I'd better check on it."

"I can. I'm dressed for it."

"Yeah, I noticed your tennis shoes."

She started toward the front door. "I don't have slippers, and I'm not accustomed to the cold."

"But you're from Chicago," Colt said as she passed him.

"We are seven thousand feet up the side of a mountain in December, and, besides, I've never been accustomed to the cold, even being from Chicago." Glancing at the alarm system, she noticed he'd turned it off. She grasped the handle and opened the door. As she stepped out onto the front deck, Colt followed her. "I've got this." *Leave it to a pro.* The urge to say those words was strong, but she bit them back.

"You're kidding. I'm not letting you come out here alone. What if someone is here? Who do you take me for?"

"Someone who only has pants and a T-shirt on and no shoes, not even socks. That's who." She ground her teeth together, wanting to draw her gun as she checked the area out. But he was probably right about it being one of the dogs.

"I'm used to the cold. I'm coming. End of discussion."

Patience. I could use a dose of it, Lord.

"Fine. Stay close behind me."

He chuckled in her ear. "Yeah, sure." Skirting around her, he descended the steps, quickly heading into the wisps of fog snaking along the ground.

Where's a stun gun when I need one? Ellie hurried after Colt who moved quickly from the cold concrete drive to the warmer lawn. "Wait up."

He didn't slow his pace, but she caught up with him about ten yards from the house. When she glanced back and spied the unprotected place, lit with security lights, she clamped her hand around his arm.

He halted, his face unreadable in the shadows.

"Go back and make sure no one goes into the house. I'll finish checking out here." Her fingers itched to draw her gun, but Mr. Jefferson didn't want Colt to know why she was here.

"And leave you alone? This is my home, not yours. What kind of man would I be?"

"A smart one. What about leaving your grandmother alone?"

"Then you should go back and—"

Barking blasted the chilled air.

Ellie withdrew the Glock from its holster and started toward the sound to the left.

"Where did that come from?" Colt asked.

"Mr. Jefferson."

"Harold?"

"I'll explain later. Go back to the house, lock the door and don't let anyone in until I check out what caused the dog to bark. Do not follow me."

"Who are you?"

No more secrets—at least with Winnie's grandson. "A bodyguard hired to protect Winnie." She glanced over her shoulder to make sure no one was trying to get into the front of the house. "Go. Now."

In the cover of night that surrounded them, he stared at her, or at least she felt the drill of his gaze, then he whirled around and rushed back toward the deck. She moved toward where the sound had come from, retrieving her small pocket flashlight in case she needed it. Right now she let the half-moon and security lamps by the house light her path since it would be better if she didn't announce her approach if someone was inside the fence.

In the distance she heard the cry of a mountain lion. She'd seen evidence of a big cat on one of her daily power walks with Winnie. Was that what spooked the dog? She'd gone into enough situations with incomplete intel to know the heightened danger that could cause.

Her heart rate kicked up a notch as she drew closer to the perimeter on the west side of the house where the eight-foot chain-link fence was. Another roar split the air. Closer. The sound pumped more adrenaline through her body. Every nerve alert, she became hyperaware of her surroundings—a bird flying away to the right, the breeze rustling the evergreen foliage.

Away from the house the only illumination was the faint rays of the moon. Not enough. She switched on her flashlight and swept it across the area before her. Just outside a cut part of the fence, its glow fell upon the mountain lion, its big eyes glittering yellow in the dark. Her light captured the predator's menacing stance.

The rumble of a mountain lion nearby froze Colt as he mounted the last step to the front deck. He knew that sound from the many years he had lived here. He didn't know who Ellie St. James really was, how capable she was or why she would be protecting his grandmother, but he couldn't leave her out there to face a solitary predator by herself. No matter what she ordered him to do.

He rushed into the house to a storage closet where Winnie kept some of his possessions. He used to have a hunting rifle. Wrenching the door open, he clicked on the overhead light and stared at the mountain of boxes that he had stored there. He delved into the midst of the containers filled with his memories. Where was the gun?

Panic urged him deeper into the large, walk-in closet to the shelving in the back. There he saw something he could use. Not the rifle but a speargun, a weapon he was even more familiar with and actually quite good at using.

He snatched it up and raced toward the foyer, grabbing a flashlight on the way. Before leaving, he set the alarm, then locked the front door behind him. Another growl announced to anyone around that this was the big cat's territory and not to trespass.

As Colt ran toward the west side of the property, he hoped there weren't any trees the mountain lion could climb that allowed him access to the area inside the fence. Usually the eight-foot barrier kept dangerous animals out, but it had certainly sounded like it was close to the house, possibly inside the fence.

Then a yell pierced the night. "Get back. Get away."
Those words from Ellie prodded him even faster.

Ellie never took her eyes off the mountain lion. It was still on the other side of the fence with his head sticking through the part that had been cut and peeled back to allow something big—like a man—through the opening. She waved her arms around. She didn't want to shoot the animal because it was a beautiful creature. But she would if she had to.

Its snarls protested her order to leave.

Still it didn't move back. Its golden gaze seemed to assess its chances of leaping the four or five yards' distance between them.

Bracing herself, Ellie lifted her gun and shone her flashlight into its eyes. It continued to stare at her.

Behind her she heard something rushing toward her. Another mountain lion? But they were solitary animals that guarded their territory. One of the dogs? The one that had barked earlier? Where were the other two?

She was calculating her chances with the mountain lion, then the new threat, when she heard a war cry, a bloodcurdling sound. The mountain lion shifted its golden regard to her right for a few seconds, then stepped back out of the hole and sauntered away as though out for an evening stroll. Some of the tension siphoned from her.

She threw a glance over her shoulder and saw a light in the dark moving her way. Colt. An intruder wouldn't announce his presence with a flashlight or a war cry.

She spun around and started for him. "What are you doing? You were supposed to stay at the house." Her light found him in the night, carrying a speargun. "*This time* you need to stay here and guard this hole. I need to make sure Winnie is okay."

When she passed him, he clasped her arm and halted her progress. "Hold it. Winnie is fine. I set the alarm and locked the door. What's going on?"

She stared at his hand until he dropped his arm to his side. "Did you check on her?"

"Well, no. But we never went far from the house."

"I'm going to check on her, then I'll be back. Will you stay here and make sure the mountain lion doesn't come back? And this time stay where you're supposed to be. I could have shot you." She peered at his speargun. "A bit odd to be carrying around on dry land, but it should stop the cat if it returns. That is, if you can use it."

He pulled himself up straight. "I'm quite good with this. And it's very effective if you know what you're doing. Which I do." Each word was spoken with steely confidence.

"Good." She hurried away, at the moment her concern for Winnie's safety paramount.

What if this was all a diversion? What if someone got into the house when they weren't looking? Different scenarios bombarded her. All she knew was she had to lay eyes on Winnie to be reassured she was all right.

She unlocked the front door and immediately headed for the alarm to put in the code. Then she took the stairs two at a time. When she saw Winnie's door open, she finally breathed.

A strong scent of urine—probably the big cat's—pervaded the air as Colt neared the gap in the fence. He stuffed the flashlight through a chain-link hole, and its glow shone into the wooded area outside of Winnie's property. After leaning the speargun against the fence within his quick reach, he pulled the snipped sides back into place, enough that he hoped would discourage the mountain lion from plowing its way inside.

Then he examined the ground.

Footprints were barely visible on the dry ground, but about five or six feet away, tire impressions in the dead weeds and grass were clearer. Someone had pulled a vehicle up to the fence.

He swung around and swept his flashlight around his grandmother's property and then it hit him: Where were the dogs? Why weren't they over here?

Ellie entered Winnie's bedroom, her gun drawn but at her side in case the older woman was in the room unaware of what was transpiring outside. She didn't want to frighten her with a gun being waved in the air—not two nights in a row. Halting a few feet inside, Ellie stared at the messy covers spilling over onto the floor, the empty bed. As she raised her weapon, she circled the room, checking for her client. After opening the bathroom door, she noted the spacious area was empty.

As much as she would like to rush back outside and search the grounds for Winnie or any clue to her whereabouts, she had to check the house first.

As she started with the room next to Winnie's, prayers for the woman's safety flooded her thoughts. When she reached Colt's bedroom, she hesitated, feeling awkward to intrude on his privacy. But she had a job to do. She pushed open the door and looked inside.

This is ridiculous. If the man had followed her orders, she wouldn't have to do this right now. She stepped inside and made a quick tour—noting his duffel bag on a chair, his shoes on the floor, keys and some change on the dresser, pictures on the wall from when he was young.

A picture of him coming out of the darkness with a

speargun in his hand crowded into her thoughts. She shook the image from her mind and turned to leave.

"What are you doing in my grandson's room with a gun in your hand?"

FOUR

"I was looking for you," Ellie said, putting the gun out of sight of Winnie in the doorway. "Someone has cut the fence and the guard dogs can't be found. I wanted to make sure you were all right." After picking up Colt's tennis shoes off the floor, she moved toward the exit.

"Where's my grandson? What are you doing with those shoes?" Winnie blocked her path.

"I'll explain everything after I call the sheriff and make sure Colt is okay. He's guarding the hole, making sure the mountain lion doesn't return. He's barefoot."

"The sheriff? A mountain lion? Colt barefoot in this weather? What in the world is going on?" What wrinkles Winnie had on her face deepened as she stepped to the side to allow Ellie to leave the room.

Ellie hurried toward the stairs, fishing for her cell in her pocket. At the top she paused and glanced at the older woman. "I'm going to set the alarm. Please stay inside."

Winnie opened her mouth but snapped it closed before saying anything.

Ellie rushed down the stairs while placing a call to the sheriff's office outside Bakersville. After reporting what happened, she hit the buttons on the keypad to set the alarm and hastened outside.

The crisp night air burrowed through the sweatshirt, chilling her. The thought of Colt without shoes spurred her faster toward the fence line. When she arrived, he stood by the hole he'd partially closed, holding his spear gun while hugging his arms against his chest.

"I thought you could use these." She thrust his shoes at him, then shined her flashlight on the area beyond the fence.

"Thanks. I will never again leave the house in winter without my shoes on."

"Why did you?" She examined the set of tire tracks and boot prints, wishing it wasn't so dark.

"To protect you."

"Someone needs to protect you from yourself."

"You can't deny I helped you. Someone needed to guard this hole. Since you're back out here, I'm assuming Winnie is all right."

"Yes, and I called the sheriff's office." Ellie backed away, realizing there was nothing she could do until morning other than talk with the deputy who was on the way up the mountain. She had half a mind to call Harold Jefferson and wake him up with the news, but she would wait and give him a full report first thing in the morning. "Do you think there's anything at the house I can use to finish closing the bottom of this hole?"

"How about rope?" Colt started for his childhood home.

"That'll do." Ellie followed him. "I'm sure the mountain lion is long gone with all this activity, but I'll feel better when we have the hole completely closed."

"You don't think the person who cut the fence is inside here?"

"Probably not. Maybe the mountain lion scared him off or maybe his intent was to take the guard dogs. He could have tranquilized them. The ground looked like something was dragged toward the car."

"Why hurt the dogs?"

"It would take a while to get trained guard dogs to replace them. Maybe it was to scare Winnie like the threatening letters. When I find him, I'll ask him."

"When *you* find him? And what threatening letters?"

She reminded herself going after the person who was trying to harm Winnie wasn't her job. "I mean when the police find him, they'll ask him."

Colt unlocked the front door and hurried to the keypad to turn off the security system. Winnie sat on the third step on the staircase, her face tensed into a frown. She didn't move when both Colt and Ellie turned toward her.

"I need to check the house then I'll explain what's going on." She peered at Colt. "Would you stay here with your grandmother?"

He held up the speargun. "Yes. But the security system was on the whole time."

"This one can be circumvented quite easily if you know what you're doing. We have to assume whoever is after Winnie knows what he's doing," Ellie said in a low voice.

Winnie pushed to her feet. "Someone's after me? Who?"

Colt took a step toward his grandmother, glancing at Ellie. "I'll take care of her. Do what you need to do."

"What is going on, young man?" Winnie asked as Ellie hastened her exit.

As she went from room to room, she heard Colt trying to explain when he really didn't know much other than what she had told him. From her responses, Winnie was clearly not happy. Ellie decided not to wait until morning to call Harold.

"What's wrong?" the chief financial officer of Glamour Sensations asked the second he answered his phone.

After she explained what happened with the dogs and the fence, she said, "Not only does Colt know, but so does Winnie. I've called the sheriff's office, and one of the deputies is on his way."

"I'm calling Sheriff Quinn. Knowing him, he'll come, too. He lives halfway between Winnie's and Bakersville. It won't take him long to get there. I'll be there as fast as I can."

"You don't need to until tomorrow morning. After the sheriff leaves, I hope to get Winnie to go back to bed." She didn't want a three-ring circus at the house with so many people coming and going. That could be hard to secure.

"She won't do that. Maybe I should call her doctor, too."

"She seems okay." Ellie looked through the dining room into the living room where Colt had taken his grandmother. "She's sitting on the couch, listening to Colt."

"Fine. I won't call the doctor, but I'll be there soon."

Ellie pocketed her cell and made her way to the pair in the living room. "The house is clear."

Winnie shifted on the couch until her glare zeroed in on Ellie. "Who are you?"

"I told her you're here to protect her. That Harold hired you. But I don't know much more than that." Colt finally sat in the chair across from his grandmother.

With a sigh, Ellie sank onto the couch at the other end from Winnie. "I work for Guardians, Inc. It's a security company out of Dallas, staffed with female bodyguards. Mr. Jefferson came to my employer about his concerns that someone was threatening you. You have been receiving notes for the past six weeks, each one more threatening. He finally knew he had to do something when one included a photo of you on your power walk, dressed in what he discovered you'd worn the day before."

"Why didn't he come to me?" Winnie's mouth pinched into a frown.

"He's on his way, and he can answer that. I believe he thought it might interrupt your creative process and since the deadline is looming, he—"

"So that man kept it from me." Winnie surged to her feet. "I am not fragile like everyone thinks. Goodness me, I've been through enough and survived. That ought to give you all a hint at how tough I can be." She pivoted toward Ellie. "Is that why he neglected to tell me my new assistant was really a bodyguard?"

Ellie nodded. "I prefer full disclosure, but he was afraid of how—"

Winnie waved her quiet. "I know. I will take care of Harold. He promised my husband he would watch out for me, and he's taking his job way too seriously."

"Winnie, I don't know that he is." Colt leaned forward, clasping his hands and resting his elbows on his thighs. "Someone did cut the fence and the dogs are missing. Not one of them came up to us while we were outside. They always do."

Winnie blanched and eased down onto the couch. "So you really think there's a threat?" She looked from Colt to Ellie.

"Yes, especially after tonight." Ellie rose at the sound of the doorbell. "I'll get it."

She let the deputy and sheriff into the house. "I'm Ellie St. James. I was hired by Harold Jefferson to protect Mrs. Winfield."

Sheriff Quinn shook her hand. "Harold called me and told me. I understand the Bakersville police chief is looking into the matter of the threatening letters."

"Yes. I believe the person has upped his game. I haven't had a chance to search the whole property outside, but I feel the dogs have been taken. I did search the house and it's secured."

The sheriff turned to his deputy and said, "Take a look outside. Miss St. James, which part of the fence was cut?"

"The west side about halfway down."

"Let me know, Rod, when you're through checking the premises and the doghouse." Then to her, the sheriff asked, "Where's Winnie?"

"In the living room."

When the sheriff entered, Winnie smiled. "I'm so glad you're here, Bill. Did Ellie tell you what went on tonight?"

"Harold filled me in. It's a good thing Miss St. James and your grandson were here." The sheriff nodded toward Colt. "You couldn't have picked a better time to be home."

Winnie blew out an exasperated breath. "It would

have been even better if they had clued me in on what was going on. Goodness, Bill, I've been out power walking. The man took a picture of me while I was."

"Maybe with all that has happened you should curtail that for the time being. It's gonna snow this weekend if the weather reports are correct." Sheriff Quinn sat on the couch where Ellie had been.

She assessed the law enforcement officer. He was probably in his early fifties but looked to be in excellent physical condition, well proportioned for his medium height with none of the potbelly she'd seen on others as they grew older and less active. She'd worked with her share of good ones and bad ones. From all of Harold's accounts, the sheriff fit into the good category. She hoped so because tonight the person after Winnie had stepped up his game.

She filled him in on what she'd seen outside. "Someone pulled a vehicle up to the fence recently. It rained hard a couple of days ago. The tracks could have been left maybe up to a day before, but they aren't deep enough for any longer than that. But I'm pretty sure it was this evening. We walk the perimeter every morning, and I haven't seen any evidence on the other side of the fence like what is there now. Also there are drag marks and a few paw prints beside those left by the mountain lion."

"So you think the tracks were made this evening?"

"Yes, Sheriff. That's the way it looks, but in the light of day we—you—might find more."

He smiled. "I'll take a look now. I've got a high-powered flashlight. I'll see where the tire tracks lead. The west side of the fence isn't the closest to the road out front."

"But it's the most isolated," Colt interjected.

Sheriff Quinn headed for the foyer. "When he gets back I'm gonna leave Rod here. I'd like you to come with me, Miss St. James."

"Would you mind, Winnie?" Ellie asked her client, eager to go with the sheriff.

"No, go. I'll be well protected with Colt and the deputy."

As Ellie left, Colt told Winnie that he'd escort her to her bedroom. Ellie chuckled when the woman said, "Not on your life. I want to know what they find out there."

The doorbell sounded again while Ellie crossed the foyer. She'd relocked the door after the deputy had left. When she answered it, Harold stood there with the young officer.

He charged inside, slowing down only long enough to ask, "Where is she?"

"In the living room."

While he went to Winnie, the deputy came into the house. "I couldn't find any signs of the dogs. They're gone, Sheriff."

Quinn grumbled, his frown deepening. "Rod, stay with Mrs. Winfield." To Ellie, he said, "I don't like this. They were excellent, well-trained guard dogs."

"Yeah, that was the only part of the security here I liked." Ellie went ahead of the man onto the front deck.

"And possibly the only threat the person behind the letters needed to get rid of."

"Maybe. Something doesn't feel right."

"Any thoughts on what?"

"No. Just a vague feeling we're missing something." Ellie slipped into the sheriff's car.

As he drove to the road then toward the west part of

the property, he said, "Harold told me the Bakersville police chief is looking into past employees. I can't believe one of them would be this angry with Winnie. She's the reason Bakersville is so prosperous. People around here love her."

"Someone doesn't. Maybe they aren't from around here. Maybe it's something we haven't thought about yet. Harold is having a private investigator look into Glamour Sensations' competition."

"Corporate sabotage?"

"It's a possibility. Winnie is the creative force behind the new line. From what I hear Endless Youth will change the playing field. It's not unheard of that a competitor will try to stop a product launch or beat a company to unveiling their own similar product."

"Mr. Winfield was the guy who talked me into running for sheriff twenty years ago. The best move I ever made. I owe the Winfield family a lot." He eased off the road and parked on the shoulder, directing a spotlight from his car toward the area where someone had driven off the highway and over the terrain toward the back of Winnie's property. "We'll go on foot from here."

Following the tire tracks led to the hole in the fence. Ellie knelt near the place where she'd seen the mountain lion's prints as well as smaller dog prints. No sign of blood or a struggle. When she had shined the light on the big cat earlier, she hadn't seen any evidence it had killed a dog. And she hadn't heard any noise to suggest that. So it meant the dogs had been taken recently by whoever drove the vehicle.

"These tire tracks look like they're from a truck or SUV. I'll have a cast made of them and see if we can narrow down the vehicle." The sheriff swung his high-powered light on the surrounding terrain. "These boot prints might help, too."

"It looks like about a size nine in men's shoes."

"Small man."

"Or a woman with large feet."

Ellie rose and searched the trees and brush. With some of the foliage gone because it was winter, she had a decent view. "No sign the dogs went that way."

"It doesn't look like it, but in the light of day we'll have better visibility and may find something. At the moment, though, I think the dogs were stolen. They're valuable. Maybe someone has kidnapped them."

"I don't think so. This is tied to the threats against Winnie somehow." Ellie ran her flashlight along the ground by the fence and caught sight of something neon green. She stooped and investigated closer. "Sheriff, I found something partially under this limb. I think it's from a dart gun. It would explain how he subdued the dogs so quickly."

The sheriff withdrew a small paper bag and gloves, then carefully picked up the long black dart with a sharp tip and a neon green cap on the opposite end. "Yup. I'll send this to the lab and see if there are any fingerprints on it. Hopefully they can tell us what was in the dart— poison or a knockout drug."

"At least there are a few pieces of evidence that might give you a lead."

As they walked back to the sheriff's car, Ellie kept sweeping her flashlight over the ground while Quinn scoured the terrain.

When he climbed into his patrol car, he said, "I have a friend who can repair the chain-link fence. I'll have him out here first thing in the morning. You don't want the return of the mountain lion."

"I'll be talking to Winnie and Harold about electrifying the fence and setting up a system to monitor the perimeter. If it hadn't been for the dogs, we might not have known about the hole in the fence for a while. That area is hidden by thick foliage from the house. We might not have seen it on our power walk in the morning, either."

"Yeah, she's definitely gonna have to beef up her security. She's been fortunate not to have problems in the past." As the sheriff returned to park in front of the main house, lights blazed from it. He chuckled. "She must have gone through and turned a light on in every downstairs room."

"I can't blame her. She all of a sudden realizes someone is after her."

Colt watched his grandmother as Harold explained his reasons for not letting her know what was going on with the letters. After he saw to Winnie, he was going to have a few words with Ellie and Harold. He should have been contacted right away when his grandmother first was threatened.

"The bottom line, Winnie, is that I didn't want you to worry about it when you have enough to deal with," Harold said.

Colt nearly laughed and pressed his lips together to keep from doing that. Harold was pulling out all the stops to persuade his grandmother not to be angry with him.

Her back stiff as a snowboard, Winnie narrowed her gaze on Harold, her hands clasped so tightly in her lap the tips of her fingers reddened. "I'm not a child, and you'd better remember that from now on, or no matter how long we have worked together, you'll be fired."

Harold swallowed hard. "My intentions were to protect you without worrying you. I have the police chief in Bakersville and a private investigator working on finding the person behind the letters."

"So you would never have told me if this hadn't happened. Was that your plan?"

Harold dropped his gaze to a spot on the carpet at his feet. Finally he nodded.

"I have to be able to trust you to inform me of *everything* that goes on at Glamour Sensations. Now I don't know if I can. What else are you keeping from me?" She lifted her chin and glared at her longtime friend.

Harold held up his hands, palms outward. "Nothing. But, Winnie, I promised Thomas I would look after you."

"I can look after myself. I have been for seventy-three years." Her rigid shoulders sagged a little.

Colt rose. "Winnie, let me escort you upstairs. We can hash this all out tomorrow."

She turned her glare on him. "Don't you start, young man. I don't need to be mollycoddled by you, too. I'll go to bed when I want to."

Harold interjected, "But you're starting the final tests tomorrow and—"

She swiveled her attention to him. "Losing a little sleep won't stop me from doing that. I'm not the fragile person you think I am. I want to hear what Sheriff Quinn has to say about the situation before I retire for the night. Or I wouldn't sleep a wink."

Colt heard the deputy greeting someone in the foyer. "I think they've returned."

Not five seconds later Ellie and Quinn came into the living room. Colt couldn't read much into Ellie's bland expression, but the sheriff's indicated there were problems, which didn't surprise him given what had happened an hour ago.

Sheriff Quinn stood at the end of the coffee table and directed his attention to Winnie. "Your guard dogs were drugged and stolen. We found a dart they used and tire tracks where they came off the main road, probably in a good-size four-wheel drive. Can't tell if it was a truck or SUV yet. A cast of the tire tracks might narrow it down for us."

Colt's gaze latched onto Ellie. She focused on Winnie, too, except for a few seconds when she slid her attention to him. But her unreadable expression hadn't changed. He saw her military training in her bearing and the way she conducted herself. Ellie had certainly performed capably tonight, but what if the person after Winnie upped his tactics to more lethal ones?

When the sheriff finished his report, Winnie shook his hand. "Thank you, Sheriff Quinn. As usual you have done a thorough job. I want to be informed of any progress." She shifted toward Harold. "I want the Bakersville police chief and the private investigator you hired to be told that, too. No more secrets. Understood?" Her sizzling stare bore into the man.

Harold squirmed on the couch but locked stares with Winnie. "Yes, on one condition."

"You aren't in a place to dictate conditions to me. For several weeks you have kept me in the dark about something that concerned me. Don't push me, Harold Jefferson."

The color leaked from Harold's face. "I won't," he bit out, his teeth snapping closed on the last word.

"Good, I'm glad we understand each other now. That goes for you, too, Ellie and Colt. Also, I don't want this common knowledge, and I certainly don't want anyone to know that Ellie is a bodyguard. She is my assistant."

"Agreed," Harold said quickly. "Sheriff, can you keep this quiet?"

"Yes. All my deputies need to know is that someone took your dogs. Nothing about the reason or who you are, Miss St. James. We'll play this down."

"I appreciate that. I don't want a media circus until I'm ready to unveil my new line, and then I want the focus on Endless Youth, not me."

The sheriff nodded toward Winnie. "We'll be leaving. I'm going to post Rod outside your house."

"You don't have to do that. I have the very capable Miss St. James." Winnie winked at Ellie.

"Humor me, ma'am, at least for tonight."

"Fine."

Colt hid his smile by lowering his head. His grandmother would have her way in the end. The deputy would be gone by the morning, but Colt planned to have some other security measures in place by tomorrow evening.

Harold stood. "I'll show you out, Sheriff, and give you the name of my P.I. working on the case."

"I'm sorry that Harold put you in the position he did. He told me you wanted to inform me from the first. We'll proceed as usual, but my grandson will return your gun. I don't like weapons, so I'll ask you to keep it out of view." His grandmother struggled to her feet.

Colt rose quickly but didn't move toward Winnie.

She would rebuke his offer to help, especially when he had made it obvious that he considered her fragile. In her mind she equated that to weak. His grandmother was anything but that. After all these years, Harold really didn't understand Winnie like Colt's grandfather had. If Harold had come to him, he would have told him his grandmother could handle anything.

He started toward the door when Winnie did.

She peered back at him. "Don't you buy into Harold's thinking I'm fragile. I hate that word. I am not going to break. Endless Youth was Thomas's project. I will complete it. I can find my own way to my bedroom. I have been doing that for years now."

Colt stopped and looked toward Ellie. Her mouth formed a thin line, but her eyes danced with merriment.

When Winnie left the room, Ellie took a seat on the couch. "I think she told you."

"It wasn't as bad as Harold got. He mismanaged this situation. All because he's in love with Winnie and doesn't really know her like he should."

"That's sad."

"I have a feeling my grandfather knew Harold has been in love with Winnie since the early days. That's why he asked Harold to watch out for her. He knew he would. But Harold envisions himself as her knight in shining armor coming to her rescue. My grandmother is not a damsel in distress."

"What happened when your grandfather died?"

"She did fall apart. She'd nursed him back to health after his bout with cancer and was planning a month long vacation with him when he fell asleep behind the wheel and went off the mountain. For a short time, I saw her faith shattered. I was worried, but Harold was frantic and beside himself. He went into protective mode and hasn't let up since then."

Hearing footsteps nearing the doorway, Colt put his finger to his lips.

Harold came through the entrance, kneading his neck. "Winnie didn't even say good-night when she went upstairs. She really is mad at me."

"I'm afraid so." Colt waved his hand at the bouquet of flowers on the coffee table. "She isn't delicate like these roses. As soon as you accept that, you might have a chance with Winnie."

"A chance?" Harold opened his mouth to say more but clamped it shut.

Colt grinned. "Just so you know it, you have my blessing to court my grandmother. I've known for a long time how you felt about her, and once this line is out, she deserves something more than working all the time. She's been driving herself for the past few years."

"What makes you think..." Harold's fingers delved into his neat hairstyle, totally messing it up.

"Because I see how you look at her when she isn't looking."

Harold's face flushed a deep shade of red. "She thinks I'm too young for her."

"You're sixty-five. That's not too young." Colt settled into his chair again. "Sit. We need to talk about securing the house and grounds."

"You stole my line," Ellie said as she angled toward Harold at the other end of the couch. "You need to electrify the fence, put in a new security system *tomorrow* and, since she doesn't want people to know what is going on, at least replace the guard dogs. That may be the biggest challenge. They need to be here with a handler right away."

Colt spoke up. "I have a high school friend who trains dogs. I'll give Adam a call tomorrow. If he has a dog for us, he only lives in Denver so he should be able to help us right away." He leaned back, trying to relax his body after the tense-filled past hour.

"This place needs a minimum of two dogs. Three would be better." Ellie looked at Harold. "How about the security system? The one in place is old and can be circumvented."

"I'll have someone here tomorrow. With the right kind of monetary incentive, I'm sure they could start right away. Maybe tomorrow afternoon. They probably could take care of the fence, too." Harold glanced toward the entrance into the living room. "Do you think Winnie will forgive my judgment call on this?"

"Her faith is strong, and she believes in forgiveness. I wouldn't be surprised if she isn't fretting right now about who she has angered enough to do this to her. Knowing her, she'll be praying for that person, whereas I would like to get hold of him and…" Colt let his words fade into silence, curling and uncurling his fists.

They didn't need to know he struggled with forgiving someone who had wronged him. He still couldn't forgive his father for all but abandoning him and going his merry way, living it up as if he didn't have a son and responsibilities. Winnie forgave his dad a long time ago, but after his mother had died, Colt had needed his only parent, and he hadn't been there for him.

"Well," Harold said, slapping his hand on the arm of the couch and pushing up, "I'd better be going. We all have a lot to do tomorrow."

"I'll walk you to the door and lock up after you leave," Ellie said, trailing after him.

Quiet settled around Colt like a blanket of snow over the landscape. Resting his head on the back cushion, he relished the silence, realizing this was what he needed after months on a small ship with cramped quarters. As thoughts of his job weaved through his mind, he knew he had to make a decision. Stay until Winnie was safe or leave and let others protect his grandmother. There wasn't really a decision, not where Winnie was concerned.

A movement out of the corner of his eye seized his attention. Ellie paused in the entrance, leaning her shoulder against the doorjamb. "Have you warmed up yet?"

"Finally I've thawed out. I may be used to living here in the winter, but remind me never to go outside in winter without shoes."

"You seemed lost in thought. I want to assure you I will do everything to protect Winnie. In the short time I've gotten to know her, I see what a special lady she is." She crossed the room and took her seat again across from him.

"We probably should follow Harold's example and get some rest, but I'm so wired right now with all that's happened."

"I know what you mean. Your adrenaline shoots up and it takes a while to come down. But when it does, you'll fall into bed."

"I imagine with your job you've had quite a lot of experience with that. I can't say I have."

"One of the fringe benefits of being a bodyguard."

He laughed. "Never looked at it like that. How long have you been a bodyguard?"

"Three years. I started after I left the army."

"What did you do in the military?"

"For the last few years of my service I was in army intelligence."

"So that's where you learned your skills."

"Yes, it comes naturally to me now. Sometimes I only had myself to rely on when I was working alone in an isolated situation."

"Which I'm sure is classified top secret."

Her brown eyes lit with a gleam. "You know the cliché. If I told you, I'd have to kill you."

"I'm curious but not that curious. What made you go from army intelligence to being a bodyguard?" She intrigued him. It wasn't every day he met a woman who protected people for a living.

She shrugged. "It was my time to re-up, and I thought I would try something different. I had a friend who put me in touch with my employer. When I met Kyra, I knew this was what I wanted to do. I like protecting people who need it. I like the challenge in security."

"Why not police work?"

"I like to go different places. Kinda like you. I have a feeling you've seen a lot of the world through your work."

"Yes, and I've enjoyed it, but I've been on a ship a large part of that time."

"Tired of life on a boat?"

Am I? He hadn't stopped long enough to think about it. "The past few years have been hectic but fulfilling. I've learned a lot about sea life aboard the *Kaleidoscope*. But if Winnie had her way, she'd want me to use my knowledge for Glamour Sensations. She tells me I've inherited her nose."

Ellie studied that part of his face and frowned. "I think you look more like your grandfather." She gestured toward the portrait over the mantel.

"But I have her supersensitive smelling ability," he said with a chuckle. "Every time I come home, I get the spiel about taking over the family business. But if she goes public, it won't be a family business anymore."

"How do you feel about that?"

"I don't know. It's good for the company, but it means we'll be in the big leagues and I don't know how Winnie will really like that. This is Harold's plan, and I understand why he is pushing to go public. The Endless Youth line will take us in a different direction. The expansion of the company will be good for this area."

Ellie tilted her head and smiled. "Do you realize you keep saying 'us' as though you are part of the company?"

"You'd make a good detective. Did you get your interview skills in the army?"

"I owe the army a lot, but I think I've always been nosy. It got me into trouble from time to time when I was growing up."

Colt yawned, the earlier adrenaline rush completely gone. "I guess that's my cue to get some sleep. Jet lag has definitely set in."

Ellie rose. "You've had two very hectic nights since you got here. This wasn't probably what you were expecting."

As he covered the distance to the foyer, he stifled another yawn before she thought it was her company. Because that was the furthest from the truth. If he wasn't so exhausted from months of nonstop work and traveling over a day to get home, he could spend hours trying to get to know Ellie St. James. And he had a feeling he wouldn't even begin to understand the woman.

He started up the stairs and she continued walking toward the dining room and kitchen area. "You're not coming upstairs?"

She peered back over her shoulder. "Not until I've checked the house again and made sure we're locked up as tight as we can be."

He rotated toward her. "Do you need company?"

Her chuckle peppered the air. "I've been doing this for a long time. It's second nature. Always know the terrain around you. In this case, this house. If I have to move around it in the dark, I need to know the layout."

"I never thought about that. I'm glad Winnie has you. See you bright and early tomorrow."

"Good night."

The smile that curved her lips zapped him. He mounted the stairs with that picture etched into his mind. He had grown up in this house. Could he move around it if the power went off and not run into every piece of furniture? Her skill set was very different from his. He could leave and be assured Winnie was in good hands.

That conclusion didn't set well with him. It niggled him as he got into bed, and it stayed with him all night.

After securing the house, Ellie ascended to the second floor. Walking toward her bedroom, she paused outside Winnie's room and pressed her ear against the door. Silence greeted her. She continued to hers two doors down. She couldn't shake the feeling they were vulnerable even with the deputy outside.

She immediately crossed the window that overlooked the front of the property. She studied the parked patrol car, glimpsing the man sitting in the front seat. She didn't leave her welfare or a client's to others. She hadn't vetted the deputy. She didn't even know him.

That thought clinched her decision. She went to her bed and gathered up a blanket and pillow then headed for the hallway. Outside Winnie's room, she spread her armload out on the floor then settled down for the night, fitting her gun close to her. This accommodation was four-star compared to some she'd had in the army.

She was a light sleeper, and anyone who wanted Winnie would have to go over her to get her client. She fell asleep with that knowledge.

Only to have someone jostle her shoulder hours later.

She gripped her gun. Her eyes inched open to find Colt stooping over her.

He leaned toward her ear and whispered, "I don't want to disturb Winnie, but Rod is gone. He's not in the car and hasn't been for a while now."

FIVE

Ellie was already on her feet, slipping on her shoes as she moved toward the stairs. "Stay here. It might be nothing but stretching his legs."

As she crept down the steps, avoiding the ones that creaked, only the light from the hallway illuminating her path, her eyes began to adjust to the darkness swallowing her at the bottom of the staircase. She saw the red glow on the security keypad across from her.

Before going outside to search for the deputy, she crept through the rooms on the first floor, using the moonlight streaming through the upper part of the windows that weren't draped. When she reached the kitchen, she had to switch on a light to inspect the area and check the back door.

When she returned to the foyer, she flipped on the light and punched the alarm off then went to the bottom of the steps. "Colt."

He appeared at the railing overlooking the foyer.

"I'm going outside and resetting the alarm. Don't leave there."

"You shouldn't go by yourself."

"I need you to stay there. Don't follow me. Understand?"

He nodded, but his jaw clamped in a hard line.

Ellie set the alarm, hurried toward the front door and slipped outside. She examined the patrol car, still empty. Rod's hat sat on the passenger's seat. That was the only evidence the man had been in the vehicle.

For the second time that night she made her way toward the west side of the property. Had the mountain lion returned and somehow got inside the fence? Earlier they had patched it the best they could. Now she noticed the rope they had tied across the opening had been cut and the fence had been parted again. Alert, she inspected the blackness beyond the property. Her eyes were fully adjusted to the dark, but a good pair of night-vision goggles would have been preferable. She swung around slowly, searching every tree and bush.

Something big lay on the ground near a group of firs. She snuck toward it. The closer she came the more sure she was that it was a body. From the size, probably a man. The body lay still, curled on his side, his face away from her. Was it the deputy? Was he dead?

Removing her small flashlight from her pocket, she increased her pace as well as her alertness in case this was a trap. Someone had cut those ropes.

The person on the ground groaned and rolled over. He tried to sit up and collapsed back. Another moan escaped him as Ellie reached his side.

"Rod? Are you okay?"

"Someone…hit me over the head." He lifted his hand to his hair and yelped when he touched his scalp. Blood covered his fingers.

"Why were you out here?"

"I heard something. I came to see what it was and found one of the dogs lying under the thick brush." He pointed beneath some large holly bushes. "The next thing I knew, I was hit and going down." He struggled to sit up.

Ellie helped him. "Take it easy. I'm phoning this in."

After she placed a call to the sheriff's office, Rod asked, "Is the dog gone?"

Using her small flashlight, Ellie inspected the bushes. "There's no dog here."

"There was a while ago. Its whimpering is what drew me."

"Whoever hit you must have taken the dog. The ropes on the fence were cut and the hole opened up again."

"They came back for the third dog?"

"I guess. Why do you say 'they'?"

"I don't know. It could have been one person or several. The dog weighed sixty or seventy pounds, so one person could have carried it, I guess."

"Or dragged it." She thought of the boot prints, about a size nine in a men's shoe, which meant probably a man of medium height or a large woman. "Can you walk back to the house?"

"Yes. I just need to take it slow."

Putting her arm around him, she assisted him to his feet. "Okay?"

"Yeah, except for a walloping headache."

She checked her watch. "Backup should be here soon."

"I didn't see that dog last night, but it was hidden by the holly bushes. I've got to admit I didn't think a dog was still here. I should have searched more thoroughly." He touched his forehead. "I've learned my lesson."

"It's only an hour or so to sunrise. We can search the whole grounds more thoroughly then."

"Why did whoever took the dogs come back for one of them? That was risky."

"Can't answer that." Although she had an idea. Last night Winnie had been extremely upset about the missing dogs. They had been special to her husband. So the person behind taking the animals might have had two reasons: to hurt the security around Winnie and to hurt her personally. "It does mean someone was watching the house for the right moment to come back."

"Except that I got to the dog before they could."

"It's looking that way."

The deputy gripped the railing as he mounted the steps to the front deck. "Does the sheriff know?"

"Probably."

Before she could unlock the door, Colt opened it. He took one look at Rod and stepped aside to let them inside. "What happened?"

Winnie hurried across the foyer, taking hold of the young man. "Come into the kitchen. Let me clean this gash."

"Ma'am, I'll be okay."

"Not until you see a doctor, and it still needs to be cleaned up. I have a first-aid kit in the kitchen." Winnie tugged the man forward.

Colt stood in Ellie's way. "What happened?"

She shut and locked the door, then faced him. "He heard a sound coming from the west side of the property and went to check it out. When he found one of your dogs on the ground under some bushes, he was hit over the head."

"One of our dogs wasn't taken?"

"It has been now, or at least I think it has. The dog was gone when I got there. The ropes were cut and the fence opened back up."

"Maybe there's another dog on the grounds?"

"In a couple of hours when it's daylight, we can search more thoroughly and see."

"We'd probably better go rescue Rod. My grandmother can get carried away with a cut or gash. Once she wrapped my calf for a small wound on the back. A bandage would have worked fine."

Ellie had taken a few steps when the doorbell rang. "I'll take care of this. It's probably the sheriff."

After looking through the peephole and seeing Sheriff Quinn, she opened the door. "The deputy should be all right, but he needs to be checked out at the hospital. He was hit over the head. Winnie is tending to him in the kitchen."

As they walked toward the room, Ellie explained where the deputy had been found and about the dog under the bushes.

Winnie glanced up when they entered. Frowning, she finished cleaning up the deputy's head wound. "Someone has stolen my dogs. Come on my property. Threatened me. And now hurt your deputy. I hardly see you, and in less than six hours you've been at my house twice. Neither a social call."

"I have one deputy outside right now and another on his way. Should be here any minute." He turned to Rod. "He can take you to the hospital. Get that head injury examined by the doc."

"Fine by me, but I want to work on this case. When this person came after me, he made it personal." Rod slowly stood and smiled at Winnie. "Thank you, ma'am, for seeing to me."

"Dear, I'm so sorry. You take care of yourself, and you're welcome back here anytime."

Before the sheriff followed his deputy from the room, he said, "If it's okay with you, Mrs. Winfield, I'd like to stay until sunrise and then thoroughly search the grounds."

"Of course. I'll get some coffee on and fix something for breakfast. I have a feeling we'll all need our energy for the day to come." Winnie washed her hands at the sink, then began making some coffee.

"I'll be back as soon as I see to Rod and post my other deputy. We need to discuss who would do this to you, Mrs. Winfield."

After the sheriff left, Winnie finished with the coffee. With her back to them, she grasped the counter on both sides of her and lowered her head.

"Winnie, are you okay?" Colt asked, coming to his grandmother's side and laying his hand on her shoulder.

The woman straightened from the counter, turned and inhaled a deep breath. "I will be once we find this person. If we get a ransom demand for the dogs, I'll pay it. I want them back. But what if…" Her bottom lip quivered, and she bit down on it.

"We'll do everything we can to get your pets back. I know how much they mean to you."

"I remember all the walks your granddad and I took with our dogs. It was our special time together. I think it was what helped me bounce back from my heart attack."

Colt embraced Winnie. "I'm not going back to the ship until this whole situation is resolved. Your safety means everything to me."

Winnie's eyes glistened. "That means so much to me. You're my only family now."

Behind her Ellie heard footsteps approaching the kitchen. She turned around, her hand on her gun in case it wasn't the sheriff returning. But when he came into the room, she dropped her arm to her side.

"Just in time for some coffee, Sheriff." Winnie stepped away from Colt and busied herself taking four mugs from the cabinet. "If I remember correctly you take yours black."

"Yes, I sure do."

Winnie poured the brew into the mugs then passed them out. "I've been trying to think of anyone who would do this to me. I can't at the moment."

"Let's all sit and talk this out. Sometimes that helps."

Ellie took a chair next to Colt while Sheriff Quinn and Winnie sat across from her. "Who have you fired recently?" she asked.

"No one." Her eyebrows scrunched together. "Well, I haven't personally. Harold and the human resources department handle those kind of things. There are days I don't even go into the office. I prefer working here. That's why I have a fully stocked lab in the basement."

"So you can't think of any disgruntled employees?" The sheriff blew on his coffee then took a sip. "Let's say in the past year."

Her head down, Winnie massaged her fingertips into her forehead. "You need to get a list from Harold. There have only been a few people I know personally who have left the company in the past year or so."

"Who?" Sheriff Quinn withdrew a small pad along with a pen from his front shirt pocket.

"About a year ago one of the chemists working with

me. I wasn't aware of this problem, but two different female employees in the lab accused him of sexual harassment. Glamour Sensations has always had a strict policy against it. Harold fired Dr. Ben Parker. He was difficult to work with but a brilliant chemist. When he came to me and complained, I supported Harold's decision. Frankly, I told him I was disappointed in him and…" Winnie averted her head and stared at the blinds over the window near the table.

"What else?" Colt slid his hand across the table and cupped his grandmother's.

"He said some ugly things to me, mostly directed at Harold and the company rather than at me. I will not repeat them." Squaring her shoulders, she lifted her chin.

The sheriff wrote down the man's name on the pad. "Okay, Winnie. We have one we can check on. Anyone else?"

"The only other who I had any contact with is the driver I used to have before my current one." She paused for a long moment. "I guess I was directly responsible for his dismissal. He came to work one day drunk. I knew he'd been having marital troubles so I was willing to give him a second chance. We all need those, but Harold was adamant that we don't. In the end I agreed with Harold."

"Harold was right. You can't be driven around by a person who has been drinking. What's his name?"

"Jerry Olson."

"Any more?" The sheriff took another drink of his coffee.

Winnie shook her head. "None. But there are a lot of departments I don't have any interaction with."

"How about someone who's been passed over for a

raise or promotion?" Ellie cradled her mug between her cold hands. "This person doesn't necessarily have to be gone from the company."

"Well..." Winnie patted her hair down, her mouth pursed. "We did have several candidates to be the spokesperson for Endless Youth. Christy actually wasn't in the running. I'm the one who decided she would be perfect. She might not be considered beautiful by a model's standard, but she conveyed what I wanted to communicate to the everyday woman. There were two young women before Christy who were in the final running for the position. Mary Ann Witlock and Lara Ulrich. I suppose neither one was happy when they weren't picked. They don't work for Glamour Sensations. Lara Ulrich lives in Denver, and Mary Ann Witlock lives in Bakersville. Several members of her family work for Glamour Sensations, but she works as a waitress at the restaurant not far from the company's main office."

The sheriff jotted down the additional names. "If you think of anyone else, give me a call. I'll be meeting with Harold and the police chief in Bakersville to see who they're looking at."

"Have you all thought this could be simply a kidnapping of my dogs?" Winnie asked. "They are valuable. But even more so to me. Anyone who knows me knows that."

Ellie nodded. "True, but they're even more valuable to you because you care for them so much. That could be the reason the person decided to steal them." She downed the last swallow of her coffee and went to get the pot and bring it back to the table. "Anyone else want some more?"

Colt held up his mug, as did the sheriff. Winnie shook her head.

The sheriff closed his notepad. "After I look around, I'll go back to the office and track down these people."

"How's an omelet for breakfast?" Winnie left her nearly untouched drink and crossed to the refrigerator.

"Wait until Linda comes to prepare breakfast." Colt pulled the blind to let in the soft light of dawn. "When she sees all the cars out front, she'll be here early."

"No, I need to keep busy. Besides, I don't get to cook like I used to. Thomas loved my omelets. Now to remember how to make them."

"I'll help."

Colt shifted his attention to Ellie. "You cook?"

"Yes, some. I have to eat so I learned how."

One of his eyebrow arched. "A bodyguard who can cook. A woman of many talents."

"I'd love your help," Winnie said. "Be useful, Colt, and take this cup of coffee to the deputy outside."

He passed Ellie as he left with a mug and whispered, "Watch her. She once almost set the kitchen on fire. That's why Granddad insisted she hire Linda to cook."

"I heard that, young man. At least I don't go outside barefoot in winter."

Ellie slanted a look toward Colt as he left. In the doorway he glanced back and locked gazes with her. Then he winked.

Heat scored Ellie's cheeks. She'd never been around a family like the Winfields. She would have loved having the caring and the give-and-take between her and her mother. What would it have been like to grow up in a loving family? She could only imagine.

* * *

Ellie watched the last workmen leave, the black iron gates at the end of the drive shutting closed after the truck passed through the entrance to the estate. The sun disappeared completely below the western mountains, throwing a few shadows across the landscape. She surveyed the nearly fortified property, her muscles still tense from all the activity that had occurred during the day.

"What do you think?" Colt asked, coming up behind her.

"I'd rather have been in the lab with Winnie than out here supervising."

"The sheriff put a deputy on the door to the lab. Your expertise was needed making sure everything went in correctly. Winnie needed her security system updated even without the threat to her."

"I agree. She thinks being isolated keeps her protected. On the contrary, that makes her more vulnerable." She threw him a grin. "I just hate it when I need to be in two places at once. But you're right. I needed to keep an eye on the workers and the job they were doing. After tomorrow I'll breathe even easier."

"When they mount the cameras and put in the monitoring station?"

"Yes. The only one up and running right now is at the front gate. I'm glad Winnie agreed to let us use that small room off the kitchen for the monitoring station. It's a good location. Even at night we'll be able to tell what is happening outside on the grounds."

"That would have been nice last night." Colt lounged against the railing, his gaze fixed on her.

The intensity in his look lured her nearer. It took all

her willpower to stay where she was. "I'm hoping the electrified fence will keep people and large animals away. If someone tries to circumvent the power on the fence, the company monitoring it will notify the house. The jolt won't kill, but it will discourage someone or something from touching it."

"Tomorrow the two guard dogs from the trainer in Denver will arrive, but with the fence up and running and the new security system for the house, we should be all right."

He hadn't phrased it as a question, but his furrowed forehead indicated his lingering doubts. "No place can be one hundred percent safe, but this will be a vast improvement over yesterday. I wasn't sure how much they would accomplish today, but it helped that Winnie could afford to pay for a rush job."

"I got through to the *Kaleidoscope* and told them I have a family emergency. Just when you think you're indispensable, you find out they'll be all right without you. But then I figure you don't feel that way too much in your job. I know Winnie needs you. Yesterday proved that." He snapped his fingers. "I almost forgot. The sheriff called. He's on his way from Bakersville to give us an update on the people they're checking out."

"So he'll be here about the time Harold arrives. He wants us to have photos of the people Winnie mentioned and some he thought of. He wants us to convince Winnie not to attend the lighting of the Christmas tree in Bakersville tomorrow night."

Colt straightened, his movement bringing him a step closer. "I'll give it my best shot, but I don't think Winnie will change her mind. Bakersville is honoring Grand-dad and her at the tree lighting for all the work they've done for the town. That's important to her. Bakersville has been her home a long time since she married my granddad and came to live here."

"As important as her life?"

"My grandmother can be a stubborn woman."

"Tell me about it. She didn't want the deputy in the basement. She thought he could sit in the kitchen where he would be more comfortable. I told her that workers will have to come down there and that I can't follow every worker around. The deputy stands at the door to her lab or inside with her."

"I know she balked at that. She doesn't even like me in there. Anybody in the lab is a distraction, and she is determined to complete the project in time. She believes it's tied to who is after her. She thinks it's a competitor."

"That's still a possibility. The P.I. is looking into that. Maybe Harold will have some information."

Colt nodded his head toward the gate. "That's his car now and it looks like the sheriff is behind him."

"Nothing is assured until I check the monitor," Ellie said as she hurried inside and to the small room off the kitchen.

She examined the TV that showed the feed from the front gate. Harold waved at the camera. After clicking him through, she observed the Lexus as it passed the lower camera that gave a view of anyone in the vehicle. It appeared Harold was alone. Then she did the same thing with the sheriff.

When she glanced up, Colt stood in the doorway, his arms straight at his side while his gaze took in the bank of TV monitors. "We need someone to be in here 24/7 until this is over with."

"I agree, and I'm hoping you'll help me convince your grandmother of that in a few minutes."

"So you gathered the forces to help you?"

"Yes. She may be upset with Harold for not telling her sooner, but she trusts him. And she respects the sheriff."

"You are sly, Miss St. James, and I'm glad you are. In a week's time you have gotten to know Winnie well."

"I got a head start. On the plane ride here, I studied a file Harold provided me on her. From what he wrote, I could tell how much he cares about her. In army intelligence, I had to learn quick how to read people."

He closed the space between them. "That means you can't be fooled?"

"I'd be a fool to think that."

His chuckle resonated through the air. "Good answer. I like you, Ellie St. James."

The small room seemed to shrink as she looked at the dimple in his left cheek, the laugh lines at the corners of his eyes. She scrambled to form some kind of reply that would make sense. But as his soft gaze roamed over her features it left a tingling path where it touched as if he'd brushed his fingers over her face.

The doorbell sounded, breaking the mood.

"I'll get Winnie," he murmured in a husky voice.

She stepped to the side and rushed past him to the foyer. Her heartbeat pounded against her rib cage, and her breath was shallow as she peered through the peephole then opened the door to Harold and the sheriff.

"Colt's gone to get his grandmother," Ellie told them. "She wanted to be included in the update."

"How's she holding up?" Harold asked as they made their way into the living room.

"Fine, Harold." Winnie answered before Ellie could. "Worried? Is that why you didn't answer your private line today when I called?"

With his cheeks flushed, the CFO of Glamour Sensations faced Winnie coming down the hall. "I've been busy working with the police chief, to make sure we have a thorough list of people who could possibly be angry with you."

The older woman's usual warm blue eyes frosted. "I've always tried to treat people fairly. How many are we talking about?"

"Including the ones you gave the sheriff, in the past two years, ten."

Her taut bearing drooped a little. "That many? I've never intentionally hurt someone."

"It might not be you per se but your company. Tomorrow I'm going to look back five years."

"Why so far back?" Winnie looked from Harold to the sheriff, her delicate eyebrows crunching together.

"It's probably no one that far back, but I'd rather cover all our bases. It's better to be safe than—"

Winnie held up her hand. "Don't say it. It's been a long day. It was nearly impossible to think clearly with all the racket going on earlier. This may throw me behind a day or so. Give me the facts, and then I need to go back to the lab to finish up what should have been completed two hours ago." She came into the room as far as the wingback chair but remained standing behind it.

"Winnie, the workmen will be gone by midafternoon tomorrow. They're mounting cameras all over the estate and activating the monitoring system. The only one right now that works is the front gate." Ellie took a seat, hoping her client would follow suit. The pale cast to Winnie's face and her lackluster eyes worried Ellie.

Sheriff Quinn cleared his throat. "We've narrowed the list down to the three most likely with two maybes." He withdrew his pad. "The first one is Lara Ulrich. Although she lives in Denver, that's only an hour away, and she has been spotted in Bakersville this past month, visiting her mother. I discovered she's moving back home because she can't get enough work to support herself in Denver. Jerry Olson is working when he can but mostly he's living off his aunt, who is losing her patience with him. He's been vocal about you not giving him that second chance you're known for. The last is someone Harold brought to my attention. Steve Fairchild is back in town."

Winnie gasped.

SIX

Winnie leaned into the back of the chair, clutching it. "When?"

"A few weeks ago," Harold said, getting up and moving to Winnie.

Ellie glanced at Colt. A tic in his jaw twitched. She slid her hand to his on the couch and he swung his attention to her as she mouthed, "Who is that?"

He bent toward her and whispered, "She blamed him for causing Granddad's death."

"Why is this the first time I've heard about him?"

"Right after my grandfather died he left Bakersville to work overseas."

"Because I drove him out of town," Winnie said in a raw voice, finally taking a seat. "I said some horrible things to the man in public that I regretted when I came to my right mind." A sheen of tears shone in her eyes. "I wronged him and thought I would never have a chance to apologize. I must go see him."

"No." Colt's hand beneath Ellie's on the couch fisted. "Not when someone is after you. Not when that someone could be him."

Winnie stiffened, gripping both arms of the chair.

"Young man, I will do what I have to. I will not let this wrong go on any longer. I need to apologize—in public. My words and actions were what caused people to make his life so miserable he left town. Wasn't it bad enough that Thomas had fired him that day he died?"

"I need you to tell me what happened." Ellie rose, her nerves jingling as if she felt they were close to an answer.

"Steve Fairchild messed up a huge account for Glamour Sensations. Thomas lost a lot of sleep over what to do about him. That day he fired Steve, Thomas stayed late trying to repair the damage the man had done to the company. I blamed Steve Fairchild for my husband falling asleep behind the wheel. That was grief talking. I now realize Thomas made the choice to drive home when he could have stayed at his office and slept on the couch."

Harold pounded the arm of his chair and sat forward. "Winnie, the man was at fault. We took a hard knock when that client walked away from our company. It took us a year to get back what we lost. You only said what half the town felt, and then on top of everything, he dared to come to Thomas's funeral. You were not in the wrong."

Winnie pressed her lips together. For a long moment silence filled the room. "This is the last I'm going to say on the subject. I owe the man an apology, and I intend to give it to him." She swept her attention to the sheriff. "What about Mary Ann Witlock?"

"I'm still looking for her. She's not been seen for a week. She told her neighbor she was going to Texas to see a boyfriend. That's all I've been able to find out so far."

"And you don't think Dr. Ben Parker is a threat?"

"No, he's in a nursing home in Denver."

"He is? Why?"

"He had a severe stroke. He can't walk and has trouble talking."

"Oh, dear. I need to add him to my prayer list."

"He wouldn't leave the young women in his lab alone," Harold muttered, scowling.

Winnie tilted up her chin. "That doesn't mean I shouldn't pray for him. You and I have never seen eye to eye on praying for people regardless."

Listening to the older woman gave Ellie something to think about. She was a Christian, but was her faith strong? Could she forgive her mother for her neglect or the bullies that made her brother's life miserable? She didn't know if she had that in her, especially when she remembered Toby coming home crying with a bloodied face.

"We'll continue to delve into these people's lives. I'm just glad the police chief is handling it quietly and personally," Harold said with a long sigh. "He's trying to track down how the letters came to your office. There was no postmark. He's reviewing security footage, but there are a lot of ways to put a letter in the interoffice mail at your company. Some of them aren't on the camera."

"Fine." Winnie slapped her hands on her thighs and started to push up from her seat. "I've got a few more hours of—"

"Grandma, we have something else we need to talk to you about." Colt's words stopped her.

Ellie noticed the woman's eyebrows shoot up.

"Grandma?" Winnie asked. "Is there something else

serious you've been keeping from me? You never call me Grandma." Her gaze flitted from one person to the next.

Ellie approached Winnie. "I'm strongly recommending that you not go to the lighting of the Christmas tree tomorrow night."

"I'm going, so each of you better accept that. Knowing you, Harold, you've hired security. I wouldn't be surprised if every other person in the crowd was security. I won't let this person rob me of all my little pleasures." She stood, her arms stiff at her sides. "Just make sure they don't stand out."

Evidently Colt was not satisfied. "Grandma—"

"Don't 'Grandma' me. I will not give in to this person totally. I'm already practically a prisoner in this house, and after tomorrow, this place will be as secure as a prison." She marched toward the exit. "I'll be in my lab. Have Linda bring my dinner to me. I'm eating alone tonight."

Quiet ruled until the basement door slammed shut.

"That worked well," Colt mumbled and caught Ellie's look. "What do you suggest?"

"Short of locking her in her room, nothing. I'd say strengthen the security and pray. I won't leave her side. Harold, have you found a few people to monitor the TVs around the clock here at the house?"

"Yes. With the police chief and Sheriff Quinn's help, I have four who are willing to start tomorrow. One is a deputy and two are police officers. They need extra money. My fourth one is the retired police chief. He's bored and needs something to do. They will be discreet."

"Perfect." Although the police chief and sheriff

vouched for the men, she would have her employer do a background check on them. She'd learned to double-check everything. "I'd like a list of their names."

The sheriff jotted them down on a piece of paper. "I personally know all these men, and they will do a good job."

"That's good. Did you discover what kind of vehicle could have left those tire tracks?"

"The tire is pretty common for a SUV, so probably not a truck."

"What was in the dart?" Ellie held her breath, hoping it wasn't a poison. Winnie still thought there was a chance to get her dogs back.

Sheriff Quinn rose. "A tranquilizer. We're checking vets and sources where it can be purchased. But that will take time."

Time we might not have.

After Ellie escorted the two men to the front door then locked it when they left, she turned to see Colt in the foyer, staring at her. The scent of roasted chicken spiced the air. Her stomach rumbled. "I just realized all I had today was breakfast."

"It looks like it will be just you and me tonight."

The sudden cozy picture of them sitting before a roaring fire sharing a delicious dinner stirred feelings deep inside her she'd fought to keep pushed down. She'd purposely picked this life as a bodyguard to help others but also to keep her distance from people. She was more of an observer, not a participant. When she had participated, she'd gotten hurt—first with her family and later when she became involved with Greg, a man she had dated seriously who had lied to her.

Colt walked toward her, a crooked grin on his face.

"We have to eat. We might as well do it together and get to know each other. It looks like we'll be working together to protect Winnie."

"Working together? I don't think so. I'm the body-guard, not you. You're her grandson. You are emotion-ally involved. That can lead to mistakes, problems."

He moved into her personal space, suddenly crowd-ing her even though he was a couple of feet away. "Being emotionally involved will drive me to do what I need to protect my grandmother. Feelings aren't the enemy."

They aren't? Ellie had her doubts. She'd felt for her mother, her brother and Greg, and ended up hurt, a lit-tle bit of herself lost. "Feelings can get in the way of doing your job."

"It's dinner, Ellie. That's all. In the kitchen."

"I know that. I'm checking the house one more time, then I'll be in there to eat." She started to leave.

He stepped into her path. "I want to make it clear. I will be involved with guarding Winnie. That's not ne-gotiable."

She met the hard, steely look in his eyes. "Every-thing is negotiable." Then she skirted around him and started her room-by-room search, testing the windows and looking in places a person could hide. She'd counted the workmen as they'd left, but she liked to double-check.

As she passed through the house, she placed a call to her employer. "I need you to investigate some law enforcement officers who are helping with monitoring the cameras I've had installed around the estate. The sheriff and police chief vetted them."

Kyra Hunt laughed. "But you don't know if you can trust them?"

"No. You taught me well. I can remember a certain police officer being dirty on a case you took."

"I've already looked into Sheriff Quinn and the police chief. Nothing I can find sends up a red flag."

Like the background checks Kyra did on Harold Jefferson, Linda and Doug Miller, and Christy Boland. She knew nothing was completely foolproof, but she would be a fool if she didn't have these background checks done on people who came in close contact with Winnie. After she gave the four names to Kyra, she said, "Also look into Colt Winfield. He came home unexpectedly and is now staying."

"Mrs. Winfield's grandson? Do you suspect him?"

"No, not really, but then I can't afford to be wrong."

"I'll get back to you with what I find."

When Ellie finished her call, she walked toward the kitchen, the strong aroma of spices and roast chicken making her mouth water.

"Linda, I'll take care of the dishes. Go home," Colt said as Ellie came into the room.

Linda nodded. "I imagine Doug is asleep. Today was an early one, and with all that's been going on, he didn't have much chance to even sit." She removed her apron and hung it up on a peg. "Winnie said she'll bring up her dinner tray later."

Ellie crossed to the back door and locked it after the housekeeper left. She watched out the window as the woman hurried across the yard toward the guesthouse where she and her husband lived. "I haven't had a chance to tell her today that any guests she has will have to go through me first. I'll do that first thing to-morrow." She pivoted, her gaze connecting with Colt's.

"We talked about it. She's fine meeting anyone she needs in town for the time being."

"Just so long as her car is inspected when she comes back."

Surprise flashed across her face. "You think Linda might be involved?"

"No, but what if someone managed to hide in her car? Then when she drove onto the property they would be inside without us knowing. It's necessary until we know how the new dogs are going to work out."

"You have to think of everything."

"My clients depend on it. As we speak, I'm having the men who are going to monitor the security system vetted by my employer. Nothing is foolproof, but there are some procedures I can put in place to make this house safer, so Winnie won't have to worry about walking around her own home. I've had everyone who comes into close contact with Winnie on a regular basis checked out."

"Harold?

"Yes, just because he hired me doesn't make him not a suspect."

"Me?" Colt pulled out a chair for her to sit in at the kitchen table set for two.

"Yes, even you."

"I'm her grandson!"

"I know, but some murders have been committed by family members."

He took the chair across from her. "Do you trust any-one?" he asked in a tightly controlled voice.

"I'm paid to distrust."

"How about when you aren't working? Do you go around distrusting everyone?"

"I trust God."

"No one else?"

Ellie picked up the fork and speared a slice of roasted chicken. Who did she trust? The list was short. "How about you? Who do you trust?"

His intense gaze snared hers. "I trust you to protect my grandmother."

"Then why are you wanting to do my job?"

"Because I trust myself to protect my grandmother, too. Isn't two better than one?"

"Not necessarily."

After he scooped some mashed potatoes onto his plate he passed her the bowl. "You never answered my question about who you trust."

"I know." Her hand gripping her fork tight, she dug into her dinner. His question disturbed her because she didn't have a ready answer—a list of family and friends she could say she trusted. Could she trust Colt?

The chilly temperature and the low clouds in the dark night promised snow when they arrived at the tree lighting. Ellie buttoned her short coat and checked her gun before she slid from the front passenger seat of the SUV. "Winnie, wait until I open your door."

While Colt exited the car, Ellie helped his grandmother from the backseat. The whole time Ellie scanned the crowd in the park next to City Hall, her senses alert for anything out of the ordinary. Lights blazed from the two-story building behind the tree and from the string of colored lights strung from pole to pole along the street, but too many of the townspeople were shrouded in darkness where the illumination didn't reach.

Ellie flanked Winnie on the right side while Colt took the left one. "Ready?" she asked.

"I see Harold waving to us from the platform near the Christmas tree." Colt guided his grandmother toward Glamour Sensations' CFO.

"No one said anything about you standing on a platform," Ellie said. The idea that Winnie would be up above the crowd—a better target—bothered Ellie. She continued her search of the faces in the mob, looking for any of the ones the police were looking into as the possible threat to Winnie.

"Oh, yes. I have to give a speech before I flip the switch. I'll keep it short, dear."

Ellie wasn't sure Winnie took the threat against her as seriously as she should. "How about you skip the speech and go straight to turning on the lights so we can leave?"

Winnie paused and shifted toward Ellie. "I've lived a long, good life. If I go to my maker tonight, then so be it."

"Winnie," Colt said in a sharp voice that reached the people around them. They all turned to watch them. Leaning toward his grandmother, he murmured, "I'm not ready to give you up. I'd care if something happened to you."

Winnie patted his arm. "I know. But I want you two to realize I have a peace about all of this. That doesn't mean I will fire Ellie—" she tossed a look toward Ellie "—because I won't give the person after me an easy target. But, as I'm sure she knows, there is only so much you all can do. The only one who can protect me is the Lord."

"But you know He uses others to do His bidding. I fall into that category. If I tell you to do something, just do it. No questions asked, okay?" Ellie wished she could get Winnie to take this whole situation more seriously.

"Yes, my dear."

"If I see a threat in the crowd, I'm going to get you out of here. Then later you can chalk it up to a crazy assistant getting overzealous in her job if you need to spin it for the press. Let's get this over with."

Up on the platform as Winnie approached the podium and the cheering crowd quieted, Colt whispered to Ellie, "You make this sound like we've come for a root canal."

"How about several? I don't like this at all." She gestured toward one area of the park that was particularly dark. "Why couldn't they have the lighting of the tree during the daytime?"

Her gaze latched onto a man in the front row reaching into his coat pocket. Ellie stiffened and put her hand into her own pocket, grasping her weapon. But the guy pulled out a cell and turned it off.

Five minutes later when Winnie completed her short speech thanking Bakersville for the honor to Thomas and her for naming the park after them, she stepped over to flip the first switch. Suddenly the lights went out in City Hall and the only ones that illuminated the area were the string of colorful lights along the streets and around the park. Next Winnie flipped the switch for the lights on the twelve-foot Christmas tree and their colorful glow lit the area.

"That's why it's at nighttime."

The tickle of Colt's whisper by her ear shot a bolt of awareness through Ellie. Her pulse rate accelerated, causing a flush of heat on her face. Someone in the crowd began singing "Joy to the World" and everyone joined in, including Colt and Winnie. Ellie sang but never took her attention from the people surrounding Winnie. Harold had said he would have people in plain-clothes scattered throughout the attendees in addition to the police visible in the throng.

Ellie moved closer, intending to steer Winnie back to the SUV. But before she could grasp her elbow, women, men and children swamped Winnie.

"Thank you for what you've done for Bakersville," one lady said.

Another person shook Winnie's hand. "When the economy was down, you didn't lay off anyone at the company. We appreciate that."

After five long minutes of the same kind of praises, Ellie stepped to Winnie's right while Colt took up his position on the left.

Winnie grinned. "Thank you all. Bakersville is important to me. It's my home."

People parted to allow Winnie through the crowd. Suddenly a medium-built man stepped into Winnie's path. Ellie inched closer to Winnie while she gripped her weapon.

Winnie smiled. "I'm glad to see you, Mr. Fairchild. I heard you were in town."

"Yeah. Is there a problem with me being here?" He pulled himself up straight, his shoulders back.

"No, on the contrary, I meant it. I'm glad I ran into you." She raised her voice. "I wanted to apologize to you for my behavior right after Thomas died. I was wrong. I hope you'll accept my apology."

The man's mouth dropped open. The tension in his stance eased. "I—I—"

"I would certainly understand if you don't, but I hope you'll find it in your heart to—"

"I made mistakes, too," Steve Fairchild mumbled. Then he ducked his head and hurried off.

"Let's go, Winnie," Ellie said and guided her client toward the car.

The closer they got to the SUV the faster Ellie's pace became. Her nape tingled; her breath caught in her lungs. The person behind the threats was here somewhere—she felt it in her bones. Possibly Steve Fairchild, in spite of how the encounter had turned out. Not until Winnie was safe in the backseat and Colt was pulling out of the parking space did Ellie finally exhale.

"I thought that went very well, especially with Steve Fairchild, and nothing happened at the lighting of the tree," Winnie said from the backseat.

We're not at your house yet. Ellie kept that thought to herself, but her gaze continually swept the landscape and the road before and behind the SUV.

Winnie continued to comment on the event. "The Christmas tree this year was beautiful. Not that it isn't every year, but they seemed to have more decorations and lights on it. You were here last Christmas, Colt. Don't you think it was bigger and better?"

Ellie tossed a quick glance at Colt. In the beam of an oncoming car, she glimpsed his set jaw, his focus totally on the road ahead.

"I guess so. I never thought about it."

"Isn't that just like a man, Ellie?"

"Yes, but I've found a lot of people don't note their surroundings unless there's a reason." Ellie couldn't help but notice that Winnie hadn't said much on the ride down the mountain, but now she wanted to chit-chat. That was probably her nerves talking. "You'll be all right, Winnie. I won't let anything happen to you."

"I know that. I'm not worried."

"Then why are you talking so much?" Tension threaded through Colt's question.

"I'm relieved nothing happened and pleased by the kindness of the people of Bakersville. I even got my chance to apologize to Mr. Fairchild in public. I wish I could have stayed longer. I probably should call the mayor tomorrow and apologize that I couldn't linger at the end. I usually do."

Behind the SUV a car sped closer. Ellie couldn't tell the make of the vehicle from the glare of the headlights.

"I see it." Colt slowed down.

The car accelerated and passed them on a straight part of the winding road up the mountain. The Ford Focus increased its distance between them and disappeared around a curve. Ellie twisted to look behind them. A dark stretch of highway greeted her inspection.

She sat forward, her hand going to her gun. She took it out and laid it on her lap.

"Expecting trouble?" Colt asked.

Although it was dark inside the SUV, with only a few dashboard lights, Ellie felt the touch of his gaze when he turned his head toward her. "Always. That's what keeps me alert."

"Oh, my goodness, Ellie," Winnie exclaimed. "That would be hard to do all the time. When do you relax, my dear?"

"When I'm not working."

"I noticed you slept outside my bedroom again last night. You can't be getting rest."

Ellie looked back at Winnie. "Now that the security system is totally functioning and someone is monitoring it at night, I can go back to my room. But I'm a light sleeper on the job whether in a bed or on the floor in front of a door." After checking behind the SUV, she rotated forward. "You don't need to worry about me."

"Oh, but, my dear, I do. How do you think I'd feel if anything happened to you because of me?"

Again Colt and Ellie exchanged glances. She'd never had a client worry about her. If Harold hadn't hired her, she doubted Winnie would have, even knowing about the threatening letters. That thought chilled her. The woman would have been an easy target for anyone.

As the SUV approached the next S-curve, the one where Winnie's husband went off the cliff, Colt took it slow, leaning forward, intent on the road.

When they made it through without any problem, Winnie blew out a breath. "I hate that part of the road. If I could avoid it and get down the mountain, I would. That's a particularly dangerous curve."

"It's not much farther. Which is good since they're predicting snow tonight." Colt took the next curve.

Halfway through it Ellie saw the car parked across both lanes of the road. With no place to maneuver around it, Colt slammed on his brakes and Ellie braced for impact.

SEVEN

Ellie gasped as the brakes screamed and Colt struggled to keep the vehicle from swerving. She muttered a silent prayer just before they collided with the car across the road. The crashing sound reverberated through the SUV. The impact with the side of the Ford Focus jerked Ellie forward then threw her back. The safety belt cut into her chest, holding her against the seat.

"Are you okay?" Ellie fumbled with her buckle, released it and shoved open the door.

"Yes." Colt swiveled around to look at his grandmother.

"I'm fine," she said from the backseat.

Ellie panned the crash site as she hurried toward the car. She couldn't get to the driver's door because of the SUV so she rounded the back of the vehicle and opened the front passenger's door to look inside. Emptiness mocked her.

She straightened and turned to Colt. "Have Winnie stay inside."

Standing by his car, Colt nodded and went around to Winnie's side.

"No one is in the car. Call it in." Keeping vigilant,

Ellie scanned the landscape and then made her way back to the SUV. She stood outside the vehicle.

"He said he was fifteen minutes away," Colt told her from the backseat where he sat next to his grandmother.

"Winnie, would you please get down," Ellie chided. "No sense giving anyone a target to shoot at."

"You think he's out there waiting to shoot me?"

Ellie looked around. "Could be. Someone drove this car here and left it across the road in just the right place for anyone coming around the curve to hit it. If this had been car trouble, where is the driver?"

"Walking to get help?" Winnie's voice quavered.

"But there's no reason to have it stalled across the road like this and not to leave the hazard lights flashing."

When Winnie scooted down on the floor, Colt hovered over her like a human shield.

"No, I'm not going to let you do that. I won't let you be killed in my place. Colt, sit back up."

"No. I won't make it easy for them."

"You're going back to your ship tomorrow." Anger weaved through Winnie's voice.

"We'll talk about this when we're safe at the house."

"Don't placate me. I'm your elder."

Ellie heard the back-and-forth between them and knew the fear they both were experiencing. She had a good douse of it herself. But she planted herself beside the back door, her gun raised against her chest. "Shh, you two. I need to listen."

Not another word came from inside the SUV. Ellie focused on the quiet, occasionally broken by a sound—something scurrying in the underbrush on the side of the road, a sizzling noise from under the hood, an owl's hoot. Finally a siren pierced the night. Its blare grew closer. Ellie smiled. She liked how Sheriff Quinn thought. Let whoever might be out here know that help was nearby. Through the trees on the cliff side, Ellie caught snatches of the red flashing lights as two patrol cars sped up the winding highway toward them. Help would be there in less than two minutes.

Even when the sheriff arrived at the wreck site, Ellie concentrated on her surroundings, not the patrol cars screeching to a halt and the doors slamming shut. Finally she slid a glance toward Sheriff Quinn marching toward her while three of his deputies fanned out.

"Is everyone all right?" The sheriff stopped, reaching out to open the back door.

"Yes, but I need to get Winnie to the estate." Ellie backed up against the SUV. "I don't think anyone is going to do anything now, but she isn't safe out here."

The sheriff pointed to his deputies. "One of you get behind that car. Let's see if we can push it out of the way. Wear gloves. We'll want to pull fingerprints off the steering wheel if possible. Someone left this baby out here." He waved his hand toward the car. "And I intend to find out who did this."

Colt climbed from the backseat, closing his grandmother inside and positioning his body at the door.

While the deputies moved the car off to the side of the road, the sheriff switched on his spotlight, sweeping the area. Ellie followed the beam, delving into the shadows for any sign of someone still hanging around.

Then the sheriff moved his car up along the SUV, rolled down the windows and said, "Winnie needs to get out on this side and into my car. If anyone was here, they'd be along the mountainside, not the cliff side of the highway. It's a sheer drop to the bottom."

"I'll take care of it," Ellie said to Colt. "When Winnie and I are in the sheriff's car, take the front seat."

Colt stepped to the side as Ellie slipped inside the backseat of the SUV, then he shut the door and resumed his position.

"Winnie, did you hear the sheriff?"

"It's hard not to. He was shouting."

"I'm going to follow you out of this car. We'll sit in the back of the patrol car."

"Do I hunch down in there, too?"

"It wouldn't hurt. We don't know what we're up against. Caution is always the best policy."

Winnie crawled across the floor to the other side of the backseat. She gripped the handle and pulled it down. "Here goes." The older woman scrambled out of the SUV and into the patrol car two feet away.

Ellie followed suit, and Colt jumped into the front.

The sheriff gunned his engine, maneuvering up the road with expert precision. "We had a report of a stolen Ford Focus from the parking lot near City Hall. A family came back from watching the tree lighting and found their car gone."

So someone had been at the celebration and decided not to go after Winnie in a crowd. Instead, he chose a dark, lonely stretch of road to cause a wreck. Was that someone Steve Fairchild? He had been at the tree lighting and he'd made a point to see Winnie. Was that his way of taunting her before he made his move?

If Colt hadn't been as alert as he had and his reflexes quick, the crash would have been a lot worse. Ellie peered at Winnie's face. She couldn't see the woman's expression, but she held her body rigid. Tension poured off Winnie.

Ellie felt a strong urge to comfort the woman. "You're almost home."

"Someone hates me that much. We could have gone off the road like…" Her voice melted into the silence.

"We'll find the person." Sheriff Quinn stopped at the main gate to the estate and peered back at Winnie. "This is my top priority. I'm leaving two deputies here, and I'm not going to take no for an answer."

Ellie pushed the remote button to allow them inside. As they headed for the main house, the two dogs followed the car as trained.

"Fine, whatever you think is best," Winnie said, the words laced with defeat.

Ellie covered Winnie's clasped hands in her lap. "If someone was trying to stir memories of your husband's wreck, then he would have picked the S-curve for it to happen. His intent would have been clear if he had done that. There still could be a logical explanation that has nothing to do with you. It could be kids joyriding who got scared and ditched the car."

"Do you really believe that?" Winnie asked, her hands tightening beneath Ellie's.

"It's a possibility. That's all I'm saying. Until I know for sure, I don't rule out anything." But something she said to Winnie nibbled at the edges of her mind. Was there a connection to Winnie's husband somehow? What if he didn't fall asleep at the wheel? What if it had been murder five years ago?

A couple of hours later, Ellie entered the kitchen where the sheriff and Colt sat at the table, drinking coffee and reviewing what had occurred.

"How's Winnie?" Colt walked to the carafe and poured Ellie a cup of the black brew.

She took a deep breath of the aroma. "She's bouncing back. I think the similarity to what happened to her husband is what got her more than anything."

"I agree. It worries me, too. A few threatening letters and cut-up pictures aren't nearly as menacing as trying to re-create the same kind of accident. My first instinct was to swerve and avoid the car. If I'd done that, we could have gone off the cliff." Colt slumped into his chair, releasing a sigh.

Ellie sat beside him. "That has me thinking, Sheriff. Your department handled Thomas Winfield's accident. Are you one hundred percent sure it was an accident?"

"Yes, as sure as you can be. When all this began with Winnie, I reviewed the file. Nothing to indicate he was forced off the road, no skid marks. The tire tracks on the shoulder of the road were from Thomas's car. No one else's. No stalled car like this evening. We checked for drinking and drugs, too. He had no alcohol or drugs in his system."

"He shouldn't have," Colt said. "Granddad didn't drink, and his medicine wouldn't have made him sleepy."

"I know, but there was a report of a car weaving over into the other lane a few miles from where the wreck occurred. The man who reported it honked and the driver of the other car swerved in time to miss him. That person watched that car drive off, and it was going straight, no more weaving. He called it in, anyway. His description wasn't detailed, but what he said did fit your grandfather's car."

"So you're saying in your opinion it was an accident?" Ellie took a large swallow of her coffee.

"Yes. Besides, nothing has happened in five years. Why something now? Why Winnie?"

Colt raked his fingers through his hair. "How in the world do you two sit calmly and talk about this kind of stuff?"

"Because it's good to talk about all the possibilities. Brainstorm theories." The sheriff stood. "Ellie, I'll take another look at the file, but I don't think there's a connection. While you were checking on Winnie, two of my deputies arrived after processing the scene of the wreck. The Ford Focus was towed, and we'll go over it, check for fingerprints in the front seat and door. Maybe something will turn up. Also the SUV was towed to the garage in town to be fixed. I'm posting one deputy inside at the front door and the other at the back. Don't want the two new dogs to mistake them for an intruder."

Ellie started to get up.

Sheriff Quinn waved her down. "I'll send the deputy in here and see myself out."

When he left, Colt looked at her. "Let's go into the den."

Too wired to go to sleep yet, she nodded, topped off her coffee and trailed after Colt.

In the den, he stoked the fire he'd made when they had first come home. Winnie had been cold and sat by it until she'd gone to bed. Ellie observed the strong breadth of his shoulders: his movements were precise, efficient, like the man. She liked what she saw.

When he sank onto the couch next to her, he picked up his mug and sipped his coffee. "I never thought my brief vacation was going to turn out like this."

"I can imagine. No one plans for this."

He angled so he faced her, his arm slung along the back of the couch. "What if Harold hadn't acted quickly on those letters? What if Winnie's assistant hadn't alerted Harold about the threats? I know Winnie. She would have dismissed it. She wants to think the best of everyone. This could have been totally different, especially tonight."

"We can't think about the what-ifs. It's wasted energy."

"Which is precious right now. At least the house and grounds are secure. Winnie won't be happy seeing the deputies here tomorrow morning. She's worried the press will get hold of the fact that she's been threatened and make a big deal out of it. That could jeopardize the company going public. So far the people involved have remained quiet. That won't last long. I know Harold will have to notify certain people if nothing is solved by Christmas. Maybe that is the point of all of this."

"If the news does go public, that might actually help Winnie. Most of the people in this town love Winnie and will want to help her. Someone might come forward with information they don't realize could help the police find who is behind this."

"But rumors get started and get blown all out of portion, twisted around. It happened years ago when Granddad divorced his first wife. Not long after that he married Winnie. For a while people thought she had taken him away from his first wife, but that wasn't the case. It took years for her to correct those impressions. People had to get to know her to understand she would never come between a man and his wife. It hurt her enough that when I asked her about something I'd heard, she told me what happened."

"I know. I've seen similar cases on the national level, even ones I worked behind the scenes over in the Middle East. The truth often is twisted and blatantly altered."

His hand brushed against her shoulder. "So you see why she's trying to keep all this quiet. Already too many people know about it. I'm afraid she won't be able to. Which brings me to our next problem."

The feel of his fingertips touching her lightly sent her heart racing. His nearness robbed her of coherent thought for a few seconds until she forced herself to concentrate on what he was saying. "I'm afraid to ask what."

"You afraid? All I've seen is a woman cool under pressure."

"There's nothing wrong with being afraid. It keeps me on my toes."

"This Friday night is Glamour Sensations' Christmas Gala. I know my grandmother. Even with what happened tonight, she'll insist on going. She's supposed to introduce Christy as the face of Endless Youth and tease the press with what's going to come in February and the rest of next year."

"I was hoping she would decide not to go and let Harold take care of it."

"My grandmother has always been the spokesperson for the company. Any change will fuel speculation. Glamour Sensations will need the infusion of money by going public if we're to launch and produce the new line the way it should be. If she doesn't show up, some people will think she was badly injured in the wreck."

"Do you think that could be the reason for the wreck?

Some competitor wanted to damage what the company is planning to do?"

"Could be." Colt scrubbed his hands down his face. "I wish I knew what was going on. It would make it easier to fight."

"Let me think about what we can do. I certainly don't want to drive to the gala."

"I doubt Winnie would, either, especially with the reminder of Granddad's accident. It took a long while to get over his death. Her heart attack didn't disrupt her life like his dying." He took her hands. "When this is all over with, Harold needs a raise for hiring you. Winnie trusts you. Maybe she'll listen to you about the gala."

"I'll do what I can. Meanwhile I have an idea about how to get her down this mountain without driving."

"How?"

"Use a helicopter. There's plenty of room for it to land in front of the house."

His eyes brightened and he squeezed her hands. "I like that. Winnie should agree, especially given the alternatives."

"I can talk to the sheriff tomorrow to see about who to hire in the area." Then she would have to vet the person in only a few days. But it could be done with her employer's assistance. "If there is no one in the area he'd recommend, we could check Denver or Colorado Springs."

Colt lifted one hand and cupped her face. "You're fantastic."

The gleam in his eyes nearly unraveled her resolve to keep her distance. When this was over with, she would move on to another job and he would return to his research vessel. She needed to remember that. But when his thumb caressed her cheek and he bent toward her, all determination fled in the wake of the soft look in his eyes, as though he saw her as a woman like no other. Special. To be cherished.

His lips whispered across hers before settling over them. He wound one arm around her and brought her close. Her stomach fluttered. Then he enveloped her in an embrace, plastering her against him as he deepened the kiss. Her world tilted. She could taste the coffee on his lips. She could smell his lime-scented aftershave. She could feel the hammering of his heartbeat. Heady sensations overwhelmed her, tempting her to disregard anything logical and totally give in to the feelings he stirred in her.

The realization frightened her more than facing a gunman. She wedged her hands up between them and pushed away from him. The second their mouths parted she missed the feel of his lips on hers. But common sense prevailed. She moved back, putting several feet between them.

"I know I shouldn't have kissed you," Colt said, "but I've wanted to since that first night when you attacked me in the hallway. I've never quite had that kind of homecoming before." One corner of his mouth quirked.

She rose, her legs shaky. "I need to check the house, then go to bed. There's still a lot to do tomorrow."

Before he said or did anything else, she spun on her heel and rushed toward the exit. She considered going outside for some fresh air but decided not to. Instead, she went through the house, making sure the place was secured. Heat blazed her cheeks. She'd wanted the kiss, even wished it could have continued. That would be dangerous, would complicate their situation. But she couldn't get the picture of them kissing out of her mind.

With his hands jammed into his pants' pockets, Colt stood in front of the fireplace in the den and stared at the yellow-orange flames. He'd blown it this evening. He'd had no intention of kissing Ellie, and yet he had. Against his better judgment. What kind of future could they have? He lived on a research vessel in the South Pacific. It wasn't as if he could even carry on a long-distance relationship with a woman. He'd learned from his past attempts at a relationship that he wanted a lasting one like his grandparents had had. Anything less than that wasn't acceptable.

Was that why he'd given up looking for someone? What kind of home could he give her? A berth on a ship? He didn't even call it home. This place on the side of a mountain would always be his home.

He heard her voice coming from the foyer. She said something to the deputy Colt couldn't make out. Peering at the mantel, decorated with garland and gold ribbon for the holidays, he glimpsed the Big Ben clock and the late hour. He needed to go to bed, but he waited until Ellie finished talking with the deputy. He gave her a chance to go upstairs before him because frankly he didn't know what to say to her.

He would have continued the kiss if she hadn't pulled away. His thoughts mocked his declaration to stay away from Ellie St. James, a woman who was fiercely independent and could take care of herself. He'd always wanted someone who would need him. Someone to be an equal partner but rely on him, too.

After taking care of the fire, he moved toward the

staircase. Coming home always made him reassess his life. Once he was back on the research vessel he would be fine—back on track with his career and goals.

A few days later Ellie waited for Colt and Winnie in the living room right before they were to leave for Glamour Sensations' Christmas Gala. Dressed in a long black silk gown with a slit up the right side and a gold lamé jacket that came down to the tops of her thighs, she felt uncomfortable. The only place she could put the smaller gun was in a beaded bag she would carry. After all, to the world she was Winnie's assistant, there to make things run smoothly for her employer.

A noise behind her drew her around to watch Colt enter wearing a black tuxedo. She'd only seen him in casual attire. The transformation to a sophisticated gentleman who moved in circles she didn't unless on the job only confirmed how different they were. Yes, he was working on a research ship, but he came from wealth and would inherit a great deal one day. She was from the wrong side of the tracks, a noncommissioned officer in the army for a time and now a woman whose job was to guard others.

He pulled on his cuffs then adjusted his tie. "It's been a while since I wore this. I was all thumbs tying this."

Ellie crossed to him and straightened the bow tie. "There. Perfect."

His smile reached deep into his eyes. "Sometimes I think I need a keeper. I'm much more comfortable in a wet suit or bathing suit."

His remark tore down the barriers she was trying to erect between them. "Tell me about it. I don't like wearing heels. It's hard to run in them."

We'd like to send you two free books to introduce you to the Love Inspired® Suspense series. These books are worth over $10, but are yours to keep absolutely FREE! We'll even send you two wonderful surprise gifts. You can't lose!

Each of your **FREE** books is filled with riveting inspirational suspense featuring Christian characters facing challenges to their faith...and their lives!

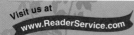

GET 2 FREE BOOKS!

HURRY!
Return this card today to get 2 FREE Books and 2 FREE Bonus Gifts!

YES! Please send me the **2 FREE Love Inspired® Suspense books** and **2 FREE gifts** for which I qualify. I understand that I am under no obligation to purchase anything further, as explained on the back of this card.

PLACE FREE GIFTS SEAL HERE

❑ I prefer the regular-print edition
123/323 IDL FNRT

❑ I prefer the larger-print edition
110/310 IDL FNRT

FIRST NAME   LAST NAME

ADDRESS

APT.#   CITY

STATE/PROV.   ZIP/POSTAL CODE

▼ DETACH AND MAIL CARD TODAY!

® and ™ are trademarks owned and used by the trademark owner and/or its licensee. © 2012 HARLEQUIN ENTERPRISES LIMITED. Printed in the U.S.A.

LIS-IV-12C

"Let's hope you don't have to do that tonight."

"I talked with the police chief and his men are in place as well as security from Glamour Sensations. They're checking everyone coming into the ballroom. Thankfully that doesn't seem as out of place as it would have years ago."

She should step away from him, but before she could, he took her hand and backed up a few feet to let his gaze roam leisurely down her length. When it returned to her face, he whistled.

"I like you in heels and that black dress."

She blushed—something she rarely did. "Neither conducive to my kind of work."

"I beg to differ. The bad guy will take one look at you and be so distracted he'll forget what mayhem he was plotting."

Ellie laughed. She would not let his smooth talking go to her head. Two different worlds, she reminded herself. She could see him running Glamour Sensations one day, especially when he told her yesterday he used to work at the company until he finished his college studies.

A loud whirring sound from the front lawn invaded the sudden quiet. She used that distraction to tug her hand free and go to the window. The helicopter landed as close to the house entrance as it could. The dogs barked at it even when the pilot turned it off. Doug Miller called the two Rottweilers back. They obeyed instantly.

"Doug is great with the dogs."

"He was as excited as Granddad when he brought home Rocket and Gabe. Although I don't know if these new ones can ever replace the German shepherds in

Doug's and Winnie's hearts. I was hoping we would get a ransom demand or someone would come forward."

"So did I with the nice reward Winnie offered." Ellie rotated from the window and caught sight of the older woman behind her grandson. "You look great, Winnie."

Dignified in a red crepe gown, she walked farther into the room. "I heard the helicopter. Probably our neighbors heard it, too. Never thought of using one to go to a ball."

"It's the modern-day version of Cinderella's coach." Colt offered his arm to his grandmother.

"In that case I fit the Fairy Godmother rather than Cinderella. That role needs to go to you, Ellie."

"Which leaves me as Prince Charming." He winked at Ellie.

Fairy tales were for dreamers, not her. Ellie skirted around the couple and headed for the foyer before she let the talk go to her head. "Well, our version of the story will be altered a tad bit. This Cinderella is taking her Fairy Godmother to the ball and sticking to her side. But I definitely like the idea of us leaving by midnight."

"I may have to go, but I don't have to stay that long."

Ellie stopped and hugged Winnie. "Those were the best words I've heard in a while."

"After dinner I'll make the announcements, stay for questions then leave. We should be home by eleven. I know you aren't happy about me going to the gala, but I owe all the people who have worked years for my company. They'll benefit so much when we go public. A lot of employees will get stock in Glamour Sensations for their loyalty."

Ellie climbed into the helicopter last and searched the area. Where was the person after Winnie? Watching them here? Waiting for Winnie at the hotel or in the ballroom? She clutched her purse, feeling the outline of her gun. Was their security enough?

As employees and guests entered the ballroom, Winnie stood in a greeting line between Colt and Ellie, shaking everyone's hand and taking a moment to talk with each person attending the gala. At first Ellie wasn't thrilled with her client doing that, but it did give her a chance to assess each attendee.

When Christy moved in front of Winnie, her smile grew, and instead of shaking the woman's hand, Winnie enveloped her in a hug. "How was your trip to L.A. for the commercial?"

"A whirlwind. I never knew all that this position would involve. Peter picked me up from the airport late last night, and since I woke up this morning, I've been going nonstop. I'm going to cherish the time we sit down and have dinner tonight."

Winnie took Christy's fiancé's hand and shook it. "It's nice to see you again, Peter. Christy will be in town at least through Christmas. But afterward she'll be busy. I hope you can arrange some time to go with her on some of her trips. I never want to come between two people in love."

Dr. Tyler held Winnie's hand between his for a few extra seconds. "When it's snowing here, I plan on being on that beach when Christy shoots her second commercial next month."

"Perfect solution. I love winter in Colorado, but that beach is beginning to sound good to these old bones."

"Tsk. Tsk. You don't look old at all. It must be your

products you use. You should be your own spokesperson."

Colt leaned toward his grandmother. "I've been telling her that for years. She looks twenty years younger than she is. What woman her age wouldn't like to look as youthful?" He gave her a kiss on the cheek.

As Christy and Peter passed Ellie, she said, "You two are seated at the head table. There are place cards where you're to sit."

Peter nodded his head and escorted Christy toward the front of the room, which was decorated in silver and gold. Elegance came to mind as Ellie scanned the spacious area with lights glittering among the rich decor.

Thirty minutes and hundreds of guests later, Winnie greeted the last person. "Every year this event gets bigger."

"This year we have an extra dozen media people here, including our own film crew." Harold took Winnie's arm and started for the head table.

"I guess it's you and me." Colt fell into step next to Ellie, right behind Winnie. "Did you see anyone suspicious?"

"Actually several I'm going to keep an eye on. Did you realize Mary Ann Witlock's brother is here?" Ellie asked, recalling the photo she'd seen in connection with information on Mary Ann Witlock.

"Bob Witlock? He's worked at Glamour Sensations for years."

Winnie paused and turned back. "He's in marketing and agreed that Christy would be better than his younger sister for the position. Before I made the announcement, I talked to him. I wanted him to know first. For that matter, Jerry Olson's daughter works for

Glamour Sensations and is here. She's married. I won't hold someone accountable for another's actions, even a close relative."

"Who is Jerry's daughter?" The reports from the sheriff hadn't said anything about that.

"They have been estranged for years, but it's Serena Pitman. She works in the research lab."

If she'd had the time she would have run her own investigation into each of the prime suspects with grudges against Winnie, but she couldn't do everything, which meant she had to rely on information garnered from reliable sources. Sometimes, though, those sources didn't give her everything she might need.

Winnie continued her trek toward the front of the room. Ellie racked her mind with all the guests who had passed before her, trying to remember who Serena Pitman was. Her visual memory was one of her assets. Face after face flitted through her thoughts until she latched onto the one that went with the name Serena Pitman. Red hair, almost orange, large brown eyes, freckles, petite. She searched the crowd of over two hundred until she found Serena at a table three away from the head one.

When Ellie sat down, her back to the stage, she faced the attendees with a clear view of Serena and her husband. The suspects the police had narrowed down as a viable possibility had not shown up—at least they hadn't come through the greeting line. The security and hotel staff were the only other people besides the guests, and she had made her rounds checking them when she had first arrived before the doors had been opened.

Sandwiched between Winnie and Colt, Ellie assessed each one sitting at the head table. Across from her sat

Christy and Peter. Next to the couple was a reporter from the Associated Press and a fashion editor from one of the industry's leading magazines. A Denver newspaper editor of the lifestyle section and a Los Angeles TV show hostess took the last two seats. Harold took his place next to Winnie.

Halfway through the five-course dinner, Colt whispered into Ellie's ear, "Is something wrong with the food?"

"No, it's delicious. I'm not that hungry." Ellie pushed her medley of vegetables around on her plate while her gaze swept over the sea of people, most intent on eating their dinner.

"Everything is going all right."

She slanted a glance at Colt, said, "For the moment," then returned her attention to the crowd.

"Remember, you're Winnie's assistant."

"One who is keeping an eye on the event to make sure it's pulled off without a hitch."

The editor from the Denver newspaper looked right at Winnie and said, "I heard someone earlier talking about a wreck you were involved in. Is that why you arrived here in a helicopter?"

Winnie managed to smile as though nothing was wrong. "A minor collision. It didn't even set off the air bags. A car left stranded in the middle of the highway. Tell me how the drive from Denver was. It was snowing when we arrived."

The man chuckled. "This is Colorado in December. We better have snow or our resort areas will be hurting."

"You're so right, Marvin. Being stranded here isn't too much of a burden. Mountains. Snow. A pair of skis.

What more could you ask for?" Winnie cut into her steak.

Harold winked at Winnie. "A warm fire."

"A hot tub," the TV hostess added.

"A snowmobile since I'm probably one of the rare Coloradoans who doesn't ski," Marvin tossed back with the others at the table throwing in other suggestions.

When the conversation started to die down again, Colt asked the Denver editor, "Do you think the Broncos will go all the way to the Super Bowl?"

Ellie bent toward him. "Good question. Football ought to keep the conversation away from the wreck," she whispered.

The mischievous grin on his face riveted her attention for a few long seconds before she averted her gaze and watched the people at the table.

By dessert the conversation morphed from sports to the latest bestsellers. As Peter expounded on a thriller he'd finished, Ellie half listened as she watched the various hotel staff place the peppermint cheesecake before the attendees around the room.

Four tables away Ellie spied a woman who looked vaguely familiar. Was she in one of the photos she'd seen over the past few days? She didn't want to leave Winnie to check the woman out, but she could send a security officer standing not far from her.

"Excuse me, Winnie," Ellie leaned closer to her and whispered, "I'll be right back. I need to talk to your head of security."

Winnie peered over her shoulder at the man at the bottom of the steps that led to the presentation platform. "A problem?"

"I want him to check someone for me. Probably nothing. Be right back."

"We'll be starting our program in ten minutes. The waiters are serving the dessert and coffee."

The head of Glamour Sensations' security met Ellie halfway. "Is there a problem?"

"The dark-haired woman on the serving staff at the table two from the left wall. She looks familiar. Check her out. See who she is and if she has the proper identification."

He nodded and started in that direction. The woman finished taking a dessert plate from a man, put it on a tray and headed quickly for one of the doors the servers were using. The security chief increased his pace. Ellie slowly walked back toward Winnie, scanning the rest of the room before returning to the woman. The dark-headed lady set the tray on a small table near the door then rushed toward the exit, shoving her way through a couple of waiters. The security chief and a police officer Ellie recognized gave chase.

A couple of guests rose, watching the incident unfold.

Ellie leaned down to Winnie. "You should think about leaving. I think the lady I spotted is who we're after."

Winnie turned her head so no one at the table could see her expression or hear her whisper, "I saw. If she's gone, she can't do anything. I'll start now and run through the program then we can leave."

"Did you recognize her?"

"I couldn't tell from this distance. My eyesight isn't as good as it once was."

"Okay. Then let's get this over with. I'll be right behind you."

Winnie was introducing Christy when the head of security came back into the ballroom. He shook his head and took up his post at the foot of the steps to the platform. Ellie noted that all the doors were covered so the woman couldn't return to disrupt the presentation.

Christy came up to stand by Winnie, their arms linked around each other as they faced the audience clapping and cheering. Behind the pair, the screen showed some of the Endless Youth products being released in February. At the height of the event the confetti guns shot off their loads to fill the room with red-and-green streamers. A festival atmosphere took hold of the crowd.

Through the celebration Ellie hovered near Winnie, fixing her full attention on the crowd. Not long and they would all be back in the helicopter returning to the estate. She would be glad when that happened.

Some colorful streamers landed near Ellie, followed by a glass vial that shattered when it hit the platform. A stinking smell wafted up to her. Coughing, Ellie immediately rushed to Winnie's side as more vials mixed in with the streamers smashed against the floor throughout the ballroom, saturating the place with an awful, nauseating stench. People panicked and fled for the doors. The gaiety evolved into pandemonium almost instantly.

EIGHT

Over the screams and shouts, Colt hopped up onto the platform and reached Winnie's side just as Ellie tugged her toward the steps.

"We need to get out of here," she told them. "This would be a great time to strike in the midst of this chaos."

Colt wound his arm about his grandmother. Winnie faltered at the bottom of the stairs. He caught her at the same time Ellie turned and grabbed her, too. Their gazes met.

"We can get out this way." Ellie nodded toward a door behind the staging area. "It leads to an exit. All we have to do is get to the helicopter."

"But the announcement and celebration are ruined," Winnie mumbled, glancing back once before being ushered through the door and down a long hall.

His grandmother looked as if she were shell-shocked. He couldn't blame her. He, too, had hoped they could make it through the evening without incident.

"Once I get you home, I'll check to see what happened. Knowing the police chief and the sheriff, they are already on it." Ellie removed her gun from her purse.

The sight of the lethal weapon widened his grandmother's eyes at the same time the color drained from her face. He tightened his arms about her. She was a remarkable woman, but anyone could hit a wall and fall apart. He was afraid she was there.

At the door that led outside, Ellie held up her hand to stop them. "Wait. Let me check the area out." She searched the long hallway. "Be right back."

He looked over his shoulder at a few people rushing down the corridor toward the exit.

A couple of seconds later, Ellie returned. "Let's go. The helicopter is around the corner. People are pouring out of the hotel, but it's clear on this side."

"Not for long." Colt tossed his head toward the people coming down the hall.

With her hand on Winnie's right arm, Ellie led the way. She'd seen the pilot in the chopper and his instructions earlier were to start the engine the second he saw them approaching. Colt flanked his grandmother on the left and slightly behind her as though shielding her from anyone behind. Ellie did this as a job. He did it because he loved his grandmother enough to protect her with his life.

As she neared the front lawn of the hotel, Ellie slowed, panning the terrain for any sign of someone lying in wait. The woman who could have been behind what occurred in the ballroom might have planned the chaos so she could get to Winnie easier outside in the open. Ellie wouldn't allow that to happen.

Peering around the corner of the hotel, Ellie scoped out the crowd emerging from the front entrance, many with no coats on, who stood hugging themselves. The biting cold penetrated the thin layer of her lamé jacket. The people behind them in the hallway burst from the exit, their loud voices charged with fear and speculation.

"Let's go." Ellie started across the snow-covered ground.

A man hurried toward the helicopter as the blades began to whir.

Her gaze glued to the exchange between the pilot and the stranger, Ellie shortened her strides, waiting to see what transpired. When the man ran back toward the crowd, she increased her speed again. The sound of sirens blasted the chilly air.

At the chopper Colt assisted Winnie up into it while Ellie kept watch on the surroundings. After Colt followed his grandmother into the helicopter, Ellie climbed in and the pilot lifted off.

Over the whirring noise, Ellie spoke into her headset. "Who was that man?"

"Hotel security letting me know what happened in the ballroom. I figured you'd be outside soon." The pilot made a wide arc and headed toward the estate.

Ten minutes more. Ellie didn't let down her guard. Sitting forward, she scanned the terrain below. A blanket of white carpeted the ground, lighting the landscape. A helicopter ride she'd taken during one of her missions in the army flashed into her mind. Insurgents on the ground had fired on it, wounding one person in the backseat.

"Winnie, move as far over toward Colt as you can."

As her client did, Colt wrapped his arms around her. Again trying to shield her as much as he could.

Nine minutes later the pilot brought the chopper down as close to the main house as possible. Ellie scrambled out and hurried to Winnie's side to help her. The second she placed her feet on the drive, Ellie shepherded the woman toward her front door while the dogs barked at the helicopter.

Colt gave a command, and they quieted. He came up behind Ellie as they mounted the steps to the deck. Doug threw open the front door, and Ellie whisked Winnie inside.

"The sheriff called and said he's on his way," the caretaker said. "He briefly told me what happened so I came over. I figured you'd be back soon."

Through the fear that marked Winnie's face, she smiled. "I can always count on you and Linda."

"She's in the kitchen preparing some coffee. She'll bring it into the den. I'll let the sheriff in when he's at the gate."

On the way to the den, Ellie paused in the doorway of the small control room. "Have you seen anything unusual?" she asked the ex-police chief who monitored the security feed.

"Nope. Quiet."

Ellie caught up with Winnie and Colt as they entered the den. While Ellie walked from window to window, drawing the drapes, her client collapsed onto the couch, sagging back, her eyes sliding closed.

"Winnie, are you all right?" Colt sat beside her.

"No. This has got to stop. Everything was ruined tonight. Poor Christy. This was her big debut, and some mean, vicious person destroyed her moment."

Ellie positioned herself in front of the fireplace close to Winnie but facing the only entrance into the room. She still clutched her gun as though it were welded to her hand.

"I want to thank you for getting me out of there, Ellie. I'd still be standing on stage, stunned by the lengths a person will go to hurt another."

Ellie moved to the couch and sat on the other side of Winnie. Not until she took a seat did she relax her tightly bunched muscles. "I was only doing my job."

"You've done much more than that for me. The Lord sent you to me at this time." Winnie patted Colt's leg. "And you were there for me, too. I have truly been blessed having two people like you seeing to my welfare." Tears shone in her eyes.

Ellie thanked her. "I got a look at someone I suspect may be the one causing the trouble. Hopefully this might be over before Christmas. I'm still not sure from where I know that woman at the gala tonight, but when security approached, she ran. That's not the action of an innocent person." The sound of footsteps returned Ellie's attention to the door, her hand tensing again on her gun.

Linda entered with a tray of four mugs and a coffeepot. "Doug let the sheriff in the front gate. He should be here any minute. After he arrives, we'll leave unless you need me for anything, Winnie."

She shook her head, a few strands escaping her usual neatly styled silver-gray bun at her nape. "You two are up late as it is. I'm glad you didn't go to the Christmas Gala. Not after what happened."

"Doug and I felt we needed to stay here and make sure nothing went wrong from this end. He patrolled the grounds with the dogs. You know how he is when it starts snowing. He'd rather be outside than in the house." Linda placed the tray on the table in front of the couch. "Do you want me to pour the coffee?"

Colt scooted forward. "I'll do it. Tell Doug thanks."

Doug appeared in the entrance with the sheriff. Linda crossed to them and left with her husband.

Sheriff Quinn grabbed the mug Colt held out to him. "It's getting cold outside."

Winnie didn't hesitate to ask her questions. "Bill, what happened? Is everyone all right? I'm assuming since I don't feel sick that what was released into the air wasn't poisonous."

"You're right, Winnie. Thankfully they were only stink bombs. The police are still trying to determine how many. There were five confetti guns, and it looks like each one shot at least one vial out of it. Maybe more."

"Any injuries with the stampede for the doors?" Ellie cradled her hot mug between her palms. She'd been caught up in a riot once and knew how easily people could get hurt when everyone was trying to flee a place.

"Right before I arrived, the police chief called to let me know he has access to the security feed at the hotel. He said so far it looks like ten injuries, mostly minor stuff. One woman is being sent to the hospital, but I don't think she will stay long."

"It could have been a lot worse." The firm line of Colt's jaw and the extra-precise way he set his mug down attested to his tightly controlled anger.

The sheriff looked at Ellie. "The police chief wants you to look at the tapes of the event. He understands from Glamour Sensations' security head that you think you recognized someone who fled out the staff door. We need to ID that person."

"Sure. I'll do anything I can, but I don't want to leave the estate. Not when Winnie is in danger."

"I thought you would say that. We'll have access to the tapes by computer. It'll be a good time for you all to look over the footage and see if anyone is out of place."

"Anything, even watching hours of tape," Colt said. "I want this to end. My grandmother has been through enough. All I can say is that I'm glad her last product development has been concluded."

"Hon, I'm fine, especially with you and Ellie here." She patted Colt's hand. "Dear, get my laptop from my lab downstairs, will you please?"

Right before he disappeared down the hall, Colt threw a look at Ellie while Winnie and the sheriff talked. In that moment Ellie saw how worried Colt was for his grandmother. Again, she found herself wishing she had that bond with someone.

Sheriff Quinn interrupted her thoughts. "The police are rounding up the staff to question them. If we could have a picture to show them, that will help."

Ellie closed her eyes and imagined the woman from across the ballroom. "She's about five feet six inches with long dark hair. I couldn't tell her eye color specifically, but I think a light color. She was dressed as a server—even had a name tag on like the others."

"I'll let the police chief know that. See if anyone is missing a uniform. If not, it could be one of their staff even if the person wasn't supposed to work that event. Did you see who Ellie is talking about?" he asked Winnie.

"No, sorry. I was trying to keep the conversation at the table going in the right direction. As I suspected, a few rumors have been flying around. The AP reporter wanted confirmation the position of the stolen car indicated it was probably left deliberately, possibly to block our way home."

"Sheriff, did you find any fingerprints on the stalled car the other night?" Ellie leaned over, refilled her mug and poured some more coffee into Winnie's.

"The report came in. No fingerprints the owner couldn't verify weren't someone's who has been in the car lately. So no help there."

Colt came back into the den and handed the laptop to the sheriff to pull up the site with the security footage on it. When he had it, he turned it around and set it on the coffee table, then walked behind the couch to watch.

Sheriff Quinn pointed to a link. "Click on that."

Colt did and a scene from inside the ballroom popped up on the screen. They watched that angle, but Ellie couldn't find the woman or anyone else that appeared suspicious. Colt went to the next link and brought it up.

Ten minutes into it, Winnie yawned. "I'm sorry. I don't know if I can stay awake."

As her own adrenaline rush had subsided, obviously Winnie's had, too. Ellie was used to the ups and downs, but her client wasn't. "Sheriff, can she review it tomorrow morning? I may want to see them again, too."

"Sure." He turned to Winnie. "I can escort you to your room."

Colt paused the tape while Winnie struggled to her feet, sighed and stepped around her grandson. "No, you should stay. At least this person hasn't come into my home and threatened me. If I couldn't walk freely in my own house, I don't know what I would do."

When Winnie left, Ellie murmured, "I didn't have the heart to tell her there is no place one hundred percent secure."

Colt scooted over so the sheriff could sit on the couch. "You don't think it's safe here?"

"Basically it is, as much as it can be. Or I wouldn't let Winnie walk around by herself without me right there. But in any situation I've learned to be wary."

"On the research vessel we've had two run-ins with pirates in different locales, which keeps us on the watch wherever we go, but nothing like this." Colt clicked to continue viewing the security footage.

"It's sad," Ellie said, focusing again on the tape. "These kinds of things are what keep me in business."

"Pause it. That's her!" About an hour into the footage Ellie bolted forward, pointing at a dark-haired woman on the screen who was carrying a tray with coffeepots and a water pitcher. "The same height, hairstyle. Can we zoom in on her?"

Colt clicked several keys and moved in closer.

"That's who ran out of the ballroom when the security head made his way toward her. We need a still of that, and see if someone can make the photo clearer." Her image teased Ellie's thoughts.

"I'll see what I can do and bring it back to you tomorrow." Sheriff Quinn wrote down how far into that tape they were while Colt started the footage again.

On closer examination, Ellie saw surprise on the woman's face when she spied the two security men coming toward her. She glanced toward a table near the head table, then hurried toward the exit. "Back up. Who was she looking at?"

Colt found the spot and zeroed in on the table next to the one where they'd been sitting. "Take your pick who she's staring at."

"Maybe no one." The sheriff rose.

"Or maybe one of the people whose back isn't to the woman," Ellie said. "There are four men and three women. Is there any way we can find out who was sitting at the table? There were only a few tables reserved and that wasn't one of them."

"I'll see what I can find out tomorrow morning when I meet with the police chief. In the meantime, I'm leaving two deputies with you again. One is in the foyer. The other is driving up the mountain as we speak. Rod will let him in. We'll have a long day tomorrow so get some sleep. That's what I'm gonna do. I'm determined we'll find out who it is. We have a picture now. That's better than before."

"Sheriff, I love your optimism. I hope you're right. I could be home in time for Christmas." She walked with him out to the foyer where Rod stood.

"Where is home?"

"Dallas, when I'm between jobs."

"Family there?"

"No. It'll just be me, but my boss hosts Christmas dinner for anyone who's in town." Which was the closest she came to having a family during the holidays.

"I have a son coming in for Christmas with his three children. I can't wait to see them. It's been six months, and they grow up fast."

When Ellie returned to the den, Colt gathered up the closed laptop and bridged the distance between them. "I heard what you said about Christmas. Do you think this will be over by then? That we'll have a peaceful Christmas?"

"I'm hoping. Winnie has been great dealing with what's been happening to her, but it's taking its toll."

"I'm glad she's finished in the lab. She doesn't have to worry about that at least."

"But that will mean she'll focus totally on what's happening. That may be worse."

"Then we'll have to create things for her to do. We haven't decorated the house like it has been in the past. Tons of decorations are still in storage in the basement."

Ellie couldn't remember decorating for Christmas in years, and even as a child, they often didn't have a tree. Her mother didn't care about the holiday, but Toby and she had tried to make their apartment festive. Then Toby had died and Ellie hadn't cared, either. "Sure, if it will help take Winnie's mind off the threats."

"Christmas is her favorite time of year. She's been so busy she's not had the time to do what she usually does. This will be perfect." Colt strode to the staircase with Ellie.

As she mounted the steps to the second floor, she wondered what a family Christmas was really like. At the top of the stairs, she looked around and started laughing. "I can't believe I walked all the way up here when I haven't checked the house yet."

"It must have been my charm and wit that rattled you."

"I hate to burst your bubble, Colt, but it's exhaustion." The sound of his chuckles sent a wave of warmth down her length.

"I'll put this laptop in my room and come with you. I wouldn't want you to fall asleep while making your rounds." He turned toward the right.

Ellie clasped his arm. "I'll be okay. I may be exhausted, but that doesn't mean I'll fall asleep."

He swung around. His gaze intent, he grazed his fingertips down her jaw. "What keeps you from sleeping?"

She shrugged one shoulder. "The usual. Worries."

"Winnie would tell you to turn them over to the Lord."

"What would you say?"

"Winnie is right, but I've always had trouble doing that. I still want to control things."

"Me, too. I know worrying is a waste of time and energy, but I've been doing it for so long, trying to control all aspects of my life, that I don't know how to give it totally to God."

"Practice."

"Have you ever practiced and practiced and never accomplished what you set out to do?"

"Not usually." He snapped his finger. "Except ballroom dancing. I have two left feet."

"I'll remember that if you ever ask me to dance." She took a step back. "Seriously, you don't need to come with me. At least one of us should get some sleep. I'm not going to bed until the second deputy arrives, anyway."

"I can keep you company if you like."

She would, but as she stared into his face, a face she'd looked forward to seeing each morning, she knew the danger in him staying up with her. Each day she was around him she liked him more and more. The way he loved his grandmother, handled a crisis—the way he kissed. "No, I'm not going to be long." She backed up until her heel encountered the edge of the staircase.

Like the first night they met, he moved with a quickness that surprised her, hooked his arm around her and tugged her to him. He planted a kiss on her lips that melted her resolve not to be around him. Then he parted, pivoted and started down the hallway. "Good night, Ellie. I'll see you in the morning."

Why did you do that? She wanted to shout the question at him but clamped together her tingling lips that still felt the remnants of his kiss. Coupled with her stomach fluttering and her heart beating rapidly, the sensations from that brief joining left their brand on her. She hurried down the stairs, sure the only reason she was attracted to the man was because it was that time of year when she yearned for a family, for a connectedness she'd never had except with her twin brother, Toby.

As Ellie went from room to room, making sure the house was secured, she forced her mind back to the case. She visualized the picture of the woman on the computer in her mind. She'd seen her before. By the time she reached her bedroom, she strode to the photos the sheriff had shown them of the possible suspects. She flipped through the pictures until she came upon Mary Ann Witlock. Covering up the woman's long blond hair, Ellie visualized her in a dark brown wig. And that's when she knew. Mary Ann was the bogus server at the gala tonight.

"Hot chocolate for everyone," Linda announced the next afternoon as she brought in a tray with the drinks and a plate of frosted Christmas sugar cookies.

For the past couple hours Ellie had been decorating a tree with Colt and Winnie and Harold and Christy. Now she climbed the ladder to place the star at the very top. When she descended to the floor, she viewed the ten-foot tree Doug and Colt had cut down that morning. The scent of pine hung in the air.

"This is turning into a party. I love it." Winnie backed away from the tree in the living room centered in front of the large picture window. "I might not be able to leave, but I appreciate you all coming here to help cheer up an old lady. This is just what I needed."

Colt slung his arm over his grandmother's shoulders. "Old? Did I hear you admit you're old? Who has stolen my grandmother?"

Winnie punched him playfully in the stomach. "I am seventy-three."

Colt arched a eyebrow. "So?"

"Okay, I admit I've let the threats get to me. But not anymore. The sheriff is closing in on the woman who, it looks like, has been behind everything."

"I can't believe Mary Ann is behind this. If I'd known what would happen, I'd have turned down the opportunity to be the spokesperson for Endless Youth." Christy took a mug of hot chocolate and a cookie off the tray. "I didn't realize she needed the money."

Winnie frowned. "Neither did I. If she had come to me, I would have loaned her the money."

"We don't know for sure it's her behind the threats," Harold said as he planted himself in a chair. "All we know is she was disguised last night as a server and then ran from security when approached."

"That's the action of a guilty person. And why was she wearing a dark wig if she was innocent?" Linda asked as she left the room.

"What do you think, Ellie?" Winnie removed some tinsel from a box and passed it out.

"She needs money and lost a chance at making a lot. She is missing right now. The police went to her house and haven't been able to locate her. Maybe the search warrant will produce something more concrete." Ellie carefully draped a few strands of tinsel on a branch. Probably the person Mary Ann was looking at before fleeing the ballroom was her brother, sitting at the table next to them. When Winnie had identified him this morning on the video, that was at least one mystery taken care of. Sheriff Quinn was investigating Bob Witlock to make sure he had no involvement, but he didn't think the brother did because he and Mary Ann had been estranged for several years.

Colt came up beside Ellie. "At the rate you're going, Ellie, it'll be midnight before we finish decorating the tree. This is the way we do it." He took some of the tinsel and tossed it onto several limbs. "See? Effective and fast."

"But it's not neat."

"That's okay. It's fun, and our tree isn't what you would find in a magazine. It's full of our past—not fancy store-bought ornaments." Colt gave her some more tinsel. "Give it a try."

Ellie did and laughed when half ended up on the carpet. "There must be an art to it, and clearly I don't have the toss method down."

Colt stepped behind her and took her arm. "It's called losing a little control and just letting go at the right time," he whispered into her ear.

She was glad no one else could hear him; his words caused her pulse rate to accelerate.

As he brought her arm back then swung it forward, he murmured, "Let go."

In the second she did and the silvery strands landed on various branches haphazardly, but none on the floor, something inside her did let go. It had nothing to do with the activity. It had to do with the man so close to her his scent engulfed her. The brush of his breath against her neck warmed her.

Quickly she stepped away. "I have no idea when I'll use this new skill again, but thanks for showing me how to do it properly." She tore her gaze from his and swept it around the room, taking in the faces of the people, all of whom were watching them.

The chime of the doorbell cut through the silence that fell over the room. Ellie thrust the remaining tinsel into Colt's hands and hurried to answer the door. She'd let him get to her. Let him give her a little glimpse at what she was missing. And she became all soft.

She opened the door to allow the sheriff inside. "I hope you have good news for us. What did you find at Mary Ann's house?"

He faced her with a grim expression. "We found a lot of evidence that points to her being the person threatening Winnie—one letter Winnie received was on Mary Ann's computer, along with pictures of Winnie. There was also a suicide note from Mary Ann. When I turned the computer on, that was the first thing that came up."

"Suicide? You found her body?"

"No. No one has seen her since last night. The Bakersville police and my office are still searching for her. There were also a couple of large dog crates in her garage and mud-caked boots, size nine men's shoes, although that isn't the size she wears. Also, there was a stack of unpaid bills on her kitchen table. She received a foreclosure notice a week ago."

"Winnie won't be safe until Mary Ann is found. I hope alive. But what about the dogs? If she took them, where are they?" Out of the corner of her eye she glimpsed Colt coming across the foyer toward them.

"Good question," the sheriff replied. "She could have gotten rid of them or sold them perhaps to someone not from around here. She needed money, so that would be my guess."

"So there's no telling where the dogs are, then?"

Colt stopped next to her. "Winnie was concerned something has happened."

"It has. It looks like Mary Ann is the person threatening Winnie, but she's disappeared." Ellie tried not to look at Colt directly in the eyes. Something had changed between them earlier in the living room, and she didn't know what to think or what to do about it.

"Which means Winnie is still in danger."

"Afraid so," the sheriff said, removing his hat and sliding the brim through his hands.

Winnie paused in the doorway into the living room. "Bill, why are you all standing out here? Come join us. Harold is here and Christy. Peter is coming after his last patient. We're getting ready for Christmas finally."

"I hate to intrude—"

"We've got hot chocolate and Christmas cookies."

"Well, in that case, I'll stay for a little while." The sheriff made his way toward Winnie, grinning from ear to ear. "Linda makes great cookies. I bought a box of them at the cookie sale at church."

"Why, Bill Quinn, I could have made them."

Both of his eyebrows rose. "Did you?"

Winnie giggled. "No, you're safe from my cooking. Why do you think I hired Linda in the first place?"

"Your husband insisted."

As the two entered the living room and their voices

faded, Ellie hung back with Colt. "I wanted to let you know what the sheriff told me when they went to Mary Ann's house." After she explained what they found, she added, "There was a suicide note on her computer."

"But she wasn't there?"

"No. The woman isn't in her right mind. She's desperate. What she did last night is an act of a person falling apart. An act of revenge."

"And the dogs? Any idea where they are?"

"They're valuable dogs. No telling where they are now. She most likely sold them since she was in debt for thousands of dollars. The police chief is checking with the bank in Bakersville where Mary Ann had an account to see if she was paid a large amount of money lately."

"If that's the case, couldn't she take care of some of her debt, if not all?"

"I did some research on some of the suspects, and I remember she had extensive dental work six months ago. I saw a before and after picture. Her teeth and smile were perfect afterward. It made a big difference in her appearance. I wonder if she did that hoping she would get the spokesperson position for Endless Youth."

"If that were the case, I can see why Winnie wouldn't hire her. She wouldn't want anyone who'd recently had work done to her face, even dental. The press could take it and focus on that rather than on Endless Youth. I've seen it before. Where the intended message is side-tracked by something that really had nothing to do with it."

"She had a huge dental bill and her waitress salary probably barely covered her necessities."

Winnie appeared in the living room entrance and

peered at Colt. "We have guests. You two can talk after they leave. I imagine you're speculating about Mary Ann, and I would like to hear what you have to say. She needs our prayers, the troubled girl."

"Sorry, Winnie," Colt replied. "We didn't want to say anything in front of the others."

"It's only Christy and Harold. They're family. Oh, that reminds me. I've got to let the person monitoring the gate know to let Peter in when he arrives. I thought we'd have an early dinner before sending our guests down the mountain. And the sheriff is staying, too. It seems his office can run without him occasionally." Winnie hurried toward the monitoring room.

"Are you sure she is really seventy-three?" Ellie asked as she headed for the living room.

"That's what her birth certificate said. I saw it once before she whisked it away from me. That was when she wouldn't tell anyone her age."

"She should be the spokesperson for Endless Youth."

"You know Harold mentioned that to her, and she laughed in his face. I could never see my grandmother purposely putting herself in the public eye."

"Because of what happened when she married your grandfather?"

"Partly, and the fact that Winnie is really shy with most people."

"Shy? I don't see much evidence of that. Look at last night with the media before everything fell apart."

"She's learned to put on a front and can do it for short periods of time, but, believe me, the evening drained her emotionally beyond the threats and what happened with the stink bombs."

"No wonder I like her so much. She and I have a lot in common."

"I know. That's why I like you."

His words took flight in her heart until she shot them down. They didn't mean anything. Really.

Soft strains of Christmas music played in the background. The fire blazed in the hearth in the living room while the hundreds of lights strung around the tree and a lone lamp gave off the only illumination. Colt settled on the couch next to Winnie, with Harold at the other end. Ellie sat directly across from him. Cuddling as two people in love did, Christy and Peter shared an oversize lounge chair. Sheriff Quinn had left hours ago.

Cozy. Warm. Almost as if there had been no threats, no attempts on Winnie. Almost. But the thought had edged its way into Colt's mind throughout the day, souring a day meant to forget the incident at the gala and to focus on Christmas. Then he would look at Ellie and the outside world wouldn't mean anything.

Doug came into the room. "Before Linda and I leave, I thought I'd let you know that it has started snowing again. We're not supposed to get too much."

"Thank Linda for another wonderful dinner." Winnie set her coffee on a coaster on the table.

"We enjoyed sharing the celebration tonight with all of you, but I want to check on the dogs," Doug said. "We both hope they find this Mary Ann Witlock soon so this is all over with." After saying his goodbyes the caretaker left.

Colt had always felt his grandmother was in good hands with the couple who had become more a part of the family with each year. "I wish the sheriff would call us with some good news. Maybe Mary Ann fled the area."

"Sheriff Quinn said they checked the airports in the vicinity, but Mary Ann's car is gone so she might have. They have a multistate search out for the car." Ellie leaned back and crossed her long legs.

The movement drew Colt's attention, his eyes slowly making their way up her body to her face. The soft glow of the lighting in the room emphasized her beauty. What was it about Ellie that intrigued him? That she could take care of herself in just about any situation? He knew strong women, even worked with several on the research vessel, but other than respecting their intelligence, there was no draw for him—not like with Ellie.

"We all know there are plenty of places to hide in the mountains around here. Back roads to use." Peter shifted then circled his arm around Christy.

"Yeah, but it's winter and snow will make that more difficult," Harold said.

Peter came right back with, "We haven't had as much as usual so far this year. She may be long gone by now."

"True. And when you're desperate, you sometimes do things you wouldn't normally do." Ellie's gaze fixed on Colt as though there was a secret message behind her words.

"I know she was at Glamour Sensations a lot for the Endless Youth position, but she was always so quiet and reserved. I didn't really know her at all." Christy peered over her shoulder at Peter. "You did her dental work. Didn't you see her for a follow-up a few weeks ago? What do you think her frame of mind was like?"

"She was agitated. She asked me to extend the time she could pay off her bill. I did, but she still was upset when she left. If I'd thought she would commit suicide, I'd have said something, but…"

"Peter, we can't always tell what someone is thinking or is going to do. I know we all would have said something if we had known. I'm still praying the police will find her alive and hiding." Winnie's hand quivered as she brought her cup to her lips.

Colt slid his arm around his grandmother. "You'd be the first one to help her if you'd known. If she's found, I wouldn't be surprised if you pay for a good lawyer to defend her. That's one of the things I love about you."

A frown puckered Christy's forehead. "Can we change the subject? I don't want to spend any more time on this horrid situation. I feel bad enough about Mary Ann."

Winnie patted Colt's thigh, then smiled at Christy. "You're right. Let's talk about our plans for Christmas. Only three days away."

Ellie's cell rang. She looked at the number then rose, leaving the room. Colt heard her say Sheriff Quinn's name and followed her into the foyer.

As he neared her, she ended the call and lifted her gaze to his. "They found Mary Ann's body."

NINE

Ellie slipped her cell into her pocket. "Her body was found at the bottom of a cliff by cross-country skiers right before dark. Her car, parked near the top of the cliff, was found by a deputy a little later."

"Suicide?"

"That's what they think, but Sheriff Quinn will know more tomorrow after the medical examiner looks at the body and they have more time to thoroughly search the scene below and above. The preliminary processing supports a suicide, especially in light of her note and state of mind."

Colt blew out a long breath. "Then it's over with."

"It's looking that way."

"Let's go tell everyone." Colt held his hand out to her.

She took it, realizing by tomorrow or the following day she could be on her way back to Dallas. Just in time to spend a lonely Christmas at home. At least she'd have a few hours with Kyra and her husband on the twenty-fifth.

When they reentered the living room Colt sat next to Winnie. "Ellie heard from the sheriff. They found Mary

Ann's body at the bottom of a cliff. They think it was suicide but they'll make a ruling probably tomorrow."

"It's over. That's great." Standing at the fireplace, Harold dropped another log on the blaze. "The best news I've heard in a while."

"Harold! How can you say that? A young woman killed herself." Tears glittered on Winnie's bottom eyelashes.

The CFO flushed, redder than the flames behind him. "You're right. I was only thinking about you and your situation."

"She did try to kill you." Peter sat forward. "There are people last night who were hurt because of her rage. *You* could have been hurt in the stampede to leave. Or when you were outside. Surely the stink bombs were a ruse to get you outside."

Winnie pushed to her feet. "I don't care. I can't celebrate a woman's death."

Colt stood up beside her. "Grandma, I don't think Harold really meant that. He was just showing how happy he is that it's all over."

Harold crossed to Winnie and took her into his arms. "I'm sorry. I never meant to cause you any pain. Please forgive me."

She raised her chin and looked at him. "I know you didn't. I only wish I'd known what was going on in Mary Ann's head. I could have helped her."

Could she forgive like that? Ellie wondered. She still couldn't forgive her mother for her neglect as she and Toby grew up. If Toby hadn't had Ellie, he would have had no one to look out for him. He'd needed extra care, and their mother couldn't be bothered.

"I applaud you for wanting to help the woman, but

she did try to hurt you." Peter shook his head slowly. "Aren't you just a little bit angry at her? That's a natural human response to someone who does something to you."

Winnie withdrew from Harold's embrace. "Did I ever feel anger toward the person behind the threats? Of course, I did. I'm no saint. But if I let that anger take over, I'm the one who is really hurt by it."

Peter snorted. "You're really hurt if they succeed in their plan. I'm sorry. I think people should be held accountable for what they do."

"I have to agree with Peter," Colt said. "Mary Ann had choices. I can't make excuses for what she put you through. I certainly won't celebrate her death, but I'm relieved it's over with. We can all have a normal Christmas." He looked from Winnie to Ellie.

Silence hovered over the group as his gaze drew her to him. Ellie gripped the back of a chair and remained still, finally averting her eyes.

"We'd better head home. I don't want to get caught out in a snowstorm." Peter rose right after Christy and put his arm around his fiancée. "Our time is limited since Christy found out she needed to go back to L.A. for a couple of days."

"Since when?" Winnie asked.

"Since last night." Harold kneaded her shoulder. "I forgot to tell you. I meant to first thing this afternoon, then we started decorating the tree. She is going to appear on *Starr's Take*. The talk show hostess felt bad about what happened last night and wants to highlight Christy for a show at the first of the year. That is, if Christy will fly to L.A. tomorrow and tape the segment first thing the next day."

"I'll be back midafternoon Christmas Eve. I don't want to miss my first one with Peter." Christy clasped his hand. "We had plans, but he's been so good about it."

"Harold, I can't believe you didn't tell me the second you walked into my house," Winnie said.

"If you remember correctly, you dragged me over to the box of lights and told me to untangle them."

Winnie's eyes twinkled. "Oh, that's right. In that case, I know what it's like to be distracted. I've had my share of distractions these past few weeks. No more. I'm diving into Christmas. I might even persuade my grandson to go up to my cabin like we used to."

"Not unless the sheriff approves, Winnie." Harold gave her a kiss on the cheek and prepared to leave.

Winnie walked with Harold, Peter and Christy to the foyer while Colt stayed back, snatching Ellie as she started to follow his grandmother. "I can't believe this may be over."

"If it is tomorrow, when are you going back to your research vessel?"

"I'm definitely staying through Christmas now. I want to make sure Winnie is all right. She can beat herself up when she finds out someone is hurting and she didn't do anything about it. I don't want her to start blaming herself for not anticipating Mary Ann's reaction to not getting the job with Endless Youth."

"We can't control other people's reactions, only our own."

Winnie strode into the room. "You two don't have to worry about me. I'm going to be fine, especially if I can spend some time at the cabin like we used to every Christmas."

"So you really are thinking about going up the mountain?" Colt asked.

"Yes, I know we spent the day decorating the house, but all of this has made me yearn for those simpler days. Thomas and I loved to escape life by going to the cabin."

"My fondest memories are of our Christmases spent there."

"So you'll agree to go?" Winnie picked up the coffee cups and put them on the tray Doug had left earlier.

"Yes."

Winnie looked up from the coffee table. "How about you, Ellie? I'd love for you to join us. You're part of the reason I'm safe and able to go to the cabin. It would be nice to share it with you."

"I hate to intrude—"

"Nonsense. I remember you saying that you don't have family to spend the holidays with. Consider us your family this year." Winnie started to lift the tray.

Colt hurried forward and took it from her. "I agree with Winnie. After all the time you've spent protecting her, let us show our appreciation. Please."

The look he gave Ellie warmed her insides. She wasn't quite ready yet to say goodbye to him or Winnie. Which, if she thought about it, was probably a mistake. Clearly she had feelings for them—and she didn't do emotions well. Still, maybe it was time just to do something impulsive. "I'll join you, if you're sure."

"Well, then it's settled. We'll go if the sheriff thinks it's okay." Winnie walked toward the hallway. "I'm suddenly tired. It's been quite a day—actually, quite a week."

After she left to retire for the night, Colt's gaze

seized Ellie's, a smoldering glint in his gray-blue eyes. "What about you?"

"I'm surprised I'm not tired. Maybe I had one too many cups of coffee. Caffeine usually doesn't affect me, though."

"I'll be right back. I'm known around the *Kaleidoscope* as the night owl, the last to go to sleep and definitely not the first to wake up in the morning."

As Colt left with the tray, the warmth of the fire drew Ellie to the sofa nearest the fireplace. She decided that for a short time she was going to enjoy herself. Real life would return when she flew back to Dallas and took another assignment.

Settling herself on the couch, she lounged back, resting her head against the cushion. The faint sounds of "Silent Night" played in the background. She remembered a Christmas Eve service she went to years ago where at the end the lights were switched off and only candlelight glowed in the dark church. She reached over and shut off the lamp nearby, throwing the room in shadows with only the tree and fire for illumination.

With a sigh, she relaxed, though she knew she couldn't surrender her guard totally. Nothing was official concerning Mary Ann. The sheriff still had a few loose ends he wanted cleared up.

She heard Colt move across the room toward her. The air vibrated with his presence although he was quiet. The cushion gave in when he sat on the sofa only inches from her. His scent vied with the aromas of the fire and the pine tree.

"Ellie," he whispered as though he might wake her up if he spoke any louder.

"I can't fall asleep that fast." She opened her eyes and

rolled her head to the side to look at him. "I was enjoying the sound of the music and the crackling of the fire."

"I can always leave you—"

She touched her fingertips to his lips. "Shh. The sound of your voice is even better. Tell me about what it was like growing up with Winnie. What happened to your parents?"

He leaned back, his arm up against hers. "I never really knew my mother. She died shortly after I was born. A massive infection. I guess my father tried to raise me—or more like a series of nannies did. One day when I was four Winnie showed up at the house and found the nanny drinking my dad's liquor. Winnie took me home with her, and I never left after that."

"What about your father?"

"I saw him occasionally when he wanted something from his parents. Mostly I just heard about his exploits from the servants or sometimes from the news. He played fast and furious. Never cared about the family business. One day he mixed drugs and alcohol, passed out and never woke up. Winnie told me he was mourning my mother's death. According to my grandmother, he loved her very much and fell apart when she died."

"How do you feel about your dad?"

Colt tensed, sitting up. "I hardly knew the man, so how can I answer that?"

"Truthfully. You might not have known him well, but that doesn't stop you from forming an opinion, having feelings about him."

For a long moment he sat quietly, his hands clasped together tightly, staring at the coffee table. "The truth is I don't have much feeling toward him at all. He was the man who happened to sire me, but he wasn't my fa-

"I'm a good listener. When you want to talk about your parents, I'm here."

She strode across the foyer, making sure the alarm system was on and working. Then she began with the dining room, examining the windows to verify they were locked. Not many people had ever told her they would listen to her about her past, but then she'd rarely given anyone the chance. Colt was scaling the walls she kept up around herself. Was it time to let him in?

Late the next afternoon, not long before the sun went down, Ellie propped her shoulder against a post on the porch of the mountain cabin. The Winfield place was nothing like the image of a tiny log cabin she had in her mind. Though the bottom portion was made out of logs, the three-bedroom A-frame was huge and imposing. The smoke from the huge stone fireplace, its wisps entwining with the falling snow, scented the crisp air. A large mug with Linda's delicious hot chocolate, which she'd sent with them before they'd climbed into the four-wheel-drive Jeep and trekked up to the top of the mountain, warmed her bare hands.

The cabin door opened and closed. Colt came to stand beside her with his own drink. "It's beautiful up here. The view when it isn't snowing is breathtaking."

"Will this snow be a problem?"

"The weather report says this system should move out fairly fast. We'll probably get six or seven inches. Nothing we can't handle. But we have enough food for four or five days. We always come prepared with almost twice what we need and there are staples left up here. Doug and Linda use the cabin throughout the year."

"I was glad to see you had a landline. I knew the cell

reception was nonexistent this far up the mountain. I don't want to be totally cut off from civilization."

"Mary Ann can't hurt Winnie anymore. The ME ruled it a suicide, and the sheriff couldn't find anything to indicate she wasn't working alone. Winnie is tickled they have a lead on where the dogs could have been sold."

"That'll be a nice Christmas present for Winnie if they find the dogs and they're back at the estate when she comes down off the mountain."

"If it's possible, Sheriff Quinn and Doug will make it happen."

"Winnie has a lot of people who care about her and watch out for her. That says a lot about her."

Colt's gaze snared hers. "How about you? You told me once your brother died when you were young. Do you have any more siblings?"

"Nope. It was just him and me. He was my twin."

"That had to be extra hard on you."

"Yes it was. He had a congenital heart defect that finally got the best of him."

"How old were you?"

"Thirteen."

"How were your parents?"

Suddenly the cold seemed to seep through the layers of clothing Ellie wore. She shivered, taking a large swallow of the now lukewarm chocolate. "I'd better go back inside before I freeze."

In the cabin, Winnie sat in a chair before the fire, knitting. Ellie stopped a few feet into the great room.

Winnie glanced up. "These past few years I haven't gotten to knit like I used to. I found my needles and

some yarn and decided to see if I remembered how."
A smile curved her mouth, her hands moving quickly.

"It looks like you remember."

"Yes. A nice surprise. The second I stepped inside
the cabin I felt like a new woman. My product line is
finished, at least for the time being, and the person after
me has been found. I'd say that was a wonderful Christmas gift." She lifted the patch of yarn. "And now this.
Have you ever knitted?"

Laughing, Ellie took the chair across from her. "I
wouldn't be able to sit still long enough to do it. That's
something I'll leave to others."

"I might just make this into a scarf for you. That way
you won't forget me when you get back to Dallas and
go onto another assignment."

"Forget you?" Ellie shook her head. "That's not
gonna happen. You're an amazing woman."

A hint of red colored her cheeks. "Where's my grandson?"

"Communing with nature," Ellie said with a shrug.

"I'm glad you didn't change your mind about coming." Winnie paused and leaned toward her, lowering
her voice. "I was sure you would."

"Why?"

"I saw you yesterday while we were decorating and
celebrating. You weren't totally comfortable with the
whole scene. I imagine since you go from one place
to another because of your job, you don't do much for
the holidays. Who did you spend Thanksgiving with
this year?"

"No one. I microwaved a turkey dinner and cele-
brated alone. I have a standing invitation to Kyra's, but

I hate always intruding on her and her husband. They're practically newlyweds."

"Kind of painful sometimes being around a couple deeply in love when you aren't."

"That's not it. I just…" *Just what?* she asked herself. In truth, Winnie was probably right. Kyra and Michael were always so good to include her in whatever they were doing, but she saw the looks exchanged between them—full of love that excluded everyone else in the room. She'd never had a man look at her like that—not even Greg, who she had thought she would marry one day. "It's not that I want a relationship, but there are times I get lonely."

"We all do. And why don't you want a relationship? You have a lot to offer a man."

Ellie peered at the front door, relieved it was still closed and Colt was outside. "I don't think I'd be very good at it. I've always depended on myself for everything."

"Everything? Not God a little bit?"

"Well, yes. I know He's there, but I'm not sure He's that interested in my day-to-day life."

"Oh, He is."

"Then where was He when I was growing up? Having to raise myself? Take care of my brother because our mother couldn't be bothered?" She finally said the questions that had plagued her ever since she gave herself to Christ.

"Look at the type of woman you've grown into. You're strong. You can take care of yourself. You help others have peace of mind when trouble happens in their life. I for one am thankful you came into my life.

Sadly, an easy road doesn't usually hone a person into what they need to be."

The door finally opened, and Colt hurried inside, stomping his feet. Snow covered his hair and coat. "I forgot something in the Jeep and went out to get it." After shrugging out of his heavy jacket, he put a sack on the table near the chair he settled into. "It's really snowing now. Too much more and we'll have whiteout conditions."

"It sounds like the weatherman got it wrong." Ellie eyed the bag. "What did you forget?"

"A surprise."

"You know a bodyguard doesn't like surprises."

"This is a good one." He quirked a grin, his eyes sparkling. "You and Winnie have to wait until Christmas morning."

"It's a present? I didn't get you anything." An edge of panic invaded Ellie's voice. A gift from him made their…friendship even more personal.

"It's nothing. And I don't want anything. That's not why I'm giving you this."

Winnie laughed. "Ellie, enjoy it. Colt loves giving gifts. He's just like his grandfather. I used to be able to find out what it was before Colt gave it to me. But not anymore. He's gotten quite good at keeping a secret."

"So, Winnie, what are we having for dinner?" Colt combed his fingers through his wet hair.

Winnie gave him a look. "Are you suffering from hypothermia? You want *me* to fix dinner?"

Colt chuckled. "Not if I want to eat anything decent. I was teasing you. Ellie and I will cook dinner for you." He rose and offered Ellie his hand.

She took it and let him tug her up. "You do know I don't cook a lot for myself. I'm not home that much."

"But I cook. We all take turns on the ship, and if we weren't accomplished, we quickly learned or the rest of the crew threatened to toss us overboard."

Ellie examined the contents of the refrigerator. "Grilling is out," she said as she glanced back at Colt. "Which, by the way, I am good at. So I guess the steaks can wait for a less snowy day."

"From the looks of it outside, I don't know that's going to happen before we leave. We can use the broiler in the oven."

"So how are we going to get out of here if it snows that much?"

"We have a snowmobile in the shed out back and skis."

"Winnie skis?"

"She did when she was younger, but she'll use the snowmobile. How are you on skis?"

"Never tried it. I live in flat country."

"We have some cross-country skis. Flat country is fine for that."

"But the way down isn't flat. I might not make a pretty picture on skis, but I'll do what I have to." She took the meat out of the refrigerator. "Okay, steak it is. I can actually prepare them and put them in the broiler. So what are you gonna cook?"

His chuckle spiced the air. "I see how this is going to go. I'm going to do most of the work. I thought you said you could cook."

"Simple things like steaks. Let's say you're the head chef and I'm the assistant. Believe me, you all will be much better off."

"Well then, let's make this simple. Baked potatoes and a salad."

"I'm all for easy."

Surprisingly Ellie found they cooked well as a team, and by the time they sat down to eat she'd laughed more at the stories Colt told her about life on the research vessel than she had in a long time. Her jobs were serious and left little room for the lighter side of life.

"I'm glad you two talked me into coming up here," Ellie said when Winnie finished her blessing. "I've worked a lot in the past few years and have had little downtime. I needed this and didn't even realize it. No bad guys out there stalking a client. That's a nice feeling"

Winnie agreed. "That's how I'm looking at these next three days. A minivacation that I needed a lot. I'm too old to work as hard as I have been with Endless Youth. But it's mostly done, and I've accomplished what Thomas and I set out to do all those years ago. Once the company goes public, I'm stepping down as CEO of Glamour Sensations."

Colt dropped his fork on his plate. "You're finally retiring? I've been wanting you to slow down for years."

Winnie pursed her lips. "I would have if a certain young grandson had decided to use his degree in chemistry and come into the business. I figure Harold can take over the CEO position until he grooms someone for the job."

Ellie picked up on the sudden tension that thickened at the table between grandson and grandmother. She swallowed her bite of mushroom-covered steak and said, "What are you going to do with all your free time?"

"I won't completely turn the company over without keeping an eye on it. But I figure I could knit, read, wait for great-grandchildren."

Colt's eyes popped wide. "Winnie, now I know why you insisted on coming up here. Did you have something to do with all this snow, too? We won't be going anywhere until it stops. Visibility is limited."

His grandmother smiled. "I have a lot of skills, but controlling weather isn't one of them. I figured the circumstances were just right for me telling you this now rather than right before you go back to the *Kaleidoscope*. You'll inherit my shares in the company so you'll have a stake in it."

"What's this about great-grandchildren? This is the first time you've bought that up in a long time."

Winnie pointedly looked at Ellie before swinging her attention to Colt. "Just a little reminder. After all, I'm getting up there. These threats made me realize I won't be around forever. I need to make plans for the future."

Colt's eyebrows slashed downward, and he lowered his head, as though he was enthralled with cutting his steak.

"The threat is over and you should have many years before you, Winnie," Ellie said, trying to defuse the tension vibrating in the air.

"I'm planning on it, but it's in the Lord's hands."

The rest of the meal Winnie and Ellie mostly talked, with a few comments from Colt. What part of the conversation had upset him? Ellie wondered. The part about Harold becoming CEO or the great-grandchildren?

At the end Ellie rose. "I'll take care of the dishes. That I know how to do at least. When I was first in the army I was on mess duty a lot."

"Colt will help you," Winnie offered. "You're our guest. We certainly can't let you do it alone."

As Ellie walked into the kitchen she heard Colt say in a strained voice, "I know what you're doing, and you need to stop it."

"Stop what? If you want, I'll help her."

The sugary sweet sound of Winnie's voice alerted Ellie to the fact that the woman was up to something, and she had a pretty good idea what it was. When Colt came into the small kitchen, his expression reflected his irritated mood toward his grandmother. Ellie worked beside him in silence for ten minutes.

As she washed the broiler pan, she asked, "What's going on with you and Winnie? Are you upset about her retiring and Harold taking over?" She didn't think that was it.

"I'm glad she's retiring, and Harold's a good man. Don't tell her, but lately I've been thinking about what I need to do. I don't see me living on a research vessel for years."

"So you might help with the company?"

"Maybe. I have an obligation that I need to finish first to the research team."

"Then what has you upset? And don't tell me you aren't. It's all over your face."

"She hasn't played the great-grandchildren card in ages. I thought she'd learned her lesson the last time."

"What lesson?"

"Come on. You're smart. Don't you see she's trying to play matchmaker with us?"

"It did cross my mind, but I think it's cute."

"Cute! The last time she did, I went out with the woman to make her happy. On the surface she seemed all right until we stopped dating and she began stalking me. That's one of the reasons I took the job on the *Kaleidoscope*. It's hard to stalk a person in the middle of the Pacific Ocean. It turns out I've enjoyed the work I'm doing and the woman went on to marry and move to New York, but Winnie isn't usually that far off reading people."

"We're all entitled to a mistake every once in a while. Besides, she had your best interests at heart—at least in her mind."

"I told the lady I wasn't interested in a serious relationship. She was and didn't understand why I wasn't. Hence the stalking to discover why she wasn't Mrs. Right."

"Don't worry. I don't stalk. I protect people from stalkers. And I'm not interested in a serious relationship, either. So you're perfectly safe. Your grandmother's wiles won't work on me." Ellie wiped down the sink. "So if you know that your grandmother has done that in the past, why did you talk me into coming this morning when I voiced an objection?"

He blew out a frustrated breath. "Because I like you. I've enjoyed getting to know you, and I didn't like the idea that you would spend Christmas alone."

"Oh, I see."

"Do you? Winnie needs to realize a man can have a friendship with a woman. She keeps insisting Harold is just a friend, so surely she can understand we can be friends."

Ellie laughed. "You don't have to convince me. Just Winnie."

"Yeah. Besides, after Christmas, I'll go back to *Ka-*

leidoscope and you'll go on another assignment. We'll probably be halfway around the world from each other."

"I agree. Forgive the cliché, but we're like two ships passing in the night."

"Exactly." He draped the dish towel over the handle on the oven. "And I think I'll go in there and explain it to her. Want to back me up?"

"Sure."

Colt stalked into the great room and found it empty. He turned in a full circle, his gaze falling on the knitting project in the basket by the chair his grandmother had been sitting in. His forehead crinkled, and he covered the distance to the hall, coming back almost immediately. "She went to bed. It's just you and me, and it's only nine o'clock."

"I think that was her intention."

"I know." A chuckle escaped Colt. "And I'll have a serious word with her tomorrow. In the meantime, want to play chess or checkers?"

"I can't play chess, so it has to be checkers."

Colt retrieved the board and game pieces and set it up at the table where they had eaten their dinner. "I'll have to teach you how to play chess. It's a strategy game. I have a feeling you'd be good at it."

"Maybe tomorrow. After the past few weeks, I don't want too tough a game to play tonight." Ellie took a chair across from him. "After an assignment I go through a mental and physical letdown, and after a particularly hard job, I almost shut down for a couple of days."

"Is this your way of telling me you're going to lounge around and do nothing but eat bonbons?"

"If you have any, I might. I like chocolate." Ellie moved her red checker forward.

"What else do you like?" Colt made his play, then looked up into her eyes, trapping her with the intensity in his gaze. Electrifying. Mesmerizing.

"Protecting people," she somehow managed to reply. "I really do like my work. Making sure a place is secure. Trying to figure out all the ways a person can get to another."

"I can understand liking your job. I like mine, too."

"What do you like about your job?"

"Finding unique species. Trying to preserve the ocean. The challenge of the job. That's probably what I like the most. I want a job that forces me beyond my comfort zone."

"We have a lot in common."

Colt answered her move by jumping her red checker. "You said you became a bodyguard because you want to help those who need protection. Why is that important to you?"

"King me," Ellie said when she slid her first red piece into his home base. "Because my twin was bullied. I wasn't going to allow that to happen to others if I could do something about it."

"He was but you weren't?"

"No. I had a rep for being tough and not taking anything from anyone."

He cocked his head to the side. "How did you get that reputation?"

"By standing up to the people who made fun of my brother. Toby was slow. He was the second twin. He became stuck in the birth canal and was deprived of oxygen, which caused some medical and mental problems."

"When did you start championing him like that?"

"When we started school. Kindergarten."

"What did your parents think?"

Ellie looked at the board and made a move without thinking it through. With his next turn, Colt jumped her pieces until she had to crown his black checker.

"Obviously the subject of your parents isn't one of your favorites," he said. "Like me."

Ellie swallowed the tightness in her throat. Recalling her past never sat well with her. "No. I never knew my father. He left my mother when Toby and I were born. He never once tried to get in touch with us. And for different reasons from your dad, my mother was less than stellar in the parent department. I basically raised Toby and myself. I didn't have grandparents like yours."

"So you and I have another thing in common."

There was something about Colt that drew her. She hadn't wanted to admit that to herself, but she couldn't avoid it any longer. They were alike in a lot of ways even though their backgrounds were very different. He came from wealth and was college educated. She'd graduated from high school and had been educated on the job in the army.

Ten minutes later Colt won the checkers game. She wanted to think it was because her mind hadn't been on the game, but that wasn't true. He was good and she wasn't. She hadn't played since she was a kid and the old man next door used to challenge her. She hadn't won then, either, but she had enjoyed her neighbor's conversation about the different places she could see around the world. So when the U.S. Army recruiter came to her school, she'd thought it would be a good way to go different places.

"Another game?" Colt asked.

"No, one beating in a night is enough. My ego can only take so much."

He threw back his head and laughed. "I have a feeling your ego is just fine."

"Okay, I hate to admit that Winnie has the right idea about going to bed early. What's even nicer is that I don't have to walk through the house and check to make sure we are locked up tight. No one in their right mind would come out on a night like this." Ellie made her way to the window and opened the blinds to look at the heavy snow coming down.

"Near blizzard conditions," Colt said close to her ear.

The tickle of his breath on her nape zipped through her, but she stayed still. There was nothing stopping her from turning around and kissing him. No job. No threats against Winnie. This was her time that she'd chosen to spend with Winnie and Colt. His presence so near to her tingled her nerve endings and charged her, demanding she put aside her exhaustion and give in to the feelings bombarding her from all sides.

"Yes, I haven't seen this much snow in a while." Her reply ended in a breathless rush.

"It makes this cabin feel even cozier." His soft, whispered words caressed her neck.

She tensed, trying to keep herself from leaning back against him.

"Relax. We'll be perfectly fine in here. If we need rescuing, people know where we are and will come when we don't show up the day after Christmas."

His teasing tone coaxed the tension from her. She closed the blind and swung around at the same time she stepped away. "I think I can survive being snowbound in a large, warm cabin with enough food for a week. My boss doesn't expect me to come into the office until the day after New Year's."

"I wish I could say the same thing. I have to get back to the ship."

His comment reminded her of their differences. She was a bodyguard. He worked on a vessel in the middle of the Pacific Ocean. Not conducive to a relationship. "Good night, Colt."

"Coward."

"Oh, you think?" She'd been accused of being many things. Being a coward wasn't one of them.

"When it gets personal, you leave."

"That's what this is?" She drew a circle in the air to indicate where they were standing.

He moved to the side, sweeping his arm across his body. "Good night, Ellie. We'll continue our conversation tomorrow when you're rested."

On her way to her bedroom, the searing heat of his gaze drilled into her back. Every inch of her was aware of the man she'd wanted to kiss but didn't. It was better this way. Now she only had a few more days and she could escape to Dallas.

Ellie hurriedly changed into her sweatpants and large T-shirt then fell into bed. She expected sleep to come quickly. But she couldn't stop thinking about Colt. At some point she must have gone to sleep because the next thing she realized a boom shook the cabin, sending her flying out of bed.

TEN

Ellie fumbled in the dark for her gun she kept on the nightstand out of habit. When her fingers clasped around it, she raced into the hallway at the same time Colt came out of his bedroom.

"Check on Winnie," she said and hurried into the great room. The cabin seemed intact, but when she peered toward the large window that overlooked the front of the place, she saw an orange-yellow glow through the slats in the blinds as though the sun had set in the yard. She yanked open the door, a blast of cold rushing in while flames engulfed the Jeep nearby in the still-falling snow.

Gun up, she moved out onto the porch. When she stepped into the snow blown up against the cabin, she glanced down and realized she had no shoes on. In spite of the biting cold battering her, she scanned the white terrain. Although night, it was light and eerie. The storm had died down some but still raged, as did the fire where the Jeep was.

From behind a hand clamped on her shoulder. She jerked around, her gun automatically coming up.

Colt's eyes grew round, his hand falling back to his side.

"Don't ever come up behind me like that, especially after something like this." Using her weapon, she gestured toward the flames. "I could have shot you."

With her toes freezing and the sensation spreading up her legs, she hotfooted it into the cabin and shut the door, locking it. "How's Winnie?"

"I'm fine."

Ellie glanced over Colt's shoulder. Winnie hovered near the hallway, wrapped in a quilt. "You know what this means."

She nodded. "Mary Ann didn't send those threats."

"Possibly. Or someone was working with her and maybe killed her to keep her quiet. It's possible to make a murder look like suicide. That's what the police wanted to determine when her body was discovered."

"The Jeep couldn't have exploded on its own?" Winnie came farther into the room.

"Not likely."

Colt parted a few slats on the blinds and peeked outside. "The fire is dying down with all the snow falling, and the wind has, too. We need to call the sheriff."

Ellie marched to the phone and picked it up. "No dial tone. This is definitely not an accident."

"So we're trapped in this cabin with no way to get help." Colt strode into the kitchen and peered out the window. "I see nothing on this side."

Ellie checked the other sides of the cabin, calling out from her bedroom, "Clear here." *For the time being.*

"What do we do? Who is behind this?" Winnie's voice quavered.

Ellie reentered the great room. "At the moment the

who isn't important. We need to come up with a plan. If he blew up the Jeep, he could try something with the cabin and we can't guard all four sides 24/7. He might have destroyed the Jeep to get us out of the house."

"How can we leave?" Winnie pulled the blanket closer to her.

"The snow is starting to let up," Colt said. "Maybe I could make it down the mountain and get help. You could stay here with Winnie and guard her. I know these mountains and have the best chance of getting out of here."

Ellie faced Colt. "How are you going to walk out of here? Over a foot of snow was dumped on us in the past twelve hours."

"We have snowshoes I can use. Or I'll get to the snowmobile in the shed and use that."

"What if he's out there waiting to shoot anyone who leaves?" This was a situation where she wished she were two people and could stay and protect but also go and get help.

He clasped her arms. "I've fought off pirates. I can do this. Besides, the visibility isn't good because it's still night and snowing."

"Exactly. It won't be good for you, either." Thinking about what could happen to him knotted her stomach.

"But I know this area well. I doubt the person out there does. This is Winfield land. Not much else is up here. This isn't debatable. I'm going. You're staying." A determined expression carved harsh lines into his face.

She nodded. She didn't like the plan, but they didn't have a choice.

Colt started for his bedroom.

Winnie stepped into his path. "Colt, don't do this. I

don't like you being a target for this person. You're my only family left."

"I have to go. I'm taking Granddad's handgun with me." He looked back at Ellie. "I'm leaving his rifle in case you need it."

"Fine. Bring it out here with ammunition. I'll keep you covered for as long as I can." The helplessness Ellie experienced festered inside her. Protection was her job, not his.

Winnie turned large eyes on Ellie as Colt disappeared down the hallway. "I'm glad Thomas taught Colt to shoot. At that time it was for him to protect himself if he came upon a bear or cougar in these mountains— not a person bent on killing me."

"You won't as long as I have a breath in me." Ellie's hands curled into fists.

Nor Colt. I won't let him die, either. He means too much to me. That realization stunned her for a moment, then because she had no choice, she shoved it into the background. She couldn't risk her emotions getting in the way of whatever she had to do.

When he reemerged from the hallway, dressed in a heavy overcoat and wool beanie, carrying snowshoes, thick gloves, goggles and the rifle, he thrust the latter into Ellie's hand then dug for a box of shells and laid them on a nearby table. "More ammunition is on top of my bureau."

He put on his goggles, wrapped a scarf around his neck and lower face, donned his snowshoes and gloves, then eased the back door open. Cracking a window that overlooked the back of the cabin, she took up guard as Colt trudged his way toward the shed two hundred feet away.

Her nerves taut, she shouldered the rifle, poised to fire if she needed to. Ellie scoped the terrain for anything that moved. All was still. Not even the branches of the pine trees swayed from wind now.

"What's happening? I don't hear the snowmobile," Winnie said behind Ellie.

"Nothing. He's inside the shed." *But is he safe?* What if the assailant was waiting for him? Ellie couldn't leave Winnie. That might be what the person wanted. But what if Colt needed—

The side door to the shed opened, and Colt hurried back toward the house, his gaze scanning the area.

"What happened?" Ellie asked at the same time Winnie did when Colt reentered the cabin.

"The snowmobile won't start. Someone disabled it."

"Are you sure? Does it have gas?"

"There's a hole in the tank. The gas leaked out all over the ground. The ski equipment and anything else we might use to leave here is gone. He's cut us off."

Trapped. She'd been trapped before and gotten out. She would this time, too, with both Colt and Winnie. "Okay. For the time being let's fortify the cabin, find places to watch our surroundings while we figure out what we should do."

"I still think I should try leaving here on foot," Colt insisted.

"Maybe. What's up in the loft?" Ellie pointed to a narrow staircase.

"Storage mostly, but it might be a better vantage place to watch the area from," Colt said.

"I'm going to fix some coffee. We need to stay alert. I don't think there's going to be any more sleep tonight."

"Thanks, Winnie. I could use a whole pot." Colt kissed his grandmother on the check.

When she left, Ellie moved toward the stairs. "Keep an eye on her while I look at the loft."

Colt stepped closer and whispered, "Ellie, I don't think Winnie could make it out of here, so all three of us going is not an option. She might have power walked around the perimeter of the estate, but sloshing through the deep snow even with snowshoes is totally different. It's exhausting after a few hundred yards. And snow-shoeing can be treacherous going downhill over rough terrain, especially with her weak knees. Not to mention leaving her exposed for the person to shoot."

"And you don't think you'll be."

"What's the alternative? Waiting until we're missed? That could be days. No telling what would happen in that time."

"I'll be back down in a few minutes. Check the windows and doors to make sure they're locked. Put some heavy furniture up against the two doors. Shutter the windows we won't use for a lookout."

"What are you two whispering about?" Poised in the entrance into the kitchen, Winnie planted her fists on her waist. "If you're worried about me, let me inform you I'll do what I have to. I won't let this person win. Any planning and discussions need to include me. Understand?"

Ellie exchanged a glance with Colt before he pivoted and headed toward his grandmother, saying, "We were just discussing our options."

Ellie clambered up the stairs. The whole loft was one large room with boxes and pieces of furniture stored along the walls. Two big windows overlooked the west and east part of the landscape. One person with little effort could keep an eye on over half the terrain. That could leave Winnie and Colt covering the north and south. That might work. But then as she started back down the stairs, questions and doubts began tumbling through her mind like a skier who lost her balance going down a mountain.

The scent of coffee lured her toward the kitchen. She poured a mug and joined Winnie in the great room before the dying fire. She gave the older woman a smile, hoping to cajole one from her.

But Winnie's frown deepened. "I've been trying to figure out who would go to such lengths to get me. I honestly can't imagine anything I've done to cause this kind of hatred. I feel so helpless."

Ellie remembered that exact feeling a little while ago. It never sat well with her. "I've been thinking."

Colt suddenly came from the hallway with his arms full of warm clothing, snowshoes and other items. "If we need to leave suddenly, I want this on hand. I'm separating it into piles for each of us."

"I say we have two options. All of us leave and try to make it down the mountain. Or I go by myself and bring help back." Ellie sat on the edge of the sofa, every sense attuned to her surroundings.

"Those aren't two options in my opinion," Colt said. "I'm going it alone. I can move fast. I should be able to get back with help by dark if I leave right away. The best place for me to try and get to is the estate. I think that's the best—"

"No, Colt. You're not going by yourself. I won't have you get killed because of me. There is a third option.

We stay here. That's what I want." Winnie pinched her lips together and pointedly looked at each one of them.

Colt surged to his feet. "Sorry. I love you, Winnie, but the longer we spread this out the more this person has a chance to accomplish what he wants to do. Kill you and in the process take us all out."

"I agree with Colt about us all waiting, but I'd rather be the one going for help. I know how to avoid being a human target. I was trained in that."

"Winnie is your client and first priority."

"I know. That's the dilemma I—"

Thump!

"What was that?" Ellie rose and started for the window by the front door. She motioned Colt to check the back area.

Again she heard the sound—like something striking the side of the cabin. Ellie parted the blinds to peer outside. Nothing unusual but the sight of the charred Jeep.

Thump!

"That's coming from the north side." Colt rushed down the hallway.

Ellie helped Winnie to her feet and followed him. "Do you see anything?"

He whirled from the window. "We've got to get out of here. He's firing flaming arrows at the cabin."

Ellie stared out at the evergreen forest, which afforded a lot of cover along the north area of the property. Another arrow rocketed toward the cabin, landing on the roof. "He's burning us out. Either we leave or die in a fire."

Colt ushered them out of the room. "Let's go. If we can get away, I think I know a place you two can hide.

It's defensible, only one way in. We need to dress as warm as possible."

"He's on the north side. We'll use the window facing south to get out of here. He can't watch all four sides at once."

Winnie halted before her pile of garments. "Unless there is more than one."

"We have to take our chances and pray the Lord protects us." Ellie quickly dressed, then stuffed useful items into a backpack—flashlights, a blanket, matches, weapons, some bottled water and food.

"He'll be able to track us, but the cave system isn't too far away and it's beginning to snow again. I hope the conditions worsen after we get to the cave. The way I have to go is down. I can do that even in less-than-favorable visibility." Colt prepared his backpack then slung it over one shoulder.

The noise of the arrows hitting the cabin increased. The scent of smoke drifted to Ellie as they hurried into the laundry room. A three-by-three window four feet off the floor beckoned her. She pulled a chair to it and opened their escape route. A blast of cold air and snow invaded the warmth of the small room.

Ellie stuck her head out the opening. It was at least six feet to the ground. "I'll go first, then you, Winnie. Colt can help lower you to me."

After tossing her backpack out the hole, Ellie leaped up and shimmied through the small space, diving head-first and tucking into a ball. The snow cushioned her tumble to the ground. She bounced up and positioned herself to guide Winnie, breaking her fall. While Colt wiggled through the opening and followed Ellie's example, she and Winnie put on their snowshoes. Colt donned his as fast as he could.

The thumping sound thundered through the air.

Winnie started to say something. Ellie put her finger up to her mouth. Colt's grandmother nodded that she understood.

Colt pointed in the direction he would take, then set out in a slow pace with Winnie mirroring his steps, then Ellie. The less snow they disturbed the faster the falling flakes would cover their tracks.

When Colt reached the edge of the forest that surrounded the cabin, Ellie paused and glanced back. The stench of smoke hung in the air, but she couldn't see any wisps of it coming from the cabin because of the heavy snowfall. Even the indentations they'd made were filling in, though still evident.

Then the sound of the arrows striking the cabin stopped. Ellie searched the white landscape but saw no sign of the assailant. She turned forward and hurried as fast as she could to catch up with Colt and Winnie.

Fifteen minutes later, the wind began whipping through the trees, bringing biting cold to penetrate their layers of clothing. Even with so little skin exposed to the chill, Ellie shivered and gritted her teeth to keep them from chattering.

A cracking noise reverberated through the forest, followed by a crash to their left. Ellie looked up at the snow- and ice-burdened limbs on the pines and realized the danger of being beneath the heavy-laden branches. Winnie barely picked up each foot as she moved forward. Her pace slowed even more.

When Winnie stumbled and fell, Ellie whispered, "Colt," and rushed toward the woman.

The wind whisked his name away. He kept trudging forward.

"Colt," she said a little louder as she bent over to help Winnie to her feet, one snowshoe coming off.

He glanced back, saw his grandmother down and retraced his steps as quickly as he could. He assisted Winnie to her feet while Ellie knelt and tied the snowshoe back on Winnie's foot. Snow-covered, the older woman shook.

Another crack, like a gun going off, resonated in the air. A pine branch snapped above them and plunged toward them. Ellie dove into both Colt and Winnie, sending them flying to the side. The limb struck the ground a foot away from them.

Dazed, Winnie lay in the snow, then pain flashed across her face.

"What's wrong, Winnie?" Ellie asked, pushing up onto her hands and knees next to the woman.

"I think I did something to my ankle," she murmured, her voice barely audible over the howl of the wind through the trees.

Colt knelt next to Winnie. "I'll carry you the rest of the way. The cave isn't far."

"I'm so sorry, Winnie." Ellie peered at the large branch on the ground.

"Don't you apologize. I could have been hurt a lot worse if that had fallen on me."

While Colt scooped up his grandmother, Ellie used her knife to cut a small branch off the big one. She used the pine to smooth out the snow behind them as much as possible and hide their tracks.

Ten minutes later, Colt mounted a rocky surface, went around a large boulder and stooped to enter a cave.

Ellie stayed back to clear away their steps as much as possible, then went inside the dark cavern, reaching for her flashlight to illuminate the area. A damp, musky odor prevailed.

Colt set his grandmother on the floor, took a blanket out of his backpack and spread it out, then moved Winnie to it. Kneeling, he removed the boot from the injured foot and examined it. "The ankle's starting to swell. I don't think it's broken. But a doctor will have to look at it when we get home. The faster I leave, the faster you'll get the medical care you need."

Ellie slung her backpack to the ground near Winnie and sat on it. "We'll be fine. I'll make Winnie comfortable then stand guard near the entrance."

"I should be back before dark. If I can get to the house, I can get help. It's a little out of the way, but I think it would save time in the long run. I know I can find help there." Colt started to stand.

Winnie grabbed his arm. "I love you. Don't you dare take any more risks than you absolutely have to. If you have to take your time to be safe, then you've got to do that."

"Yes, ma'am." He kissed her forehead. "I have a good reason to make it safely down the mountain."

Ellie rose and walked with him a few feet. "Ditto what your grandmother said. I have food and water. We have a couple of blankets. We'll be fine." She tied his scarf, which had come loose, back around his neck. Suddenly emotions jammed her throat. She knew the dangers in store for Colt. Not just the rough terrain in a snowstorm but a maniac bent on killing them.

He clasped her glove-covered hands and bent his head toward hers. A smile graced his mouth right before his lips grazed across hers once then twice. Then he kissed her fully. She returned it with all her needs and concerns pouring into the connection that sprang up between them.

In a raw whisper, she said against his mouth, "Don't you dare get hurt. We have things to talk about when this is over."

"If I hadn't been motivated before, I am now." He gave her a quick peck on her lips then departed, striding toward the cave entrance.

Ellie watched him vanish around the corner, then went back to Winnie to make sure she was comfortable before she stood guard at the mouth of the cavern.

"He'll be all right," Winnie assured her. "He knows these mountains well. Hopefully better than whoever is after me."

Ellie nodded at Winnie, remembering the grin Colt gave her before kissing her. The memory warmed her cold insides. "Yes. After all, he's fought off pirates before."

Winnie chuckled.

The warmth died out when a gunshot blasted the air and the mountain over them rumbled.

ELEVEN

Colt exited the cave, scanning the terrain for any sign of their assailant. Through the curtain of snow falling a movement caught his full attention. Suddenly a shadow rose from behind a rock and aimed a rifle at him. Colt dove for cover as the white-camouflaged figure got off a shot, the bullet ricocheting off the stone surface behind him.

A noise rocked the ground—like a huge wave hitting shore in a thunderstorm. Colt had only heard that sound one other time, right before tons of snow crashed down the mountain, plowing through the forest, leaving nothing behind in its wake.

The entrance of the cave a few feet away was his only chance. He scrambled toward it as rock, snow and ice began pelting him.

Winnie went white. "An avalanche!"

Ellie hurried toward the entrance. "Stay put," she said, realizing Winnie didn't have a choice.

As she rounded the bend in the stone corridor, she saw Colt plunge toward the cave, then a wall of white swallowed him up. The force of the avalanche sent a swell of snow mushrooming into the cavern.

When the rumbling stopped, snow totally blocked the cave entrance and she couldn't see Colt. She rushed to the last place he'd been and began digging with her hands. Cold and wet invaded the warmth of her gloves, leaving her hands freezing. She didn't care. Nor did she care Winnie and she were trapped. She had to find Colt.

Please, Lord, let me find him. Please.

Over and over those words zoomed through her mind.

But all she uncovered was more snow.

Stunned, with limited oxygen, Colt tried to unfurl his body so he could use his hands to dig his way out before he lost consciousness. But the snow encased him in a cold coffin. He had a small pocket of air, but it wouldn't last long. He finally dislodged his arm from beneath him and reached it toward the direction of the cave, but he could move it only a few inches.

Lord, help me. Winnie and Ellie are in danger.

"I'm in here," he called out, hoping that Ellie was free on the other side.

"Colt!"

The sound of Ellie's voice gave him hope she could dig him out before he ran out of oxygen. "I'm here."

"I can hear you, Colt. Hang on."

He focused on those words and tried to calm his rapid heartbeat, to even his breathing in order to preserve his air. A peace settled around him as if God enclosed him in an embrace.

* * *

"Ellie, what happened?" Winnie called out. "It sounded like an avalanche."

"It was. I'm assessing our situation." Ellie kept digging near the area where she'd heard Colt and prayed he wasn't buried too deeply.

If he was almost to the entrance of the cave, he would have been sheltered from the worst of the avalanche. Concerned for Colt, she hadn't thought about their situation till now. They were trapped in the cave. It would be days before a search party was sent out, and then would the rescuers even realize they were trapped in the cavern? And if they did, would it be in time? She had a couple of water bottles and a little food, but what worried her the most was the cold. A chill infused every crevice of the cave.

Although tired from shoveling the snow with her hands, she didn't dare take a break. "Colt, are you there?"

"Yes," his faint response came back and a surge of adrenaline pumped energy through her body.

Her hand broke through the snow and touched him, and relief trembled down her length. She doubled her attack as though sand was running out of an hourglass and she only had seconds left to free him. Soon his arm was revealed. He wiggled it to let her know he was okay. She kept going, uncovering more of him until he could assist her.

When he escaped the mound of snow, Ellie helped him to stand, then engulfed him in her arms. "Are you all right? Hurt anywhere?"

"I feel like an elephant—no, several—sat on me, but other than that, I'm in one piece."

She leaned back to look into his dear face, one she had thought she would never see again. "I heard a gunshot then the rumble of the avalanche. What happened?"

"Our assailant found us and shot at me when I came out of the cave. That must have triggered the avalanche. I dove back into the cave. He might not have been so fortunate."

"Then he could be buried under tons of snow?"

"It'll depend on where he was and how fast he reacted, but it's definitely a possibility."

"Come on. Winnie is worried." Ellie grasped his gloved hand in hers and relished the connection. She'd almost lost him. That thought forced her to acknowledge her growing feelings toward Colt. There was no time to dwell on them now, but she would have to in the future. Every day she was with him, the stronger those feelings grew.

Winnie's face lit up when she saw Colt. "You're alive."

"Yes, thanks to Ellie." He slanted a look at her before stooping by Winnie. "Are you doing okay?"

"Now I am. What happened?"

As Colt told his grandmother, her face hardened more and more into a scowl.

"I hope he's trapped in the avalanche," Winnie blurted out at the end. "Evil begets evil."

One of Colt's eyebrows lifted. "No forgiveness for the man?"

Winnie pursed her mouth. "I'm working on it, but his actions are making it very hard. It's one thing to go after me, but he was trying to kill you. He needs to be stopped, and if the avalanche did it, so be it."

Ellie sat, her legs trembling from exhaustion. "We

need to come up with a plan to get out of here. Colt, you said there's only one way into this cave. You've explored this place completely?"

"There's another way in that is blocked on the other side. This system goes through the mountain we are on."

"What do you mean by blocked?"

"Years ago there was a rockslide. There's an opening, but it isn't big. I'm not sure I can fit through it. For all I know the rocks may have shifted and closed it completely off."

"Or opened it up some more. Would the assailant know about the back way into this cave?" Ellie slid her glance to Winnie, who pulled the blanket around herself, her lips quivering.

"Unless you're really familiar with the area, you wouldn't know about it. Like I said, this is Winfield property."

"Let's hope he isn't because I don't think we can wait around to see if anyone finds us and digs us out."

"Agreed."

"Winnie, if Colt and I help you, do you think you can make it through the cave to the other side?"

She lifted her chin. "Don't you two worry about me. I'll do what I have to. If I can't make it, you can leave me and come back to get me after you find a way out."

"We can't leave you alone." Colt wrapped his arms around his grandmother.

"I'm not afraid. The Lord will be with me."

"It may not be an issue if I can carry you."

Ellie gathered up all the backpacks and supplies and led the way Colt told her to go while he carried his grandmother in his arms. Dripping water and their breathing were the only sounds in the cavern. The chill burrowed into Ellie's bones the deeper they went into the heart of the mountain.

"How long ago were you last here?" Ellie asked as the passage became narrower and shorter.

"At least ten years ago."

Ellie glanced back at Colt. Winnie's head was cushioned against his shoulder, her eyes closed. "Was there any crawling involved?"

He nodded. "Come to think of it, the cave gets tight in one area."

When Ellie reached a fork in the cave system, she stopped. "Which way?"

Colt shut his eyes, his forehead wrinkled. "I think to the right. This probably isn't the time to tell you I'm lousy with telling you the difference in right or left."

"There's no good time to tell me that," she said. "I could go a ways and see what I find."

"No, we'll stay together. If it's the way, you'd have to track back." Colt shifted Winnie some in his embrace and winced.

"Are you all right?"

"I hurt my arm when the whole mountain came down on me."

"Just your arm? Let's take a rest, eat something and drink some water."

"We should keep going."

"Our bodies need the rest, food and water." Ellie plopped the backpacks down on the stone floor and helped Colt lower his grandmother onto a blanket.

"You two don't have to stop for me," Winnie murmured, pain etched into her features.

"We're stopping for all of us." Ellie delved into her backpack and found the granola bars and a bottle of water. "It may be freezing, but we still have to keep ourselves hydrated."

"Just a short break." Colt removed his gloves and rubbed his left arm.

Shivering, Winnie took the first sip of water then passed it to Ellie. When she gave it to Colt, the touch of his cold fingers against hers fastened her attention on him. In the dim lighting his light blue eyes looked dark. Shadows played across his strong jaw. But the sear of his gaze warmed her as though she sat in front of a flaming blaze.

"I wonder if the cabin caught fire." Colt bit into his granola bar.

"If it did, maybe someone will see the smoke and investigate. They might be concerned about a forest fire." Winnie began unlacing the shoe she had put back on when they'd started the journey through the cave.

"Maybe, but we're isolated up here and the conditions down the mountain might be worse than up here." He popped the last bite into his mouth.

Winnie took off her boot to reveal a swollen ankle, worse than before. "I can't wear this anymore. It's killing my foot. Oh, dear, that was a poor choice of words."

"But true. I've had a sprained ankle, and it does hurt to wear close-fitting shoes." Ellie unwound her scarf and wrapped it around Winnie's foot.

"I can't take your scarf. You need it."

"Nonsense, you need it more than me. One layer of socks isn't warm enough. I find feet, head and hands get cold faster than other parts of your body. If you keep them covered it helps you feel warmer."

Winnie smiled, but the gesture didn't stay on her face more than a second. "I can hardly keep my eyes open."

"Then keep them closed. I'm carrying you, anyway." Colt rose. "Ready."

"Are you sure?" Ellie mouthed the question to Colt, touching his hurt arm.

He nodded.

"If the cabin is gone, I won't get to see what you brought in the sack for me and Ellie." Winnie snuggled close to Colt's body.

"What if it isn't burned down?"

Ellie replied, "I think you should tell us, anyway. Don't you, Winnie?"

"Yes."

He exaggerated a sigh, but the corners of his mouth quirked up, his left dimple appearing in his cheek. "Doug carved a German shepherd like Lady for me to give to you, Winnie, and I found my mom's locket in my belongings in the closet when I put my speargun back." His gaze fastened onto Ellie. "I hope you'll accept it."

Her throat closed, emotions she couldn't express rushing to the surface. "I shouldn't. It's your mother's."

"She'd want you to have it. You've gone above and beyond your duties as a bodyguard."

"I totally agree, Colt," Winnie said. "I hope you'll accept it, Ellie, if it didn't burn."

"I'd be honored," she murmured.

Colt cleared his throat. "We'd better get going."

As Ellie continued their trek, the ceiling dropped more until Colt had to bend over while carrying his grandmother through the passage. When Ellie peered at the pair, she noticed Colt's back kept scraping the roof of the cave. Strain marked his features as he struggled to stay on his feet with Winnie in his arms. Ellie rounded a corner in the passageway and came to a stop.

"Does this look familiar, because if it doesn't maybe we should try the other path?" Ellie waved her hand ahead of them at a tunnel about four feet wide and three feet tall.

Colt paused behind her and put his grandmother on the floor. "Yes. I'd forgotten I had to crawl part of the way toward the end. I've been in a lot of caves through the years. They kind of all run together."

"Let me wait here while you two check it out," Winnie said. "I'll be fine. I can catch a catnap. If it turns out to be a way out, you can come back for me. If it doesn't, then we don't have to try and get me through there."

"I don't want to leave—"

"Ellie, we're trapped in a cave with a mound of snow standing between us and the person after me. I think I'll be perfectly safe here by myself."

"I'll go alone, and if it's the way out, I'll come back and get both of you." Colt moved toward the narrow passageway. "Rest, Winnie. It's not far from here so I shouldn't be gone long."

Ellie helped make Winnie more comfortable. Since this ordeal had started, she had appeared to age a couple of years. Ellie was concerned about her. Winnie had been working so hard the past year on the Endless Youth products and then to have to run for her life… It might be too much for even a tough lady like her.

Although her eyes were closed, Winnie huddled in the blanket up against Ellie and said, "Since this began I've been thanking God for sending you to me. Now I'm thanking you for staying for Christmas. I doubt it's your idea of how to celebrate Christmas, but I'm mighty grateful you're here, and if I'm not mistaken, so is my grandson."

"Here we are trapped in a cave and you're match-making."

"You can't blame a grandmother for trying. I've got a captive audience," Winnie said with a chuckle, some of her fight surfacing.

"I like Colt." *A lot.*

"What I've seen makes me think it's more than just like. Or is that wishful thinking on my part?"

Ellie opened her mouth to say, "Yes," but the word wouldn't come out because it wasn't the truth. "No, there is more, but Winnie, I just don't see how..." She didn't know how to explain her mixed-up feelings even to herself, let alone someone else.

"I know you both have separate lives, but even when two people live in the same town and their lives mesh together, a relationship can be hard. Colt needs someone like you in his life."

"You're right about the hurdles between us."

"Thomas and I had hurdles, too, but we overcame them. He'd just divorced his wife a couple of months before we started dating, but we'd known each other and worked together for several years. People took our openly dating as a sign we'd been having an affair while he was married, especially his ex-wife. She made our lives unbearable for a while, then thankfully she decided to move away and we began to have a normal relationship. Thomas was a wonderful stepfather to my son. In fact, he adopted him when we got married."

Marrying. Having a relationship. Where does that fit in my life? She'd spent her years just trying to survive and have a life with meaning. Her work and faith had given her that. But if she gave in to her feelings concerning Colt, everything would change. So much of her life had been one change after another and she had needed some stability, which her vision for her life had given her—until now.

The passageway narrowed even more. Colt flattened himself and pulled his body through the stone-cold corridor. Although pain stabbed his left bicep, he kept going because a freezing wind whipped by him, indicating there was a way out of the cave up ahead. Reaching forward to grasp something to help him slither through the tunnel, he clutched air. Nothing. He focused the small flashlight on the spot in front of him and saw a drop-off.

Dragging himself to the edge of the opening of the passageway, he stared down at a black hole where the floor of the cavern should be. Across from him, not thirty feet away, light streamed into the darkness. He swung his flashlight toward the area and saw the rocks he remembered piled up where the second cave entrance used to be.

So close with a thirty-foot gap between him and freedom.

"What's keeping Colt? He should have been back by now." Winnie's teeth chattered.

Ellie rubbed her gloved hands up and down Winnie's arms. "It might have been farther than he thought. It hasn't been that long." She infused an upbeat tone into her voice because she knew the cold was getting to Winnie. "Tell me some more about your marriage to Thomas. It sounds like you two were very happy."

"Don't get me wrong. We had our problems, especially concerning Colt's father, but we always managed to work them out. As long as we had each other, we felt we could deal with anything."

"That's nice. No wonder you're a romantic at heart."

"Me? What gave you that idea?"

"Oh, the flowers in your house, a tradition your husband started and you continued. The way you talk about Thomas. But mostly some of the products your company sells with names like Only Her and Only Him."

"You aren't a romantic?"

"Never had time for romance in my life."

"Why not?"

Ellie ended up telling a second person about her childhood. "What is it about a Winfield demanding to know stuff I've never shared with others?"

"It's our charm." Winnie grinned, a sparkle in her eyes for the first time since they'd started on this trek hours ago. "That and we care. People sense that about us. Hard to resist."

"That could be it."

A sound behind Ellie turned her in the direction of the tunnel. Colt crawled out of the hole, his features set in grim determination.

"Something wrong?" she asked.

He shook his head. "The tunnel is narrower than I remember, but if I can get through, you two can. Anyone larger than me won't, though. When I reached the other end, there is a sheer drop-off at the opening that wasn't there before, but the hole in the cavern is only four feet deep. I'll be able to lower myself to the floor and make my way to the entrance. It's still partially blocked. I may have to move a few rocks, but I'll be able to get through the hole."

"So bring back some skinny people to help us," Ellie said.

He laughed, then gathered what he was going to take with him—snowshoes, gun, tinted goggles. "I'll keep that in mind. Stay here. It's warmer in this cavern than the other one."

At the entrance to the tunnel, Ellie placed her hand on his arm.

He turned toward her.

"Keep safe. If an avalanche happened once, it can again."

His smile began as a twinkle in his eyes and spread to transform his earlier serious expression. "I like this role of knight in shining armor."

"Well, in that case, here's a token of my appreciation." She produced his scarf he'd left on the floor and put it around his neck. "It's cold out there."

"It's cold in here."

"True, but not as much wind." Her gaze linked with his. "I mean it. Don't take any unnecessary risks."

"Then it's okay to take necessary risks?"

"I'll be praying."

"Me, too, Colt," Winnie said from where she was sitting against the wall of the cave.

Colt stepped around Ellie, made his way to his grandmother, whispered something to her then kissed her on the head.

When he returned to Ellie, he caught her hands and brought them up between them, inching toward her until they touched. "I probably won't be back for a while."

"I know."

He leaned down and claimed her mouth in a kiss that rocked Ellie to her core, mocking her intention of keeping herself apart from him. It was so hard when he was storming every defense she put up to keep people away.

He pulled back, stared at her for a long moment then ducked down and disappeared into the tunnel. She watched him crawl toward the exit, his light fading. *What if I never see him again?* Her heart lurched at that thought.

Lord, keep him safe. Please. You're in control.

Although the temptation was great to check out the front of the cave and the cabin, Colt couldn't. That would eat into time he didn't have if he was going to get help back up the mountain before dark. He didn't know how long Winnie could last in this freezing weather. She had never tolerated the cold like he and his granddad had.

When he wiggled himself through the opening in the cave, he emerged into more falling snow, but at least it wasn't coming down too hard. Actually the snow could work to his advantage by covering his tracks if the assailant was still alive and out there waiting.

The scent of smoke hovered in the air. He looked in the direction of the cabin but couldn't see any flames. A dense cloud cover hung low over the area.

In his mind he plotted the trail he would take to the estate. Once there, he could use the phone and call for help. Then he and Doug could start up the mountain even before a rescue team could form and make it up to the cave.

Hours later, only a short distance from the house, Colt pushed himself faster. It would be dark before he could get back up the mountain if he didn't move more quickly. Although his legs shook with fatigue, he put one foot in front of the other, sometimes dragging himself out of a hole when he sank too far into the snow. But once he made it over the last ridge he would nearly be home. That thought urged him to pick up speed yet again.

When he put his foot down in front of him, the snow gave away, sending him tumbling down the incline. When he rolled to the bottom, he crashed into a pine tree, knocking the breath from him. Snow crusted him from head to foot. He wiped it away from his goggles and saw two snow boots planted apart. His gaze traveled upward past two legs and a heavy coat to a face covered in a white ski mask.

"Do you think Colt is all right? What if the bad guy didn't get caught in the avalanche and was waiting for him? I can't lose my grandson." Winnie took a sip from the bottle of water then passed it to Ellie.

"Colt can take care of himself." She prayed she was right.

"I know. I shouldn't worry. It does no good but get me upset."

"In a perfect world we wouldn't worry." Ellie worried, too. So many things could go wrong.

"We're safe in here while he's—"

A roar split the air, sending goose bumps flashing up Ellie's body.

Winnie's eyes grew round and huge. "That's—that's a…" She gulped, the color washing from her face.

"A bear. Nearby."

"In this cave!" Winnie sat up straight, the blanket falling away from her. "What's it doing in here?"

"It's a cave and wintertime. Hibernating?" Ellie

quickly gathered up all their belongings and stuffed them into one of the backpacks.

"What do we do?" Winnie asked at the same time another deep growl echoed through the cave.

"Get out of here."

"How? It sounds like it's coming down the passageway we used."

"We're going through the tunnel. Chances are it can't get through there. It's probably still fat since it's only December." Ellie felt for her gun at her hip. "If I have to, I will shoot it. Do you think you can crawl through the tunnel?"

"If I have to, I will."

Ellie helped Winnie to her feet, then supported most of her weight as the woman hopped toward the escape route. "You go first. I'm going in backward so if the bear follows, I can take care of it. From what Colt said, there is no room to turn around. Okay?"

Taking one of the flashlights, Winnie knelt before the entrance and began crawling forward. Ellie backed into the tunnel, pulling the backpack after her. Through the opening she glimpsed a brown bear loping into the area where they had been, sniffing the air. It released another roar, lumbered to the hole and stuck its head inside.

Colt started to spring up when a shovel crashed down on top of him, glancing off his head and striking his shoulder. His ears rang. The whole world spun for a few seconds. The man lifted the weapon again. Colt dropped back to the ground and rolled hard into the man. The action sent a wave of dizziness through Colt, but toppled his assailant to the snow.

Facedown, Colt fumbled in his coat pocket for his

gun, fighting the whirling sensation attacking his mind. Before he could pull it out, his attacker whacked the shovel across his back. Again, pain shot through his body. Someone yelled right before blackness swallowed him up.

"That's the bear!" Winnie said behind Ellie in the tunnel.

"A big one thankfully. I don't think it can get in here. Keep moving as fast as you can just in case."

Keeping her eye on the bear and her gun aimed at it, Ellie listened to Winnie's struggles as she made her way. Ellie didn't want to go any farther until she knew what the bear was going to do. Even if the animal tried to fit into the narrow passage, it wouldn't be able to do much. She calmed her speeding heartbeat.

Wiping first one sweating hand then the other against her coat, she locked gazes with the beast, giving it the most intimidating glare she could muster. "I'm not letting you pass. Don't make me hurt you." A fierce strength coated each word.

The bear released another growl. Its long teeth ridiculed her statements. The animal pushed forward a few inches but didn't go any farther because the walls sloped inward at that point. Finally it gave one last glower then backed out of the entrance into the tunnel.

"There's a really narrow part," Winnie said behind her.

When the bear disappeared from her view, Ellie scooted backward toward the other end. Sounds of the animal drifted to her, but it hadn't returned to the tunnel. A chill pervaded the passage, especially the closer she came to the exit. The thought that it was even colder than where they had been worried Ellie. Winnie needed medical attention and warmth. Ellie couldn't give her either.

"Colt." A familiar male voice filtered into Colt's pain-riddled mind.

The first sensation Colt experienced besides the drumming throb against his skull was the chill penetrating through his clothing. He opened his eyes to find someone kneeling next to him. With his cheek pressed against the snow, frigid, biting, Colt fought the urge to surrender again to the darkness.

"Colt, I was checking the grounds when I heard a noise and looked up the rise. I saw someone attacking you."

Relief that it was Doug pushed Colt to keep himself as alert as possible. Winnie and Ellie were depending on him. Moaning, he lifted his head and regretted it instantly. The world tilted before him. He closed his eyes, but it still swirled. He didn't have time for this. He forced down the nausea churning his stomach and slowly he rolled to face upward. Snowflakes pelted him, but the storm had lessened. Which meant whoever attacked him could possibly find the other entrance into the cave because his footprints weren't totally covered by the falling snow.

"Winnie and Ellie are trapped in the cave system near the cabin, the one I told you about." Somehow he strung together a sentence that made sense.

Doug looked up at the mountain. "That's the way your attacker fled."

Colt struggled to prop himself up on his elbows, searching for the tracks the man made. If he moved slowly, the world didn't spin too much. "I was coming to the house to call for help. There was an avalanche and it blocked the front of the cave. I used the back way in on the other side of the mountain. It's blocked, but I managed to remove a few rocks and wiggle out of the opening."

"Let's get you to the house and call 911, then I'll go up there."

"No, you go back. We're almost into cell range. Alert the sheriff then follow my tracks. I have to go. If that man finds Winnie and Ellie, he'll kill them. He tried to burn the cabin down."

"But wasn't Mary Ann Witlock the one threatening Winnie?"

"Maybe this guy was helping her."

Taking it slow, Colt tucked his legs under him then pushed himself to stand. Doug hurried to assist him. Colt's body protested with his every move, but he managed to remain upright. Then he put one foot in front of the other and started up the mountain, following his assailant's tracks.

He glanced back at Doug and the man was almost to the fence line at the estate. Help wouldn't be too far behind, but Colt had to quicken his pace if he was going to stop the attacker from harming Winnie and Ellie.

I need Your help, Lord. I can't do this without You. Anything is possible with You.

While Winnie stayed on the ledge at the tunnel, Ellie lowered herself over the cave shelf, clinging to a protruding rock. When her feet touched the floor, she let go of the stone, then positioned herself near the wall.

"Okay, Winnie. I'm going to guide you down and hold you so you don't put any weight on your bad foot."

"I still hear the bear. Do you think it can get through that tunnel?"

"No. It's angry we got away. Come on. We'll find a place to settle down and wait for Colt where we can also keep an eye on the tunnel."

After Winnie made it to the floor of the cavern, Ellie swung her light around to find the best place to wait. Puddles of icy water littered the area. Wind blew through the opening.

"The good news is that the water isn't totally frozen so the temperature isn't much below freezing."

Winnie snorted. "Tell that to my body."

Ellie pointed to a place a few feet away. "It's dry there and it looks like it'll shelter us from the wind. And I can see the tunnel."

Shielded from the wind slipping through the opening, Ellie cocooned Winnie in as much warmth as possible. She even used the backpack for her to sit on. "There. Now it's just a matter of a couple of hours. Everything will be over."

"No, it won't. We don't know who is after me. Who might have worked with Mary Ann?"

"I know we looked into her background and no one stood out. She didn't have a boyfriend, and the couple of members of her family who worked for Glamour Sensations didn't have much to do with her."

"One of the reasons I didn't pick her to be the spokesperson for Endless Youth was the way she always came across as though she were ten or fifteen years older than she was. An old soul but not in a good way. Weary. Unhappy. That wasn't the image I wanted to project for this line. Christy is the opposite of that. Young at heart although she is thirty-two. I didn't want a woman who was too young, but I wanted one who had an exuberance in spirit about her. I was so happy when Christy started dating Peter. She'd been engaged once before, and he was killed in a motorcycle accident." Winnie hugged her arms against her chest.

Ellie needed to keep her talking about anything but the situation they were in. "I understand that Christy became engaged to Peter right after you chose her as the spokesperson. Will that interfere in your advertising plans for the product?"

"No, Peter assured me he would do whatever Christy needed. He's been a great support for her. I was surprised at how fast he moved. They'd only been dating a couple of months. I think secretly—although he would never admit it—that he was afraid once the world saw her another man would snatch her right up. Men and claiming their territory." Winnie chuckled. "But I can't complain. Thomas was just like Peter. We only dated a few months, too. Of course, we worked together for a while before that."

"They know a good woman when they see her," Ellie said over the howl of the wind, its force increasing through the cave.

"Yes, and I'm hoping my grandson follows in his granddad's footsteps."

Even in the shadows created by the dim light, Ellie could see Winnie's gleaming eyes. "I have a very persuasive boss who has tried her best to fix me up with a couple of men she knows in Dallas. So far I've not succumbed to her tactics."

"Colt needs someone like you."

"I refuse to say anything to that. I'm sure there is a better subject than my love life."

Winnie's forehead crinkled. "You know, I've been thinking. Not many people knew we were coming up here. We really didn't make the final decision until we talked with the sheriff yesterday. Remember?"

"Yes. We were having a late breakfast. But only Linda was in the room besides the sheriff and us."

Winnie gasped. "It couldn't be Linda, Doug or the sheriff."

A sound above Winnie drew Ellie's gaze. On top of the ledge stood a man dressed in white wearing a white ski mask with a gun aimed at Winnie.

TWELVE

"Who are you?" Ellie asked the man on the ledge.

He cackled. "I'm not telling you. You two can die wondering who I am, especially after all the trouble you've put me through today."

"Why me?" Winnie lifted her face toward her assailant. "What have I done to you?"

"You continually have ruined my life," he said in a voice roughened as if he disguised it.

"I couldn't have. I haven't done that to anyone. I would know about it."

"Well, obviously you don't," the man shouted, his gun wavering as anger poured off him.

Ellie glanced at her gun lying on the ground next to her. She gauged her chances of grabbing it and getting a shot off before he did.

"Don't think about it. I'd have Winnie dead before you could aim the gun."

The voice, although muffled by the ski mask some, sounded familiar to Ellie. She'd heard him before— recently. Could it be Doug? The sheriff?

"Why me?" Winnie asked the gunman. "Don't you want me to know why you're killing me? What satisfaction can you have in that if I don't know why, especially if I wronged you as you say?" A mocking tone inched into Winnie's voice.

Ellie needed to keep the man talking. "As far as we know you're a maniac who belongs in a mental—"

His harsh laugh cut off the rest of her sentence. "Colt isn't coming to your rescue. I left him for dead and followed his trail to you two. How accommodating he was to show me where you all were."

No, Colt can't be dead. He's psyching me out. Trying to rattle me.

"I guess you should know why, Winnie." He said her name slowly, bitterness dripping from it. "You stole my father from my mother."

Winnie gasped.

"If you hadn't come along, my parents would have gotten back together. I would have had a father who would acknowledge me. Instead, he wouldn't have anything to do with me. You poisoned him. You kept him from me."

"Thomas didn't have a child. Thomas couldn't have one."

"Liar!"

"The doctors told Thomas it was impossible, and we never could have children." The pain in Winnie's voice was reflected in her expression, too.

"I am Thomas Winfield's son. My mama showed me my birth certificate. It was right there on the paper. There wasn't a day that went by that I wasn't reminded I wasn't good enough to be a Winfield. He discarded my mother and me like we were trash."

"Are you talking about Clare, Thomas's first wife?"

"Yes. He decided to divorce her for you."

"No, he didn't. We didn't start dating until after the divorce."

"That's not what my mama told me. Why in the world would I believe you? My father wasn't the only one you took away from me. Everything I wanted you came after. Well, not anymore. I'm putting an end to you." He lowered the gun a few inches and pointed it right at Winnie's heart.

Ellie yanked Winnie toward her at the same time a shot rang out in the cave. Snatching her weapon from the floor, she raised it toward their attacker while putting herself in between Winnie and the man. But Ellie didn't get off a shot. Instead, his arm fell to his side, the gun dropping from his fingers. It bounced on the stone surface, going off, the bullet lodging in the wall. Blood spread outward on the white jacket he wore as he crumbled to the ground.

As Ellie scrambled up, she glimpsed Colt diving through the hole and springing to his feet, his gun pointed at their assailant.

"Ellie, Winnie, are you two all right?"

"Yes," they both answered at the same time.

Ellie swiveled toward Winnie. "Are you really okay?"

She nodded. "At least I'm not cold anymore. Fear will do that to you."

Ellie headed up the sloping side to the ledge above Winnie and joined Colt as he knelt next to the gunman. He removed the man's goggles then his white ski mask to reveal Peter Tyler, blinking his eyes at the light she shone on his face.

Ellie stared at the glittering Christmas tree in the living room at Winnie's house. Although it was Christmas Day, there had been nothing calm and peaceful so far. Winnie had spent time with Christy, consoling her over her fiancé. Harold and Colt had been behind closed doors a good part of the morning, then Colt insisted Winnie rest before the sheriff came this afternoon. He had an update on what Peter Tyler had said after he came out of surgery to repair his shoulder where Colt had shot him. Colt and Doug had gone up to the cabin to see what was left of the place. Colt had wanted her to come, but she'd felt she needed to stay with Winnie. After what had occurred with Mary Ann, she wasn't quite ready to relinquish her bodyguard duties with Winnie until she had reassurances from the sheriff.

Then she would return to Dallas. And try to put her life back together. She finally could admit to herself that she loved Colt, but how could she really be sure? Even if she was, that didn't mean he cared about her or that they should be together. He lived on a research vessel in the middle of the ocean. She could never imagine herself living like that.

When the doorbell rang, she hurried across the foyer to answer it. Stepping to the side, she let the sheriff into the house. "I hope you're here to tell us good news."

"Yes," he said as Winnie descended the stairs and Colt came from the kitchen.

"Would you like anything to drink? We have some cookies, too." Winnie gestured toward the living room.

"Nope. Just as soon as we talk, I'm heading home. My son and grandchildren are there waiting for me so they can open presents. I haven't quite had a Christmas like this year in—well, never." Sheriff Quinn stood in front of the fireplace, warming himself. "I came right from the hospital after interviewing Peter. I laid it on the line. We have him dead to rights on three counts of attempted murder, arson and a number of other charges. I told him the judge would look kindly toward him if we didn't have to drag this out in a lengthy trial. He told me what happened."

Winnie frowned. "What was his involvement with Mary Ann?"

Colt hung back by the entrance into the living room, leaning against the wall, his arms folded over his chest. Ellie glanced toward him, but his expression was unreadable, his gaze fixed on his grandmother.

"He encouraged her to act on her feelings and gave her suggestions. When she was his patient, they got acquainted. He listened to her when she ranted about not getting the spokesperson job, then began planting seeds in her mind about how she had not been treated fairly. The threatening letters were Mary Ann's doing and the stink bombs at the Christmas Gala. He helped her kidnap the dogs because he told her that she could get some good money for them and get back at Winnie."

"Your lead didn't pan out about the dogs. Does he know where they are?" Colt asked, coming farther into the room and sitting next to Winnie.

"Yes, because he connected her with the person who took them to sell in Denver. The police there are paying that gentleman a visit today before he gets rid of them. You should have your dogs home by tomorrow."

"Unless someone bought them for a Christmas gift." Exhaustion still clung to Winnie's face, especially her eyes.

"Then we'll track each purchase."

"Winnie, they're alive. That's good news." Colt took her hand in his.

"So Peter Tyler was responsible in part about the dogs. How about the car left in the middle of the road the night of the Christmas tree lighting?" she asked.

"That was him. He didn't care whether you went off the cliff like Thomas or got upset by the similarities between the two events."

Winnie sat forward. "Wait. He didn't have anything to do with Thomas's accident, did he?"

"No, at least that's what he said, and all the evidence still points to an accident, Winnie. He wasn't even living here at that time. He moved back not long after he saw in the newspaper about Thomas dying. His mother had passed away a few months before your husband. According to Peter, she was still brokenhearted after all the years they were divorced. She fed Peter a lot of garbage about you coming between her and Thomas. I told him that wasn't the case. You two worked in the lab together, but so did my mother and she said it was hogwash what Thomas's ex-wife was saying."

Winnie smiled, and even her eyes sparkled with the gesture. "Your mom is a good friend."

"She sends her regards from sunny Florida. I can't get her back here in the winter. Too cold."

Winnie laughed. "I heartily agree with her. I may go visit her and warm these cold bones."

"We didn't make the final decision to go to the cabin until you told us it was safe. How did Peter know we were there?" Ellie asked Sheriff Quinn.

"He knew there was a chance, based on the talk the night before. He planned ahead, staying in a small cabin not far from you on the Henderson property. Then he came back to watch and see if you went." The sheriff held his hands out over the fire and rubbed them together.

Ellie liked seeing Winnie's smile and hearing her laugh. The past weeks' ordeal had taken a toll on the woman. After the doctor at the house had checked out Winnie, she'd slept for twelve hours last night. Winnie had insisted Colt go to the hospital and have some X-rays on his arm. Ellie had taken him but little was said. In fact, Colt dozed on the trip to the hospital where the doctor told him he would be sore for a while, but he hadn't fractured his arm. Colt had also suffered a mild concussion, but he'd refused to stay overnight.

"Winnie, you could always return with me to the *Kaleidoscope*. We're in warm waters. In the South Pacific, it's summer right now."

"Not if I have to live on a boat."

Colt smiled. "It's a ship."

"Not big enough for me. You know I can't swim. You didn't get the swimming gene from me."

"Speaking of genes. Is Peter my uncle?"

Winnie shuddered. "Good grief, no. I don't know who his father is, but Thomas was sterile. For some reason she used Thomas to blame all her woes on. I guess that was easier for her than changing."

"I'm heading home to salvage a little bit of Christmas with my family." The sheriff crossed the room to the foyer, and Colt walked with him to the front door.

Winnie pinned Ellie with an assessing look. "You've been quiet. I imagine you're glad this is over with about as much as I am."

"I'm usually like this when a job is finished. It takes me days to come down from the stress. How's Christy?

She looked much better after she talked with you this morning."

"At first she wanted to step down from being the spokesperson for Endless Youth, but I talked her out of that. I told her she's not responsible for other people's actions. She isn't to blame for Peter or Mary Ann. Christy told me she talked with Peter before he went into surgery. What sent Peter over the edge was that Christy got the job that would demand a lot of her time—time away from him. He came to Bakersville after years of being told I was the one who caused all the trouble for him and his mother. He struggled to make it through school and has a huge debt from college loans he's still paying back. He saw the money he thought he should rightly have as Thomas's only living son. It festered inside him. The trigger was Christy getting the job and getting all the attention. But it was Peter's problem, not hers."

"Can you forgive Peter for what he did?"

"Probably when I recover from the effects of yesterday. Hanging on to the anger will only hurt me in the long run. Look what happened to Peter and his mother when they held on to their anger."

Listening to Winnie's reasonable explanation of why she would forgive Peter made Ellie think about her mother. She hadn't talked to her in years, and that had always bothered her. Maybe she should call her tonight and wish her a merry Christmas.

Colt reentered the living room. "I'm glad this is all wrapped up. I got a message from the *Kaleidoscope*. Doug gave it to me this morning. I'm needed back there to finish up a study we've been running on the seal population in the area where we're anchored."

"When?" Winnie rose.

"Day after tomorrow. I want to make sure you're all right and things are really settled after what's happened."

"At least we have a little more time together. I think I'll take my second nap today. See you two at dinner."

After Winnie left, Colt took the couch across from Ellie. He stared at the fire for a long moment before looking at her. "One thing my grandmother isn't is subtle. For being tired, she can move awfully fast."

"I think she's still trying to process it all. Having not just one but two people angry with you to the point they wanted to harm you is hard on even the toughest person. Imagine Peter's mother lying to him for all those years."

"It just makes me realize how fortunate I've been to have Winnie and my granddad to raise me."

"I'm going to call my mother tonight. It's about time I did. I don't expect warm fuzzies, but I need to take the first step to try and mend our relationship. She's all the family I have. I see the relationship you have with Winnie, and although we'll probably never have that kind, we can at least have a civil one."

"You get a chance to do that. I don't have that. My father is dead."

"You can forgive him in your heart. That's what is important."

"You're right." Colt stood and bridged the distance between them. "Speaking of relationships, what are we going to do about us?"

"Nothing."

He clasped her hands and hauled her up against him. "You can't deny we have a connection."

"No, I can't. But this isn't real. This whole situation

heightened all our senses. I've seen it before with others and their relationships didn't last. You and I live very differently. I couldn't live on a research vessel even if it's classified a ship. I need space. I would go crazy. How could a relationship last with you in the Pacific Ocean and me flying all over the world for my job? I think we should cut our losses and go our separate ways."

"How do you feel about me? Forget about what you just said. All the logical, rational reasons we shouldn't be together." He placed his hand over her heart. "How do you feel in there?"

"I love you, but it isn't enough. A lasting relationship is much more than love. We haven't had any time to think about our feelings. We've been on a roller-coaster ride since you arrived."

He framed her face. "I love you, Ellie. I don't want to let you go. I realized that when I was trying to get back to you and Winnie in the cave. I thought I was going to lose you when I saw Peter pointing the gun at you."

His declaration made her hesitate, her resolve wavering. Finally she murmured, "Someone has to be the logical, rational one. I guess I'm that one. I need time to figure out what I want. You need time. You have a job that needs you right now and so do I."

He bent toward her and kissed her. All the sensations he could produce in her flooded her, making her want to take a risk. When he pulled back, sanity returned to Ellie.

"Why not give the *Kaleidoscope* a chance? You might like it."

She shook her head.

"No, I'm leaving tomorrow morning to return to Dallas. Maybe sometime in the future we'll meet again under less stressful circumstances."

He released a long breath. "You're right. These past few weeks have been unreal. Reality is our everyday lives. Will you promise me one thing?"

"Maybe."

He chuckled. "Why am I not surprised you said that? Where's the trust?"

"That's just the point. I don't trust easily and these new feelings could all vanish with time."

"Winnie will be having an Endless Youth gala to launch the new line on Valentine's Day. In spite of what happened the last time, she'll be having it at the same hotel that evening. Come back. Meet me there if you think we have a chance at what we started here. That's seven weeks away."

"I promise I'll think long and hard on it."

"You do that," he said. "And I hope I'll see you then."

Colt stood at the double doors into the hotel ballroom on Valentine's Day. The event was in full swing. Laughter floated to him. A sense of celebration dominated the atmosphere of the Endless Youth gala. The music, soft and romantic, filled the room. Couples, dressed in tuxedos and gowns, whirled around the dance floor to the strains of a waltz.

None of the gaiety meant anything to him.

The ball was halfway over. Ellie wasn't here. She wasn't coming.

"Colt, why aren't you dancing?"

He forced a smile for his grandmother, but inside his heart was breaking. "You sent Ellie the invitation?"

"For the third time, yes, and I know she received it."

"I gave her the space she wanted."

"Then you've done what you can. Have faith in what you feel, what you two shared at Christmas. I saw how she felt about you. Give her time to work it out. Why don't you dance with your favorite grandmother?"

"You're my *only* grandmother."

"True."

"You know dancing isn't my thing. Harold is so much better than me, and he is your date for tonight."

"Just because Harold and I are dating doesn't mean I should neglect my grandson." She laughed, a sound Colt loved to hear from his grandmother. "I can't believe I'm dating again. I thought that would never happen after Thomas."

"Why not? You're seventy-three years *young*."

"You're right." Winnie held her hand out to Colt.

He threw a last glance over his shoulder at the hotel lobby. No Ellie. After three days on the *Kaleidoscope* he'd known what he'd felt for her was the marrying kind of love. There was no thrill and excitement in his job. He wanted to share his life with Ellie. He'd completed his research project and resigned. It was time for him to put down roots. Alone, if not with Ellie.

He whisked his grandmother out onto the dance floor and somehow managed to sweep Winnie around the ballroom to some love song without stepping on her foot or stumbling.

Then he saw her, dressed in a long red gown, across the room in the entrance to the ballroom. Ellie had come. He came to a standstill. Their gazes linked together, and his heart began pounding against his chest.

"Go to her," Winnie whispered, backing away from him.

Colt headed toward Ellie at the same time she did. They met on the edge of the dance floor. He was sure he had some silly grin on his face, but Ellie's smile encompassed her whole face in radiance.

"You look beautiful. Want to dance?" He offered her his hand.

She clasped it and came effortlessly into his embrace. The feel of her against him felt so right.

"I'm sorry I was late. My flight was delayed then we had to change planes and—"

He stopped her words with a kiss. When he drew back and began to move about the floor, he said, "You're here. That's all that's important."

They flowed as one through the crowd of dancers. All he could do was stare at her. He never wanted to take his eyes off her again.

"Seven weeks was too long to be apart. When I returned to the *Kaleidoscope,* my life wasn't the same. I wanted different things. I love you, Ellie."

"The same for me. I went back to Dallas. I even went on an assignment in Rome. I love Rome. I stayed a few days after my job was finished, but Rome wasn't the same without you. I tried to talk myself out of my feelings, but I couldn't, not in seven weeks. That's when I knew I had to see you again. Be with you."

The music stopped. Colt grabbed her hand and hurried off the dance floor out into the lobby. He found a private alcove and pulled her back into his arms.

"I want to be with you, too," he said.

"Our jobs—"

He put two fingers over her lips, the feel of them against his skin everything he remembered. Warm. Soft. Her. "I resigned from the *Kaleidoscope.* I'm slowly going to take over for Winnie. She wants to retire completely in a year or so. She says she's ready to lie around and eat bonbons."

Ellie laughed. "That'll be the day. She'll hole herself in her lab in the basement and create some other sensational product."

"As the soon-to-be CEO of Glamour Sensations, I'm hoping she will. What would you say if we hired you as the head of our security? The company is growing. I need someone with more experience than our current guy. Security will become more important than ever before. And there will still be some travel involved so you won't always be confined to here."

She snuggled closer. "I like being confined to here if you're here, too."

"Right by your side. I hope as your husband." Then he kissed her with every emotion he'd held in check for the past seven weeks without her.

"I think I can accommodate that."

* * * * *

Dear Reader,

Christmas Stalking is the fourth in my Guardians, Inc. series, where the women and men are both equally strong characters who know how to deal with dangerous situations. I've had readers write to me about how much they enjoy seeing a woman play a tough role and still be soft and vulnerable enough to fall in love. I have two more books coming in this series for Love Inspired Suspense. Look for them in the future.

I love hearing from readers. You can contact me at margaretdaley@gmail.com or at 1316 S. Peoria Ave., Tulsa, OK 74120. You can also learn more about my books at www.margaretdaley.com. I have a quarterly newsletter that you can sign up for on my website or you can enter my monthly drawings by signing my guest book.

Best wishes,

Margaret Daley

Questions for Discussion

1. Trust is important in a relationship. Ellie doesn't know how to trust because of what she has seen in her work as well as in her past. Has anyone caused you to distrust them? Why? How did you settle it?

2. Who is your favorite character? Why?

3. Ellie is self-reliant, and has to be in her job. But when she protects Winnie, she comes to depend on Colt—at first reluctantly, later because she has no choice. Do you consider yourself independent, needing no one? Is it possible to go through life not needing anyone? Ellie discovers she must depend on others at times. Who do you depend on and why?

4. How do you feel about the resolution at the end between Colt and Ellie? How would you have liked the book to end?

5. What is your favorite scene? Why?

6. Colt is torn between two jobs—working for the family business and being a marine biologist. Have you ever been torn between doing two different jobs? How did you resolve it? Are you happy with your choice?

7. Ellie's relationship with her mother is nonexistent because of their past. She hasn't been able to for-

give her mother and move beyond her anger. Do you or someone you know have a similar relationship with a parent? How have you or that parent dealt with the situation?

8. Colt couldn't forgive his father. He was neglected as a child and then his dad died without any resolution between father and son. Although he is loved by his grandparents, Colt has an emptiness inside. Is there someone in your past that has done that to you? How can you get past that?

9. Winnie's life is in danger. This is hard for Colt to handle. When life seems impossible, what do you do? Who do you turn to for help?

10. Although Ellie knew she should forgive her mother, that God wanted her to, she couldn't. Have you ever done something you know you shouldn't or avoid what you knew you should do? How did that situation turn out?

11. Who did you think was after Winnie? Why?

12. The villain was motivated by revenge. How can we get past wanting to retaliate against someone who we thought hurt us?

13. Winnie has a hard time believing someone wants to kill her. She has never intentionally hurt anyone enough to make a person want her dead. She doesn't know how to deal with it. What would you do if someone felt that kind of anger toward you?

14. Winnie felt she owed Steve Fairchild a public apology because of what happened when her husband died. Others didn't feel she did. The first opportunity she had she made the apology. Have you ever done that? How did the person react? How did you feel afterward?

15. Ellie's brother was bullied when he was alive because he was slow and different. Ellie became tough in order to protect her twin brother. Have you ever stood up to a bully to protect yourself or another? How did it turn out for you?

REQUEST YOUR FREE BOOKS!

2 FREE RIVETING INSPIRATIONAL NOVELS
PLUS 2 FREE MYSTERY GIFTS

Love Inspired®
SUSPENSE

YES! Please send me 2 FREE Love Inspired® Suspense novels and my 2 FREE mystery gifts (gifts are worth about $10). After receiving them, if I don't wish to receive any more books, I can return the shipping statement marked "cancel". If I don't cancel, I will receive 4 brand-new novels every month and be billed just $4.49 per book in the U.S. or $4.99 per book in Canada. That's a saving of at least 22% off the cover price. It's quite a bargain! Shipping and handling is just 50¢ per book in the U.S. and 75¢ per book in Canada.* I understand that accepting the 2 free books and gifts places me under no obligation to buy anything. I can always return a shipment and cancel at any time. Even if I never buy another book, the two free books and gifts are mine to keep forever.

123/323 IDN FEHR

Name _____ (PLEASE PRINT) _____

Address _____ Apt. # _____

City _____ State/Prov. _____ Zip/Postal Code _____

Signature (if under 18, a parent or guardian must sign)

Mail to the **Reader Service:**
IN U.S.A.: P.O. Box 1867, Buffalo, NY 14240-1867
IN CANADA: P.O. Box 609, Fort Erie, Ontario L2A 5X3

Not valid for current subscribers to Love Inspired Suspense books.

**Are you a subscriber to Love Inspired Suspense
and want to receive the larger-print edition?
Call 1-800-873-8635 or visit www.ReaderService.com.**

* Terms and prices subject to change without notice. Prices do not include applicable taxes. Sales tax applicable in N.Y. Canadian residents will be charged applicable taxes. Offer not valid in Quebec. This offer is limited to one order per household. All orders subject to credit approval. Credit or debit balances in a customer's account(s) may be offset by any other outstanding balance owed by or to the customer. Please allow 4 to 6 weeks for delivery. Offer available while quantities last.

Your Privacy—The Reader Service is committed to protecting your privacy. Our Privacy Policy is available online at www.ReaderService.com or upon request from the Reader Service.

We make a portion of our mailing list available to reputable third parties that offer products we believe may interest you. If you prefer that we not exchange your name with third parties, or if you wish to clarify or modify your communication preferences, please visit us at www.ReaderService.com/consumerschoice or write to us at Reader Service Preference Service, P.O. Box 9062, Buffalo, NY 14269. Include your complete name and address.

LISUS11B